STARLIGHT CHILD

NANCY J. COHEN

Copyright ©1995 by Nancy J. Cohen
STARLIGHT CHILD
Published by Orange Grove Press
Printed in the United States of America
Digital ISBN: 978-1-952886-08-9
Print ISBN: 978-1-952886-31-7
Cover Design by The Killion Group, Inc.
Interior Design by Formatting4u.com

Chapter One

A woman's high-pitched screams of anguish tore through the night. The piercing cries lanced into Mara's sleep-numbed mind and awakened her.

Sitting up abruptly in bed, she listened acutely. Dead silence filled the room.

Her gaze swept the bedchamber, resting upon her modern built-in shelving unit with its holovid array, the chest of carved wooden drawers from her home planet Tyberia, and the display case with her collection of sculptures. The room's illumination had brightened automatically when she sat up, but still her heart raced and her spine chilled with fear.

Could the awful sounds have come from Hedy? An urgent need to check on her roommate propelled her out of bed, but a glimpse of the petite brunette sleeping next door reassured her that all was well.

After a hasty search of the rest of the apartment, Mara concluded she'd been dreaming. Letting out a breath of relief, she grabbed a wrap from her chamber and told herself to calm down. But the agonized cries kept reverberating in her mind as though they were real, and she couldn't dismiss the uneasy feeling that something was wrong.

Trying to shake off the remnants of her nightmare, she strode to the fabricator in the living area to conjure a warm drink, hoping it would soothe her sensitized nerves. She stood watching the alcove in the wall as her beverage materialized in a large ceramic mug. Drinking a cup of wagmint tea always calmed her when she felt tense, and it had been a particularly aggravating day at work. Maybe that was why her sleep had been disturbed.

As soon as the notion came to her, she dismissed it. She hadn't awakened because of insomnia. A woman's screams had torn her from the fabric of slumber. They had sounded as real to her as the mug in her hand. Although it had been synthesized from a molecular matrix, the mug was solid. She believed the sounds she'd heard were just as substantial. It couldn't have been a dream. And if not, then whose distress was so great that it had touched her while asleep?

She was just raising the cup to her lips when a loud chime shattered the heavy silence.

"Computer, open channel," she said, her voice trembling. "Hello? Who is it, please?" Holding her breath, she waited for the response.

"It's Sarina," said her friend in a tense tone. The video was off, so Mara couldn't see her face. "Can you come over?"

Her throat constricted. "It's two-thirty in the morning. What's wrong?"

"I can't explain over the commlink. Oh God, Mara, what am I going to do?" Sarina's voice cracked. "Please, come quickly!"

"I'll be there." Mara terminated the link, set her mug down, and obtained a set of lace underwear and a plum stretch jumpsuit from the fabricator. As she pulled them on, she wondered what could have happened.

Her imagination ran wild with all sorts of ominous possibilities, making her fingers quake so badly that fastening her jumpsuit required a major effort.

After sparing a brief glance at the reflector to straighten her long hair, she strode into the foyer. Her shiny black boots were where she'd left them beside the door. As she shoved her feet inside, she composed a voice message for Hedy. Normally her roommate slept as soundly as a hibernating bear, but Mara didn't want Hedy to worry should she awaken alone.

Outside, the dark sky above the biosphere's crystal domed

ceiling was studded with stars. Breathing in the cool, crisp air, she focused on determining the quickest route to Sarina's. They lived some distance from each other even though Bimordus Central was relatively compact.

Taking an airbus or a people mover meant she'd have to change vehicles along the way. It might be more expedient to walk three blocks to the transport terminal and requisition a speeder.

Making her decision, she strode at a fast pace along a paved walking path dimly lit by low footlights. Her surroundings faded into the background of her preoccupied mind. Wrinkling her brow, she wondered what could have happened to cause Sarina such anxiety.

Was her daughter ill? Seven months old, the pretty blond-haired, blue-eyed babe already showed signs of her exceptional heritage. Jallyn Diana bore the sacred sign of the circle on her palm in the same manner as her gifted mother.

Although Sarina was the legendary Great Healer, Mara knew that her healing power was limited. She hoped Jallyn hadn't been stricken with a disease Sarina couldn't cure. As the child's godmother, she felt very close to her.

Moisture pricked her eyes and she sought to divert her concern by examining different possibilities. Perhaps Jallyn was not the cause of Sarina's trouble. Could Sarina herself have been attacked? She'd made her share of enemies while becoming the Great Healer. Briefly, Mara reviewed the story that had become nearly as familiar to her as her own history.

Sarina had been abducted from Earth by Captain Teir Reylock of the Coalition Defense League. As ordered, Teir had delivered her to the High Council on Bimordus Two for her marriage to Lord Rolf Cam'brii. Through this union, it was believed Sarina would fulfill an ancient prophecy and become the Great Healer.

Mara could hardly believe that a mere two annums had passed since the horrible plague called the Farg had swept through

Coalition space, followed by the dreaded Morgot conquerors. The Morgots had sought to stop the prophecy's fulfillment. They'd hired Cerrus Bdan, a Souk slave trader, to eliminate Sarina and Teir, who was acting as her bodyguard. Bdan failed to meet his objective. When Sarina fell in love with Teir, her power activated and she became the Great Healer. She eradicated the Farg and chased the Morgots from Coalition territory.

Beside the Souks and the Morgots, who else would have reason to resent Sarina's interference in their affairs? Mara supposed former Councilor Daimon could be considered a contender. The powerful statesman had been a leader of the Return to Origins faction, a secessionist movement that had gained favor during previous crises.

Daimon tried to have Sarina and Lord Cam'brii assassinated to prevent their marriage from taking place, fearing the legend's fulfillment would strengthen Coalition unity. When Sarina became the Great Healer, Daimon was forced to resign. But Mara had heard his followers were active on other worlds.

As she mulled over the alternatives, her gut feeling told her that none of these pertained to Sarina's current distress. Something else was involved here.

She'd just have to wait to learn the answers.

Twenty minutes later, she stood at the entrance to Sarina's residential tower, a cylindrical structure made from glittery pink stone and white marbelite. An unusual number of security personnel patrolled the well-lit perimeter.

A middle-aged man with a stern visage stepped in her path as she neared the entrance.

"Can I help you, mistress?" The man wore a nondescript khaki jacket but his stiff military posture and firm voice proclaimed his authority.

"I'm Mara Hendricks, here to see Sarina Reylock." Her heart thumped in her chest. She'd been here before at night and had never encountered any resistance. This couldn't signify anything good.

The man examined a file on his hand-held datalink. After a moment, his face brightened, and he offered her a smile. "The Great Healer expects you. I'll let you in."

Her feeling of dread deepening, she entered the lift from the atrium lobby.

"Fourteen," she spoke aloud, and the door slid shut. The different levels passed by in a blur as the lift sped upward. By the time it reached the fourteenth floor, her knees were shaking.

A pair of guards stood in front of Sarina's door, frightening her with their fierce expressions. One of them announced her arrival over the comm unit.

Inside, Sarina rushed to greet her. "Mara, I'm so glad you're here."

After giving her a brief hug, Mara stood back, regarding her friend's tear-streaked face and disheveled appearance. Sarina's gray eyes were wide with shock. Her blond hair was in rumpled disarray, her nightclothes haphazardly covered by a crimson robe. A faint, sickly sweet odor was in the air. The casements were wide open, letting in a cool breeze that ruffled the hairs on Mara's skin.

Her stunned gaze swept the living area, alighting on a tall, bearded figure seated on a double lounger in front of a black crystalline table. Glotaj, the supreme regent, was here.

He wasn't the only guest. Lieutenant Wren, one of Teir's crew, stood in front of the holovid entertainment center studying the flashy dials. He'd been injured on a recent mission and was on medical leave.

Great suns, had something happened to Teir that they were both here? The captain was away on assignment. Why else would Glotaj and Wren have come together if not to deliver bad news?

"What's happened? Teir, is he—" She couldn't get beyond those words.

Sarina shook her head. "It's Jallyn. She's been kidnapped." Sinking onto a chair, the Great Healer covered her face with her hands.

Mara's jaw gaped. "What?"

Glotaj rose from the lounger to greet her. "Mara," the older statesman said, regally inclining his head. Wings of gray fanned his temples, flanking a forehead creased with worry lines. A pair of dark, piercing eyes met hers. Without preamble, Glotaj launched into an explanation.

"Someone showed up at Sarina's door pretending to deliver a bouquet of flowers. She thought they were from Teir and opened the portal, wherein the delivery person disabled her with a noxious fume sprayer. When her life-form readings dipped, the automated sentry sent out an alarm. A security team found her out cold on the floor. We've already done a sweep of the apartment. Traces of quantum resolution activity were found in the baby's chamber."

He scowled as though that had a significance Mara didn't understand. "The other results won't be available for a few hauras yet," Glotaj continued. "The security team picked up unusual readings by the stairs in the lobby."

"Who do you suspect is responsible?" She wavered between talking to Glotaj and rushing to Sarina's side. Her friend was in dire need of comfort.

"Speculation can wait," Sarina snapped, lifting her head. "Will you do a separation, Mara? I have to know if Jallyn's all right."

As a Tyberian, Mara possessed extrasensory ability, but her power went beyond the norm for her people. She could actually separate her spirit from her body and jump into another person's life space.

This allowed her to see what the other person saw and to experience their viewpoint as events unfolded. It was a gift she was loath to use because it had caused her an unhappy childhood. But in this case, she would do anything to help Sarina.

"Of course, I'll help." To ease her mind in preparation, she rested her gaze on various art pieces around the living space, souvenirs from Sarina's travels. They would be meaningless if her baby daughter was lost.

"I need an object that's touched Jallyn," she reminded Sarina gently.

"Of course." Sarina rushed from the room, returning a moment later holding a lavender woven blanket.

Mara took it from her and clutched it to her chest. Her eyes closed, and she began the inner flight along the astral plane. As she concentrated, a vibration hummed through her body, expanding outward. A buzzing noise rang in her ears.

She felt herself lighten as the sound altered, changing to a rushing noise like water gushing through a narrow gorge. All at once, her essence separated from her body and floated upward. She hovered a moment, feeling as airy as a feather. It was an incredible sensation and she wanted to savor it, to remain immersed in the peace and warmth of her new state.

Unencumbered by a physical body, she could go anywhere. Freedom beckoned her. The dimensions of time and space didn't pose any restraints to her spiritual being. She still had a form of sorts, but it was different, like an energy signature of what she had been.

She focused her thoughts on the baby, on the pretty blond-haired child who'd be frightened and bewildered without its mother. She could feel its vibrations emanating from the blanket, guiding her. Almost instantly, she was with Jallyn, popping into her head.

Confusion struck her. Seeing through the baby's eyes, it was difficult to make out the view in Jallyn's perspective. She was lying on her back, squirming, her diaper wet and uncomfortable. Overhead a bright light shone in her face. When her head twisted to the side, rows of painted wooden strips obstructed her view. Beyond the slats was a curved metal wall.

Footsteps sounded. A woman's face appeared, peering at her with a frown. Jallyn saw a large set of violet eyes, a pale complexion, brown hair knotted in a low bun. As the face neared, the nose seemed to expand, threatening to jab into her. She began to cry.

"Not now," Mara whispered to herself. She couldn't see well through the moisture in Jallyn's eyes.

Huge hands grasped her pudgy legs, raised them, removed the wet diaper. She was cleaned and dried, then rediapered. As Jallyn was turned onto her stomach to have her back rubbed, Mara glimpsed a small round casement set high in another metal wall. A viewport, and outside all was dark.

Having seen enough, Mara separated. Instantly, she found herself back in Sarina's apartment being sucked into her physical body.

She opened her eyes. The feeling of weightlessness had gone, but the serenity she'd experienced remained with her. Once more encumbered by her physical being, she took a moment to adjust.

"Jallyn is lying in a crib. A woman is caring for her," she told Sarina, trying to keep the emotion from her voice.

Sarina stared at her, wide-eyed. "Thank God someone's looking after her." Her composure shattered, and tears streamed down her face. "Jallyn… Oh, dear God, what am I going to do?" Her face paled, and she slumped down onto the nearest lounger.

"She needs a medic," Mara said in alarm. "Let's call Hedy." With the supreme regent's permission, she gave Wren the coded signal that would trigger Hedy's bedside alarm. Her roommate, a respected physician, could be relied upon for discretion.

Reassured that Hedy was on her way, Mara obtained a sedit beverage from the fabricator and handed it to Sarina.

"Drink this. It'll help." As her friend drained the contents, Mara wondered if she should get one for herself. It might help stem the flood of tears that hovered at her eyelids.

"What else did you notice?" Glotaj asked in an impatient tone.

"I saw a viewport and a metal bulkhead."

"That sounds like a ship." The supreme regent narrowed his eyes. "Computer, open channel. Get me the control center for Spaceport Operations." When the connection came through, he identified himself. "I want the manifest checked for all departures within the past two hauras."

"I'll get right on it, Your Excellency," said the controller. "Do you wish to wait on the line?"

"No, call me back." Abruptly, he terminated the link and addressed the women. "If Jallyn isn't on Bimordus Two, it will take us longer to find her, and the Elevation Ceremony is scheduled for sixty days hence. It will be disastrous if Jallyn fails to appear. We must keep this situation under wraps until she's found."

"I agree," Wren said in a quiet voice. He'd been listening off to the side but now walked over to join them. "If Jallyn's abduction becomes public knowledge, it will frighten the Auranians. They'll fear they are still in danger from those who would oppose them."

Glotaj nodded solemnly. "They might be deterred from revealing their legacy for another millennium. Jallyn has to be found so she can make her scheduled appearance."

Mara considered his words as she took a seat next to Sarina. The Auranians were people of ancient descent who'd been persecuted because of their ability to mentally manipulate the aura surrounding living matter. Forced to flee their home planet of Shimera, they'd scattered among the stars, hiding their heritage to avoid further repression.

Sarina's ancestors had been Auranians who'd landed on Earth. Teir was thought to be of Auranian descent as well. Ever since their joining, Auranians had been coming forward to share their legacy. Jallyn's birth symbolized the reemergence of their race. The Elevation Ceremony would serve to recognize their right to freedom of expression, and Mara prayed Jallyn would be found in time to be there.

"Do you think Jallyn was taken because someone wants to discourage the Auranians from returning to power?" she asked, puzzled. She didn't think the Auranians would pose a threat to anyone. Those who had come forward were learning long-forgotten skills based on Sarina's experience. They were healers, albeit on a more limited scale than Sarina.

"Who would be against us?" Sarina's voice rose barely above a whisper. "My people just want to live in peace." Her fingers plucked at her crimson robe, opening and closing the folds in a nervous, repetitive motion.

Mara gripped Sarina's cold hand in her own to offer reassurance. "Why else would someone take Jallyn? Do you think Sarina is in danger, too?" she asked Glotaj. A weight settled in the pit of her stomach at the possibility.

Glotaj shook his head. "The abductors had the perfect opportunity to take her, but she was left untouched. No, it was Jallyn they wanted." The supreme regent paced the room, his hands folded behind his back.

Wren swept a sympathetic glance toward Sarina and Mara, and she drew strength from his presence. A strong, confident male, Wren was a Polluxite who served as Teir's navigator aboard the *Valiant*. Like his captain, he ignored military convention and opted to wear leather breeches and a white shirt half open at his muscular chest.

Her gaze scanned his liquid hazel eyes and then rose to his layered eyebrows. A white streak was sandwiched between two chestnut layers darker than his head of brown hair. Combined with the rugged angles of his face, the unusual brows gave him a striking appearance.

Beside her, Sarina gave a tremulous sigh. Mara shot her a sharp glance, wishing Hedy would hurry up and get there. She squeezed Sarina's hand, willing her to be strong. Her own heart fluttered rapidly in her chest. Jallyn… the poor child.

"Does Teir know?" Mara asked.

Glotaj responded. "He's on a special assignment and can't be reached. They have orders to observe radio silence."

A cry of anguish escaped Sarina's lips. The empty cup slipped from her fingers, tumbling onto the carpeted floor. Mara caught her by the shoulders just as she slumped to the side. "By the faith, she's passed out."

Wren hurried over. With his big arms, he scooped the Great

Healer into his protective embrace. "She's had a terrible shock. I'll put her in her chamber until Dr. Te'larr gets here," he said, using Hedy's formal name.

As he headed away, Mara swiped at her moist eyes with the back of her hand. Emptiness beckoned at her mental doorstep, partly from fear for the missing child and partly from sharing her friend's anxiety. She felt powerless when events were unfolding so fast and wished there were more she could do to help.

"I think we should consider different angles," Wren said when he'd returned, his expression somber. "Jallyn could have been taken for reasons other than the Auranian issue."

His tense state was betrayed by a large set of muscular wings that suddenly sprouted from his back. With a grimace of annoyance, he forced them to fold and retreat.

"Why are you looking at me?" he asked his audience. "You should be thinking of other possible culprits.

"Like who?" Glotaj queried, spreading his hands.

"This could be another ploy by the Morgots. Their leader, K'darr, tried to capture Sarina before she became the Great Healer. He could hope to gain through the infant what he failed with her mother."

Mara gazed at him askance. "You mean, he'll attempt to use Jallyn's power for his own purposes?"

Wren nodded, his expression pained. "The extent of Jallyn's ability is unknown at this stage. She may not even possess the healing gift despite the sign of the circle on her palm."

"Jallyn does have the gift," Mara stated. "I've sensed it in her, and she might be capable one day of doing even more than healing. The light of the aura is strong in that child."

"Revenge could be a motive for the Souks," Glotaj added, his face pensive. "They have reason to resent Sarina's interference in their affairs."

"I doubt they're involved," Wren retorted. "After Lord Cam'brii's secret mission to Souk last annum, the pashas who gained power have been friendlier to the Coalition."

"Where is Rolf?" Mara asked, aware that Lord Cam'brii and his bride had become good friends to Sarina and Teir.

"He and Ilyssa are visiting his family on Nadira," Glotaj answered. "They know nothing about this. The fewer people who hear about it, the better."

"What about former Councilor Daimon? Could he be making a replay for dominance?"

Glotaj stroked his bearded jaw. "I don't see how stealing Sarina's baby would fit into his scheme of things. The Return to Origins faction is a secessionist group." His shoulders slumped, betraying his state of distress.

Normally the Coalition leader's demeanor was calm and poised, as it had been through all the crises that had afflicted them recently. It proved how much he cared for Sarina that he let his emotions show.

"I've got it," Wren said, jabbing a finger in the air. "It's a ransom demand."

"That's absurd." Mara's head throbbed, and she rubbed at a pulsating point on her temple. "Sarina and Teir don't have a lot of credits. What would someone stand to gain? In my opinion, you're both off track. There's something else we're missing."

The chime from the comm unit sounded, breaking the resultant silence.

"Greetings. This is Glotaj speaking," the statesman said over the speaker system.

"It's Controller Brecch from Spaceport Operations, Your Excellency. I have the information you requested. Three ships have launched within the past two hauras. One belongs to Fromoth Trun and the Yanuran delegation. They are returning to Yanura. Another craft is owned by Gregorski, a pilot who's applied for mining rights to the Doby asteroid belt. The third is Ambassador El'Rik's ship. He's returning to the Minx system."

"That's very helpful, Controller. Thank you for your assistance." Glotaj signed off, his brows furrowed in thought.

"I've been representing the Yanurans before the Admissions Committee," Mara mentioned. "Their departure was expected."

Glotaj nodded absently. "I'd like to have a private conversation with Admiral Daras Gog. I'm sure Sarina won't mind if I use her upstairs office."

While he was gone, the door chime rang and Hedy was admitted. Her haste in getting there was apparent in her disheveled appearance. She wore a pair of leggings and a pullover sweater, and she'd fastened her brown hair into a ponytail.

"Thank the stars you're here," Mara cried, rushing to her. Quickly, she filled Hedy in on what had happened.

Hedy's face paled and her lips compressed. When Mara finished, she rummaged in her bag for her mediscan unit. "I'll tend to her right away," she said. Turning on her heels, Hedy headed toward Sarina's sleeping chamber.

Mara paced the living area. Her mind filled with the issues they'd discussed. Had anything been left out, any item of small significance that would apply to the situation?

A thought struck her, and her heart raced. "Lieutenant Wren!"

Wren was at the holovid unit, studying Teir's new image crystallizer. At her summons, he glanced up.

"The kidnappers knew Sarina would open her door to receive a bouquet of flowers, yet Earth isn't advanced enough to be a member of the Coalition. First contact hasn't been made. How would they know about the Earth custom of delivering flowers? It would have to be someone like me who's studied their culture."

Wren raised his layered eyebrows. "Has anyone discussed this topic with you recently?"

She regarded him thoughtfully. She worked as a cultural specialist for the Department of Interstellar Relations in the Diplomatic Affairs Bureau, representing new alien cultures applying for admission to the Coalition. In addition, she attended interdisciplinary team rounds at the wellness center, offering her knowledge of alien customs as they pertained to medical care.

"I don't recall anyone mentioning Earth's cultural practices. Then again, the database in the study center is open to all." The main library on Bimordus Two had a huge directory, receiving input from over five hundred worlds.

"This could be an important clue," Wren remarked, his voice a pitch higher with excitement.

"What could?" Glotaj descended the spiral staircase. When Mara explained her idea, he nodded his agreement. "You're right. On Bimordus Two, we consider it a sacrilege to snip blooms and deprive them of their short lifespan. The kidnappers used a specific knowledge of Earth customs to trick Sarina. We'll have to look into this possibility more thoroughly."

He strode down the last few steps. Though dressed casually in a short tunic and trousers, his lined face, sharp gaze, and proud posture displayed his status as a member of the royal House of Raimorrda.

Teir also claimed lineage from that respected ruling family, Mara remembered. Was it possible the baby had been abducted by someone working against the Raimorrdans?

No, it couldn't be. Destroying the Elevation Ceremony would harm Auranians, not those of Raimorrdan blood. She was grasping at straws. Hanging her head, she felt discouragement wash over her.

"I've notified Admiral Gog about the traces of quantum resolution particles found in the nursery," Glotaj said, staring at a Carellian thorn vase displayed on a pedestal.

Mara followed the direction of his gaze. Pink veins highlighted the translucent white vase, while thorny prominences decorated the curved upper edge. It had been one of the best pieces she'd ever sculpted. The day when Sarina and Teir had accepted her gift with lavish praise had been one of her proudest moments.

Her eyes wandered to the holographic image of Jallyn fixed on the wall. The baby gurgled with laughter, her tiny hands and feet waving with uninhibited joy as the camera had captured her. She remembered how Sarina had beamed with pride when she showed her the picture, and her eyes misted.

Pushing aside her emotions, she focused on what Glotaj had said. "What's the significance of quantum resolution particles?" she asked.

Glotaj's mouth tightened as he moved closer to where she stood. "It means the abductors used transporter technology to escape. We've determined there were two of them, but our scans are inconclusive for further details."

Her jaw gaped. Transporter technology? As far as she knew, their scientists were only able to transport a roomful of objects from one location to another, but they hadn't perfected the technique enough to transfer people.

Transporter technology was not related to the molecular alteration process that ran their fabricators or allowed shuttles to be disguised in different configurations.

She stared at Glotaj. "How is this possible?"

"We know of several nonaligned species who possess technical knowledge in advance of our own," Glotaj said, his face grim. "The Rakkians, Fire Weavers, and Bolons come to mind."

"They should all be checked out," Wren stated, frowning. "One thing I don't understand—why the ruse with the flowers if the abductors could have gotten in using the same transporter method?"

"Apparently, they arrived downstairs in the lobby. They must have been uncertain as to the location of Sarina's apartment. But once they found it and gained entry, they beamed directly out."

"Is there any way to trace the pattern to learn where they went?" Mara asked.

Glotaj shook his head. "We don't have that capability. We do know the child was taken aboard a ship. Admiral Gog is sending patrols after Boris Gregorski and Ambassador El'Rik. The Yanuran delegation is another matter. Their situation requires a closer look, so I'm sending a special team to Yanura."

At Mara's look of puzzlement, he explained. "The Yanurans have applied for admission to the Coalition. You've been helping them with the application process, so you're more familiar with their situation. But Wren may not know the details."

He directed his attention to the Polluxite. "Fromoth Trun, the Yanuran leader, has offered to share the formula for Vyclor, a miracle age-preserving drug derived from seaweed, as a trade incentive. The data seems conclusive, but the Admissions Committee requires a fuller investigation before reaching a decision."

"The Yanurans don't need a trade incentive to enter the Coalition," Wren said. "So why are they offering something so valuable?"

"They're demanding immediate access to our technology instead of having to wait the usual probationary period of one annum. This approval can only be granted if they're given special trade status. We need to conduct a more thorough examination first."

"If you ask me," Mara interrupted, "the Admissions Committee is looking for an excuse to deny their application. No one likes their smell, and I think that's why the committee is delaying its response."

The Yanurans exuded a fishy odor that may have prejudiced the committee against admitting the amphibian race to the Coalition. Fighting intolerance had become Mara's passion in life after her own personal experiences in this regard. In her opinion, the Yanurans were being discriminated against without reasonable cause.

Glotaj compressed his mouth. "I'm sending a team to Yanura regardless of your views, Mara. The mission will confirm the data regarding the drug and see if their delegates had anything to do with Jallyn's disappearance."

"Then I'm going. I've been working with Fromoth Trun for the past five weeks, and I'm familiar with his preferences. You won't find anyone else better acquainted with Yanuran culture."

"Agreed," Glotaj said almost too quickly, as though he'd expected her to volunteer. "Lieutenant Wren, you'll join the group as navigator. Consider your medical leave canceled."

"We'll need a medic," Mara said. "Ask Hedy to go."

A smile cracked the supreme regent's face. "Excellent idea. Lieutenant Ebo, a Sirisian, will serve as communications officer. He's also a qualified engineer. Lieutenant Commander Deitan Sage will serve as pilot and mission leader."

Wren's eyes widened. "Commander Sage? He's a diving specialist in the SEARCH Force. We've worked together before."

"What's the SEARCH Force?" Mara asked, unfamiliar with that branch of the Defense League.

"SEARCH stands for Sea & Aerospace Command Detachment," Wren answered. "It's a commando unit whose operatives are trained to function in all types of environments. Commander Sage joined our crew last annum for a mission to Souk."

"I think Sarina briefly mentioned this to me. You had to transport a couple of people off the Isle of Spears in the Scylla Sea?"

"That's right. The commander dropped at forty kilometers offshore, swam to the island and laid out the laser markers to guide the rest of us in with our chutes. Luckily for us, Commander Sage took out a squadron of Hortha guards that would have pinned us on the beach. I don't know anyone else who could have taken them on single-handedly without leaving one of them alive to sound the alarm."

"Great," she muttered. Just what they needed—a gung-ho soldier in charge of a mission requiring diplomacy and tact. She knew the best way to deal with the Yanurans, and muscle power was not the approach of choice.

Hopefully, Commander Sage was a reasonable man who would respect her opinions. But if he took an aggressive stance, she'd have to deal with him in the only way he might understand.

She loved a good fight, as long as the weapons were words.

Chapter Two

"Be careful. Those fish squirt acid if they're handled improperly," Lieutenant Commander Deitan Sage warned through the commlink embedded in his face mask. Beyond the glimmer of his lamp, it was difficult to follow the movements of his fellow divers. The reef stretched into the inky blackness and his vision extended only as far as his light source.

He checked his own net that had caught a school of flatfish. Careful not to touch any of them with his gloved hand, he twisted the net opening around a tensile bar knot to seal it.

He'd much rather be exploring the reef that teemed with marine life instead of capturing fish destined for Defense League research. Flatfish could change colors to match their background. The military hoped to isolate the chemical process responsible and apply it to camouflage uniforms. No longer would it be necessary to issue desert wear for dry terrain or white parkas for frozen ice lands or forest green bodysuits for verdant planets. Enhanced with a chemical color changer, a standard-issue uniform could be created to suit all types of missions. It wasn't the kind of research Deke prided himself in.

For nearly the entire span of his thirty-five annums, he'd been fascinated by the watery depths. Having grown up on Eranus, where most people lived in floating cities atop vast oceans, that was easy to understand. But his father, the director general, had hoped Deke would follow in his footsteps with a military career. Jon Sage had enjoyed being a warrior, but not his son. Deke excelled at swimming and diving, and he chose marine biology for his career path. Despite his father's disappointment, Deke had coaxed Jon into sending him to the Institute for Marine Studies.

The chancellor, Samuel Ho Chin, had recognized his potential and encouraged him to pursue the research that fascinated him. Deke had advanced rapidly and earned his doctorate. When he heard Sammy intended to retire, Deke considered applying for the position. His area of study focused on deep-sea vents, but to continue his work, he needed a large grant. Securing the chancellorship would get him the required funding.

He knew many other qualified people would be in competition for the position, and it would help if he could stand out from the crowd. Jon advised him to accept a commission in the Defense League. Serving in the military would provide him with a well-rounded experience and should win him points over the academicians applying for the chancellorship.

He'd joined the elite SEARCH force as a diving expert. Although he accomplished his missions with a high rate of success, the end of his two-annum term of service was rapidly approaching. Meanwhile, Sammy's contract was due to expire in six months, and a rival was being considered for the job. Deke needed to distinguish himself before his best career opportunity dissolved.

He wouldn't be earning any bonus points in these murky waters. Collecting schools of fish was a total waste of his time and talent.

His glance snagged on a patch of long, whitish tubes with blood red tips glimmering in the cast of his light beyond a piece of brain coral. The ghostly cluster swayed gently in the current. Nearby, small crabs crept among a rise of rocks while an eel slithered off into a crevice.

Great stars, could those be giant tube worms?

His pulse accelerating, Deke swam over. He'd never seen the eight-foot-long tube worms in the absence of hot sulfur-rich water before. Did this mean they could exist in environments other than a deep-sea vent community? Or was there something special about this reef that made the red-tipped creatures show up here?

He yanked a specimen container off his weight belt and had just obtained a sample of ocean water when an agonized scream sounded from the commlink in his ear. He looked up in time to spot one of his colleagues sinking to the seabed in a flurry of bubbles.

After snapping the collection jar onto his belt, he took off with the efficiency of a strong swimmer. Deke kicked his legs and thrust water out of his path with powerful strokes to reach his fallen comrade. One glance at the ruptured air-supply hose showed him that a flatfish had spewed its acid. Nueva was barely conscious.

Deke ripped the woman's mouthpiece out and replaced it with his own. Sharing breaths, he revived her enough to get her to cooperate when he put his arm around her waist. He ascended toward the surface, his muscles straining. They stopped every few meters so he could give Nueva several intakes of air. Sweat dripped inside his dive suit, and his heart raced in a thumping rhythm. The passing minutes seemed like hauras as they slowly neared the light at the surface.

At last, they broke free. One quick glance, and his crewmates on the boat realized what had happened.

"Get her on board," yelled Larse, the team medic. The bearded man helped haul her onto the dive platform. It wasn't easy considering her weighted gear and the boat's rocking motion.

Deke looked skyward. The weather was deteriorating, according to the moisture-laden clouds scudding overhead. A stiff wind created high crests that battered his face.

A pretty redhead appeared at the rail. Carmin, a biochemist from Eranus, was as unrestrained in bed as she was masterful over a microscope. She and Deke had gotten to know each other quite well during this voyage. She must have noted the oncoming weather since an orange slicker covered her body.

"Where do you think you're going?" she hollered as he broke away from the dive platform.

"I have to check something below," he called, meaning to obtain a tube-worm specimen.

"No, you don't," a fierce male voice said. Commander Brigarde strode into view. The executive officer's large bulk was impressive even in his rain gear. His heavy dark brows furrowed in an angry line. "A message has come through from Command. You're to report to the captain's stateroom immediately."

Annoyance rippled through him. "What? I can't leave now. I've just found something—"

"Get your ass up here," Brigarde shouted, his face reddening.

"Yes, sir." Deke flipped onto the dive platform and removed his headgear. The clouds chose that moment to burst. Rain splashed his face and cascaded down his neck as he wrestled with the rest of his equipment on the swaying deck.

Still wearing his insulated wet suit, Deke clutched the specimen container in his hand and headed for the captain's quarters. His thoughts raced as he wound his way through the gray metal corridors of the ship's interior.

A message awaited him from Command. Did that mean he was needed for a SEARCH operation? It would sure beat floating around here and hunting schools of fish.

He identified himself on the comm unit, and Captain Manseur's gruff voice invited him to enter. Deke stepped inside, closing the door behind him. Then he turned and gave a crisp salute.

"You can dispense with the formalities, Commander. What's that?" The captain eyed the collection jar in Deke's hand.

Deke grinned, appreciating Manseur's blunt manner. "I found tube worms by the reef, sir. This is the first time I've seen them in this type of environment. I took a water sample so I could test its properties." He ran a hand through his damp hair, wondering if he'd be allowed time in the ship's lab.

Captain Manseur gave a curt nod. A stern military man who possessed a keen sense of humor, he was in charge of the fleet of oceangoing research vessels that Defense League maintained on Setai IV. The world was mostly water with a few land masses, much like Eranus. Setai IV was being explored with the possibility of colonization in the near future.

The captain didn't claim to be a science scholar. He preferred fine wines, gourmet foods, and beautiful women as his hobbies. With Deke receiving new orders, no doubt he'd concentrate on getting to know the voluptuous redhead when Deke transferred off his ship.

"You'll have to leave your specimen for our biochemists. Here are your new orders." Captain Manseur handed a datalink to Deke.

Deke activated the device and peered at the contents displayed on the screen. He was to report for duty at the Defense League station on Bimordus Two, the Coalition capital. He'd be taking charge of a special mission. A space voyage of sixteen days duration was involved.

"What is this? Why me?" Deke stared at the datalink in stunned silence. His missions had always utilized his diving expertise. He belonged at sea, not piloting a starship. Appalled, he glanced at the captain as though his superior officer could change his orders.

"A transport vehicle is scheduled to arrive for you within the next haura, Lieutenant Commander. I suggest you pack your things."

"The hell I will! This isn't the kind of mission I'm normally assigned."

"You wish to contact Vice Admiral Rutta to protest your orders?"

"They're not from Rutta, sir. The Supreme Regent sent this message." Deke didn't care what the mission entailed. He wanted to remain on Setai IV to investigate those tube worms. Perhaps it was all a mistake. "May I use a secure line, sir? I'd like to learn more details so I'll know what equipment to bring."

"As long as you're ready when the shuttle arrives, you can stop by the comm center."

Deke nodded and snapped a salute. "It's been a pleasure serving with you, Captain." Still clutching his specimen container, he left the captain's stateroom.

Detouring by the ship's lab, he gave his valuable water sample to one of the biochemists before heading to the comm center. The duty officer left him alone so he could make his call in private.

Glotaj came on the line right away. Deke faced the older man on the monitor screen. From the background view, he could see the supreme regent was in his office.

"Sir, I don't understand why you've put me in command of this mission," Deke said. "My skills are better utilized in undersea operations."

"Your diving expertise is one of the reasons why I selected you to lead the team to Yanura, Deke."

He drew in a breath. He hadn't known their destination. "Yanura? Why there?"

Glotaj patiently explained the purpose of the voyage. When he was finished, Deke let out a long breath. He had reasons of his own for wanting to visit the planet, so he didn't need to be convinced. But he was still puzzled as to why Glotaj had chosen him as team leader. "Why didn't you just assign me as science officer?" he asked.

"As you know, your father and I are friends. He's spoken to me about your interest in the chancellorship. I thought I'd give you the chance to demonstrate your leadership skills. I've been following your career since you entered the service, Deke, and I believe you have the potential to go far."

"Thank you, sir." Deke's voice choked with emotion. This could be the opportunity he'd been needing to distinguish himself from the other candidates. He'd better make sure his team accomplished their mission objectives. "The shuttle is expected at any moment, and I have to prepare for departure. I appreciate your faith in me, Your Excellency."

Glotaj's lined face creased into a smile. "May the Light of the Aura grace your voyage. By the way, the name of the vessel you'll be taking to Yanura is the *Celeste.*" His eyes twinkled mischievously. "You'll find she's different, but that can have its advantages. Glotaj out."

As soon as the supreme regent terminated the link, Deke went to his cabin to gather his personal belongings. While automatically piling his things into a single worn case, he thought about the problems Glotaj had mentioned.

He looked forward to investigating the seaweed farms on Yanura. Mariculture was familiar to him from his home planet, so he knew what to expect. If the Yanurans were fooling anyone with their story about an age-preserving drug, they wouldn't get past him. And should the Yanurans be involved in Jallyn's abduction, he'd find her, too. He wouldn't let them get away with any more of their dirty tricks, not after what had happened to Larikk.

His good friend and colleague had disappeared on Yanura three annums ago. Deke had reason to believe foul play was involved, but the Yanurans had effectively blocked any attempts at an investigation. At the time, they were not members of the Coalition, so he couldn't pursue the case. But now that they were applying for admissions status, they'd come under Coalition provisional law.

He halted his packing and gritted his teeth. If the Yanurans were being deceitful—and he'd be willing to bet this was the case—Deke would quickly and ruthlessly ferret out the truth.

****

"I know we're on the wrong track, Hedy," Mara said to her roommate. "Fromoth Trun was extremely courteous in all my encounters with him. I'm sure the Yanurans have nothing to do with Jallyn's disappearance."

"We'll find out when we get to Yanura," Hedy replied.

They were home packing for the trip ahead. Hedy had finished stuffing her case and had wandered into Mara's room. The medic sat on the lounger, examining her painted fingernails for flaws.

"I'm looking forward to seeing their planet after working so closely with Fromoth Trun. They're an interesting species." Mara folded a stack of data cards into her bag. "Did you know they are nocturnal? We'll have to adapt to their way of life. It'll be quite fascinating."

Hedy rolled her green eyes. "I'm more excited about spending time in close quarters with that handsome Polluxite, Lieutenant Wren. Did you see his shoulders? By the corona, I've never met a man with a physique like his before."

"Oh, yeah? How about that Fraisirian messenger from the finance ministry? Didn't you say the same thing about him?"

Hedy shrugged. "That was last week."

"Hedy! This mission is serious."

The petite brunette grinned. "No one said we couldn't have fun along the way."

"Lieutenant Wren is a member of Captain Reylock's crew. Normally he ships out on the *Valiant.*"

"So what? He's barely recovered from a disrupter wound he got on their last mission." She heaved a long sigh, her gaze heavenward. "I wish I had been his medic."

Mara snorted. "You're impossible. I keep telling you men are nothing but trouble, and you won't listen."

Her most recent relationship had been a disaster. She and Pietor, an advocate in the Enforcement Bureau, had been seeing each other for seven months when he'd invited her to his home planet to meet his parents. They'd taken one look at her dark hair and olive complexion and voiced their disapproval. Mara was nothing like the albino beauties on Sonoria. How could Pietor have taken up with someone like her?

Instead of coming to her defense, Pietor had told them about her special gift. The memory of his mocking words still cut her deeply.

"Pietor wasn't worthy of you," Hedy said gently. "If he'd really loved you, he would have appreciated your ability."

"I was nothing more than an exotic plaything to him. What a fool I was to believe he cared about me."

"He was weak, Mara. Be glad he didn't marry you first and

then take you home. You were lucky to get rid of him." Hedy gave her a teasing grin. "Loosen up and you'll have more fun on this trip."

"I'm not joining this delegation to have fun. I intend to prove to the Admissions Committee that the Yanurans deserve an unbiased approval of their application."

She threw a few cosmetics into her case despite her knowledge that the *Celeste* fabricators could supply most of what they'd need. She still preferred to bring along certain favorite items.

"I wonder what Lieutenant Commander Sage will be like," Hedy mused. "I hope he's not one of those stiff protocol types."

"Wren speaks very highly of him," Mara pointed out.

"We're not in the military. He can't order us around."

Mara heard the note of defiance in her roommate's tone. "We are under his command while on this mission, Hedy."

Hedy raised her eyebrows. "Spoken like a real trooper. I can't wait to see how you react when he gives you an order." She rose, smoothing the skirt of her minidress. "In the meantime, I'm going to get ready to meet that gorgeous Lieutenant Wren again." She indicated her brown waves of shoulder-length hair. "Do you like this style or should I straighten it?"

Mara raised her hands in mock despair. "What am I going to do with you?"

Hedy flashed her a brilliant smile. "Try having a lighter outlook. It'll work wonders on your psyche. Say, maybe you could jump into Wren's viewpoint the next time we meet. You'll be able to sense how he feels about me."

That did it. Mara picked up a pillow and threw it at her roommate.

Hedy dodged the hit with a squeal and ran out. Mara stood looking after her, her hands on her hips, wondering how she was going to stand hearing Hedy's ramblings about Wren for the entire trip.

Despite their teasing banter, Mara knew Hedy was just as worried as she was about Sarina and the baby. It seemed to be an unspoken agreement between them to focus on the political aspects of the mission and not the personal angle. Otherwise, thinking about Jallyn could paralyze them both with anxiety.

Mara packed her last item, the baby's blanket. She'd need it to do separations to check on Jallyn's status. Her heart filled with pain as she pictured the tiny infant girl, so sweet and innocent.

May the Light of the Aura shine upon us, she prayed. *We'll need all the help we can get.*

Hedy was a competent healer, and Mara knew she wouldn't be diverted by her attraction to Wren when her skills were required. Despite her passionate nature, Hedy could be quite serious when the occasion demanded it.

Mara, on the other hand, was always serious. She drove herself hard and needed to be constantly busy. On this trip, as cultural specialist, she'd be responsible for ensuring the Yanurans were greeted properly, according to their customs. It was a role she looked forward to with great anticipation. Hopefully the crew, and Lieutenant Commander Sage in particular, would be receptive to her suggestions.

Chapter Three

"Hedy, what's the problem?" Mara asked, frowning.

They'd just stepped off the moving walkway at launch bay 72 and were facing the air lock that would take them out of the protective domed section of the city. The whine of engines and roar of thrusters coming from outside hurt Mara's ears.

"I forgot something." Hedy's arms were loaded down with bundles. She'd dashed into a few of the shops along the spaceport concourse and now paused, staring at Mara. "I have to go back."

"Oh, for heaven's sake." Mara glanced ahead, eager to get aboard the *Celeste.*

"You can go on. I won't be long. Did you remember to call Sarina and tell her we were leaving?"

"Yes, I did. She's so disappointed she couldn't come along."

Hedy raised an eyebrow. "Glotaj reminded her that she needs to stay home in case the kidnappers contact her."

"He's right, but I wish we could offer more in the way of support. With Teir and us gone, she'll have no one else to confide in. Glotaj has clamped down on letting the news leak out."

"Stop feeling guilty," Hedy chided her. "You know you're excited about this trip."

Mara smiled sheepishly. "Yes, and we should be moving along. At least let me carry some of those packages."

Hedy handed over several of her bags. "I'll see you on board the ship," she said before turning away and heading back toward the shops.

Mara stepped inside the air lock. A steel door hissed shut

behind her, followed by a whoosh of air that clogged her ears. Another door slid open on the opposite side. She strode out into the late afternoon sunshine, shivering from the sudden drop in temperature.

Stopping in her tracks, she stared at the fat, cumbersome spacecraft standing on the launchpad.

"Great suns, what kind of ship is that?"

Instead of the sleek vessel she'd expected, the *Celeste* reminded her of a manatee, an Earth mammal she'd read about in her studies. Maneuverability for a ship this size and shape had to be minimal. She took in the reflective black surface. Maybe its purpose was to provide some sort of protective camouflage. With its odd design, the ship seemed more suitable for hauling cargo than for taking a crew into a potentially dangerous situation.

Not that she thought they'd run into hostilities from the Yanurans. On the contrary, the amphibians were sure to welcome the Coalition team, since this visit would give them the chance to prove their claims about a miracle drug. Fromoth Trun had left Bimordus Two to make the necessary arrangements for receiving an official inspection team.

Actually, it made sense for them to arrive in a civilian vessel. If they showed up in a warship, it would alert the Yanurans that more was at stake than a mere scientific expedition. Still, considering the hazards of space travel, she'd have felt better if the ship had been designed for speed and maneuverability. Pirate attacks may have diminished since the Souk slave runs had ended, but the thought of pirates still unnerved her. There were other rogues and thieves out there unrelated to the Souk conflict.

A security detail checked her in and directed her up the gangplank to board the *Celeste*. The embarkation area was located near the cargo hold on D deck. She spotted a schematic diagram of the ship on a far wall and hastened over to figure out where to go.

The bridge was located on deck A and the engineering section on deck C. Staterooms were to be found on deck B, two levels up. There were six private cabins, she noted. How would she know which one had been assigned to her and Hedy? Deck B also had a holovid lounge, a physio lab, a dining and conference facility, and other public areas that weren't labeled.

Anxious to explore, she entered the turbolift. "Deck B," Mara commanded, and the door slid shut. Hopefully someone was around who could tell her which cabin was hers. Odd that there wasn't any reception committee to greet the civilians.

The lift rose, and a moment later, it came to a smooth halt. Its steel door opened to reveal a long, narrow corridor with soft lighting and ivory painted walls.

Balancing the packages in her arms, she stepped into the corridor. As she moved forward, a door to her right shot open and a tall, dark-haired man walked directly into her.

Crying out, Mara dropped her bundles and teetered backward. His arm shot out, catching her at the waist.

"What do you think you're doing?" he snapped.

Pulled against him, she found herself staring into his face. Nearly a head taller than she, he reached a good six-feet-two-inches in height. They were so close she could smell the musky scent of his aftershave.

"I was just getting out of the lift."

His glance drifted to her slightly parted lips. "You should watch where you're going."

"So should you," she retorted, flustered.

Her senses flared as she regarded him, unable to move away. The man's features were angular and even, sculpted like one of her art forms. He had heavy brows, a straight nose, and a perfectly chiseled mouth. His jawline was firm with just the hint of a shadow.

Imagining what it would be like to smooth her fingers over the planes of his face, her artistic persona itched to touch him. With that desire came the stirrings of something unwanted deep inside her. Her heart hammered in a rapid tempo of response.

"Ships have confined spaces," the man said in a low, suave tone. "There isn't room for tight maneuvers."

"I can see that." Her breath came short as she felt every point of contact between them.

"Try to be more careful, or we might run into each other again." His mouth curved into a grin as though it would be a pleasurable event.

Gods, when he smiled, his brown eyes warmed like melted chocolate and two adorable dimples appeared in his cheeks. Never in all of her twenty-eight annums had she met a man this handsome.

"Who are you?" she demanded, barely recognizing the husky tone as her own.

His grin widened. "Lieutenant Commander Deitan Sage at your service. You can call me Deke."

He was Commander Sage? She'd expected him to be a stiff soldier, not a rakishly attractive devil with a smooth tongue. Warning bells rang in her mind. This voyage might be more dangerous than she'd anticipated.

"Release me," she ordered. Struggling to free herself, she tilted her neck back and found his mouth hovering centimeters above hers.

"This could prove to be an interesting journey… Mara." His eyes danced as he continued to hold her without any apparent inclination to let her go.

"How do you know my name?" She tried to ignore the sudden weakness in her limbs.

"I've read your dossier. I know quite a bit about you." His arm tightened. "But not as much as I'd like to know. You feel quite good in my arms."

Someone cleared their throat behind them and Deke let her go. She sprang back with a guilty expression. Hedy stood grinning at them in front of the open turbolift car. Her arms were loaded with bundles.

"Pardon me for interrupting," she cooed.

"Hedy, this is Commander Sage," Mara said, struggling to regain her composure. "Can you tell us which cabin is ours?" she asked him, her tone icy.

"Your stateroom is the third one on the left," he told her, tugging his maroon and gray uniform into place.

Her skin heating under his scrutiny, she stooped to pick up the bundles she'd dropped. He bent over to help, and their heads collided.

"My, you do enjoy personal contact, don't you?" he said, picking up the scattered packages.

Her heart somersaulted as he gave her another disarming grin. If he kept displaying those dimples, she'd be lost.

"Thank you." She took the remaining bundles from him.

Deke nodded at Hedy. "You must be the medic. That stateroom is yours." He pointed to the closed door opposite Mara's.

"We have our own cabins?" Mara exclaimed. This bonus was unexpected.

"Yes, we want our guests to be comfortable. What is all this stuff you're bringing aboard?"

"I went shopping," Hedy replied. "Wait until you see the travel games I bought. We're going to have a great time. I picked up some snacks, too, along with extra music chips."

Deke's brows drew together. "This is not a pleasure cruise, ladies. I suggest you use the next couple of hauras to stow your gear and familiarize yourselves with the ship's interior. We'll be meeting in the conference room at eighteen hundred hauras for a mission briefing."

With an abrupt turn, he strode toward the hatchway at the opposite end and disappeared into another compartment.

"Whew," Hedy said. "If this isn't a pleasure cruise, he sure has a strange way of greeting his new crew. You two didn't waste any time getting acquainted."

Mara grimaced. "We accidentally ran into each other. It's like he cast a spell on me. I couldn't move."

"Uh-oh, this sounds serious."

"The only thing that's serious is our mission." For all the fun things Hedy had brought, they shouldn't lose sight of their purpose.

"I need to make sure my equipment arrived intact," Hedy

said. "I suppose they put our luggage in our cabins. Did you check to see if your foot pan arrived?"

Mara winced. She couldn't fathom why Hedy kept referring to her sculpting tray as a foot pan. "I figured it would be too big to fit in the cabin, so I had it delivered to the cargo bay. Do you want to take a tour with me after we're settled in?"

"Sure. Maybe I'll run into Lieutenant Wren the same way you met Commander Sage."

Hedy's green eyes sparkled with mischief as her mood shifted from somber to lighthearted. It was one of the features about her that Mara admired. Dealing with pain and suffering on a daily basis, Hedy was able to walk away from her job and enjoy herself on her time off.

After unloading Hedy's packages, Mara entered her cabin and shut the door. She wished she could be as blithe about life as her friend, but one cause or another always seemed to attract her attention. This latest one with the Yanurans threatened to undermine her goals. Her push for the Yanurans to be admitted into the Coalition offended certain influential parties. This attitude impeded her chances of getting promoted, but she wouldn't sacrifice her ideals for selfish reasons. The Yanurans were being mistreated and it was up to her to prove their sincerity, regardless of the consequences.

Yet she had her doubts. Fromoth Trun's emotions had been impossible to read. She had relied mostly on her impressions of the Yanuran leader to form an opinion. Even Hedy had advised her to be more discriminating in her judgments, but after experiencing prejudice firsthand, Mara felt compelled to support the Yanuran cause. She was as firm in her commitment as that ruby crystalline table was rock solid.

Her gaze swept from the low table to the plush sitter upholstered in a rose and beige pattern that sat behind it. Hanging on the wall above was a painting with colorful geometric designs. The sharp lines didn't appeal to her artistic sense. She preferred the rounded rims and graceful curvatures of her sculptures.

Through an archway beyond, she spotted the firm double lounger that served as a bed. Her case had been placed beside it on the carpeted floor. Built-in shelves, a lighted vanity, and a fabricator alcove completed the decor. Off to one side was the entrance to a private sanitary.

Not bad for a spaceship, she thought, going to use the facilities. The sanitary was roomy, and the sonic shower was big enough for two.

With a sigh, she remembered the voyage to Antarus IV, Pietor's home planet. The ship Pietor had leased was small but comfortable. Taking advantage of the autopilot, they'd spent most of the time in their cabin. The spacious shower had been an added attraction. All had gone well until they arrived at his home world and she met his parents. She could still feel the sting of their disapproval.

Not only was her complexion dark compared to their people, but she was… different. It was a label she'd suffered throughout her childhood, but she'd never expected to hear it from Pietor's lips. The painful memories were still fresh in her mind.

As she washed and dried her hands, she focused on more current issues. It had been a while since she'd checked on Jallyn's status. Glotaj had requested she do periodic separations to see if the baby's location had changed. Mara unpacked her case until she came to the baby's blanket. Clutching it in her hands, she sat on the lounger and closed her eyes.

The astral plane beckoned her, and her essence left her body. She floated upward and concentrated on receiving vibrations from the blanket. A strange sensation tugged at her, something dark and unpleasant. Disturbed, she ignored it and concentrated on Jallyn. The next moment found her inside the baby's head.

Jallyn was asleep. Her eyes were closed, and somnolence started to overwhelm Mara as she absorbed the infant's tranquil state. She dissolved back into the astral plane, recalling that Sarina's hands had touched the blanket. How was her friend faring?

Instantly, she was zipping through non-dimensional space

and popping into Sarina's perspective. The Great Healer sat alone by the comm unit inside her residence. Her gaze was fixed on a framed image of Jallyn that hung on the wall. Staring at the happy vision through tears swimming in her eyes, Sarina's heart twisted with anguish.

Abruptly, Mara separated. She couldn't bear to share her friend's pain and not be able to help. Sarina would have liked to come with them, but there were no guarantees they'd find Jallyn. The baby could have been taken aboard one of the other two ships that left that day. Mara still didn't believe the Yanurans were involved but intended to fulfill her duty. Glotaj wanted all possibilities checked out, and she would play her part.

Returning to her body, she prayed Jallyn would be recovered quickly. At least the baby appeared unharmed. She'd have to do more frequent separations in case the situation changed. How terrible for Sarina, waiting by the comm unit for the chime to sound, worried about her beloved daughter. Mara's eyes flooded with moisture.

She covered her face with her hands, yielding to her fears when someone knocked on her door. Thinking it was Hedy, Mara called out, "Come in."

Commander Sage swept inside her cabin. He took one look at the tears streaking her face, and his handsome visage blanched. "I'm dreadfully sorry. I didn't mean to intrude." He stepped back as though meaning to leave.

"It's all right." Mara managed a smile. "I was just thinking about Jallyn." Uncertain of how much he knew about her, she didn't mention the separation.

Standing, she appraised her visitor. His thick dark hair swept his forehead in a casual style. His eyes held a look of sympathy. Her gaze fell to his uniform. The fabric stretched tautly across his broad shoulders and tapered over a wide chest, trim waist, and narrow hips. His pants tucked into a pair of polished black boots.

"I came to ask if you'd received your bags," Deke remarked, his tone light.

"Yes, I did, Commander. Thank you for your concern."

"I said you could call me Deke." His eyes crinkled with amusement.

"Very well… Deke." She felt strange using his first name, and uncomfortable when he was so near. His bulk seemed to take up half the space in her cabin. Swallowing, she tried to look anywhere but into his eyes.

"You're the alien culture specialist, but you're also a friend of Sarina and Teir's?" he asked.

"That's right."

"And the medic, I understand you and she room together on Bimordus Two?"

"Hedy and I met at the conservatory where we both took exobiology. Hedy branched off into multispecies medicine, and I went into cultural studies."

"I see." Deke studied her, his expression oblique.

Mara wondered what he was thinking. It didn't take her long to find out.

"I'd like to get to know you better," he said, taking a step closer.

"What do you mean?" She backed away until her legs hit the upholstered sitter. "You read my dossier, so I assume you're aware of my professional qualifications."

"You know that's not what I'm talking about." A sexy grin lit his face as he regarded her.

She took one look at his dimples and melted. Her gaze locked with his. "Shouldn't we discuss our mission?" she asked in a desperate attempt to deflect his interest.

"We'll do so at the briefing." He moved closer.

Noting the look in his eye, she realized he intended to make a pass at her and she wasn't sure how to respond. Her nerve endings tingled in anticipation of his touch. What would be the harm in it? He knew she was a professional. His opinion of her as a crew member shouldn't be influenced by her response.

"Don't worry," he said, placing his hands on her shoulders,

"we'll have plenty of time to talk business later. Let's get acquainted."

His eyes pierced hers with a seductive warmth that stole her breath. She couldn't tear her gaze away. But before she gave in to her yearnings, she sought to free her mind of lingering concerns.

"Do you think we'll succeed?" she asked.

"Succeed? At what?"

"Our mission to Yanura."

"Our mission is obvious, although how we're going to face down the Yanurans in this unwieldy ship is beyond me. We'll find a way." He bent his head toward her, clearly wishing to dispense with small talk and get on with his seduction.

Her anger flared. "What do you mean by *facing down* the Yanurans?"

Deke's face folded into a frown. "Our weapons array shows minimal configuration. The amphibians are sure to cause trouble. I'd have preferred a vessel with more armaments."

She twisted out of his grasp. "Why should you think they'd cause a problem? They're eager to be accepted into the Coalition. May I remind you that we're not planning a commando raid? Our visit to Yanura is a diplomatic affair."

"That's what the Yanurans are supposed to think, but we're searching for a missing child. We have to be prepared for any contingencies."

It annoyed her that Deke anticipated hostilities. Why would Fromoth Trun, the Yanuran leader, spend over a month on Bimordus Two pleading his case with the Admissions Committee if he planned to harm the inspection team?

"I'm sure the Yanurans will be happy to cooperate with us," she said in a stiff tone.

"Well, I'm not." He stepped away, his eyes blazing. "Are you so gullible that you believe those creatures? Didn't you see the preliminary survey that was done when they first mentioned joining the Coalition? Glotaj told me that hints of political unrest came to light, but the extent and nature weren't known. He wants us to find out more about it. Jallyn's disappearance might be related to whatever problems the Yanurans are having at home."

"How preposterous! I don't see any connection between the Yanurans and Jallyn."

"Oh, no? Fromoth Trun's vessel launched shortly after Jallyn's abduction took place. Are you denying he's a suspect when you saw for yourself that Jallyn was on a ship?"

So the commander did know about her separations. "Two other ships also left the spaceport at that time. You're just prejudiced against the Yanurans like everyone else. I thought you were selected to command this mission because of your diving expertise. You're supposed to check out their seaweed farms and confirm the data on Vyclor."

"That's only part of our mission."

"It's the most important part. As soon as you verify their claims regarding the drug, we can make a favorable recommendation to the Admissions Committee."

He shook his head. "It's not as simple as that. We still have to locate Jallyn."

"Why don't you come right out and say you believe the Yanurans are guilty of her abduction?"

"We'll find out soon enough." He gave her a smug look.

"How dare you accuse them of such a grievous crime without having any experience in their affairs." She glared at him in righteous indignation.

"Oh, but I do have experience," he said quietly, his brown eyes intense.

"How so?"

"I'll explain during the briefing."

"Fine, then you can leave now."

Deke's mouth tightened. "This isn't over."

"Yes, it is. I'll see you later, Commander." She stared after him as he left. Rage constricted her throat. Who in Zor did he think he was—a judge, jury, and executioner? How dare he accuse the Yanurans of wrongdoing when he couldn't prove anything. She wondered what experience he'd had with them that made him so biased in his views. Regardless of his reasons, his attitude could be a hindrance to their mission.

She considered contacting Glotaj and registering a complaint, but then she remembered Deke had been selected by the supreme regent himself. Glotaj must have thought he was the best man for the job.

It would be up to her to persuade Commander Sage to take a reasonable approach. Hedy was always chiding her for promoting one cause or another, but she felt compelled to defend issues she felt strongly about. Instilling tolerance in Deke was going to be her next challenge.

She hadn't always expressed her opinions so openly. As a child, she used to shy away from confrontations. Because of her special ability, her relationships usually ended in hurt and rejection.

The people on her planet were naturally psychic, but in most cases the full range of their ability didn't develop until after puberty. Mara had manifested her innate talents much earlier. Although other Tyberian children were able to sense emotions at an early stage, it was rare for one so young to be able to travel the astral plane. Usually it took years of study for an adult to reach that level of consciousness.

Because she didn't know how to discipline herself, Mara would jump into her friends' viewpoints without warning. Her ability frightened her playmates, who were too young to understand. Under those circumstances, no one wanted to be her companion for long. Eventually it became too painful to make friends because she knew it would only lead to ridicule.

A special school existed for children like her who were specially gifted at an early age. Mara's parents sent her there so she could learn how to channel her psychic energy. They didn't realize their action only made her feel more alienated.

She'd applied herself to her studies so she could leave the school and enter "normal" society again. Eventually, she had learned how to control her separations. As an adult, she declined the opportunity to extend her powers and chose instead to study exobiology at the Science Conservatory on Gemini VII.

Her experiences motivated her to specialize in cultural relations. In her opinion, the key to accepting alien cultures was to understand them.

Commander Sage didn't seem to feel that way. If he approached the Yanurans with his hostile attitude, he might destroy the progress she'd made with Fromoth Trun. Mara would have to convince him to view the Yanurans more objectively.

A knock sounded on her door, and Hedy's high-pitched voice called out, "Are you ready for our tour yet? I finished unpacking."

"Yes, I'm coming." A moment later, she joined Hedy in the corridor. "Commander Sage stopped by my cabin." She glanced up and down the narrow space to make sure no one else was around to hear.

"Oh?" Hedy's eyebrows rose.

"I can't understand his attitude toward the Yanurans. The man's mind is poisoned with prejudice against them."

"Why do you say that?"

They walked toward the hatchway at the far end. "He just about accused them of being liars. He mentioned a report that hinted at political problems on Yanura and suspects Jallyn's disappearance might be related." She snorted. "I've never heard anything so absurd. Fromoth Trun assured me he had the full support of his people."

Hedy smiled. "I'll bet you gave Commander Sage your opinion."

"Of course, I did. I won't let him get away with making false accusations."

"Uh-oh. I get the feeling the poor man doesn't know what he's in for. This is just the type of challenge you enjoy." Hedy gave her a curious glance. "Why did he stop by in the first place? Was it to discuss the Yanurans?"

Mara grimaced. "He wanted to get to know me better."

"You don't say! And how did he propose to do that?"

They crossed into a section with open hatchways leading into other public areas. "I'll leave that to your imagination," Mara said dryly.

Hedy grinned as though intending to coax the details from Mara but just then she spotted someone ahead. "Stars, there's Lieutenant Wren," she squealed.

The Polluxite was ascending a spiral staircase just ahead of the main lounge.

Hedy rushed forward. "Hello, Lieutenant. It's good to see you again."

"Please call me Wren, Dr. Te'larr." The big man paused and glanced down at her.

"And I'm Hedy." Her gaze locked with his, and for once she was speechless. Clearly Hedy was mesmerized by the fellow's clear hazel eyes.

Wren cleared his throat. "Excuse me, but there's work to be done." He turned away to continue his ascent.

"Is it time for the briefing yet?" Hedy asked, her gaze fixed on his broad back and the vertical slits visible in his shirt. She'd never seen his wings sprout but Mara had told her about them. Hedy had said they sounded sexy as hell.

He glanced back at her. "Not yet. We have to leave orbit first."

Mara waved a greeting. "Hello, Wren. Would it be okay if we watched the launch from the main viewscreen?"

"Sure, follow me. The bridge is up here." He pointed to the round opening above his head. His gaze slid to Hedy. "After you, mistress."

Hedy winked at Mara and put her foot on the lowest rung. She managed to hike up her skirt as she passed him.

Wren's rugged face colored as Hedy stepped onto the landing above. She whipped around to face Wren when he reached the top. He towered above her, being at least six inches taller.

"Mistress, you're in my path," he said, stating the obvious.

"Sorry." Hedy stepped to the side, her gaze following his

movements as he headed to the nav console to begin his calculations.

Mara observed them with amusement. Those two had some serious vibes between them. She noted Deke was already on the bridge, busy monitoring one of the computer displays. Another crew member was present at the comm panel station.

"That must be Lieutenant Ebo, the Sirisian," she said to Hedy, indicating the thin humanoid who had the characteristic elastic pink skin of his race. He'd covered his bald head with a scarlet turban. As they watched, he elongated his arm to toggle a switch several meters away.

Mara introduced herself and Hedy to the fellow. He acknowledged their greeting and turned back to his task.

Deke addressed them. "I see you've decided to join us for the launch. We should be getting clearance to lift off in less than ten minutes. You may wish to hold onto those safety straps on the bulkhead. Kindly don't distract us from our work, or I'll send you to the observation lounge."

"I wouldn't think of being a distraction, Commander," Mara said in a teasing tone.

He tightened his mouth and returned his attention to his instruments. Mara stared at the back of his head, eager to hear what he'd have to say at the upcoming briefing.

Chapter Four

"The two intruders in Sarina's apartment were Rakkians," Deke said. He sat at a circular table in the dining facility that doubled as a conference room. It had a large oval viewport, bright lighting, and comfortable seating. Mara had claimed a place on his left, followed by Hedy and Wren, with Ebo on his right.

Acutely aware of Mara's presence, he tried to display disinterest toward her for the sake of his crew. It wasn't easy when his gaze kept sliding in her direction. He'd never seen a woman so stunningly beautiful. His fingers ached to thread through her long glossy hair. Straight and thick, it cascaded down her back like an onyx waterfall. Her deep blue eyes reminded him of the fathomless ocean depths, full of secrets he yearned to explore. She was more exotic than any sea creature and more alluring than any siren.

Tamping down his arousal, Deke forced his attention back to the subject at hand.

"The Rakkians were identified as Pruet and Joro, assassins who hire out their services to the highest bidders," he continued. "Glotaj is checking into their recent activities to determine their employer." Drumming his fingers on the table, he wished they had more conclusive information.

Mara glanced in his direction and his gaze slammed into hers. Her olive complexion flamed with color as she quickly averted her eyes.

"Forgive me, sir, but can you fill me in on what happened on Bimordus Two?" Ebo asked, drawing Deke's mind back to their topic of discussion. The Sirisian elongated his arm and reached to the fabricator to conjure himself a drink.

Deke explained the details of Jallyn's disappearance. "We have no idea why the child was taken. No ransom demands have been made, so we can only hope she's being kept alive for whatever purpose her captors have in mind."

"She is being cared for as though her welfare is important," Mara added. "I would guess that means her return is anticipated."

"Maybe she'll be released after the Elevation Ceremony," Hedy said with a hopeful note.

Deke didn't believe the child's recovery would be that simple. "The kidnappers have the advantage over us. The longer Jallyn is missing, the more desperate we'll become. When they do make their demands known, we'll be more likely to accede to them. She has to be kept alive so proof of her well-being can be demonstrated. Meanwhile, the two henchmen haven't resurfaced. Glotaj believes they're still with the child."

Silence fell over the room, broken by Wren. "Mara, tell them your theory about Earth customs."

Mara's eyes brightened. "Whoever sent Joro and Pruet knew about Sarina being from Earth. It's a popular courting custom there to send cut flowers to a woman. The assassins approached Sarina offering a bouquet they said was from Captain Reylock."

"Glotaj had the investigative team check the records at the study center, but no one accessed files on Earth customs within the past six months other than Captain Reylock himself," Deke said.

"Am I correct in assuming the Yanurans are not aware of our true mission?" Ebo queried.

Deke nodded, his expression somber. "The Yanuran delegation departed at the same time as two other ships following Jallyn's abduction. Defense League patrols have been sent after those vessels. We're responsible for the Yanurans. The Admissions Committee planned to send a science team there anyway, which worked in our favor."

Ebo elongated his neck to peer closely at Deke. "So while we're pretending to evaluate their admission status, in actuality we'll be searching for clues to the missing child's location?"

Deke's brows drew together. "We are the science team, Lieutenant. Part of our job is to check into the Yanuran claims about a miracle age-preserving drug."

"Commander Sage is a diving specialist," Wren contributed, hunching his broad shoulders. "Since the Yanuran drug is derived from seaweed, the Yanurans have agreed to let us inspect their underwater farms as proof of their claims. The commander was selected to lead the mission because of his expertise in this field."

Deke squinted his eyes in thought. Wren had made an important point about Deke's background, and he should approach this assignment as though it were a SEARCH operation. Then they'd be prepared for any contingencies that might arise.

"We'll break for evening nourishment and then adjourn to the ordnance room," he said. "I'll need to do a weapons assessment on each one of you."

"Weapons assessment?" Mara asked. "What for?"

Deke turned his full attention on her, watching her moisten her lips with the tip of her tongue. It was an unconscious gesture on her part, but it mesmerized him. Angry at himself for being distracted, he made his tone of voice harsher than intended.

"You need to be proficient in the use of tactical armaments," he told her, knowing she'd be riled. "Each one of us must be prepared."

"Prepared for what? Are you expecting the Yanurans to fire upon us?"

"You never know. I wouldn't put it past them to lure us to the surface and cause an unexpected accident."

"Don't be absurd. Fromoth Trun and his people will be trying to impress us so we'll recommend their acceptance to the Admissions Committee."

"The Yanurans are deceitful liars. You can't trust anything they say."

Mara knocked her chair back as she rose. "If you approach them with that attitude, you'll destroy the rapport I've established with Fromoth Trun. You'll ruin everything we're trying to accomplish."

"Perhaps I should share what I know about them," Deke said. "Sit down and I'll explain. I've had dealings with their people before."

Mara sank to her seat with an expectant look on her face.

"Computer," Deke called, "access records for Larikk, star dates 352.7 through 352.9. Display the first visual recording." He tilted his head to regard the women in the room. "Larikk was my friend and colleague. We grew up together on Eranus. His father was Dr. Ventry Muir, who discovered the relationship between hydrogen uptake and blue silico amoeba."

A holographic image sprouted from the center of the white marbelite table. Larikk, bearded and slim, wore a loose tunic and trousers. A wide grin split his face as he spoke into the camera.

"Hey Deke, how ya doing? I just got my first samples and they look good. I couldn't wait to share this with you. The region is tropical, with trees so tall you wouldn't believe it. The vegetation is thick and abundant with wildlife. I don't think the Yanurans have touched the surface of what's possible here. My initial analysis of the algae confirms what they've said. I've sent a specimen home to the lab but I wanted you to know how well it's going since you'd encouraged me to come. I'll keep you posted."

His image flickered and dissolved.

Deke's audience stared at him with blank expressions. "Larikk was researching a vaccine against Turtle Ravage," he said. "It's a disease that afflicts a species of marine turtles on our world. Preliminary studies showed that an algae from Yanura might prevent the contagion. Larikk applied for permission to travel to the planet to collect samples."

Wren raised his layered eyebrows. "And the Yanurans agreed? I thought they were closed to offworlders before this annum."

"That's not true," Mara said, the annoyance in her voice obvious. "You need to understand something before we arrive at their planet. The Yanurans consist of several different races. Fromoth Trun represents the Croags, the largest populace. They've always favored increased contact with other worlds, but until now they hadn't applied for admission to the Coalition. They're using the drug Vyclor as a bargaining chip to obtain special trade status. I think they waited until they'd refined the drug for broad-species application."

Wren nodded. "That makes sense."

"The Worts make up the other major faction on Yanura," she continued. "They're tree-dwelling cousins of the Croags who like to maintain close ties to home and are suspicious of strangers. I don't know much about them, so most of my information about the populace is based on knowledge of the Croags."

"You mean the Worts may not favor membership in the Coalition?" Deke asked, incredulous. "How can the Admissions Committee even consider their application if it only represents half the planet's population?"

"The Croags make up nearly three-quarters of the inhabitants."

"So what?" Deke ran his fingers through his hair. "Every world that has joined the Coalition has been united. Their unity indicates that they've resolved certain political and social issues and are ready to become part of a larger community. Now you're saying these differing factions on Yanura have opposing views?"

"I didn't exactly say that," Mara countered, but a trace of uncertainty hung in her voice.

He glared at her. "Glotaj told me there were hints of political unrest on Yanura, but now I'm thinking it may be more serious than he thought. We'll have to talk to a representative of the Worts when we're there. If major political differences exist between the various factions, it could be cause to reject Fromoth Trun's application. In the meantime, we're getting off track. I want you to hear this last communique from Larikk."

Deke called up another entry from the computer and Larikk's image reappeared. The bearded man kept casting furtive glances over his shoulder as he spoke.

"You wouldn't believe what I've discovered, Deke. I don't want to say anything yet because I need to gather more data, but it could prove to be a windfall. The Yanurans want to keep it all for themselves, but I think they'll be interested if I suggest the broader possibilities. We could make a fortune. The only deterrent is—" His voice garbled for a moment then cleared. "Listen, if I don't return, you'll know it wasn't an accident. Larikk out."

Deke surveyed his crewmates. "Larikk never did come home. His death was ruled an accidental drowning, but his body was never recovered. I applied for a travel visa to Yanura and it was denied. Even when I showed his message to the Department of Justice authorities, they said it was circumstantial and didn't prove anything."

"They're right," Mara agreed. "Just because your friend gave that warning didn't mean the Yanurans were to blame for his disappearance."

"I believe they wanted to keep their secrets and killed him. It might have something to do with this miracle drug we've been sent to investigate."

"Larikk could have been referring to anything."

"He went after that vaccine at my urging, and I won't have his death hanging over my head. If the Yanurans are guilty, they'll pay for it." Deke's mouth curved down, and his eyes narrowed. He'd been blocked in his attempt to investigate his friend's death before, but now nothing would stop him.

"Your attitude is unreasonable. You'll be looking for things to be wrong," Mara said.

"After Larikk's tale, you're not suspicious?" Deke asked. He couldn't believe her naiveté.

"I'm willing to be open-minded. You don't know what secret Larikk discovered, nor can you be certain the Yanurans harmed him. You're making assumptions that will bias your viewpoint and obstruct our mission." She gestured at the others, who were listening with rapt attention. "If you offend Fromoth Trun, he'll revoke our travel visas. We'll fail in the search for Jallyn, and you'll have lost any chance you might have to learn what Larikk discovered. The Admissions Committee will merely send another science team in our place."

And he'd fail to win the appointment to the chancellorship, Deke reminded himself. Ruefully, he regarded her. "As our protocol expert, I'll expect you to suggest the best approach."

"We should be able to check into Larikk's disappearance as long as we're discreet. I don't see the harm in making a few inquiries," Wren interjected.

Deke nodded, grateful for the Polluxite's support. "Let's break for evening nourishment; then we'll reassemble for the weaponry evaluation in the ordnance room."

Land's sake, Mara thought. Deke was still insisting on that absurdity. With an annoyed frown, she got up and took her place in line for the fabricator, aware that he stood behind her. The hairs on her nape rose in response. He must resent her meddling presence, but she was here to ensure the Yanurans were treated with respect.

She didn't mind if Deke checked into Larikk's activities as long as their mission wasn't jeopardized. Obviously Wren thought Larikk's disappearance was worth investigating, and maybe it would lead to something significant in regard to their own assignment. Her job was to make certain the Yanurans were given a fair evaluation.

Thinking over their earlier discussion, she admitted the relationship between the Croags and the Worts was unclear to her. Fromoth Trun had insisted the Worts' interests were being met and they wouldn't object to membership in the Coalition. She intended to meet with a Wort representative herself to confirm his words. Regardless of what Deke might think, she wasn't a complete fool.

She obtained her plate of food and headed back to the table. Hedy had chosen a vegetarian meal of pasta and salad. Mara couldn't wait to bite into her juicy steak, mashed red tuber, and calyp greens. She'd always had a big appetite and was starving. As she bit into a soft roll, she eyed the foodstuffs chosen by the others. Wren bent over a plate of berries and nuts, while Ebo forked a gooey pink substance into his stretchy mouth.

On her left, Deke sat down, resting his plate on the table. A fishy odor assailed her nostrils. Annums of training had taught her to swallow her distaste and maintain her poise when she ate in alien company. Dining with different cultures was part of her job.

Hedy wasn't so subtle. "What is that stuff?" she asked, wrinkling her nose.

"This is brown algae chowder, raw placar fish, and seaweed pudding," Deke said, pointing to each in its turn. "Want to try some?" He offered her a quivering moist white cube covered in a slimy translucent substance.

"No, thanks." Hedy grimaced and turned back to her own meal.

"You should fit in well with the Yanurans," Mara said, unable to resist the dig. "They smell like your food."

For a moment he didn't answer, and she was afraid she'd gone too far. Then his mouth curved in a devilish grin. "If you like alien cultures so much, how about trying an iced jelly? It's a popular beverage on Eranus. I'd be happy to conjure you one."

Her curiosity got the better of her. "What is it?"

"A combination of water, slab sugar, rose concentrate, grass jelly, and crushed ice." His eyes glittered as he waited for her response.

"Grass jelly?"

"A black jelly made from seaweed. Want to try it?"

Mara was never one to turn down a challenge. "Sure, why not?" Her gaze followed Deke as he rose and went to the fabricator. He certainly cut a dashing figure in his uniform. Watching him made her wonder about his background. He'd said he was from Eranus, but what kind of life had he led there? Had he always been interested in a military career?

By the time he returned with a tall, frosted glass, she'd resolved to delve into his history. It would help her deal with him more effectively if she understood his origins.

One taste of the drink was enough to scatter her thoughts. The black liquid tasted like iodine. Trying not to gag, she managed to swallow the first sip. "Delightful," she muttered.

"I can see you relish the taste," Deke remarked.

With her mouth puckered from the astringent drink, she was unable to cast a witty retort. Bending her head, she hid her discomfort by raising a forkful of warm, soft tuber to her lips. The food had a sweet, buttery-rich flavor that thankfully erased the bitterness of the beverage.

"How do you survive on such meager fare?" Hedy asked Wren. "You have such a powerful physique. Your nutritional requirements must be enormous."

Wren concentrated on his food, his brows drawn together as he hunched over his plate. Mara was amused to notice the flush that crept up his face.

"I drink Cal six times a day," he said. At Hedy's puzzled expression, he explained. "It's a high-protein, calcium-rich beverage that supplies most of what I need."

"Most of what you need? And what else do you require for satisfaction, Lieutenant Wren?"

The innuendo in her tone was clear. Mara hid a smile, listening for Wren's response. The big man stuttered and gave a noncommittal reply. Mara returned her attention to her meal. Deciding she was still hungry, she obtained a large slice of kiraberry fruit pie for dessert.

As soon as they'd cleared the table, Deke ordered everyone to the physio lab.

"I haven't digested my food yet," Hedy grumbled. "Is this going to involve anything physical?"

"Come on," Mara urged her. "Wren's going. Maybe he'll unfold his wings for you."

"Ooh!" Hedy trilled, quickening her pace.

They passed by the holovid lounge, a study center, a medical facility, and finally came to the physio lab near the end of the corridor. Inside the gleaming white room with mirrored walls was an array of exercise equipment. At the far end was a set of double tempered-glass doors that led into another section.

"This way," Deke said, guiding them through the exercise area.

The next compartment served as the ordnance room. It was brightly lit and empty except for a wide cabinet set into one wall. Deke strode to the cabinet, punched in a code on a touchpad, and the door swung open. Inside was an assortment of armaments.

"Targets," he commanded, after selecting weapons for each of them. The far wall lit with moving images.

Mara spent a grueling haura struggling with the unfamiliar equipment. She was too proud to ask for assistance, so she fumbled along, dismayed when she missed the dancing targets by meters. The shooter she held was heavy, with a recoil that nearly knocked her over. Clearly her skills didn't lead in this direction.

Hedy used her feminine wiles to coax Wren into showing her how to fire a laser rifle. She cooed and shimmied when the big Polluxite reached his arms around her to teach her the proper stance.

"I'll assign each of you ladies some practice time in here," Deke said, frowning at their obvious lack of training. "I will expect you to become proficient in using these weapons before we reach Yanura."

"That's absurd." Mara faced him with her hands on her hips. "I have no intention of setting foot on that planet bearing arms."

Deke drew her aside and spoke in a low tone so the others wouldn't hear. "You'll obey my orders, or I'll have you confined to your quarters. You will not be included in the landing party, either. Understand?"

She swallowed her anger, lifted her chin, and gave him a mocking salute. "Yes, sir, Commander."

"By the stars, it's for your own protection." His jaw clenched as he regarded her with an exasperated expression.

"I can take care of myself." In truth, she couldn't. Instead of taking self-defense courses, she'd spent her free time on Bimordus Two teaching folk dances from different alien cultures. Learning the native moves had been a joyful type of exercise. Her classes were popular. She smiled inwardly as she imagined Deke performing some of the more intricate steps.

Deke gestured to the others. "Listen up, everybody. Tomorrow, we'll meet in the conference room at ten hundred hauras for a tactical discussion. I want you ladies to put in an haura each in here first." He pointed to Hedy. "You can start at eight hundred hauras. Mara, you'll go after her."

"Eight hundred hauras!" Hedy squealed. "I sleep later than that."

"I'm usually up early. I'll trade with you," Mara offered.

"Need I remind you women that this is not a pleasure cruise?" Deke's gaze sized them up. "You'd better put some time into muscle-building exercises, too. Otherwise, you'll have trouble handling those heavy blaster carbines should it become necessary."

"I didn't come on this journey to work out every day," Mara stated.

Deke's expression hardened. "You're under my command on this ship. Do you wish to receive disciplinary action for insubordination?"

She glared at him, unable to think of a suitable response. As mission leader, his position was inviolable. She, on the other hand, could be considered an unnecessary inconvenience. Even Hedy, as medic, was more of an essential crew member than she was as a protocol expert.

"No, sir," she mumbled, vowing to find another way to defy him.

Deke gave a curt nod. "Dismissed," he said, turning away to secure the ordnance locker.

Mara fell into step beside Hedy in the corridor. "Will you come to the cargo bay with me? I want to see if my sculpting tray arrived intact."

"Sure." Hedy glanced at her. "You know, I'm beginning to be sorry I came along."

"Why is that?"

"Weapons training and exercises… this is turning out to be more of a Defense League operation than a diplomatic visit. I thought it would be exciting to visit a new planet, but the commander is making me nervous. I have no desire to get caught in a hostile situation. My specialty is multispecies medicine, not trauma."

Mara halted, catching her by the elbow. "There won't be any hostile situation if Commander Sage follows my advice."

"He seems rather hardheaded."

"No kidding. The man believes the Yanurans are guilty of murdering his friend, and that conclusion is based on a single garbled communication. If you ask me, he dislikes the Yanurans and is willing to believe anything nasty about them."

They resumed their pace, stopping briefly in their cabins to freshen up.

Once more in the corridor, they headed for the turbolift at the far end of the crew quarters. "I'd hate for Fromoth Trun to be offended by Deke's attitude. The Yanuran leader will tell us to leave before we accomplish our objectives," Mara said, rubbing a hand across her brow.

"What are you going to do about it?" Hedy asked.

"I'll have to learn more about our commanding officer. It'll help me figure out how to deal with him."

A door popped open and Commander Sage stepped into the corridor. He clutched a pack of data cards. Mara hadn't realized they'd reached his cabin. Hedy slithered past, leaving Mara facing him in the tight space.

Their eyes caught and held. "I seem to keep bumping into you," Deke drawled, sounding not at all displeased.

Mara felt a responsive rush of heat. "We're on our way to the cargo deck. I need to check on some supplies I had sent to the ship."

She tried to get around him but his bulk seemed to stretch across the whole of the confined space. As though to purposely block her passage, he closed the distance between them. Hedy give a meaningful cough from behind, but Deke didn't budge.

"You're in my way," she rasped.

"No, you're in *my* way." He gave her a devilish grin, showing his dimples.

Her knees weakened. Her blood warmed. Every nerve ending in her body sizzled. Aware he was regarding her with amusement, she ducked and shot around him and kept going until the turbolift door slid shut behind her.

"Whew!" She slumped against the rear wall, sighing in relief.

"I think he likes you," Hedy said, shooting her a glance.

Mara stared at her. "Don't be ridiculous. He views me as annoying pest."

"Then he must enjoy the verbal sparring, because he sure tries hard to get you riled."

"The only thing hard about him is his… you know. And I don't mean his head."

Hedy giggled. "I wish I could get Wren to feel that way about me."

Rolling her eyes in mock despair, Mara strode into the immense cargo bay after the lift doors opened. Crates, machinery, and canvas-covered equipment lay about, most of it bolted to the deck.

"How in Zor am I supposed to find my supplies?" she asked, spreading her hands.

"Start searching at that end," Hedy suggested, pointing. "I'll look in this corner."

Ten minutes later, Mara found her stash hidden behind a carton of spare circuitry. The items rested on a mini-levitator unit. She activated the device and guided her load into an open area. There she examined the rectangular sculpting tray, the sacks of Carellian clay, the Cr'ssian soota mud and the coloring modules. Everything appeared to be present.

"I can't imagine why you brought this stuff on board," Hedy remonstrated. "If Commander Sage finds you in here stomping in that muck, he'll assign you to clean out the connector conduits. You saw how he reacted when I mentioned bringing games and music chips with me."

"Why should he care what we do in our spare time? It's not as though we're regular crew members. We're civilians."

Hedy snorted. "That's not what you said back in our apartment when we were packing. You distinctly told me we had to obey his orders on this mission."

"Yes, as it pertains to our professional roles. Commander Sage hasn't the slightest interest in what we do in our leisure time." As she put her items away, Mara wondered about the truth of her statement. She had the feeling Deke would be concerned with everything his crew did, and for some reason, she found that oddly reassuring.

Chapter Five

The next morning, Deke stormed inside the mess hall where Mara lingered over a cup of hot wagmint tea.

He tapped the chronometer on his wrist. "What are you doing in here? It's fifteen minutes past oh-eight hundred. You're late for weapons practice."

"Am I?" She raised her eyebrows.

"We're on a tight schedule. Dr. Te'larr is due at the range in less than an haura, and then we're meeting for another briefing. You can't afford to waste everyone's time."

"Oh, I doubt Hedy will be up before ten. She's a late sleeper."

Deke's face darkened. "Don't either of you take this mission seriously?"

She met his gaze solemnly. It wasn't easy when he towered above her and she had to twist her neck to look up.

"Of course, we do, Commander, but as we see it, our visit to Yanura is a diplomatic affair. I don't believe Jallyn's disappearance has anything to do with the Yanurans. Their flight plan was filed long before the abduction took place, so I feel your military preparations are unnecessary and possibly obstructive to our goals."

She stood to face him, smoothing the sides of her forest-green belted tunic. Black leggings and short, polished boots completed her ensemble. Wishing to appear professional, she'd twisted her hair into a sleek braid. She glanced briefly at the snug fit of Deke's maroon and gray uniform. His proximity made her pulse quicken.

Deke's gaze, bold and arrogant, raked her body. "What about Larikk, huh? He was onto something and got killed as a result."

Planting her hands on her hips, she retorted, "You don't know what happened to Larikk, and even if someone did harm him, you have no right to blame an entire race. You're prejudiced against the Yanurans like everyone else. When you get to know their people, you'll see they have feelings and problems just like you do. They'll become individuals, not a faceless entity."

An impish gleam entered Deke's eyes. "The Yanurans have frog faces."

Mara stomped her foot, then realized he was grinning at her. By the Light, he was purposefully goading her. Well, she'd take the opportunity to teach him a thing or two.

"Do you know how many different species we have in the Coalition? Over five hundred worlds, and everyone has contributed something valuable to the galactic community. Take the Gomins, for example. They may look weird with their segmented bodies, roving eye, and wavy antennae, but their music has brought pleasure to billions of people."

"The Gomins have nothing to do with our situation. I'm responsible for the safety of this crew, and we need to be able to defend ourselves if the need arises. You never know when a situation might turn ugly."

The man had a one-track mind, Mara concluded. Fuming in frustration, she tried another tactic. "You're approaching this mission as though it's a commando operation. We should be discussing protocol and customs instead."

"Which is the purpose of our briefing this morning," he conceded. "I want you to tell us what to expect from the Yanurans and how we should greet them." He paced forward until he was a hairs-breadth away from her. A whiff of masculine cologne drifted toward her, tantalizing her with its spicy scent. "I'm not being unreasonable, Mara. You have to understand my responsibility in this matter."

Gazing into his piercing brown eyes, her resolve faltered. As mission leader, Deke was responsible for the safety of the crew. But did that mean he had to prepare them for a battle that might never occur? She turned away, but he caught her by the arm.

"Where are you going?"

"To my cabin."

"You're due in the ordnance room."

"Land's sake! Why do you persist in that absurdity?"

His grasp on her arm tightened. "I thought I made it clear that I expect you to follow my orders. If not, I'll have you confined to your cabin for the duration of this voyage."

She glanced at the rage smoldering in his eyes and had no doubt he'd follow through on his threat. "Very well, but who will teach me? I can't open the locker myself, and I have no idea what to do."

Deke looked at her consideringly. "Wren has agreed to play instructor for your friend. I suppose I could help you. Ebo and Wren have bridge duty, so I'm free right now."

Mara had an instant vision of Deke standing with his arms around her as Wren had held Hedy during the previous weapons practice. "That's okay, I'll manage on my own. I don't want to inconvenience you."

Deke's lips curved in a wicked grin. "It's not a problem. Please, after you." He released her and made a sweeping gesture toward the hatchway.

She preceded him down the corridor, aware of his eyes on her back… or more likely, on her swaying derriere. The man was an enigma. One moment he acted the stern commander and the next he flirted with her. How was she to respond? Was he so strict because he cared about her? He'd admitted feeling a deep sense of responsibility toward his crew, so his insistence on their proficiency in weaponry was a genuine concern to him. But how did he feel toward her personally?

She had no doubt he'd make a move on her in the ordnance room. It was too good an opportunity for a man like him to pass up when he'd have a valid reason for putting his hands on her. Her skin tingled in anticipation of his touch. But did she mean anything more to him than a handy conquest?

It would be best not to respond to his amorous overtures. If he wanted to ensure her skill with weapons, that was all he'd get.

Walking behind her, Deke saw the stubborn tilt of her head in defiance of his orders. Surely Mara understood the need to be prepared for all contingencies? It wasn't bias against the Yanurans that made him extra cautious.

He expected any crew member under his command to be able to function as part of a team. His expectations weren't unreasonable. At least, he didn't think so. Mara kept accusing him of being prejudiced, but he was just doing his job. Conversely, she considered defending the Yanurans to be her personal task. In a way, this was a form of reverse bias. She couldn't see beyond her own nose that those people should be held under suspicion. Her dedication to her ideals was admirable but misguided.

Although his purpose was to teach her how to defend herself, Deke couldn't help anticipating how it would feel to envelop her soft body in his… tutorial embrace. But when it came time to show her how to hold a blaster carbine, he found himself picturing her in a confrontation with a murderous Yanuran. As a result, he delivered his instructions in a stiff manner and ended up being overly critical of her performance. Annoyed with himself, he felt doubly remorseful at Mara's obvious relief when the session was over.

"Are you leaving?" she asked pointedly, her tone as cool as her eyes.

"I'll meet you here tomorrow morning. Be on time," Deke ordered, resolving to be more agreeable during the next round. He exited, nearly colliding with Hedy in the exercise area.

"Is Lieutenant Wren here yet?" Hedy said, breezing into the ordnance room. Her green eyes swept the empty range. "He's kindly agreed to be my instructor."

Mara rubbed her aching arms. Her muscles were unaccustomed to the workout. Maybe some strengthening exercises would be useful after all.

"Commander Sage gave me a lesson. I hope you have a more enjoyable session with Wren. I'm heading to the study center to review the data on Yanura." She fully expected Deke to give her a hard time at the briefing and wanted to review the files to refresh her mind. Her arguments should be well-grounded in factual information, testimonies, and personal observations from visitors to the planet.

Heavy footfalls announced Wren's arrival. Mara turned to greet him with a friendly smile. "Good morning, Lieutenant."

The big man was dressed in a standard uniform, probably at Deke's urging. Mara knew he didn't wear one on board the *Valiant.* His chest was even broader than Deke's, but then he had his huge wings folded into his back. His hair was carefully slicked off his wide forehead and she caught a whiff of a masculine musk scent. After acknowledging her greeting, Wren turned to Hedy. Mara was amused to see a dark flush suffuse his rugged features.

"Dr. Te'larr." He gave a slight bow.

"I told you to call me Hedy." She linked her arm into his, winking over her shoulder at Mara. "I'm looking forward to your instructions. I'm sure there are so-o-o many things you can teach me."

His color deepening, Wren sputtered a noncommittal reply.

Mara left, grinning to herself. Hedy could come on strong when a man appealed to her. Some males were put off by it, but if anything, Hedy's assertiveness seemed to encourage Wren. Mara had never asked him why he was still single, but now she wondered. Could it be that shyness lurked beneath his powerful exterior? He might need someone like Hedy to snag him. If that were the case, they'd be well suited for each other.

A wave of envy hit her, surprising her in its intensity. After Pietor, she hadn't sought a relationship with another man. She was afraid of being rejected again and for the same reasons Pietor's parents had refused to accept her. She performed "weird psychic stuff" to use Pietor's hurtful words.

Hedy blamed Pietor for not defending her, but Mara had faced prejudice before and feared it was always something she'd encounter. Hedy and Sarina were among the few friends who regarded her ability as a special gift. She doubted she'd ever find a man with their level of tolerance.

Oh my, she should have checked on Sarina when she'd done her latest separation. Earlier that morning, Jallyn had been awake, still aboard the ship. Relieved to find the baby's status unchanged, Mara had returned from her astral journey, discarding the sense of unease that had accompanied the experience.

Yesterday, Sarina had been sitting alone by her comm unit with no one to provide support. Mara wished she could be with her but it wasn't possible. She hoped the other crew members besides Hedy viewed Mara's current role as being important to their mission. It was hard to tell Deke's opinion. She wasn't sure if he respected her position or if he viewed her presence on the ship as a waste of a berth. So far, he seemed more interested in aggravating her than soliciting her professional advice. Or maybe that was how he normally reacted to women.

Glotaj had mentioned Deke was single when they discussed the mission in Sarina's apartment. Now Mara found herself wondering why a man with the commander's good looks had never taken a mate. Perhaps he preferred to play the field and avoid commitments. In that case, he wasn't coming on to her because he genuinely liked her. She was merely another conquest.

Resolved to focus on their mission, she entered the study center, taking a seat at one of the computer consoles. Using voice-activated commands, she requested data on Yanura. The upcoming briefing would give her the opportunity to show the commander she was worth her mettle. Unfortunately, the material offered nothing new. She'd been hoping to find information about the Worts that would verify Fromoth Trun's claims.

An haura later, she joined the other crew members in the conference facility. Wren, sitting next to Hedy, gave a report on their navigational status, and Ebo rattled off a series of technical calculations from the bridge. When he was finished, Deke turned to Mara.

"Okay, tell us about the Yanurans."

He sat on her right as before, and again his nearness disconcerted her. His quiet air of authority was evident in his erect posture and firm jawline. Mara moistened her lips, trying to focus her thoughts on the subject under discussion and not on the man beside her. Despite her determination not to get involved with him, she couldn't deny the way her heart hammered in his presence.

"Since the Croags make up the majority of the population on Yanura, they're the group I'm going to describe," she began, folding her hands on the table. "They have smooth, moist green skin, broad flat skulls, and prominent eyes. They're cold-blooded, meaning their body temperature varies with their surroundings. They use their skin to breathe and also to lose or absorb water. As cold-blooded organisms with porous skin, they need to respond quickly to external changes in temperature. To maintain a stable environment, the Croags live underground in a network of burrows. There it's moist and shady, protecting them from the heat of the sun and from losing moisture on the surface.

"Because they don't need to eat frequently to maintain their body temperature, the Croags only consume one meal a day. Their diet consists of insects, worms, farmed fish, a variety of small animals, and fruits and vegetables. Their senses are highly developed, including their taste buds, so they can be finicky eaters. Besides the five senses we all share, the Croags can detect ultraviolet and infrared light."

Deke held up a hand. "This is all very fascinating, but I want to know what to expect on an interpersonal level."

Mara gave him a small smile. "The standard greeting is to touch the fingers of your right hand to your forehead and give a short bow, saying *Rogi Kwantro.*"

"What does that mean?" Wren asked, shifting restlessly. His glance slid sideways toward Hedy.

"May your source of water be plentiful," Mara quoted, folding her hands on the table. "It's also polite to say the words as you are parting company from a Yanuran. Make sure you use your right hand in both instances. Performing the gesture with the left one implies a vulgar insult."

"Tell us about Fromoth Trun," Deke said.

Mara was grateful he hadn't interrupted her and seemed interested in her assessments.

"He is courteous almost to the point of obsequiousness. His style of dress is formal, his mannerisms elaborate. He enjoys being the center of attention."

"Would you say he's vain?"

"Most definitely. Fromoth Trun is the elected leader of his people, the Croags. His most powerful aide is Lixier Bryn, who was left in charge while he was on Bimordus Two. Fromoth Trun seemed anxious to return home."

"Why? Doesn't he trust this guy?"

Mara shrugged. "It's hard to tell. His entourage appeared devoted to him. The two females on his staff, the ministers of commerce and finance, raved about his accomplishments. I suspect, however, that the Yanurans are flatterers. They hide their true feelings under a veneer of rosy polish."

"What's the status of females in their society?" Lieutenant Ebo inquired. Sirisians, Mara knew, cherished the gentler sex on their planet. Possessing a more delicate constitution, Sirisian women rarely worked outside the home.

"They're considered equals," she replied. "Yanurans mate once a year." That drew startled looks from around the table. "They don't cohabitate as we know it. When a female is bearing young, she may move in with her mate for the four-month period. After giving birth, she can choose to remain or go back to her own burrow."

"Do they raise their offspring together?" Ebo asked.

"They don't have family units. In Croag society, the community is more important than the individual. Males and females work together on an equal basis. The young are raised separately, in their own section of burrows. As adults, they can bunk with whomever they choose. Communal living is the norm."

"Didn't you say they were nocturnal?" Hedy put in.

"Yes, that's right. Their workplaces are above ground. There's less danger of their skin drying out when the bright sun isn't shining overhead. We want to stage our arrival for early morning, when their workday is ending."

Silence fell over the group.

Finally, Deke spoke. "It's important that we assess the political situation on the planet. For all we know, the Worts might be vehemently opposed to joining the Coalition. You've only heard what Fromoth Trun has told you and that's the Croag viewpoint. Political instability would give us a valid reason to recommend a denial of their application to the Admissions Committee."

"That's all you care about, isn't it? You're just looking for ways to discredit the Yanurans."

"And your blind trust means you won't look beyond what you want to believe. We need to do more than verify the properties of their age-preserving drug. Glotaj mentioned the political situation. You've been ignoring it because it doesn't suit your views of the Yanurans. Well, I don't intend to do a half-assed job while we're there."

"He's right," Wren cut in. "We should assess the entire situation, and maybe we'll learn more about what happened to Larikk."

"We have to look for Jallyn," Mara reminded them.

"If she's on the planet, we'll find her," Deke stated, his tone firm.

She bit her lower lip, her emotions in turmoil. Was she the only person concerned about giving the Yanurans a fair evaluation?

Deke handed out data cards. "I've drawn up a duty roster. You're each assigned times on the firing range and in the exercise lab. Watches on the bridge are posted. Our next group session will involve a review of the Croag capital, Revitt Lake City. We'll begin a series of tactical simulations. Dismissed."

Fitting her data card into her pocket link, Mara noticed that she had nothing planned until 1430 hauras, when she was assigned an haura of exercises in the physio lab. She exited beside Hedy.

"I don't like the way the commander orders us around," Mara said, gritting her teeth. "Glotaj assigned the wrong man to be in charge of this mission. Deke is looking for trouble."

Hedy gave her a sharp glance. "The man is not discounting your advice. On the contrary, he's using it to take a sensible approach. You're too defensive where the Yanurans are concerned."

"I am not defensive! I'm upholding their rights. No one else seems to care about treating them fairly."

"Deke has to make sure all the angles are covered. It's his responsibility if anything goes wrong."

"Nothing will go wrong unless he offends Fromoth Trun."

"Hopefully, that won't happen." Hedy checked the chronometer on her wrist. "Wren has a free haura after he checks his nav instruments. He's agreed to join me in the lounge to show me a holovid of his home planet."

Mara relaxed her stiff shoulders and smiled at her friend. "I think the guy likes you. I'm heading to the cargo bay to start a new sculpture."

"Going to work off your angst? What about your nemesis?" Hedy waggled her eyebrows.

"I'm sure Commander Sage's duties will keep him fully occupied." At least, Mara hoped that would be the case. She didn't care for another close encounter with the dashing commander.

****

Mara was ankle-deep in a sculpture kneading phase, blissfully unaware of her surroundings until a clear male voice disrupted her tranquility.

"What in Zor are you doing?"

Startled, she glanced up. Deke stood watching her, a look of curiosity on his handsome face. Her pulse quickened at the sight of him.

"I'm creating a sculpture." Following the direction of his gaze, she peered down at her legs. She'd rolled up her leggings to mid-thigh. Her bare feet were covered in clay, and flecks of mud splattered her naked calves. Her cheeks heating, she realized how grimy she must look.

"You're stomping on muck in a giant tray," he said in a disbelieving tone. "What kind of art form is that?"

She wiggled her toes in the wet, gooey slime. "The clay needs to be worked before shaping. It'll harden later into a translucent material. This is the best method even though it's crude. Besides, I like the feel of wet clay on my feet and stomping on it helps me to relax."

He sidled closer, his lips curving upward. "I wasn't aware you were feeling tense."

Warmth flooded her skin. "Ah, don't you have work to do on the bridge?"

"Ebo is on duty. I thought I'd ask if you needed assistance with exercise training."

His expression didn't reveal his thoughts, and she wondered why he had made the offer. Was it a peacemaking gesture? She pounded her feet, her toes squishing in the delightfully cool muck. If she accepted, it would provide her with another opportunity to discuss the Yanurans with him.

"All right, that would be helpful, thanks." She hoped it was the right decision.

His gaze locked with hers. "I'll be looking forward to it." As his gaze trailed downward, she became aware of what kind of exercises he actually had in mind.

His words hanging in the air like a seductive promise, he pivoted and left the cargo bay.

Mara resumed her stomping with renewed vigor. She hammered her feet so hard they were burning when she finally finished. Scooping the sticky clay onto her sculpting circle, she worked quickly, molding it into a recognizable form. The heavy-lipped cup would harden into a translucent crystalline piece, delicately veined in red.

Brushing her hands off on her work apron, she stepped back to view her art. The edges were curved to perfection.

Just as she molded the clay, she'd sway Deke Sage to her viewpoint. Justified or not, his suspicion of the Yanurans rankled her. The exercise session should afford her the opportunity to discuss the situation with him further.

Putting away her supplies, Mara realized she was anticipating their next encounter with heightened pleasure.

****

Sitting in the holovid lounge, Hedy sidled closer to Wren on the wide double lounger. A three-dimensional holovid of his home planet, Pollux, was playing in full color in the center of the room. An attractive female strolled through each scenic wonder, describing it as though the viewer were actually there.

Watching the female guide made Hedy wonder about Wren. Did he have someone back home? What had made him join the Defense League? What was his family like?

She was aware of his tense posture as he sat as far away from her as possible. His shyness appealed to her. She'd never met a man before who hadn't fallen madly in love with her. Wren wasn't responding in that way and it piqued her interest.

Getting him to relax in her presence was her first objective. Learning more about him was the second goal she hoped to accomplish. Then, perhaps, she could ask him to unfold his wings. Just the thought of them sprouting behind his broad back sent delicious chills up and down her spine.

"I'd love to see your world," she told him, careful to keep her voice demure.

He risked a quick glance in her direction. "I haven't been home in annums," he said gruffly.

"Your family must miss you."

"I doubt it. They were glad when I left."

The words were spoken with such bitterness that Hedy was shocked. "Why do you say that?"

Wren clasped his hands together. "It's the truth, that's all."

Feeling she'd touched upon a nerve, she let it pass even though her curiosity was dying for satisfaction. "Tell me more about your planet. What's that area?"

She pointed to the holovid that showed a scene of high vertical cliffs overlooking a vast ocean. Children were jumping off, their wings sprouting as they soared into open space.

Wren took a moment before he answered. "Those are the Cliffs of Courage. Once you master them, you are elevated to the status of adult on our world. A ritual ceremony is attached. Everyone takes the plunge at age sixteen."

"It must have been one of the highlights of your life," she remarked as she imagined him jumping off the cliff's edge and flying for the first time.

His face darkened. "I never took the test."

"What? Why not?"

"Computer, cancel program. Lights on." The holovid dissolved and the room brightened. Wren rose and began pacing. "There's something you should know about me, Hedy Te'larr. I have a disability, and it prevents me from ever… from taking a mate."

She stared at him, dumbfounded. He appeared healthy. "What are you talking about?"

His expression echoed annums of pain. "I can't fly," he admitted, his voice so low she had to strain her ears to hear.

"You can't… Oh, for Zor's sake! What does that have to do with taking a mate?"

"To post marriage banns on Pollux, one must be of adult status. That privilege wasn't granted to me. Any female who allies herself with my household would suffer the stigma of my shame. We would not be able to consummate our union."

"You mean physically or legally?"

"In my mind, they are as one."

Hedy paused. Did that mean he'd never been with a woman? An insane impulse to wrap her arms around him and offer comfort overwhelmed her.

"A woman in love with you wouldn't care if you could fly or not," she stated.

"On my world, a female would not set the two apart."

"Why would she have to be from your world?"

"Who else would care about me? Besides, I have to join with one of my own species in order to produce viable offspring," he answered in a reasonable tone.

"That's not necessarily the case. You're humanoid, which means you share the same genetic code as many other races. Look at Sarina and Teir. She's from Earth and he's a Vilaran. It hasn't stopped them from sharing a life together."

Wren shook his head. "Even if that is so, I haven't earned the right to have a mate."

"Exactly what is the cause of your problem?" She gazed up into his troubled hazel eyes, feeling small next to his height. She wished she could offer him a measure of comfort, but Wren seemed adamant in his self-denial.

He flushed uncomfortably. "I went through a battery of physical tests and they showed nothing wrong."

She reached out and grasped his cold hand. "What happened then?"

"My parents had me see mental therapists. It was a difficult time. I-I lost my friends."

"Is that why you joined the Defense League?"

He responded with a miserable nod. "I had to get away. It was necessary to spare my parents the distress of always making excuses for me."

"I'm so sorry." She rose and drew him to his feet. With her other hand, she encircled his neck and pulled his head down. "Kiss me," she whispered against his mouth.

"No, I—"

"I know you want to." She'd seen the expression in his eyes. "Don't be afraid. Consider it a token of our friendship. We can be friends, can't we?"

With a groan, Wren swept her into his arms and pressed his mouth to hers. She reveled in the feel of his lips plundering her own, his desperate hunger evident in the urgency of his movements. She wondered how much experience he'd actually had with women, but it didn't matter. She'd take whatever he offered. Clutching her fingers in his hair, she couldn't help the small sound of pleasure that escaped her lips.

Abruptly, he released her and sprang back. "Forgive me," he apologized, an expression of self-loathing on his face. "I am forgetting myself."

"You need to forget yourself, Wren. Your problem is of no concern to me. I want to know you as a man."

"A whole man I am not, according to my kind."

"Well, I'm not a Polluxite."

He sucked in a breath. "You make this hard, *petula.*"

That had sounded suspiciously like a term of endearment. Maybe she was making some headway after all.

Wren glanced at his chronometer. "I have bridge duty in ten minutes. I regret this session must end."

"I don't believe you understand," she reiterated. "I said your problem doesn't matter to me."

"It matters to me, Doctor. That's what counts." He turned his broad back to her.

"Wren, wait." But by the time the words passed her lips, he was gone.

Hedy rushed into the corridor and through the hatchway into crew quarters, where she stopped to knock on Mara's door.

"Come in," came the answering response.

Mara had apparently just come out of the sonic shower. She'd changed into a rust-colored tunic and black leggings and was braiding her dampened hair.

"Wren kissed me, but he won't have anything more to do with me," Hedy blurted, sinking onto the lounger in the sitting area. She proceeded to tell Mara about their encounter. "I'd like to run my own medical tests on him. I can't understand why no one could discover the cause for his problem."

"Could it be psychosomatic?"

"There's always that possibility. He said he'd seen mental therapists. Apparently, they couldn't do anything for him. He views himself as half a man."

"It sounds as though he's fully functional in that regard." Mara finished tying off her braid.

"So what? His cultural taboos remain an obstacle between us. He may be able to perform, but he won't."

"You really like him, don't you?"

Hedy shrugged, her eyes downcast.

"You've just got to keep working on him," Mara insisted. "If he responded to you so strongly, he must feel a similar attraction."

"Suns, men are so difficult, aren't they?" When Mara didn't reply, Hedy pursed her lips. "Did you run into Commander Sage again?"

Mara nodded, averting her eyes. "I'd started a sculpture. Deke caught me with my feet in the clay."

Hedy smiled as she pictured the scene. "I'll bet he was entertained."

Reluctantly, Mara recounted their conversation.

"So he's going to assist you with exercises? That should be exciting."

"I plan to use the time to convince him to view the Yanurans more objectively."

"Sure, whatever you say." Hedy figured they would discuss more than the Yanurans. "I'll talk to you later. I need to organize my medical supplies."

****

The appointed haura for Mara's stint in the physio lab approached, but when she arrived, Deke was nowhere in sight. Wondering if he'd been detained on the bridge, she paged the command center. Wren, who was on duty, suggested she try his cabin or the study center.

She found him in the ship's library, peering at a monitor screen with an intent expression on his face. Her greeting startled him.

"Sorry," he said, a sheepish grin creasing his face when she told him the time. "When I concentrate, I tend to forget everything else."

"What are you viewing?" Curious to see what had drawn his attention, she meandered inside the softly lit area and squinted at his screen. A series of mathematical equations met her puzzled gaze.

"I'm catching up on the latest computations for ionic charges of undersea coppenium in relation to water temperature fluctuations."

"Oh, I see." She hadn't understood a thing he'd said. "You, um, read this sort of stuff often?"

"I need to keep up with what's current." He switched off the computer and rose, stretching. "I could use a few exercises myself about now."

She swallowed hard. In her mind's eye, she pictured his sinewy body streaked with sweat, his muscles bulging as he lifted weights. The image unnerved her. Would he touch her, show her how to use the equipment? How could she abide being that close to him when already her heart was thudding so hard that he must hear it?

Moistening her lips, she followed him out into the corridor. By the time they reached the physio lab, she could barely breathe. As long as he didn't smile at her and show his dimples, she would be safe.

Wouldn't she?

Chapter Six

Mara stared at Deke as he removed his boots and began peeling off the fastening strip on the side of his uniform. The air in the exercise room was cool but heat coursed through her veins as she watched him, too unsettled to move.

"What are you doing?" she asked, afraid to guess.

"Getting changed. I have my activity shorts on underneath this uniform." He lifted his brows. "It won't bother you if I change right here, will it?"

"Of course not."

But her bravado dissolved into embarrassment, especially when Deke took a long time stripping off his uniform. She figured he was deliberately taunting her and when he finally stood before her in his gray knit shorts, her gut clenched in reaction. His broad shoulders and arms rippled with muscled strength. Swirls of dark hair guarded his chest in sensual patterns that made her want to tangle her fingers in them. Her gaze roamed down to his tight hip-hugging shorts and sturdy hair-covered legs.

"You finished?" Deke asked gently.

Horrified, her gaze flew to his bemused expression. She stammered for a response but ended up staring at him as he closed the distance between them. With his bare chest directly in front of her, he halted.

"Ready for the first move?" he said, his voice a low masculine rumble.

"First move?" She moistened her lips, dismayed when his gaze intently followed her tongue.

"We need to warm up our muscles. Stretch your arms out and copy what I'm doing."

Her eyes fixated on his bulging biceps as he demonstrated the exercise in front of her. His head held high and his arms stretched wide, he flexed and extended his sinewy forearms.

By the Light! This was sweet torture. To be near the man was difficult enough. To be alone with him, forced to observe his virile body half-naked and performing tests of muscular prowess, was an agonizing test of her willpower.

As a coil of desire swirled within her, she told herself his interest was purely superficial, that he'd selected her because she was a convenient target aboard ship. After the voyage was over, he'd be off to the next port and the next attractive female.

She copied his warm-up exercises, keeping an adequate distance between them. When done, she strode to an exercise machine that didn't took too difficult. But when she attempted to use the pulley contraption, it wouldn't budge.

"Let me help." Deke positioned himself at her back, leaned forward and covered her hands with his. His warm breath caressed her nape as he showed her how to use the equipment.

She sucked in a sharp breath as her body responded to his powerful chest pressed against her back. It took all her concentration to focus on the lesson and not on him. When at last he directed his attention to another machine, she exhaled a breath of relief.

For a while they worked separately, Deke using the rowing device with a holovid screen showing a lake scene and Mara manipulating the machines to fortify her arms. It aroused her just to see his muscles gleaming with sweat. His masculine essence pervaded the room, making it difficult for her to block out his presence even when she tried to think of something else. If only her body wasn't so responsive to his nearness. Nothing could come out of a relationship with the man, and yet she couldn't deny the effect he had on her.

Finally, Deke called for a rest.

Mara was astounded he wasn't short of breath after forty-five minutes of steady exercise. She felt drained, as though she'd just run a marathon and finished in last place.

"Your clothing is too heavy for this type of workout. Next time, I suggest you don suitable athletic attire," he advised.

She stared at him and swallowed. The exercise had felt good after all, and she appreciated Deke's forcing her into it. It wouldn't do to sit around the ship for two weeks growing soft.

"A dance outfit would be more comfortable," she agreed.

His brow folded into a frown. "What's that?"

"I teach folk dance classes on Bimordus Two. They're native dances from the various groups that make up the Coalition. I find the expressive movements help me to understand the cultural nuances of the different peoples."

"Is that so? Folk dancing is not a very vigorous form of exercise," he drawled. "No wonder your body needs conditioning."

Her mouth tightened. "Move away, and I'll show you one."

He retreated, giving her space. She called to the computer for music then dipped and swirled in the fast Twirl Dance of the Nagarina Watch.

"I believe there's a more intricate pattern involving a duet," he said, sauntering forward when she had finished her demonstration. "I know a few steps myself. Computer, play the first movement of Mach's symphony."

As the melodious music filled the room, Mara swallowed a sudden lump in her throat. What had she gotten herself into this time? Deke's eyes gleamed expectantly as he approached her, a devilish grin on his face. Rooted to where she stood, she could only stare at him and try to ignore the wild thumping of her heart.

He walked behind her, and put his arms around her shoulders and gently drew her against his chest.

"Lean back," he commanded.

She obliged, knowing she would regret this. But she'd never done the duet before, having had a dearth of male partners on Bimordus Two. Part of her was curious to see how it was done.

"We move our bodies like this," he said.

His hips began a slow rhythmic gyration. Swaying behind her, he clutched her closer so that she bumped against him with each rocking motion. She felt each contact like a jolt of electricity. When his fingers slid up her arms, tickling her skin, she quivered with delight.

Closing her eyes, she tilted her neck back, craving more. His hands slid to her hips, guiding them against his own in an erotic motion that made her breath come short. When he nibbled at the skin behind her ear, she gasped.

"I think we should practice this every day," he said, his voice husky.

Her mind scrambled, caught in a net of need. Unable to stop herself, she twisted around to face him. Still held in his embrace, she gazed into his intense eyes.

He pressed his midsection against her belly, sliding himself along her length in the sensual rhythm of the dance. Her body thrummed at their points of contact.

She tilted her head back and parted her lips. His mouth hovered near—

"Bridge to Commander Sage," Wren's voice boomed on the comm unit.

Deke sprang back. "Go ahead."

"Incoming message from Supreme Regent Glotaj, sir. High priority."

"I'll take it in the conference room. Sage out."

He traced a tender line along Mara's cheek with his forefinger. "Too bad about the interruption. We'll continue this later."

"Yes. I mean, no." Her face flushed hotly. "Don't think… I didn't mean—"

"I know you didn't." He gave her a gentle smile. "It's the way things are meant to be. You'll see. By the end of this voyage, we'll—"

"We'll have accomplished our mission." She drew herself upright, ashamed of her wanton behavior. Where was her professionalism, her pride? "I think we're losing sight of our purpose. We have to agree on an approach to the Yanurans. We're not on this trip to indulge ourselves. You clearly informed me and Hedy this wasn't a pleasure cruise."

"Maybe so, but if we perform a few more dances like this one, it might soften my attitude toward Fromoth Trun and the Croags." The twinkle in his eyes raised her ire.

"How dare you make light of the situation. Now you're the one who's not being serious about this mission."

He winked at her. "I'm perfectly serious, Mara, about you." After grabbing his uniform and boots, he marched out the door.

"Ooh, I hate that man." She clenched her fists in frustration. And yet, as he departed, a strange feeling of loss struck her. Could it be that she was getting used to his irritating company?

By the Light, she hoped not. The man was too damn attractive for her peace of mind.

She conjured a towel from the fabricator and wiped her brow. He'd made her sweat all right, and it hadn't been from the exercise. It had been from the closeness of his body, the hot whoosh of his breath on her temple. Suddenly her pulse was racing again and she threw the towel down in disgust.

Watch yourself, Mara. You don't want to get involved with a man like him. He's interested in a shipboard fling, nothing else.

Yet as she headed for her cabin, she wondered how long she'd be able to resist.

****

Deke compressed his lips as he listened to Glotaj's urgent pleas for haste. The supreme regent's face projected onto the far wall in the conference facility. Cameras picked up his own image and sent it along subspace frequencies to the Coalition capitol building where Glotaj spoke from his office in the Great Hall.

"Our patrols caught up with the other two vessels," Glotaj said. "Gregorski's and Ambassador El'rik's ships were clean. That leaves the Yanurans as our best lead. We're not finding anything else on Bimordus Two."

"What about those two assassins, Joro and Pruet?" He hunched forward, his elbows on the table, his hands clasped.

"They're a dead end. It's up to you now, Commander. Increase speed so you arrive at the Yanuran system within twelve days at the most. It's imperative we have Jallyn back before the Elevation Ceremony. Report to me upon your arrival. Glotaj out." His image vanished.

Deke exited and climbed the companionway to the bridge. Wren and Ebo were on duty. Briefly, Deke shared the gist of their conversation.

"Increase speed to warp eight," he told Ebo. In addition to monitoring communications, the Sirisian was responsible for the engineering console. "Let's hope this vessel can handle it."

"The *Celeste* is well built," Ebo said. "She might not look like much, but she's got power." He carried out the order. With a mild shudder, the ship responded.

Deke faced the forward viewscreen. The black emptiness of space greeted him, its velvety void punctuated by myriads of gleaming stars that showed as pinpricks of light. The vast darkness reminded him of the murky ocean depths that he considered his true home. Under the sea, diverse lifeforms thrived in the cold, dark water. Here, in the distant reaches of interstellar space, complex molecules drifted, the basic building blocks of life itself. This was where it all started, and in the oceans, living matter had formed from these molecules, developing and differentiating along the evolutionary scale. Each world evolved from its particular mix of atmosphere, temperature, gravity, and base elements available to support life. The possibilities never failed to amaze him.

At the comm station, Ebo elongated his arm, stretching it across the room to flick a switch on a distant circuit board. The Sirisian was an example of a different evolutionary path. On Ebo's home planet, the element dianine was common, and it accounted for their elastic body structure.

Wren hunched over his nav instruments. His wings were the result of an evolutionary progress from a breed of avians.

Were the Yanurans so unusual, then? Their ancestors were frog-like amphibians. Didn't they deserve the same respect as other species?

Deke frowned, debating the point with himself. He knew what Mara would say. She'd give them the benefit of the doubt. But Larikk's communique couldn't be discarded. The Yanurans had done something to him and covered their tracks. Deke was justified in suspecting them of deceit. It wasn't prejudice, no matter what Mara said. He merely sought the truth. And if she weren't so absurdly naïve, she'd see the logic of his argument.

By the stars, that woman had the power to irritate and arouse him at the same time. He would have kissed her if they hadn't been interrupted by the message from the bridge. He wanted her, and every day he was in her company, his desire increased. It would drive him crazy if he couldn't lie with her soon. Her roommate was attractive, but too small for his taste. Mara, with her smooth olive complexion and lithe, graceful body, was the one who appealed to him.

Deke couldn't recall the last time he'd been so strongly attracted to a woman. Was it more than physical lust that drew him? Her beauty was unquestionable but she was also intelligent, feisty, talented, and dedicated to her ideals. But so were many other women. What was it about her that was different?

"Commander?" Wren's voice sounded alarmed.

Instantly alert, he shifted his attention. "Yes, Lieutenant, what is it?"

Wren's layered eyebrows furrowed into a frown. "Sensors are picking up subspace distortions. I've never seen anything like this, sir. They appear to be high-energy particles directly ahead."

"Change course ninety degrees to port," he ordered, squinting at the viewscreen. He didn't observe anything unusual.

Ebo keyed in the sequence and the ship changed direction.

"Try doing a wide-pattern sensor sweep," Deke suggested to Wren.

"Aye, sir." Peering at his readouts, the Polluxite grunted.

"This entire region is pocketed with subspace distortions. I'll divert power from the quantum matrix array. That might help us fine-tune these images."

"Slow to sublight speed." Deke lowered himself into the central command chair, wishing he were as familiar with space anomalies as he was with deep-sea phenomena.

"Oncoming wave dead ahead!" Wren cried. "Brace for impact."

Before Deke could sound the alarm, a force hit the ship. The deck jerked beneath his feet. Flung from his chair, Deke landed on the solid deck with a sharp pain to his hip. Something exploded in a shower of sparks to his left. Wren shouted but Deke couldn't see him due to the smoke billowing in the air.

Coughing, he rolled to get away from the searing heat as automatic sensors initiated fire control measures over the burning console. Another jarring impact hit, and he covered his head with his arms as debris rained down from above.

"Reverse thrusters," he yelled, hoping Ebo could carry out the command. Scraping along the floor, he gripped his chair and pulled himself upright. Ebo remained at his station, having put on his safety restraint at Wren's first warning. But where was Wren?

"By the faith. Wren's been hurt." He noticed the Polluxite's boots sticking out from behind a heavy metal ceiling grating that had crashed to the floor.

Deke rushed over, alarmed to find the big man unconscious, stretched out on his back. Blood oozed from a puncture wound on his neck where he'd been struck by the sharp-edged grating. His face was uncommonly pale.

"Medic to the bridge," Deke ordered, a comm channel already having been opened by Ebo, who was communicating with the other crew members.

"Dr. Te'larr is trapped in the turbolift." The Sirisian dashed over with a first-aid kit.

"What in Zor hit us?" An acrid odor pierced his nostrils. The fire control unit had shut off, having served its purpose. Deke grabbed a fuser from the first-aid kit and stanched the flow of blood from Wren's wound.

"Analysis showed the distortions to be caused by a series of density waves," Ebo explained, his pink face puckered. "When one of them collided with us, the ship was momentarily charged as though we'd come into contact with live circuitry. It shorted out the lift actuators and some of our other systems."

"Life support?"

"Functioning on all decks." Ebo's mouth stretched in a grimace. "We have sublight power but the warp generators are off-line."

Deke uttered an oath. "Have you heard from Mara?"

"Internal sensors indicate she's in her cabin, but communications from B deck are out."

Deke was torn between tending to Wren and checking on Mara. But Wren's condition was more urgent. The Polluxite was still unconscious.

"I'll manage here. You can work on retrieving Dr. Te'larr from the turbolift. Have her meet me in sick bay."

"Aye, sir." Ebo disappeared down the companionway, heading for the engineering section.

Deke peered at the disarray around the bridge. Couplings were hanging loose. Panels were dislodged, and the charred fragments of the burnt console still smelled of smoke. There was little chance of finding a mini-levitator unit. He'd have to carry Wren.

Grunting from the effort, he hoisted the big man into his strong arms. He didn't want to fling Wren over his shoulder or it might aggravate his neck wound. Now he saw what had been hidden before. There was another gash on the rear of the Polluxite's head. That must be the one that had knocked him out. Deke staggered toward the companionway.

With great effort, he managed to make his way down the spiral stairs to the lower deck. His breath labored under his burden. He kept his head bent watching his footing, so he didn't realize someone was ahead until he heard a gasp.

"Wren's been hurt," Mara said in a frightened tone.

Glancing up, Deke noted her hair had come loose, tumbling over her shoulders. Her eyes were round and wide as she regarded him. She gripped the handrail fastened along the bulkhead in a tight vise.

"Are you alright?" He surveyed her, relieved that she appeared uninjured.

"I was in my cabin when we were hit. My comm unit is out. I was just coming to the bridge to see what's going on. Where's Hedy? Is she okay?"

"She's stuck in the turbolift. Ebo is working on getting her out. The bridge sustained damage and the warp generators are off-line." He headed down the corridor, Mara following at his heels.

She trailed him into the medical facility, helping him to ease the big Polluxite onto a diagnostic bed. Deke's muscles bulged with the strain of lowering the man gently onto the firm mattress.

"He needs your friend's medical attention," Deke answered, his face grim.

"I'm here," Hedy called from the hatchway. She took one step inside and her face drained of color. "Great suns, what happened?"

Rushing over, she jabbed at a control panel on the wall beside the bed, initiating diagnostic procedures. "He must have a concussion. That's easy to fix, but what's this?" She peered at his neck, her wavy brown hair falling across her face. "There's a fragment of something lodged in his flesh."

"He was hit by a metal grating," Deke explained with a frown. How long would Wren be incapacitated? Their crew was already minimal. He couldn't afford to lose anyone.

Hedy took a cylindrical instrument and scanned the wound on his neck.

Flat on his back again, Wren stirred to consciousness. "What…?" His eyes fluttered open.

Deke gripped his shoulder. "Lie still. You were struck by a metal grating on the bridge. Dr. Te'larr is tending you."

"I have to remove this piece of metal." She pointed to the site where blood had begun to ooze again. "I'm afraid the location is delicate. The piece is lodged close to your carotid artery."

"What does that mean?" Wren's words were forced and Deke saw him wince in pain as he turned his head.

"You'll have to remain in sick bay until the arterial wall has strengthened. A rupture could prove fatal." Hedy glanced up. "I'm going to need a surgical assistant."

"I'll help," Mara offered. She didn't seem at all fazed by the situation.

"If you don't need me, I'll be heading back to the bridge." Deke shot Mara a quick glance. She reacted well in an emergency. For the first time, he felt glad she'd come aboard the *Celeste* as a member of his crew. It wasn't her physical attributes that brought him to that conclusion. Hedy was accustomed to emergencies, but Mara was a diplomat who rarely found herself in dangerous situations. He admired her ability to muster her strength and offer assistance.

Resolving to listen more seriously to her advice once the current crisis was over, he left to sort out the chaos on the bridge.

Hedy didn't waste any time and prepped Wren for surgery. She murmured words of reassurance as she applied the anesthetic that would let him sleep through the operation.

It didn't take long. The fragment came out easily with her laser scalpel, but repairing the resultant weakness in the arterial wall took longer.

"He'll have to remain still while this area strengthens," she told Mara, finished at last. She stripped off her surgical gloves and obtained a final readout of his vital signs. The Polluxite was asleep, his face peaceful. "I'll stay with him."

Mara nodded. "If you need a break, call me. Is there anything else I can do?"

"No, I don't think so. Thanks for your help. I have everything under control for now."

"I need to stop by the cargo bay to see if my sculpture was damaged. I put it in a micro shield, so I hope it's all right. Do you want me to check on the things in your cabin? I can straighten up for you since you're stuck here."

"Yes, I'd appreciate that."

After watching her friend leave, Hedy turned to stroke Wren's forehead. It pained her to see him lying so helpless.

Two hauras later, she'd finished organizing the medical supplies and testing the emergency equipment. Satisfied that all was in order, she produced a cool fruit beverage on the fabricator and approached Wren. He'd been awake for fifteen minutes and his vital signs were stable.

"Have a drink," she offered, bending and aiming a straw at his mouth.

"I'm not a baby." He scowled at her.

"You're flat on your back, Lieutenant. You are also under my orders as long as you're my patient. Now drink. You need the fluid to replace lost blood." When she saw the obstinate set of his mouth, she warned, "If you don't cooperate, I'll have to start an IV."

Her threat produced results. Reluctantly, he parted his lips and she inserted the straw. He must have been thirsty, because he sucked the drink dry in no time.

"Thank you," he said, staring at the ceiling.

She straightened, tossing the empty container into a disposer. "You'd better stop with this stoic act, Wren. You need me."

His blazing eyes swung to meet hers. "Allow me to rise and I'll manage by myself."

"Oh, no." She wagged her finger at him. "We can't put any pressure on that blood vessel wall. And until your concussion is fully healed, you may still experience occasional bouts of dizziness. This is the best place for you. I need to run a few more tests." She flipped a few switches on a console behind him.

"What for?" he demanded, his tone gruff.

"I want to make certain your synaptic junctions are properly aligned." She averted her gaze, not wanting him to realize the true nature of these tests. She meant to investigate the physical basis for his disability and now the opportunity had dropped into her eager hands. She wasn't about to let it pass.

Wren grumbled but lay still while she performed a series of intricate diagnostic procedures. He'd been right; she was unable to discover any physical cause for his inability to fly. He was as normal as any burly Polluxite male.

Wren's stentorian throat-clearing drew her attention from her console. She hastened to his bedside. "What is it?"

His face flushed an uncomfortable shade of beet red. "I am not comfortable."

"I'm so sorry. Can I adjust your headrest? Are you too warm? What can I do for you?" She fluttered over him like a mother hen.

"I am feeling tension," he said, his posture stiff.

"Tension?" She wrinkled her forehead. He hadn't mentioned pain, so that couldn't be his problem. "What do you—" Her face flooded with heat. "Oh. I should have thought of it. You need a few moments with the sanitation vacuum. I'll just close the privacy curtain and step aside…"

"No, it's not that." His fists clenched and unclenched by his side.

Puzzled as to his need, her gaze swept over his massive body. He'd complained of a tense feeling, yet he didn't have to void. What else could be bothering him?

"You've got to help me." The words slipped from his mouth in a moan. "The pressure is building up. I'm afraid I'm going to burst."

Her eyes widened, and her gaze slid to his groin. Did he mean what she thought he meant?

"You, um, want me to help relieve the tension? That service usually isn't in my sphere of duties, but I suppose I could manage just for you."

With a nervous giggle, she sat beside him and slid a hand along his leg, thinking how much she was going to enjoy this. Maybe she could prolong his stay in sick bay.

Wren jerked away. "No! Great Power, I don't need that kind of relief."

"Suns, Wren, will you speak your mind?" She sprang up, covering her embarrassment with an irritated tone of voice.

"It's my back. I must spread my wings every six hauras. The pressure's been rising and I'm afraid they're going to sprout." He squeezed his eyes shut as though in pain.

"Good heavens. Luckily this bed is equipped with a turnaround. I can lock your neck in a brace and flip you onto your stomach on this lower surface. But you have to stay absolutely still."

"Do it," he grunted.

It took her five minutes to manipulate the contraption. Wren's panting breaths and reddened complexion alarmed her. As soon as he'd landed on his stomach, a giant set of wings erupted from his back through the slits in his uniform.

"By the moons of Agus Six!" She stared in rapture at the feathered appendages. "Can I touch them?" Reaching out a trembling hand, she remembered his condition and asked, "Sorry, are you alright?"

"Much better," he gasped, limp with exhaustion.

"Do you mind if I see what they feel like? I mean, they're wonderful. I've never seen anything so incredibly"—*sexy* was what she wanted to say—"large," she finished.

The tips of her fingers caressed the edge of one huge wing. It quivered under her touch. The feathers felt soft, like fluffy down, layer after layer on a strong muscular frame.

"Oh," she moaned, "this is wild."

Sinking onto the bed, she closed her eyes and reveled in the feel of his astounding wings. Her hands traced the outlines of the meshed barbs and tickled along the vanes, stroking the junctions, sinew, and coverts. She'd never thought she could get such a charge out of feeling a man's wings, but this was almost better than an orgasm.

She snapped her lids open, remembering her professional duties. "Sorry, we should change your position. There's too much pressure on that blood vessel wall this way. Are you ready?"

He pinched his face and his wings collapsed, disappearing into the slits in his broad back. He nodded his acquiescence and she used the contraption to return him to his supine position. His body secure, she sat next to him and stroked his arm.

"By the Gods, Wren, I've never felt so hot for a man before."

"It is not my right to enjoy a woman's attention. Please, leave me alone."

"Who said it wasn't your right? Just because you didn't jump off those cliffs on your home planet doesn't mean you can't function as a man. You're perfectly normal that I can see."

He glowered at her. "I am not normal according to my race. You waste your time with me."

She'd hoped to convince him that being with a woman from another world might work, but his mind-set against mating was so strong he refused to yield regardless of his desire. She'd never wanted anyone as much as she wanted Wren, yet she despaired of softening his heart.

"Very well," she said, afraid of turning him against her. She rose, checked his vital signs, and proceeded to the console to run another analysis of the data she'd obtained earlier. It wasn't easy to concentrate with Wren in the room.

It was going to be a torturously long interval for them both while he was confined to sick bay.

Chapter Seven

Emergency procedures were still in effect eight hauras later when Mara entered the conference room. Deke had called for another briefing. Hedy and Ebo were already in attendance. As she took her seat, Mara noted Deke's drawn face and slumped posture. She was aware he'd taken over Wren's duties as well as his own.

Deke pushed himself upright in his chair. "Dr. Te'larr, please report on Wren's condition."

"His vital signs are stable," Hedy said, her voice subdued. "His neck wound is healing well. I see no sign of complications from the concussion."

"That's good to hear." Deke surveyed each of his crew members. "I spoke with Glotaj. The Defense League patrols didn't find anything significant on the other two ships that left the spaceport after Jallyn's abduction. That means it's likely we'll find Jallyn on Yanura."

"We're not even certain the Yanurans took her," Mara cautioned. She still found it hard to believe Fromoth Trun might have had a hand in the baby's abduction but wanted more than anything to find Jallyn.

"Did you bring the baby's blanket with you to this briefing? I'd like you to do another separation while we're all present."

"I'm ready." Mara held up the lavender cloth in her hand to show the others. Clutching it to her chest, she closed her eyes and let her consciousness soar. She emptied her mind, focusing her thoughts on Jallyn. Her awareness drifted and floated from her body, hovering in the air while she tried to get a fix on Jallyn's vibrations.

Something yanked at her, a force so murky her senses couldn't penetrate it. She resisted, but the magnetic pull was too strong. Gaunt, shadowy tentacles curled around her astral body, binding her and tugging her away from her goal. She'd felt these tendrils of darkness before, and they'd strengthened with each separation. She couldn't begin to guess where they came from, nor did she want to know.

She screamed in her mind as a kaleidoscope of sensations overwhelmed her. She thought fiercely of Jallyn, clinging in her mind's eye to the child's fragile image. *Jallyn needs me. I have to go to Jallyn.*

And then suddenly she was inside Jallyn's head, safe from whatever evil had been seducing her. Shivering within her astral body, Mara turned her attention outward. The scene was the same. Jallyn was still aboard a ship. Wherever she was headed, it must be a long voyage like theirs.

Eager to return to her physical being, Mara ended the separation and gave her report in a toneless voice, omitting any mention of the dark cloud that had threatened to envelop her. A feeling of dread lingered, chilling her blood.

"Are you alright?" Deke asked, his face etched with concern.

"I'm fine." She clamped her lips shut, closing out any further inquiries. Without having anything definite to say, she didn't want to elaborate on the experience. Maybe it was the result of her own anxiety over Jallyn's safety.

Deke's steady gaze fixed on her and Mara glanced away. From his expression, she could tell he knew something was wrong. Hopefully he wouldn't probe further.

To her relief, Deke's attention switched to the Sirisian. "How long before we're up to speed?" he asked Ebo, his tone solemn.

"The warp coils need another five hauras to recharge." Ebo's elastic pink face sagged with fatigue.

"We're losing valuable time." With an exasperated sigh, Deke plowed his fingers through his hair. "At least the space dock at Revitt Lake City has repair facilities. Are you sure you can fix the aft sensors with a new set of sequencers?"

Ebo nodded. "Almost everything else is operational. We shouldn't have any trouble." He paused. "I did discover something while running a check on hull integrity. It appears the exterior coating on the ship can absorb certain radiation bands, making us impervious to sensor scans. If another ship were to scan our area of space, they'd detect nothing unless we were within visual range."

Deke's eyebrows raised. "Would that work for a planetary defense perimeter?"

Ebo nodded his turbaned head. "The function requires an energy expenditure. It's one of the commands programmed into our defensive operations."

"In other words, we have a cloaking device?"

"Aye, sir."

"Fantastic. I have the feeling we'll be needing it in the near future. Good work, Ebo."

The crew member frowned. "I was wondering why this ship hadn't been upgraded with the latest AI. We only have rudimentary computer commands. It's possible an artificial intelligence might interfere with our stealth ability."

Deke shrugged. "I don't understand how that might happen, but we'll manage with what we've got." He glanced at Hedy. "Dr. Te'larr, when do you estimate Lieutenant Wren will be ready for duty?"

Hedy twisted a lock of her hair. "Another twenty-six hauras should do it."

"Are you sure he'll be all right?"

The healer gave him a wan smile. "Wren slept well through the night. This morning, he's been as quiet as a kougra. It's difficult to tell what he's feeling when he won't admit to discomfort. The poor man hates being confined and having me wait on him."

Mara gave her a sympathetic glance. She'd stopped by sick bay late last night, offering to relieve Hedy. Hedy had confided her lack of progress with the big Polluxite. Wren wouldn't speak except in monosyllables and acted acutely embarrassed by Hedy's efforts to assist him. Mara hadn't known what else to suggest other than for Hedy to keep trying to break through his emotional barriers.

"Lieutenant Ebo, it's your watch on the bridge," Deke said. "Doctor, you may return to sick bay. Keep me posted on Wren's progress."

Mara watched uneasily as the other two crew members filed out. Did Deke have something special in mind for her to do?

"Aren't you going to offer me any advice?" he asked her. "That's part of your job, isn't it?

Her lips compressed. "I'll do what I can to help with crew duties, since Wren is out of commission. Assign me a task, Commander."

"This is only our first crisis. We have no idea what will be waiting for us when we reach the Yanuran system."

His eyes gleamed mischievously and she realized he was baiting her. Straightening her shoulders, she glared back at him, meeting his challenge.

"The Yanurans will want to impress us so they can win approval for their membership in the Coalition."

"Yes, but how will they react when we uncover their secrets? Our resources are limited. There's only five of us, and you women are poorly prepared for subversive operations. I'll have to worry about your safety instead of our mission."

"Hedy and I aren't as delicate as you seem to think. You, on the other hand, look as though you could use some rest."

"I can't afford to take a break. I have to get back to work." Shoving his chair aside, he rose.

"Let me get you something to eat, then."

"Fine; you can bring it to the bridge."

Mara watched him go with an irritated snort. The man didn't accept help easily. He was stubborn as a Tyberian rorsh.

At the fabricator, she conjured him an iced jelly and laver-bread cakes, then as an afterthought, got Ebo one of his favorite food items as well. She produced a tray to carry the meals to the bridge.

"Breakfast, gentlemen," she called out cheerfully on the flight deck. Deke manned the helm and Ebo frowned over the communications board. Both men glanced up at her entrance.

"I brought you an iced jelly," she said, holding up the carafe. "And some laverbread cakes." Laverbread was a mixture of seaweed, oatmeal, brown algae powder, raw placar fish and chopped fresh eels. Curious about the foods Deke ate, Mara had looked them up in the food selection database.

"Thanks," Deke said, rising and coming over to retrieve the tray. His look of gratitude sent a tingle of warmth through her.

"This will give you some energy. Lieutenant Ebo, I brought something for you also."

Ebo took his meal, then resumed his position. Holding the tray, Deke hesitated to move aside. He stood rooted to the spot, gazing at her. She wished she could sense his emotions, but it was impossible to read him.

Her glance drifted to the unruly lock of hair that tumbled across his forehead. Unable to stop herself, she reached forward to brush it gently off his brow.

His eyes darkened ominously. "Mara—"

"Forgive me." She sprang back, afraid she'd offended him. "I mustn't keep you from your job."

"Wait," he said as she turned away. "Perhaps you'd like to help Lieutenant Ebo monitor communications. You're skilled in linguistics, aren't you? Ebo can explain what needs to be done. That'll free him to work on repairs."

Eager to perform a useful function, she hastened to the comm panel, where Ebo explained the various components. She took over monitoring the subspace frequency, relieving Ebo until Wren was ready to return to duty.

As she bent over the comm panel, she could feel Deke's eyes boring into her back. His nearness made it difficult for her to concentrate.

It touched her that he'd admitted to being concerned for her safety. She understood now that he wasn't being unreasonable by ordering her and Hedy to engage in weapons training and muscle-strengthening exercises. He genuinely cared about their well-being. That softened her attitude toward him, and she began to wonder why he'd joined the Defense League. As soon as she had some free time, she'd check into his background.

When Ebo finished repairing the generator coils, they were able to achieve warp speed. Over the next few days, Mara's separations showed the baby's status to be unchanged. Hopefully when the child's environment altered, they could pinpoint a target within a certain radius. The Yanurans were due to arrive home a full two days before the *Celeste* reached their planet.

If Jallyn's surroundings switched before Fromoth Trun reached his home world, it would confirm Mara's belief that the Yanurans were not responsible for her abduction. As they got closer to their goal, she reiterated her arguments in support of his people.

"I'm sure their contribution to the Coalition will be meaningful," she said to Deke one day in the mess hall. "Look at some of our other member species. The Winnows gave us new theories in subspacial geometry. The Crimerans are famous as chemists. The Risivs produce specially crafted jewelry prized throughout the Coalition. Every member has contributed something significant. If Fromoth Trun is telling the truth about having an age-preserving drug, it could help billions."

"We'll find out soon enough." Deke's face creased into a smile, and he snaked his hand across the dining table to clasp hers. They were alone, and Mara's pulse rate soared. "Have you always been so devout in your beliefs?"

She stiffened, withdrawing her hand from his grasp. "I merely expect the Yanurans to receive the same fair evaluation as anyone else. You don't seem to share that notion. Your mind is already made up about them."

Deke pushed back his chair and rose. "This discussion is becoming old. You're the one who refuses to view them objectively."

"I am not." Incensed by his misjudgment of her, she followed him into the study center. The man spent every spare moment in there, perusing obscure scientific articles on oceanography. Mara couldn't correlate the serious scholar with the decisive commander and yearned to learn more about him.

"Deke, what did you do before you joined the Defense League?" She slid into the seat next to his and faced a blank computer screen.

He gave her a quick glance from under his thick brows. "I worked at one of the research centers on Eranus."

"Really? In what capacity?"

"It's irrelevant to our current mission." He returned his attention to his studies, effectively dismissing her.

Mara tried a few more inquiries but got nowhere. Refusing to give up, she waited until Deke left before calling up the database on Eranus. Her eyes widened when she read the information on her screen. *Dr.* Sage was an esteemed marine biologist who was being considered for the chancellorship at the Institute for Marine Studies.

Unable to contain her curiosity, she turned off the unit and rushed to crew quarters, where she knocked on Deke's door.

"Who is it?" he called in his rich, deep voice.

"Mara. I have to talk to you."

"Come in."

She entered and stopped just inside the door. He'd apparently been about to rest because he lounged on his sitter without any shirt or shoes. His hair was askew and she thought he looked devastatingly handsome sprawled in such a relaxed pose. The strains of a symphony played in the background.

She cleared her throat. "I, uh, just happened to call up the files on Eranus. I had no idea you were such a renowned scientist. Why didn't you tell me?"

Swinging his long legs off the sitter, he stood to face her. "I felt it unnecessary for anyone to know what I do outside of the Defense League."

"But you're too modest." Forcing herself not to stare at his broad chest with its dark swirls of hair, she fixed her gaze on his intense brown eyes. "I'd love to hear more about your work."

Deke sauntered forward, shutting the door and then facing her. "Why are you so interested in what I do?"

"I, um…" She didn't want to reveal the extent of her interest. He might take it the wrong way. "Despite our discussions, you still insist on suspecting the Yanurans of murdering your friend," she stated instead. "I was looking for something in your background that would hint at why you persist in this prejudiced attitude."

"Larikk disappeared on their *maug* planet. Isn't that enough?" His expression darkened. "You've no faith in me, have you? You can't believe I'll act with good judgment despite my suspicions, and you're too naïve to admit I might be justified in feeling the way I do. You want to learn more about me? Very well, I'll show you what you truly want to know."

He snagged her by the shoulders, pulled her close, and lowered his head. She felt the press of his mouth on hers and her first impulse was to push him away. Placing her hands on his brawny chest, she splayed her fingers and murmured a sound of protest that sounded weak even to her own ears.

She felt her inner self being pulled closer to him by a compelling magnetism that was impossible to resist. Closing her eyes, she leaned into him, enjoying the feel of his strong arms around her and the sensation of security his embrace provided.

His mouth moved urgently, demandingly over hers. He tightened his arms around her, and she swayed closer to him. He plundered her mouth with the hunger of a starving man. Barely able to breathe, she lost herself in a heady spiral of sensations.

The savagery of his kiss dissolved any resistance that might have lingered. Hadn't he mentioned this was where their relationship was leading? She hadn't wanted to succumb to his charms, but there was nothing urbane about the way he kissed her now. She could tell by the frantic motions of his lips that he soared alongside her on a hazy cloud of desire.

As his mouth gentled and he began tiny nibbling movements,

she murmured her pleasure. She fit perfectly into the hard angles of his body as she tilted her neck back, changing the angle of the kiss. He thrust his tongue into her mouth, probing and teasing until she met it with her own hesitant explorations. His masculine scent pervaded her senses and stirred her rising desire.

Unable to stop herself, she snaked her arms around him, letting her fingers explore his broad back. Heat sizzled her blood, and she longed to touch him everywhere.

"Mara, my dear." He graced her face with tiny kisses across her cheeks and the bridge of her nose, then back to her mouth. His hands roved over her, his movements urgent. He cradled the back of her head while he deepened their kiss.

When his hips rocked against her, a jolt jarred her senses. She melted into his embrace, feeling the crush of her breasts against his chest.

Wait, what? She was in *his* viewpoint, experiencing his sensations as he kissed her. How could this happen? The notion so astounded her that she could barely breathe.

After a moment, she realized this could be a golden opportunity to learn how he felt about her. She'd never taken advantage of anyone, but this occurrence had happened unexpectedly. It shouldn't cause any harm if she explored further.

She reached out, delving deeper into his psyche. Layers of consciousness peeled away under her spiritual probe. Beneath the surface, Deke was a sensitive man who cared deeply about many issues. She'd already glimpsed his concern over Wren's welfare and the reasons for his insistence that she and Hedy learn how to defend themselves. But she hadn't understood his regret over Larikk's death. Deke felt responsible, and his guilt motivated him to seek the truth. Her surprise at this insight propelled her back into her own existence.

Her eyes snapped open at the same instant that Deke jumped back, abruptly releasing her.

"What did you do?" he cried.

Mara froze, at a loss for words. She had no excuse for her behavior.

"You tried to read my mind."

"No, I can't read thoughts. I can only sense emotions, even when I'm in someone else's viewpoint. I'm not sure what happened, but you appear to have triggered a separation."

He stared at her, horrified. "What do you mean?"

Agitated, she brushed her hair off her face. "When I was younger, this sort of thing happened all the time. I had difficulty controlling my ability. But never in my adulthood have I experienced anything similar, not even with Pietor." Her heart sank at the incredulous look on his face.

"Who in Zor is Pietor?"

"My former fiancé. His parents didn't approve of me. Instead of coming to my defense, he agreed with them and said hurtful things about my gift."

Deke glowered at her. "I can understand why. Gods, does that mean this could happen again?"

She saw his fear mixed with resentment. He stared at her as if she were some sort of freak.

"You're the only person with whom I've ever had a spontaneous separation. This has to be significant. Maybe we're meant for each other."

"I only meant to take you to bed," Deke snapped, stepping back as though putting physical distance between them could prevent another occurrence. "Otherwise, there is nothing between us. You'd better leave now." His gaze frosted. "And take that as an order."

Mara stormed out, offended and hurt by his words. Coming on this mission had been a mistake.

****

Mara worked herself into a frenzy as she stomped her bare feet in a tray of mushy clay. She had to do something to wipe away the memory of Deke's lips on hers and the remembrance of how good it had felt to be wrapped in his embrace. Pounding vigorously, she contemplated the words he'd thrown at her. It was clear he feared her, and rightfully so. She'd violated her own ethical code by piercing his layers of consciousness. This was the first time she'd ever used her ability in that manner and the ease of it dismayed her.

Stricken with guilt and remorse, she wondered how she could approach Deke when he regarded her with such revulsion.

Pietor had scorned her gift, and he hadn't even experienced it in the way Deke had. She'd been devastated when she overheard him disparaging her to his parents. Would Deke share their experience with the other crew members?

Mortified at the idea, she hoped he'd have the decency to keep what happened to himself. Hedy would understand, but Wren and Ebo might regard her differently, and that would make this mission intolerable.

By the Light, what should she do? She stepped from her sculpting tray, wiped off her feet and put away the supplies. An overwhelming need to share her burden made her hasten to Hedy's cabin. Knocking loudly on the door, she heard strains of music from within.

Hedy swung the door open and the noise blared. "Mara, I was just thinking about you. Want to play one of the games I brought along?"

"No, I need to talk. Can you turn that music down?"

"Sure." Hedy complied, then swung around to face her. She wore an amber tunic with the Coalition insignia embroidered over her left breast and black trousers. It was the standard-issue uniform for medical personnel on Bimordus Two.

Without waiting for an invitation, Mara shut the door and strode to Hedy's lounger. She sank onto the softly upholstered surface and covered her face with her hands.

"What's the matter?" Hedy said with concern.

"I went to Deke's cabin to ask him about his work on Eranus. One thing led to another and we kissed." In a stumbling tone, Mara related the tale. "He probably hates me, Hedy." Depressed, she hung her head, her hands clasped in her lap.

"Nonsense, he got scared. You'd be disturbed if someone popped into your head and you weren't expecting it. He knows you have this ability."

"But I used it wrongly. I shouldn't have tried to delve deeper. I wanted to know how he felt about me."

"Why?" Hedy perched on the edge of her bunk, facing Mara.

Mara considered her response. Physically, she couldn't deny how strongly Deke's virile looks appealed to her. She liked the way his thick hair swept across his forehead, how his dark eyes gleamed with amusement whenever he challenged her to a duel of words. Their encounters were always stimulating. She'd never met a man as intelligent or charming, or as irritatingly obstinate as Dr. Deitan Sage.

"I like him," she said simply, "and I wanted to know if he felt the same toward me."

Hedy's expression softened. "Obviously he's attracted to you or he wouldn't have kissed you. I think you should tell him this means there's something special between you."

"I tried, but he wouldn't listen. He threw me out."

"But you're right. The two of you being together must have triggered the separation. If Commander Sage had any common sense, he'd realize this was important. There's no excuse for the way he treated you."

Mara shook her head. "I probed more deeply than I should have. I sensed the terrible guilt he feels about Larikk."

"You didn't mean any harm." Hedy squared her shoulders. "If he won't listen to you, I'll talk to him. Wait here!"

"No, don't bother. He won't listen." But Hedy had stalked out before Mara had a chance to say anything more.

Chapter Eight

Deke was in the study center trying to forget about Mara. What had he unleashed by his interest in her? All he'd wanted was to bed the woman, but she'd come dangerously close to stealing his identity. So what if her lips tasted like honey and her hair felt as fine as gossamer silk? Physical desires could be satisfied by any woman. He didn't need one who could invade his psyche without warning and stimulate emotions he didn't want to feel.

Maybe at least now she understood that concern for her safety was what prompted him to be so strict regarding physical training. He didn't want to worry about her well-being when dealing with the Yanurans.

The door crashed open and Hedy breezed inside. "Here you are." She grabbed a chair, turned it around, and sat astride it to confront him.

"What is it, Doctor?"

"Do you realize how badly you've hurt Mara? Your behavior was insufferably rude."

Deke studied the woman's blazing eyes and determined tilt of her chin. Despite her somewhat frivolous nature, the medic could be quite serious when the occasion demanded it.

"I don't see that it's any concern of yours," he replied in an icy tone.

"You're wrong. She's my friend, and you've hurt her. She is particularly sensitive about being perceived as different, and you nearly called her a freak. How do you think that made her feel?"

"How do you think I felt when she invaded my mind?"

"It happened spontaneously. Didn't she tell you this was the first time that's ever happened in her adult life?"

"She should exercise better control."

"Usually she can, Commander." Letting out an exasperated sigh, Hedy twisted around to sit properly in the chair. She leveled her steady gaze on him. "Mara had a difficult time growing up. Did she ever tell you her history?"

"No, and I don't see that it's relevant." He didn't want to hear this. He didn't want to know what motivated Mara or why she acted the way she did. It might make him sympathize with her, and he couldn't afford to feel that way. He needed to maintain a barrier between them so she wouldn't jump into his head again.

He rose, intending to head for the bridge, but Hedy blocked his path. "You're going to listen to me," she declared, her petite body standing between him and the hatchway.

"Move out of my way, Doctor."

Ignoring his order, Hedy said, "Mara exhibited her talent at an earlier age than most people on her world. She's from Tyberia, you know. Psychic ability is inherent in their race, but it usually takes annums of training to reach her level. Mara's parents sent her to a special school. Other children her age made fun of her and she was always lonely. After the fiasco with Pietor, she feels she'll never find happiness."

"So what? It's not my problem." He glanced beyond her, wishing himself anywhere but there.

"Mara seems to feel you triggered her separation."

"That's absurd. She lost control of her ability and violated my privacy. I won't allow it to happen again. Now unless you want to be physically removed from my path, I suggest you get out of my way."

Hedy's chin tilted stubbornly. Grunting with disgust, Deke lifted her by the waist and put her down, none too gently, off to his side.

As he stalked out, he shot her a last warning. "This isn't your affair, Doctor. Keep out of it, or I'll confine you to your cabin."

Cursing under his breath, he strode toward the companionway leading to the bridge. What did he care if Mara's life had been unhappy? It wasn't his problem.

Nor was the separation his fault, as both women seemed to believe. All right, so he'd kissed Mara. Could the physical contact between them have triggered the event? According to what she'd said, nothing like this had happened between her and Pietor. So why him?

He shrugged. It didn't matter why or how it had happened. The only way to prevent another occurrence was to keep away from her.

The thought that he was causing her grief tugged at his heart but he pushed it aside, angry with himself for even considering the idea. She was the one who'd caused him pain, dammit.

He stomped up the spiral staircase to the bridge, bottling his feelings for the woman just as he had suppressed his emotions over Larikk's disappearance when that had spun out of his control, too.

****

Mara waited anxiously in Hedy's cabin for her friend to return. She sat on the sitter, wringing her hands. By the Light, she should never have let Hedy go. What was she saying to Deke? Whatever Hedy did, it would only make matters worse.

At least Hedy was willing to come to her defense. Mara couldn't say that about anyone else she knew except for Sarina.

Hedy and Sarina were her only true friends. She could share her honest feelings with them. Thank the stars for their friendship. Moisture seeped from her eyes as she felt a depth of gratitude. Still, she yearned for closeness with another person. It wasn't that she needed a man. She just craved the intimacy of a loving relationship that she'd lacked even from her parents.

It was a goal she'd never reach. Pietor had mocked her and Deke was repulsed by her. Tears streaked her face and ran down her cheeks. No one would ever want her.

Her sobs had reached loud proportions when Hedy burst inside. "Great suns, Mara, stop that wailing at once. The man isn't worth crying over." She handed her a box of tissues and waited until Mara had blown her nose.

"What happened?" Mara asked with a sniffle.

"He's a stubborn son of a belleek. I told him you were sensitive about your ability and normally you had full control over it. He had to have been the influence that caused the separation. Deke didn't care. He told me to mind my own business or I'd be confined to quarters."

"That sounds like him," she said bitterly.

"What are you going to do? We've got seven more days until we reach Yanura. You can't avoid him the whole time."

She narrowed her eyes. "I'm not going to avoid him. Despite his lousy attitude, I do believe the man feels something other than lust for me. This has to be why the separation occurred. When he thinks about it, maybe he'll realize a significant event occurred between us, not that he would ever admit it."

Yet as the days passed, Deke managed to avoid her, or at least he avoided being alone with her. Mara never had a chance to discuss the situation with him. Whenever they were in the same room, he maintained a careful distance, as though afraid the slightest contact might make her jump into his head.

She wanted to explain that she had probed his emotions only because she wanted to learn how he felt about her. She also meant to tell him that if she inadvertently entered his mind again, she would never try to detect his feelings without his cooperation, and that they could explore the new sensations together.

But she couldn't discuss it in front of the other crew members. At least Deke didn't treat her like a pariah in front of them. He was coolly civil to both her and Hedy, and they were the only ones who noticed the change in his behavior.

****

Deke was beginning to relax, reassured that no further occurrences with Mara were going to take place, when he was summoned by an urgent call from Glotaj. Inside his cabin, he opened a scrambled channel to the supreme regent.

"Greetings, Deke. How are repairs on the ship progressing?" said the elder statesman on the monitor screen.

"Very well, sir. We're maintaining speed, and most of the systems are back on-line. I'm hoping to complete the mechanical repairs on Yanura."

"They've been alerted and will have a maintenance crew available." Glotaj paused, his expression darkening. "I just got a call from an investigator in the Justice Department. It seems an old case has been reopened. Would you know anyone named Larikk who disappeared on Yanura three annums ago?"

Deke sucked in a breath. "He was a friend of mine, sir. I filed the initial complaint. A preliminary investigation was done but nothing significant turned up. We couldn't proceed because Yanura didn't fall under Coalition jurisdiction."

"Well, it does now. Since the Yanurans have applied for admissions status, they'll be judged by our laws. The Justice Department is interested in what happened to this fellow."

"The Yanurans claimed he drowned, sir. His body was never recovered."

"Apparently Larikk vanished in the Alterland, which is Wort territory. You understand what this means?"

"Aye, sir." A muscle spasmed in his jaw. "We need to talk to the Worts. I was planning on meeting with them anyway to assess their views on Coalition membership."

"Find out what happened to Larikk. It could be significant."

Glotaj's mouth moved but Deke couldn't discern what he was saying. It sounded like a jumble of voices in his head. He shook himself. What was wrong with his hearing?

Hello, Deke.

Great suns! His eyes widened and his mouth gaped. Mara was in his head again. Had she just spoken to him? No, it wasn't distinct words he'd heard. It was a feeling that she was there.

Get out! he implored, trying to concentrate on what Glotaj was saying.

"It's imperative you find out if these rumors are true," the supreme regent concluded. "If they are, the situation is graver than we'd thought. Contact me as soon as you reach Yanura. Glotaj out."

Blast, he'd missed the rest of what Glotaj had said. And all because of Mara! She'd invaded his mind again, interfering in a sensitive communication. Did this mean he wasn't safe from her no matter where he was? Could she leap into his consciousness at any time, any place?

He ran a shaky hand over his face. At least he felt whole again. She'd left him as swiftly as she'd entered his essence. Had she heard the conversation with Glotaj?

Rage at her intrusion sent chills cascading through his body. He rose, intending to have it out with her once and for all. She had to get her ability under control. He couldn't live like this, never knowing when she was going to invade him.

After asking the ship's computer for a fix on her location, he headed down the corridor toward her cabin. Balling his hand into a fist, he pounded on her door, oblivious to the noise he made. Mara's sweet voice bade him to enter. She sat on an armchair in her sitting room, her hands folded in her lap. Her expression told him she had been expecting him.

"I'm glad you came, Deke. I've been wanting to talk to you in private. Please close the door and take a seat."

"You've got a helluva nerve to sit there calmly after what just happened. You invaded my mind again right when I was involved in a confidential communication. How do you account for this reprehensible act?"

He threw the door shut and stood in front of her, narrowing his eyes into slits. His glance scanned her body, from her loose raven hair cascading down her back to her silken wrap to her delicate bare feet. What in Zor was that thing she was wearing? The crimson and gold drape barely covered her slim form. His loins stirred as her perfumed scent drifted toward him. Aghast at his reaction, he stared at her.

She shook her head, long strands of hair caressing her face. "I can't explain it. You have to be the variant causing its occurrence." Her dark eyes pleaded with him to understand. "This has never happened to me before. Somehow you keep pulling me into your higher plane of existence."

"You're accusing me of instigating this issue? You're the one who lacks control."

"No, Deke. The first time, I took advantage to try to find out how you felt about me. I apologize for that and promise it won't happen again. Next time this happens, perhaps we should explore further and see where it takes us."

Panic swept him. "I don't want to explore anything! This is not a scientific experiment. You're messing with my mind."

It had been difficult enough for him to assert his independence through his youth, and that struggle still affected his life. His father, Director General of Eranus, was so powerful that Deke had always stood in his shadow until he chose to pursue marine biology.

His mother, Palomar, belonged to a wealthy clan that owned a global cosmetic company. His own sense of pride made him refuse to accept her family's money to fund his research. He wouldn't be dependent on his mother or anyone else. Nor would he subjugate his mind to Mara.

By the stars, he didn't want to fear her. He'd rather twist his fingers through her glossy long hair. What if she was right? If this had never happened to her before, maybe he did have something to do with it.

In any event, they couldn't go on accusing each other. They had to work together when they reached Yanura. But could he trust her to keep out of his head during sensitive negotiations with Fromoth Trun?

He hadn't been treating her very well in the interim. What was happening between them must be just as confusing to her as it was to him. He had to look at it from a scientific viewpoint. Wasn't his purpose to explore unknown phenomena?

Not when it threatened to undermine his privacy. A cold chill washed over him but it was quickly replaced by a surge of heat when Mara shifted her position and the slit in her garment exposed her smooth leg.

By the stars, she still had the power to arouse him despite his fear of her psychic ability. Never mind those erotic dreams he had of her. This was real, and her presence initiated a physical response he couldn't control. Could the same thing be happening to her, but on a mental level? How did she feel about him as a man?

"If you're ready to listen, I have news regarding Jallyn," Mara stated.

"What is it?"

She stood and began pacing, the drape she wore clinging to her hips. His gaze focused on her lush derriere as she ambled away from him.

As though sensing his interest, she turned back to face him. He perused her smooth skin, her wide almond-shaped eyes and her rosy lips. He remembered how her mouth had tasted under his, and he longed to pull her lithe body into his arms. How easy it would be to undo her garment and drop the fabric to the floor. His breath hitched as he thought about what she might be wearing… or not… beneath the clothing.

"She's been moved to a windowless room," Mara said, distracting him from his imaginary foreplay. "I can't tell if she's on a ship or on land, but I don't sense the vibrations of movement. I think her captors have reached their destination."

"I'll notify Defense League Command. This should give us more definitive information regarding possible locations."

Mara's eyes moistened. "What if Jallyn isn't on Yanura? I can't bear the thought of going home to Sarina without her."

Despite his resolve not to get close to her, his heart twisted inside him. She appeared so fragile and forlorn, like a lost child. Perceiving she needed reassurance, he pulled her to him, groaning inwardly as her body heat penetrated his uniform. Her floral perfume stimulated his senses. Nuzzling his face in her hair, he relished the softness of her silken strands.

"Mara," he whispered hoarsely, "don't do this to me. I can't get near you without wanting you."

She raised her face to his with such a pathetic expression that he dipped his head and kissed her without any thought to the possible consequences.

Her arms folded around his neck, pulling his head down closer. The urgent movements of her lips under his and the warmth of her breath compelled him to tighten his arms around her. What had begun as a comforting embrace turned into a soul-searing kiss that neither of them could stop.

Deke knew it the instant she invaded his life space, but this time he didn't push her away. He let her linger, waiting to see if he could trust her not to probe deeper. When his hand sought her breast, he sensed her joy and wonder as she shared his incredible delight. It heightened his own arousal so that his breath came in short, labored bursts.

They weren't close enough. He wanted to be part of her just as she was already a part of him. He drew his head back to regard her. Her mouth was soft and swollen from his kiss, her expression dreamy. Her soft body felt heavenly in his arms.

"This is my kind of experiment after all," he said in a husky tone. "Let's see how far we can go with it."

Mara's consciousness jerked back to reality. While he'd been avoiding her, she had longed for the teasing glimmer to return to his eyes, for a disarming grin to light his face when he glanced at her. She hadn't even realized how much she missed their sparring encounters over the Yanurans or their exercise sessions until she was bereft of his presence. Now it felt as though she'd just received a dose of ice water over her head.

She wriggled free of his embrace. "Is that all this is to you, a game? Now that you're not afraid of me, you're trying to get me into your bed again?"

"Why not? I shared your reactions to my touch. I want more, don't you?"

Disappointment washed over her like a frothing surf. What he felt for her was purely physical. She must have been wrong to think she meant anything else to him.

"Get out," she snapped, incensed by his cavalier attitude.

"Do you deny the attraction between us? You're the one who said there had to be something significant about our connection."

"I want more than a physical relationship, Deke. Until you're ready to admit you feel that way too, please leave."

After he stomped out, she wondered if his callousness was meant to repel her. For a brief moment, he'd been caring and tender, offering his strength when she'd needed it. She remembered other instances of kindness that showed his true nature but were quickly hidden. If only she could lessen his distrust, he might open up to her more. There had to be a reason why he was the only man who had triggered such a unique response.

Maybe she should try an intellectual approach. Deke had seemed pleased the first time she'd asked about his scientific career. She could use that avenue to restart a dialogue between them.

****

She had her chance later in the study center. Deke was reviewing Yanuran flora and fauna when Mara walked in and dropped into a seat beside him.

"I didn't know you were interested in alien plant life," she said, smiling benignly.

"It pays to be prepared," he replied, staring at his screen.

"Prepared for what?"

Sighing, he switched off his monitor and whirled to face her. "Survival skills. It is necessary to become familiar with the terrain, vegetation, and various forms of wildlife of a target planet when you're going on a mission like ours."

"Is there wildlife on Yanura?" Ashamed to admit it, she realized she knew little about the planet other than the cultural practices of its amphibian inhabitants.

"Yes, many animals make their home there," he answered, a look of surprise on his face, as though he'd expected her to argue with him. "There's also a wide variety of plant life. Some we've seen on other worlds, so the vegetation won't seem so different."

"How would you compare this assignment to your research back on Eranus?"

Dashing a hand through his thick hair, he grimaced. "I prefer being near the sea. At least on Yanura, I'll have a chance to inspect their mariculture farms. I miss the ocean when I'm away from it for too long."

"What made you join the Defense League? I know I'm asking a lot of questions, but if we're going to be working together on the planet, I'll need to understand your background."

He gave her an assessing glance. Seemingly taking her interest at face value, Deke explained how he needed a grant to continue his research on deep-sea vents and how he was competing for the chancellorship.

"That's why succeeding at this mission is so important to me. I have to show Glotaj and the selection committee that I can handle a leadership position."

It touched Mara that he'd confided in her. She suspected no one else among his crew knew his term of service was temporary, and she wouldn't violate his trust by informing them.

"I appreciate your telling me this, Deke. It helps me to understand you better."

He leaned forward in his chair, and his closeness warmed her. "What about you, Mara? Why are you so adamant in your insistence that the Yanurans get fair treatment? Are you that way with all your clients?"

"Everyone deserves to be treated with respect."

"Hedy said you had a difficult upbringing. Is that why you chose a career in diplomacy, to ensure other people received the respect you never had?"

His insight made her squirm in her seat. "Since you put it so succinctly, the answer is yes. Despite all our technological achievements, prejudice still exists in many parts of the galaxy. We can't achieve true harmony until all races accept each other in an honest light."

"That's an admirable but immense undertaking for one person to accomplish."

"People like you make it difficult. You're biased against the Yanurans before you even meet them."

Deke rolled his eyes. "Here we go again."

Instantly she felt contrite. "I'm sorry. Let's change the subject. Tell me about your oceanographic research."

He grinned, his face brightening. "Want to hear about the tube worms I found on Setai Four?"

****

Torn between wanting Mara and his fear of intimacy with her, Deke was alarmed that he eagerly sought her company. She was a good listener, and he enjoyed relating stories of his scientific discoveries. By listening quietly and avoiding arguments, she insinuated herself into his psyche without even jumping into his head.

You can bed her without wedding her, Deke told himself as he left his cabin one day. Sharing her sensations when kissing her was a wild experience. It heightened his own delight tenfold. And if a kiss gave such pleasure, what would their joining do?

Every time the woman was near, his heart pounded and his loins stirred. He'd be willing to have her essence enter his body just for sex. Why wouldn't she agree?

As he headed toward the bridge, he spotted her in the holovid lounge, watching a video on Anthrobie folk dances. She was relaxing on the lounger, the hem of her long skirt folded about her ankles. Her low-neckline top afforded him a tantalizing view of her unbound breasts. At his entrance, she looked up, and he was pleased to notice her expression warmed.

"Taking a break, Commander?"

He sauntered inside. "I could ask you the same thing. How come you're not studying up on the Yanurans or working on a sculpture?"

Mara glanced at his dimples and at his even, white smile. Her knees turned rubbery as she scrambled for a response.

"I needed a rest." Her gaze swept to his broad chest and his tight-fitting uniform.

Deke dropped down on the seat beside her, leaning back as though it were the most natural thing in the world for his thigh to touch her at hip level. In a fluid movement, his arm stretched across the back of the lounger, his fingers dangling just beyond her shoulder. If she took a deep breath, he'd be touching her.

Before she could protest, he stroked the sensitive inner skin of her arm, sending shivers of delight through her.

"D-Don't," she stammered, wanting to close her eyes and savor the sensations.

"Why not? It feels good, doesn't it? Why don't you relax and enjoy this? Computer, secure the door."

"Now wait a minute, I didn't say it was all right," she huffed, aware that her tone sounded weak. His fingers moved to her cleavage, teasing her into heightened arousal. Her nipples ached for his touch as a sweet tension rose inside her.

What would be the harm in letting him kiss her? It didn't mean she'd have to hop into bed with him. One kiss, just to see if the same thing happened as the last time.

She turned toward him, giving in to her rising desire. But as soon as he touched his lips to hers, her body reacted as though it had a mind of its own. Closing her eyes, she wrapped her arms around his neck, pulling his head down closer. He tasted of spice and sea salt. The mixture left her reeling with passion. She kissed him back with demanding urgency, running her hands along the broad planes of his back.

Blissful sensations coursed through him as he felt her hands roaming his skin. Deke tightened his embrace, crushing her mouth under his. She was so lovely, so different from the other women he'd met. She reminded him of a ship on a calm sea—steady and reliable, running a straight course toward land.

He'd been with plenty of women, but most of them were only interested in his father's power or his mother's wealth. None of them ran as deep as Mara. That was how he wanted to be with her, buried deep inside and rocking to the rhythm of the timeless sea.

He felt her enter his life space and wondered why it had taken so long, but it didn't matter. He could feel how her limbs melted while her blood surged with fire. Her mouth parted and he plunged his tongue inside, exploring her the way he'd search the ocean, probing and thrusting into every fissure. Her nipples ached with wanting, so he brought his fingers into play on her breasts, his own arousal soaring as their sensations merged.

Mara hadn't known how wonderful touching a woman's breasts could feel to a man. When Deke slipped his hand inside her top and stroked her bare flesh, she made a low sound in her throat. It was both an expression of sublime pleasure and a verbalization of his delight.

He moaned her name, tearing his mouth from hers to lavish her face with kisses. She gasped when he leveraged himself atop her on the lounger. He rotated his hips, pressing the bulge in his pants against her juncture.

"Mara, I want you," he said against her ear.

She knew when he became lost in the mind-boggling heat from their inflamed flesh. It was like being caught in a whirlpool. He couldn't resist the pull, and when she entered the swirling eddy of passion and spiraled with him into the dark waters, she felt her control loosen. Maybe if she allowed him to satisfy his lust, she'd gain his trust. He'd see there was nothing to fear from her.

She knew the instant he was aware of her yielding to him and felt his joy as well as a surge of triumph. At that moment, her essence flew back into her body.

She pushed him off and sat, yanking her top into place.

"You're regarding me as just another conquest, aren't you? I won't be treated that way."

He tilted his head. "You can't deny your enjoyment. We're good together."

"Maybe so, but I'm looking for a caring relationship. You won't accept me as anything more but a warm body in your bed."

"That's not true." He stroked her arm, sliding his nimble fingers up and down her skin and causing goose bumps to rise on her flesh. "I've never felt anything like what I feel with you. It's not enough to hold you in my arms and kiss you. I want to share what you're experiencing when I'm tight inside you."

His words conjured an image that tempted her beyond reason. "If we did make love, would you just walk away afterward? Is that all it means to you—another new experience to explore? You merely want to use me to enhance your own pleasure."

He got up and straightened his clothing. "We could be great in bed, but you're mistaken if you think it could ever mean more. I'd never attach myself to a woman who can invade my mind without warning. I value my privacy too much. If you can accept my limits, we'll get along fine."

"Your limits! What about mine? Do you even care about me at all?"

"It doesn't matter. We can't have it any other way. If you decide to take my offer, I'll be waiting for you to make the first move."

She stared after him as he marched out. Was this to be her fate, always alienated from those she cared about the most? Her parents had cast her aside as a child by sending her to a special school. Now Deke was telling her that she was good enough to join him in bed, but she wasn't acceptable for any other kind of relationship. Would she never be treated as a normal person?

Despair washed over her and dragged her down. Tears wouldn't help, she thought as her lower lip quivered. She'd gotten through this before, and it had only made her stronger. No man was ever going to devalue her again and get away with it.

Chapter Nine

Hedy's luminous green eyes shone with sympathy when Mara related her woes. "I'm not the best person to give advice. I haven't had much luck with Wren," she said.

"At least he's interested in you, even if his cultural taboos forbid him from acting on it," Mara remarked. She'd sought her friend in sick bay, where Hedy was busy recalibrating her instruments. She wore the regulation uniform for medical personnel.

"Deke likes you. He's just afraid of your power."

"Not anymore. He wants to use me to heighten his sexual pleasure."

Hedy put her hands on her hips. "Do you really believe that's all he wants? You have to give him time to adjust."

"To what? The idea that I can invade his privacy without warning? The realization that his feelings would be always vulnerable if he accepts me? I can't seem to exert much control when I'm around him."

Hedy peered at her. "Maybe you should examine how you feel about yourself."

Mara stiffened. "What do you mean?"

"You talk as though you're unworthy of a man's esteem. This ability is not unique to you, remember? Other Tyberians share the same gift."

"Yes, but they have annums of training."

"So what? Why can't you consider this another form of cultural diversity? You're appreciative of alien cultures. Show some respect for your own. This issue has never happened to you before. As you said, that must mean something about your relationship to Deke."

Mara brushed down her skirt. "I'll think about it. Thanks for listening, but it's getting late. I have to go."

Out in the corridor, she paused. No doubt her abrupt departure had been rude, but Hedy's insights had hit the mark. On Tyberia, she'd be considered highly gifted but not abnormal. Was it her own perception that made her regard herself as deviant?

Deciding she needed to speak to someone from home, she entered the empty conference room and opened a commlink to Tyberia. She asked to speak to Master Keenan at her former school. He'd been her last teacher, and even though she hadn't availed herself of the opportunity to advance in her studies, she respected his opinions.

His wizened face sprang onto the monitor screen. "Mara, such a pleasure! How are you?" he articulated in the refined voice she remembered so well.

"I'm fine, thank you, Master Keenan." She frowned. "No, I'm not. I seek guidance."

"Ah." His dark eyes pierced hers as though they were actually in the same room. "Speak your mind, child."

Sitting at the table, she folded her hands in front of her. In halting tones, she related her problems.

"Have you been practicing your meditation?" Master Keenan asked.

"No, I haven't wanted to stretch my powers."

"Hmm. I remember you left the seminary before you'd completed your term."

"I didn't like being considered different from my friends."

"On our world you would have been revered for your accomplishments."

"Only as an adult. When I was younger, none of my friends understood. They made fun of me."

"I don't think you ever understood how fortunate you are."

She compressed her lips. "It doesn't seem that way to me."

"And that's the crux of your problem, *karima.*" The master's face grew thoughtful. "This attraction between you and Commander Sage must be very powerful. When a man and woman forge a romantic relationship, cords grow out of the chakras to bind them. These cords exist on all levels of the auric field. Before you even approach each other physically, your higher energy fields are interacting to see if you're compatible. If you had continued with your studies, you'd be able to see the ribbons of energy crossing between you."

"What are you saying?"

The master's eyes took on a distant glaze. "Connections already exist between you and this commander. That's why you keep being drawn to him. If you could perceive it, you'd see the arcs of rose-colored light extending from his heart chakra to yours. You must meditate to expand your consciousness. Perceiving the human energy fields takes practice, my dear. You should apply yourself to your studies. Accept the Light that flows around us and through us. Open your channels and let the universal life force infuse you with wisdom."

Mara listened to his words and struggled to understand. According to her teacher, she and Deke were already bonded on the higher spiritual planes. In order to strengthen the ties between them on the lower physical and emotional levels, she had to open herself to the force that permeated the universe. But she couldn't do that unless she embraced all aspects of her being.

A flash of insight exploded in her mind. She'd wanted to reject her gift. And if she couldn't accept this part of herself, how could she expect anyone else to do the same?

Master Keenan smiled benignly at her as though he knew what was going on inside her head. Perhaps he could read her aura on another plane, one not bound by time or space.

"Thank you," she said simply. "I should have listened to you long ago."

"You weren't ready, child. Once you let go of your limited ego, your awareness will expand to the higher bodies. You'll be able to perceive what this man truly feels for you."

"I hope so. Thank you so much, Master Keenan. My gratitude is everlasting."

"May the Light shine upon you, *karima.*"

They signed off and Mara sat as still as a statue. Master Keenan's words reverberated throughout her soul. It was true she'd never accepted herself. She tried hard to appear normal and suppressed the part that made her special. Her gift should be embraced and not denied.

For the first time in her life, she appreciated the talent shared by her fellow Tyberians. Because her power had exhibited itself at such an early age, she hadn't integrated it into her self-image in a positive manner.

Now she had a sudden urge to experience the higher sensory perceptions of which she was capable. Master Keenan had said meditation was the key. Did she remember the incantations?

She hastened to her cabin, lowered the lighting and reclined on her double lounger in the sleeping chamber. Closing her eyes, she focused her thoughts on the repetitive chants learned from childhood. The goal was to loosen her fixed reality, to feel the fluid world of energy that permeated the universe.

Her thoughts drifted to her early schooling where she'd spent hauras by the lake outside the seminary. She'd practiced blending in with her surroundings as she'd been taught. At those quiet times, she'd been able to perceive things beyond the normal human range. It had been an incredible experience but it frightened her because she wasn't mature enough to understand.

Now she felt overwhelmed with regret that she'd wasted so many annums. She could travel the astral plane, but that was only the fourth auric level, the bridge between the physical and spiritual layers. She'd never been able to go beyond that space. She had to sensitize herself to the higher frequencies in order to perceive them.

The universe is whole, and I am part of the whole. I am connected to all living beings and to all matter, real and ethereal. I am like the Light, transcending the limits of time and space.

Opening her eyes, she brought her palms up, holding her hands so that the tips of her fingers faced each other. With a plain white wall in the background, she relaxed her gaze, staring at the light blue lines rippling between her hands. She moved her palms apart, then brought them together, feeling the buildup of energy. These were very basic exercises, allowing her to perceive her own aura on its lower levels.

She set herself a new goal, which she would try to achieve by the next crew briefing.

Several hauras later, Mara fixed her gaze on Deke once they were all assembled for the day's strategy meeting. She stared at the space directly above his head. Clearing her mind, she opened herself to the Light. Soon a pulsating layer became visible, centimeters from his skin. The pulsations formed a wavelike motion down his body. The auric layer was a light blue color that brightened closer to his body, with streamers coming from his fingertips and the top of his head.

As she continued her trance, she was able to discern a rose-colored light that enveloped Deke when he looked at her. *Master Keenan was right! The commander does care for me.*

Rose was the light of love.

She realized it was up to her to strengthen the cords that bound them. But how could she make him recognize that there was more to their connection than sexual tension?

Master Keenan had said Deke's higher auric layers were constantly interacting with hers. This had to be the reason why he triggered her separations. Perhaps if she joined with him on the physical plane, acceptance would follow on an emotional level. Sooner or later, Deke would have to understand they were meant for each other.

She smiled to herself, eager to put her thoughts into action. She'd wanted Deke from the first moment they'd met, and now there was no further reason to deny herself the pleasure.

****

Deke wondered about Mara's strange behavior. Sitting across from her at the conference table, his glance kept sliding in her direction. Every time he looked at her, she gave him a secretive smile. Was that an invitation he glimpsed in her eyes? How could it be, after the nasty way he'd treated her?

Guilt assailed him at how he'd contributed to her constant stream of rejections. First her parents had sent her away, then Pietor had scorned her. Now he'd added to her pain by refusing to consider her for a serious relationship. No wonder she vigorously defended other people's rights. She'd never been treated fairly herself. Was he being honest in not giving her a chance?

But she'd invaded his mind, an inner voice protested. She could distract him at a critical moment, intrude upon a private conversation, and expose feelings he didn't care to acknowledge. She gave no warning before jumping into his psyche.

Yet hadn't she said he was the only man who had ever experienced this with her?

Confused by the tumult of emotions inside him, Deke sought solace in physical exercise and study during the next few days. When he wasn't reading the latest scientific dissertations, he worked out in the physio lab in preparation for the coming mission.

The day before they were due to arrive at Yanura, he was vigorously exercising on the rowing machine when Mara breezed in, wearing a skimpy aquamarine outfit that clung to her curves. Her onyx hair cascaded down her back like strands of spun glass. He took in her long shapely legs before fixing his eyes on her face as she strode toward him.

"Here you are," she said with a musical lilt. "I was hoping to catch you alone."

Her brilliant smile nearly took his breath away. He leapt up from the machine, switched it off, and grabbed for his towel. "I was just leaving."

"I don't think so. There's something I have to show you." She sashayed closer, the seductive sway of her hips tantalizing him.

His gaze strayed to her cleavage where the swell of her bosom overflowed from a scooped neckline. A coil of desire sprang up within him. "What is it?" he asked in a husky voice. He dropped his towel onto a chair.

"I've learned the steps to a new dance. I was hoping you would partner me." Her gaze roamed over his body clad in a pair of snug activity shorts. "Come," she said invitingly, holding out her hand. "Want to give it a try?"

With her feminine scent wafting toward him, his arousal increased. Grasping her slender hand in his, he hesitated, curious to see what she would do next. He felt like a shooter primed for action, waiting for her signal to fire.

"Computer, play *Starlight Enchantment*." Musical strains filled the area. "Lower lighting." As the lights dimmed, she stepped closer. "You need to put your right arm around me."

He encircled her waist and at her murmured instructions, they began a slow slide. His body rubbed against hers as he dipped her to one side. Just the feel of her lush softness made a groan slip from his lips.

"Perhaps we should retire to a more private setting," he suggested, his heart pounding in his chest. He couldn't get this near to her without wanting to thrust inside her and become one with her.

"Your cabin or mine?" she whispered.

"Mine. Then we won't run the risk of having your good friend, the doctor, interrupt us."

"I believe she's busy in sick bay with Wren."

"The lieutenant seems to require an unusual number of medical exams since his accident," he remarked wryly. Twirling her around, he brought her up against his body. "Is this the type of move you had in mind?" He brought his mouth to hover centimeters above hers.

"Oh, yes."

Reading her expression, his heart soared. He didn't know what had changed her mind, but she appeared willing to lie with him. Their future didn't matter. For now, she was his.

He crushed his mouth down on hers. She tasted as sweet as honey wine and as soft as a rose petal. After a few moments, he raised his head and gazed at her.

"Let's go," he rasped, not even sparing a moment to grab his shirt and shoes. He led her into the corridor and toward the crew's quarters, where they entered his cabin.

He headed straight for the sleeping chamber, giving orders to the ship's computer along the way. The lights dimmed and melodious music began playing in the background. Inside, he turned to her with a grin.

"I'm glad you've made this decision. I've been going crazy with wanting you."

She sauntered nearer, closing the distance between them. "I want you, too. We're meant to be together. The cords that bind us are strong."

He brushed his finger across her lips. "Too much talking," he admonished, slipping the sleeves of her dance outfit off her shoulders. He dipped his head to kiss her swan-like neck, pleased when she tilted her chin to allow him better access. Her responsiveness increased his desire and pummeled his senses.

"Wait," she said, stepping back.

In a graceful sweeping movement, she removed her clothing. He gasped as she stood before him naked, her nipples peaked. With a low groan, he splayed his hands on her breasts. As she closed her eyes, he felt a strange sensation in his mind. She was there, her reactions mingling with his. He felt her delight as he stroked her nipples with his thumbs.

"Great stars!" he exclaimed as his own body responded to her aroused state.

Sharing his viewpoint, Mara felt the engorgement between his thighs and moaned with need. Was it her passion or his that needed abating? She couldn't tell. Her hands grasped at his activity shorts, pulling them down. He cast them aside and drew her into his embrace.

They collapsed onto the wide lounger that served as a bed.

His mouth sought hers and they kissed greedily, urgently, their bodies pressed together. Now that she'd lowered her barriers, she couldn't get enough of him. Her body, soft and pliant, molded to his heated form in a frenzy of need.

"We're going too fast." He raised himself off her, his heavy-lidded gaze raking her body stretched out on the lounger. "Gods, you're gorgeous. I could admire you all day." He reached out and cupped the mound of hair that guarded her feminine secrets.

"Please," she pleaded, writhing as his practiced strokes aroused her passion to new heights.

"I can't believe I'm sharing how this feels to you." He kept his hand in place as he lowered his mouth to hers.

She thought she'd explode as his lean, muscled body rocked against her. She turned into him, lifting his hand out of the way and wrapping her arms around him. As she pressed her breasts flat against his chest, her fingers splayed across his back. She traced the rippled muscles under his taut skin, outlined his broad shoulders, tickled his spine, and cupped his buttocks. Every time he murmured his pleasure, she shared his delight.

Mingling with his essence, she experienced the bombardment to his senses, the surge of raw masculine power that tensed his muscles, the mind-numbing effects of his arousal. And she also felt his bliss at sharing her own passionate reactions.

Expanding her consciousness, she perceived the flow of rose-colored light arcing between them, and her heart swelled with joy. If only he could see it, too. But she still sensed fear within him and was careful to limit her visitation. Once she gained his trust, all remaining barriers between them would crumple.

She shifted her position so that he lay atop her. Groaning, he plundered her mouth with renewed vigor, his hands on her breasts. Her lofty thoughts were lost as she gave in to the delightful sensations coursing through her. The ache between her thighs grew to unbearable heights and she spread her legs, relishing the feel of his hard bulge pushing against her.

"I can't hold out much longer," he gasped, his breathing ragged.

"Then do it now," she urged, rubbing her body against him.

He surged forward with a powerful thrust. As he paused, giving her a moment to adjust, she felt the tightness that encased him and her own fullness at the same time. His name burst from her lips as she clutched at his hair.

Slowly he began rocking against her and she sensed his concern that he shouldn't hurt her. A surge of tenderness overwhelmed her as she twisted her legs around him to enhance his pleasure.

A brief glimpse surfaced of his deep admiration, intense desire, and wishful longing that he wouldn't admit feeling toward her. Before she could get a handle on it, the window dissolved as lust drove all reason from her mind.

Primal grunts burst from Deke's throat as he slid back and forth. One more plunge and she cried out at the same time as Deke reached his climax. Spasms shook her body, and she felt nothing but sublime pleasure until the waves of ecstasy faded away.

She lay sprawled on the lounger, drained of energy. Her eyes still closed, she heard Deke's heavy breathing beside her. Their link had broken. She was back inside her own head, and it was an odd sensation, like something was missing.

"Are you all right?" he asked, tickling her arm.

"I've never been better. That was incredible." Blinking open her eyes, she glanced at him.

He leaned sideways on his elbow, a lazy smile curving his mouth. "I knew it would be good between us, but incredible doesn't even begin to describe what I felt. Your gift brought us to rapture."

She sat, not even shy about her nudity. "I'm glad you feel that way, because now we can seek our destiny together."

He withdrew his hand. "Wait a minute. I'm not saying anything more will come of this. We had a good time. That's enough for me."

She drew in a sharp breath. "How can you say that after the intimacy we've shared? You know our experience was unusual. I can bring you great pleasure."

He stood and reached for his shorts. "You can also bring me pain. Just because you didn't this time doesn't mean it won't happen again. I don't want to tie myself to someone who can disrupt my life without warning."

She froze at his words. She'd thought he would realize how precious their relationship was once they'd made love. Apparently, she had been very wrong.

Snatching her clothes, she dressed herself with trembling fingers. "I'm not sorry we did this, but I deeply regret your attitude. You can't keep denying what I've seen within you. We *will* be together, and until you realize it, I hope I haunt your dreams."

With those taunting words hanging in the air, she left.

****

Deke stared after her, wondering if she'd invade his mind to torment him for his callous attitude. Sex with her was beyond amazing, but who needed a woman who could rip away his sense of self?

Yet she hadn't done that, had she? Coming together with her had only enhanced his feelings, not subjugated them. So why was he still so frightened of her ability?

Perhaps because she couldn't control it. If it could be limited to sex, there wouldn't be any problem. But since he never knew when or where she might distract him, he remained wary of her. He wished they didn't have this problem.

As though she'd put a curse on him, his dreams that night were filled with her erotic image, and he yearned to take her into his arms and kiss away her sadness.

But his doubts the next morning couldn't be dispelled so readily, especially not when they were about to meet the Yanurans.

Needing desperately to sort out his feelings, he confided in Wren as the two of them were checking supplies in the cargo bay prior to disembarkation. Ebo had bridge duty for their approach into the Yanuran system.

"You're attracted to Dr. Te'larr, aren't you?" Deke asked bluntly, loading his diving equipment onto a mini-levitator unit.

The Polluxite glanced up from the survival packs he was readying. "Hedy is a unique individual."

"Have you bedded her yet?"

Wren's face reddened. "I haven't earned that privilege, Commander."

"Earned it? What do you mean?" As Wren proceeded to explain in an embarrassed tone, Deke's astonishment grew. "You're kidding. The woman practically throws herself at you, and you won't have her? You must be crazy!" He shook his head, unable to believe Wren's obstinacy.

"I've seen the way you look at her friend," Wren said, giving him a friendly nudge.

"My problem is different." Deke described their encounters and their differing viewpoints.

"You should consider yourself a lucky man. If I were in a position to accept such an offer, I would not hesitate."

"Lucky? I wish I'd never met the woman."

Deke tossed the remainder of his supplies onto the platform. Obviously he and Wren couldn't communicate on the topic when their reasoning diverged so greatly. Wren desired a lasting relationship with Hedy but denied himself because of cultural taboos. Deke wanted to be with Mara just for the sexual pleasures they could give each other. Otherwise, he wished she'd leave him alone.

What else could he do about it? He'd been cursed from the first moment they'd met. Now he couldn't get her out of his mind even when she wasn't breaking down his mental doors. Regardless of how she went about it, she continued to torment him.

Running his fingers through his hair, he decided to concentrate on work. They were due to land on Yanura in five hauras. The preparations should take up most of his time, and Mara was busy monitoring communications. He'd thought it would be appropriate if she made the initial contact as they approached the planet. Fromoth Trun already knew her and it would aid their cause if the statesman expected nothing out of the ordinary from their visit.

Chapter Ten

Fromoth Trun beat his fist against his chest and bowed deeply in front of Mara. *"Rogi Kwantro,"* he muttered in a gravelly tone.

"Rogi Kwantro," she repeated, imitating his gesture.

She wore a shimmering emerald sarong embroidered with silver threads, her hair held back from her face by a jeweled headband. The gown represented the Tyberian style of formalwear, which she thought appropriate for greeting Fromoth Trun, especially when he'd invited the crew of the *Celeste* to a banquet in their honor.

It had been worth it to dress up just to see Deke's reaction. His eyes had fired when he caught sight of her before disembarkation, but he hadn't said a word with Hedy and Wren present.

As he stood beside her, she glanced at him. He looked tall and dashing in the standard dress uniform of the SEARCH force—a maroon and gray jacket with gold braid and insignia denoting his rank, slate gray pants, and shiny black boots.

His expression impassive, he fidgeted at her side while Fromoth Trun rattled off endless flowery salutations. Mara had been surprised by the way Deke had pleasantly greeted the Yanuran leader, bowing graciously and remembering to utter the proper words. Each new aspect of his personality was like a leaf unfolding, and the fresh layers fascinated her. If only she knew how to gain his trust.

Forcing herself to pay attention to Fromoth Trun, she smiled politely. Wren and Hedy stood just behind her and Deke, completing their field team.

Deke wondered how Mara could appear so relaxed when there were so many questions to ask. If Fromoth Trun would stop spewing his meaningless compliments, they might get down to business. When would he be allowed to view the seaweed farms? What had happened to Larikk? Was Jallyn here?

The Yanuran leader wasn't in any hurry, Deke thought. He flaunted his state of office, wearing a gaudy satin robe of bright orange and red embellished with glittering cords of gold. It made his moist green skin look pale in comparison.

His amber eyes bulged in a hairless, flat skull, the horizontal pupils giving him a look of cunning. Situated behind each eye were large round disks, his eardrums. With his broad head, tall heavy body, and lavish attire, he appeared a caricature rather than a leader, but he had charisma, and the animated gestures that accompanied his speech showed he had a flair for drama as well.

The fishy odor the Yanurans emitted didn't bother him since he was used to the fragrance of the sea, but Deke heard Hedy cough behind him. He stifled a grin at her reaction. His gaze drifted beyond the Yanuran leader to a group of aides clustered off to the side. Most of the males wore belted waistcoats in topaz or rust colors and breeches in dark brown. The females, larger in stature, wore colorful dresses with full skirts and bonnets covering their heads.

At his side, Mara stood regally, draped in her seductive sarong like a nymph come to tempt him. He tried to ignore the warmth radiating from her and the urge to draw her into his embrace. Likely she wouldn't let him touch her again after what had transpired yesterday, and the possibility disturbed him. Hadn't he told the woman he'd wait for her to come to him on his terms? When she'd approached him in the physio lab, he thought she had finally come to her senses and agreed. Yet she was still insisting their relationship meant more than a fantastic interlude of great sex.

He cursed inwardly. Here he was, thinking of Mara again when he should be concentrating on what Fromoth Trun was saying. Forcing his thoughts away from her, he returned his attention to the Yanuran leader.

"I am pleased you will accept our hospitality," Fromoth Trun said with a sly smile. "Do you wish to retrieve any items of a personal nature from your ship before we move on?"

"Huh?" Deke frowned at the official.

Mara nudged him. "Fromoth Trun has kindly offered us a place to stay during our visit. I'm sure our needs will be amply met by his capable staff."

Deke stared at her. "A place to stay? But we'll be—"

"Thrilled to see the capital city," Mara concluded, giving him a pointed glance.

Deke clamped his mouth shut, angry that she'd accepted an invitation without his permission. He'd planned for them to stay on the *Celeste.* How did this happen?

Blast, he must have missed part of the conversation when he was thinking about her. Was he to be constantly distracted by this woman?

Fromoth Trun gestured toward the *Celeste,* which rested on a launchpad behind them. They were still in the spaceport, having been met by the welcome party immediately upon arrival.

"Are you certain your other crew member won't join us, Commander? Our service team can repair the damage to your ship while you visit our illustrious city."

"No, thanks. Ebo will stay aboard. He has to realign our fuel modulators," Deke said by way of explanation.

Ebo's job was to guard the ship. In the event of an emergency, he could initiate launch procedures. Plus, the Sirisian would be monitoring communications. If there was any sign of trouble, he'd notify Deke.

Fromoth Trun spoke into his personal communicator. "Lixier Bryn, is the reception center ready for our guests?"

"Preparations are complete," a female voice answered.

"Good. We'll join you for the feast." He offered his guests a cunning grin that gave Deke the impression of a shark about to snag its prey. "This way, if it pleases you." He waved his arm in an imperious manner.

Outside the domed spaceport, the warm humid air sang with the buzz of insects and the cries of birds. Before them spread a lake, its silvery surface gleaming as dawn broke the horizon.

"It's lovely," Mara said, stopping to admire the view.

Fromoth Trun beamed at her. "Beyond those trees is the business center of Revitt Lake City. Our workday has just ended, mistress. You timed your arrival well."

She inclined her head in acknowledgment. "And your residential sector?"

He pointed to the left. "See those pavilions? They are the gatehouses to our underground complex. We must descend before the sun gets too high. Our labor force works in factories during the night, then they retire below during the heat of the day. I'm glad you agreed to being our guests. You'll get a personal view of our way of life."

Deke cast a narrowed glance in Mara's direction, still annoyed by her presumptuousness yet fully aware they couldn't afford to offend Fromoth Trun by refusing his hospitality. They had too much to accomplish to risk his ire. Besides searching for Jallyn, verifying the claims of a miracle drug, and assessing the situation with the Worts, they had to learn what happened to Larikk.

An armed security detail took up position at their flanks as they headed for the living quarters. Deke wondered at their watchful stance. Who or what were they watching for?

"Why are these troops here?" he asked Fromoth Trun in an innocent tone.

"Consider it an honor guard, Commander." The statesman marched ahead, precluding any further discussion.

As they entered one of the pavilions, a device scanned them for weapons. Mara had reminded Deke this was supposed to be a scientific expedition, so ostensibly he wasn't armed. In truth, he had a twist blade strapped to his ankle inside his boot. Created specifically for the SEARCH force, it was impervious to sensor scans and wouldn't be detected unless he was frisked. Earlier, he'd stuck a couple of gas grenades wrapped in silverscreen into Hedy's medical kit, knowing she'd bring her own supplies along. He wasn't leaving anything to chance.

A vertical lift shaft took them deep into the underground city. Deke glanced around, but his sense of direction got confused in the maze of tunnels. Fromoth Trun explained that the light was meager because his species could see in the dark. In consideration of his guests, he raised the illumination provided by sconced flamelights. As the levels declined, the air grew cooler.

Mara shivered, and Deke realized she must be chilled. Surprised she hadn't brought a wrap, he resisted the temptation to put his arm around her. It wouldn't do to show Fromoth Trun that he cared for her.

The Croag's sly mannerisms made him suspicious. Or maybe he was already suspicious and read signs that weren't really there. Could Mara have been correct in saying he'd be looking for things to be wrong? If so, why were armed troops posted at regular intervals? And where were the youngsters? All the Croags they encountered were adults.

"Where are your children?" he asked Fromoth Trun, increasing his pace to stride beside the leader.

Mara had been wondering the same thing. An eerie feeling crept over her as they advanced farther into the winding tunnels. She strained her ears to hear Fromoth Trun's reply.

"Our young are raised in a separate community," he replied, blinking as he swallowed. His skin shade darkened, and she remembered that an exterior color change occurred in Yanurans in response to temperature, light, moisture, or mood. Was he lying? Somehow, she sensed there was more to his words than he let on. Or was it just the damp coldness that had caused the deeper hue?

She didn't get the chance to inquire because they arrived at the reception center. Unlike the entrances to the private burrows they'd passed, this was a public area and the foyer was large enough to contain a wide reception desk and upholstered couches.

Fromoth Trun led them into a cavern with a cathedral-high

ceiling. Rows of long tables and chairs filled the space decorated with brightly colored tapestries and potted trees.

Mara wished for the warmth of a fireplace. She'd dressed for a subtropical climate, not realizing that while it might be appropriate for the surface, down here it was cooler. She crossed her arms in front of her chest, her bones chilled.

"Excuse me," Deke said, addressing Fromoth Trim, "have you a wrap for the lady? We didn't expect the temperature drop, and I suspect she is cold."

"Indeed, we would not want her to catch a distemper," Fromoth Trun agreed, casting a speculative look in their direction. Turning to one of his aides, he muttered a few words in an unfamiliar dialect. "Zenith Krim will get you a cover. Mara, please take this seat next to me. Commander, you may be seated opposite." Hedy and Wren were placed farther down the table.

Fromoth Trun nodded at Deke as he took his seat. "Your concern for your crew does you justice, Commander. A healthy staff works more efficiently."

Fortunately for Deke, the planetary leader had interpreted his thoughtfulness as a leadership skill. He wouldn't want the fellow to recognize there was more to his and Mara's relationship than a professional one.

Wait… What did I just say? He was taken aback by his own words, but he didn't have time to ponder them because Fromoth Trun continued the dialogue.

"We aim to keep our people happy, do we not?"

"It's good for production," Deke agreed. Discomfited by the Yanuran's interested stare, he glanced around the room. Wren stuck to Hedy's side like barnacles to a pier. The big Polluxite might deny his desire for the petite doctor, but his protective instincts were in full swing. Wren leaned over to listen when she chattered something into his ear. Hedy giggled nervously, and Wren's big hand crept across the table to cover hers.

Surrounded by so many frog faces, Deke wondered how he could turn the conversation toward their mission objectives. He glanced at Mara, admiring her placid countenance. She appeared entirely at ease in this strange setting among alien hosts.

It wasn't like back home at the institute, where the mixed alien races were scientists who shared a common purpose. Nor was this similar to his usual commando mission. He was leader of a science team but they had subversive goals. He couldn't help feeling out of his element and realized that Mara's presence brought him a measure of comfort.

"Lixier Bryn, may I acquaint you with our honored guests?" Fromoth Trun said. "This is my chief aide," he told Deke and Mara.

The Yanuran female who'd been fixing the seating arrangements strode toward them. Lixier Bryn wore a sash studded with gold firestones, indicating a high badge of office, over a rose-colored gown.

As Mara uttered the standard greeting, she wondered at the female's relationship with Fromoth Trun. One of the reasons why the Admissions Committee suspected dissention was because the Yanuran leader had been so anxious to return home. She'd thought maybe he didn't trust his highly placed aide. But perhaps Fromoth Trun had been eager to return to his burrow mate instead.

In most cases, male and female Yanurans did not cohabitate. They followed the mating call once an annum, amplexus—the mating embrace—lasting for several days. After the females bore the young several months later, they had no reason to stay together. Mates usually differed from season to season, although she supposed if a couple had a particular affinity for each other, they might join more than once and even decide to reside together.

"There's someone we'd like you to meet," Lixier Bryn said with an amiable smile. Her teeth shone white against her muddy green complexion. "Lixier Maal, please present yourself."

An elderly Yanuran shuffled toward them, his arms speckled with age marks. "Commander Sage and Mistress Hendricks, view the evidence of Vyclor, our miracle drug. I am one hundred and twenty annums old."

Mara's eyes widened. Truly, the Yanuran looked well for that advanced age.

"What is your normal life span?" Deke asked, his tone curious.

"Before Vyclor, it used to be forty, young man. Now we can last up to one hundred and fifty." He cackled, a dry, mirthless laughter. "I hope to make it a few more annums."

"Can Dr. Te'larr do a medical scan? Just for confirmation purposes, you understand." At the elder's nod of approval, Deke gestured to Hedy.

She lifted her mediscan unit out of her pack. Activating it as she walked over, she scanned Lixier Maal. Astonishment crossed her features. "His molecular pattern is consistent with advanced age for a Yanuran."

A muscle twitched in Deke's jaw. "I can't wait to see the seaweed beds and production process for the miracle drug. When will we get a tour?"

Fromoth Trun frowned at him. "We'll run you out to the mariculture farms this evening. I understand you're a diver, Commander?"

"Yes, that's correct. I'll need to get my gear off the *Celeste.*"

"That can be arranged."

The dinner proceeded as Fromoth Trun introduced the rest of his staff. Mara envied Deke's aplomb as he tackled the platters of squirming worms, snails, and flapping fish placed in front of them. Lixier Bryn urged him to try some of the delicacies presented in their honor and he eagerly took a heaping forkful from each dish, including one of sautéed eel segments in jellied sauce.

He grinned at her as she watched him down one of the wriggling worms. Her face must have turned a sickly color, but she called upon her diplomatic training and managed to eat a tiny bite herself. Thankfully berries and greens were available as side dishes.

Farther down the table, Hedy whispered into Wren's ear. From the look on his face, Wren was trying hard to stifle a grin. Mara caught her friend's eye and signaled for her to engage one of the Yanurans in conversation.

Meanwhile, she turned to Fromoth Trun. "Would it be possible for us to meet a Wort representative? I'm afraid my studies of their culture have been insufficient, and I'd like to learn more about them." She reached for her water glass and took a sip. The water tasted clear and fresh without any lingering aftertaste. She wondered if it was purified.

Yanurans rarely drank at all since their skin absorbed moisture from the air. The liquid was a courtesy to her and the other crew members.

Fromoth Trun blinked at her. "I'm afraid that is not possible. We have few lines of communication open to our tree-dwelling cousins."

"And why is that?" She smiled sweetly, hoping to put him off guard with a show of innocence.

The Yanuran leader leaned back. "The Worts prefer the company of their own kind."

"How do they feel about joining the Coalition? The alliance would bring visitors here. An exchange of cultural values would be inevitable."

"They have no objections to membership in the Coalition."

"I'd like to talk to them," Deke said loudly from across the table. He'd terminated his conversation with Lixier Bryn to listen to theirs. "How come I don't see any Worts here? Aren't they represented in your government?"

"We constitute the elected officials," Fromoth Trun declared, his skin mottling as he gestured to his ministers and aides. "If the Worts wish to participate in policy-making decisions, they can join the political process. I'm afraid they prefer isolation to involvement."

"I lost a friend in the Alterland where they reside. Larikk was a biologist from Eranus sent here to research a vaccine. Do you recall the case?"

"I have a vague recollection. If your friend vanished in the Alterland, we cannot help you." Fromoth Trun flicked his sticky pink tongue out to catch a fly. He swallowed the captured insect with a smug smile.

"Can we visit the region?" Deke persisted.

"That would not be wise. I cannot guarantee your safety if you leave the city."

"Is that why you have armed guards posted everywhere?"

Standing abruptly, the Yanuran leader tugged at his robe. "You must excuse me. Our sleep cycle begins shortly, and I have to make preparations for your tour. Lixier Bryn will show you to your quarters. The lighting will be lowered in the corridors, so I suggest you use the opportunity to rest. This evening we'll visit the seaweed farms. Your colleagues might prefer to view our textile factories instead, but we can decide later. *Rogi Kwantro.*" He beat his fist on his chest, bowed and exited.

****

Lixier Bryn showed the guests into a suite of rooms on a lower level. "This is our best accommodation," she said, her tawny eyes friendly. "I hope such distinguished personages as yourselves will find our lodgings comfortable. Is there anything else you require?" She stood in the doorway, her hands folded demurely in front of her.

Deke marched inside, scanning the space. "No, thanks. Will someone come for us later?"

"At eighteen hundred hauras, Coalition standard time." Lixier Bryn turned to Hedy. "I am not ready to retire yet, Doctor. Would you like to see our medical facility? It's in another section of the burrows."

"I'd be delighted." Hedy smiled at Wren invitingly. "Lieutenant, would you care to accompany me?"

"It would be my pleasure." Casting a knowing glance at Deke, he stalked ahead into the maze of tunnels.

"Mara and I will remain here," Deke said to the aide. *"Rogi Kwantro."*

He closed the heavy carved wooden door after Lixier Bryn and the others had left. When he turned, Mara was already surveying the arrangements.

"We have two sleeping chambers with private sanitaries and a shared sitting room," she said.

Deke peered into one bedroom and then the next. Each held two lounger beds, an armoire, and a computer desk. Spotlights in varying colors converged on the molded blastbrick walls, softening the decor.

"Hedy and I can take this room," Mara remarked, strolling inside one of the sleeping chambers.

He sauntered in after her, hooking his thumbs into his belt and leaning against the doorjamb. "I'll be happy to share with you. Hedy can stay with Wren. Knowing your friend, she'd probably prefer that arrangement."

Mara's face flooded with heat as she caught a glimpse of his expression. "Don't get any ideas just because we're alone. I'm not going to bed with you again until you change your attitude."

Deke's mouth curved in a lazy grin as he approached her. "Look, you must be tense after that banquet. I promise not to do anything you don't want me to do, but how about if I massage your neck? It'll help you to relax."

She couldn't resist when those sexy dimples creased his cheeks. His mahogany hair curled enticingly onto his forehead, and his eyes captured hers so temptingly that she wanted to melt. As he stepped in front of her, her pulse quickened from his nearness. In her mind's eye, she imagined the ribbons of rose-colored light arcing between them.

"All right." She'd make sure his hands didn't wander, although the notion of them doing just that made her skin tingle in anticipation.

He moved behind her and placed his large, strong hands on her long neck. Deftly, he applied the perfect amount of pressure to relax muscles she hadn't known were tense. As his hands glided to her shoulders, she closed her eyes to absorb the pleasure more fully. Her body swayed as he kneaded her knotted muscles into pliant relaxation.

"That feels good," she said, quivering with delight when his fingers danced lightly up and down her bare arms.

"This is a lovely dress," he rasped, his hot breath close to her ear. "I like the way it fits you."

His seductive voice thrummed along her nerves, setting them on fire. Dear heaven, she wanted him again, and she didn't care about their future. Now was all that mattered.

She made a small sound of pleasure as his hands slid toward the front of her sarong and grazed her thighs. He pressed his body against her from behind, and through the fabric of their clothes she could feel his arousal. She leaned back into the hard angles of his body, sighing with contentment.

His hand smoothed the fabric of her sarong up along her thighs and across her belly, coming to rest on her breasts.

Her rapid breathing must have told him she wanted more, because he began to caress her. Her nipples peaked and hardened and she cried out with need. At once his hand was inside her sarong, cupping her bare flesh. She thought she'd swoon from ecstasy.

"Deke, I want you."

"I know." He turned her around and slipped the sarong off her shoulders and to the floor. Her thin pair of lace panties was her only barrier that remained. "Gods, you're so beautiful. I can't get enough of you."

He quickly disposed of his own clothing. Then he sank to his knees in front of her, grasping her buttocks and pulling her closer. When he buried his face between her legs, she cried out.

In a quick, practiced movement, he had her panties off. "Relax," he crooned as his tongue flicked across her sensitive nub.

Suddenly she was in his viewpoint, feeling his sublime pleasure as he sniffed her feminine scent and stroked her secret places with his tongue. His engorged organ grew even more swollen as their reactions mingled.

"I can't wait," he said, gazing at her with glittering eyes. "You're driving me wild."

He stood and guided her to one of the loungers. She stretched out, and he joined her, moving atop to plunge inside her in a swift motion.

Her head lolled back as she gave in to the marvelous tension building within her. Her perception dimmed and centered on the increasing pressure until she exploded in a needed release. When it was over, she realized Deke had collapsed on top of her, his weight pressing against her.

She sensed his calm serenity as he lay his head on her breasts. Or was it her own contentment she felt? It was hard to tell where her emotions ended and his began.

"Deke, get off," she said, breaking the spell and the separation. "You're too heavy."

Reluctantly, he rolled to his side. "I suppose we should get dressed before Hedy and Wren return, unless you agree to be my roommate?" he offered, raising himself on his elbow to gaze at her with warm eyes.

"No, thanks. Getting dressed is a good idea." But she didn't move and sighed deeply.

"What is it?"

"I wish you would trust me. See how good this is for us? You don't need to be afraid of me."

His mouth compressed. "I'll admit you're not like any other woman I've known, but I can't give you what you want. You're asking for a commitment that I'm not prepared to make."

Her mood saddened. "You don't realize what you're throwing away."

"We've been through this before." Rising, he reached for his clothes.

"Give us a chance. That's all I'm asking."

"No." With jerky movements, he yanked on his jacket and pants.

"Then I'm sorry for you, truly I am. You can't even recognize your own feelings."

"What I'm feeling is called lust. If you think there's anything more involved, you're mistaken." And without another glance in her direction, he snatched up his boots and stalked out.

Chapter Eleven

"Ebo, what's the status of the ship?" Deke snapped into his datalink, holding the palm-size device in his hand.

The Sirisian's voice rang out loud and clear. "Repairs are proceeding as planned, Commander. We should be finished with the major overhaul by tonight."

"Keep your eye on the maintenance personnel."

"Why? Is anything amiss?"

Deke grimaced. "I can't put my finger on it, but I don't trust these people. I may have you take the *Celeste* into orbit once she's shipshape."

"I'll keep the channels open, sir. Ebo out."

Replacing his datalink in his jacket pocket, Deke paced the carpeted sitting room floor. Mara still hadn't emerged from her bedroom, and he wondered what she was doing in there. Just thinking of her stirred his blood and turned his loins to fire. He wanted her again, and it distressed him how intense that need was becoming.

He hated to admit he was getting used to sharing her reactions during their lovemaking. He couldn't imagine what it would be like without that added enhancement. Even now, he felt hollow without her essence inside him, and that was more disturbing than his physical need for her. Mara drove him to distraction, and he didn't know how to deal with the situation.

It would be so much simpler if she accepted his limits and stopped badgering him about their relationship. He'd always avoided serious-minded women in the past, but then on Eranus, no one had really been interested in him that way. They'd been using him to get to his parents.

He'd become accustomed to playing the field, figuring he might as well enjoy himself. After he joined the Defense League, the females he met were only concerned with having a good time. He supposed he'd never thought about his future in terms of settling down and having a family. Becoming chancellor at the institute was his immediate goal, but someday he might seek a mate, and he hoped she'd be as lovely and special as Mara.

Special? Wait a minute. Aren't you forgetting what she can do? He shook himself, attempting to break her hold on his thoughts, but she remained in his mind, tormenting him.

He tried to look at it from her viewpoint. Didn't Mara hope the man of her dreams would appreciate her and embrace that part of herself that was unique? Her inner desires weren't much different than his. They both wanted to be accepted for who they were. A wave of compassion struck him as he viewed her with new understanding. Should he deny her the same consideration he sought for himself? In dismissing her regard, was he throwing away the chance of a lifetime?

No, he couldn't tolerate having someone intrude on his consciousness. Her psychic ability might make her an exceptional woman but he couldn't live with that kind of uncertainty. She might pop into his head at any time, aside from their physical encounters. The mere possibility of it put him on edge and distracted him from his goals.

A door chime announced the return of Hedy and Wren, and he cast aside his musings. The duo barged in with exclamations of what they'd seen. Mara must have heard them, because she entered the sitting room and joined the conversation. He noted she'd changed out of her sarong into a modest crimson top and black pants.

"What now? It's only ten o'clock in the morning," Hedy said, glancing with dismay at the chronometer strapped to her wrist.

Wren stomped around the sitting area. Suddenly his wings

sprouted. "Sorry," he said with an embarrassed grin. "I needed to stretch."

Hedy drew in a sharp breath, while Mara stared at the Polluxite with undisguised admiration.

Deke, following the direction of Mara's gaze, felt a surge of jealousy. He disliked the feeling and tried to dismiss it by telling himself Mara didn't belong to him. Annoyed nonetheless, he gave her a glowering look that she totally ignored.

Hedy rushed forward to stroke Wren's primary feathers and caress the length of his fluffy vanes. A shudder racked him, and his rugged features suffused with heat.

"Stop that," he told her. Yet he made no move to shake her off.

"You're so magnificent. I can't help wanting to touch you."

"Doctor! Will you please restrain yourself?"

Hedy shrugged. "Why don't you admit it, Wren? You like me, too."

He turned away and collapsed his wings into his back. "Excuse me, I wish to retire. Commander, which sleeping chamber is ours?"

Deke winked at Mara. "You can share with Hedy. Mara and I would like to stay together."

Mara and Wren both cried out in protest. Wearing a broad grin, Deke showed Wren which room was theirs.

"Now just a minute, you can't run away from me," Hedy called as Wren headed in that direction. She dashed after him and shut the door.

"Poor man," Deke said, shaking his head.

"Hedy really likes him." Mara tucked a strand of hair behind her ear. "I think Wren shares her feelings but he's too stubborn to admit it... much like someone else I know."

Deke ignored her meaningful glance. "He has his reasons."

"They're foolish. Hedy could make him happy. He's hung up over cultural taboos that don't apply to her."

"You're the alien culture specialist. I'm surprised to hear you talk that way. Wren is steadfast in his beliefs."

"Yes, his integrity is admirable," she said in a sarcastic tone. Wearily, she glanced around the small space. "Is there anything to eat in here?"

"You didn't have enough at the feast in our honor?" he asked, his mouth curving upward.

She grimaced. "I don't care for live seafood the way you do."

He pointed to an alcove on one side of the sitting room. "I believe there's a cooler drawer in that direction. Go see what's inside. Maybe there's fruit or other snacks."

Just then a feminine giggle came from beyond the closed chamber door.

"Hedy!" bellowed Wren before he yanked open the door and stalked into the communal space, a wild-eyed look in his eyes. "You have to get that female out of here."

Hedy, trailing after him, planted her hands on her hips and glared at the hapless man.

Deke took pity on him. "Everyone grab a seat. We'll determine our objectives for this evening and then we should try to get some rest. It won't be easy to adapt to the Yanurans' nocturnal habits."

They agreed to split up later to cover more ground. Deke would go with Fromoth Trun to view the seaweed farms. Mara would remain aboard the dive boat as his backup, while Hedy and Wren viewed the textile factories as suggested. Afterwards, they'd meet back in their suite to compare notes.

****

Hauras later, Mara stood outside watching the sun make a blazing crimson descent on the horizon. As fingers of shadows crept over the land, the warm, humid air began to cool. A sweet, fruity fragrance kissed the gentle breeze that wafted across Mara's skin and caressed her face. Goose bumps rose on her arms as her excitement grew.

Ever since her move to Bimordus Two and her job in the

diplomatic corps, she'd aimed toward an ambassadorship, hoping to be the first to step upon alien soil and study a new culture in its own habitat. This was the next best thing, being a visitor on a planet that hosted few offworlders. Feeling refreshed after a nap and a light meal courteously delivered to their room, she couldn't wait to explore.

"Where are we heading?" She surveyed the lake and the rounded red domes of Revitt Lake City beyond. The cityscape gleamed in the waning sunlight.

"We'll begin at the transport center." Fromoth Trun took the lead along a winding brick path, his heavy robe of office swaying at his feet. A squad of armed soldiers took up positions on their flanks.

Soon they came to a section of the lake with a dock. Several boat-like contraptions floated on the water's surface, bobbing up and down on the current.

"Lieutenant Wren," Fromoth Trun said, turning to the Polluxite who stood protectively near Hedy, "if you and the doctor will be so kind as to accompany Lixier Quyp, he'll be delighted to show you our textile factories and highlights of the city center. Commander Sage, I'll escort you and Mara to the *Celeste.* After you obtain your diving equipment, we'll head for Port Octaine, where a launch will take us out to sea."

"Thank you," Deke said politely, casting Wren a meaningful glance.

Wren gave a brief nod of acknowledgment. "We're using water transport to reach the city?" he inquired, raising his layered eyebrows.

Fromoth Trun smiled broadly. "I believe you'll find this means of transportation to be an extraordinary experience."

Lixier Quyp showed Wren and Hedy how to board. The vehicle had a flat base, and Wren looked askance at the floor. The greenish bottom quivered when he stepped on it. A harness arrangement provided seats for four facing forward and a driver up front. After he and Hedy had strapped in behind their guide, the driver lifted the reins. Blowing out the air sac at his throat, the Yanuran gave a long, loud croak and the vessel rose into the air.

Wren gave a startled grunt. This wasn't a transport vehicle at all, he realized. The thing was a living beast, more like a winged reptile.

"Great suns!" he cried, gripping a security bar that had lowered at their laps. He'd expected them to propel across the water, not soar into the sky. Hedy, seated beside him, clutched his arm as Deke and Mara grew smaller and smaller below.

"What kind of creature is this?" Wren said, his breath coming in short, quick gasps.

The driver gave a short series of croaks and the vehicle veered toward the city domes.

Lixier Quyp glanced back at them, his eyes crinkling with amusement. "They're called marouches. We used to eat the beasts until Mavis Kwin designed a way to put them to use. They provide transportation, and in return we protect them from predators. Of course, for long-range transport, we maintain a fleet of winged pods. They're less cumbersome and can travel at a swifter pace."

"This is swift enough for me," Wren muttered.

"What's the matter?" Hedy asked as the marouche turned at a ninety-degree angle, tossing them sideways. The wind tumbled her hair about her face and brought a flush to her cheeks.

Wren clamped his lips together and didn't speak. Squeezing his eyes shut, he gripped the security rod with white knuckles and prayed for a speedy trip.

"Wren, talk to me," Hedy urged. "What's wrong?"

He pried an eye open. "Are we there yet?"

"Almost. What is it? Are you ill?"

He shook his head, shutting his eyes again until they'd descended and come to a complete stop. His entire body shaking, he exited the craft after Hedy.

"I can't do this again. We'll have to find another way to get back," he told her. "I, um, had a dizzy spell, but I'm all right now. It must have been a residual effect from the concussion."

Her face lit with concern. "Good heavens. I'd better run a diagnostic." She swung her medpack across her chest.

His hand stopped her. "No, really, I'm okay."

"Stubborn fool." Smiling gamely, Hedy linked her arm through his so he couldn't let go. "Let's move on. I'm eager to explore. Aren't you?" She fluttered her silken eyelashes at him.

From the way she rubbed her leg against his thigh, Wren could tell the city wasn't all she wanted to explore.

"Please, control yourself in public," he said.

"Oooh! Does that mean I can do anything I want when we're alone?"

His face suffused with heat, but luckily Lixier Quyp signaled his readiness to commence their tour before Wren got himself into trouble with a retort. One of these days he'd give that woman what she deserved, and then—

What was he saying? Wren caught himself and muttered an oath. Dr. Te'larr was off-limits, same as any other female, because of his disability. Had he forgotten that?

But it wasn't any other female that tormented him. Merely the sound of Hedy's name in his mind swept him away to an enchanted place where he was a whole man who could make love to her. Why did he feel such an affinity for this human female? Was it because she'd accepted him, regardless of his inadequacy? She deserved better and should marry a mate who was her equal.

He trailed behind Lixier Quyp, his booted heels crunching on the gravel walkway. Hedy kept pace beside him, silent as though debating how to get him to respond. Was she discouraged by his rejection? He didn't want to hurt her.

Glancing sideways, he surveyed the perfection of her profile, the glossy tint of her hair, and the soft pout of her lips. He should distance himself from her, and yet he couldn't bear to cast her away.

Against his better judgment, he wrapped his arm around her slender shoulders and pressed her close until her body heat penetrated his skin to warm his heart. He wanted to flap his wings in joy but restrained himself, cooling his ardor until his emotions could come under control.

As they neared the city, he noted uniformed security personnel patrolling the streets. He'd better pay attention to their surroundings, he thought as he scanned the path ahead for potential peril.

****

Deke wondered if Wren had secreted any weapons on his person as he foraged aboard the *Celeste* for supplies. While Fromoth Trun waited outside in the spaceport, Deke collected his diving equipment and a bag of personal belongings before stopping at Wren's cabin to grab a few requested items.

He hesitated upon viewing a crossbow hung on a hook on the wall. Too bad he couldn't take that item with him, but they still had to pass a security sweep to return to the burrows.

He had been puzzled by the number of armed guards surrounding him and Mara on their way here. An honor guard was one thing, but this evening the grounds bristled with military police. Were they in some kind of danger of which they were unaware? Why else would such heavy security measures be enforced?

Fromoth Trun had been particularly tight-lipped, preferring to parry Deke's questions with meaningless compliments. Irritated, Deke had been glad for the respite aboard the *Celeste.*

Aware that Mara was busy in her own cabin, he hastened to the bridge to consult with Ebo.

"The major repairs are completed," the Sirisian told him, taking a break from monitoring the systems controls.

"Have you been able to tap into surface communications?"

Ebo bobbed his bald head under his ruby turban. "I'm picking up some interesting chatter but nothing significant. Any leads on Jallyn?"

"We haven't seen any children, which is definitely strange, but supposedly they have their own living quarters. Mara and I are going to view the underwater seaweed farms from here. Wren and Hedy have already left for a tour of the city. We'll compare notes later. Fromoth Trun is courteous but I don't trust him. We're escorted everywhere by armed guards. It's damned odd."

"Take caution, sir."

"I will. Maintain your vigilance and keep our commlink open."

He rounded up Mara after hiding a few last-minute items among his stash of diving supplies.

"Are you ready?" he said, pausing inside the open doorway to her cabin.

"I guess so." She straightened up from packing her bag and frowned at him, her eyes expressing concern. "I don't have a good feeling about all this."

"What do you mean?"

"I did another separation using Jallyn's blanket. Something dark is out there. It frightens me."

She'd confirmed his own sense of unease. "Can you elaborate?" he asked, frowning.

Mournfully, she shook her head. "No, I can't. The feeling gets stronger each time I'm with Jallyn."

"We have to find her soon. Let's not waste any more time." He gestured for Mara to depart.

She stepped closer and fixed her gaze on him. "There's something I have to say before we leave. We might not have another chance, and I need to tell you. I-I'm sorry if I've been too pushy. I shouldn't expect you to feel the same way as I do."

He put a finger to her lips, silencing her. "This is not the time or place to talk about our personal problems. We have an important job to do today. Be alert and watchful out there."

After saying a final farewell to Ebo, they left to rejoin the Yanurans. A short while later, their marouche landed at a marina by the ocean. Out on the water, a ribbon of light made the border between sea and sky barely discernible. The distinction rapidly faded along with the sunlight. A stiff, briny breeze blew across the water, and Deke sniffed it gratefully. He'd missed the salt-laden scent of the sea.

Port Octaine bustled with activity. The evening's work shift had just begun. Yanurans scurried about, intent on their tasks. Bright spotlights illuminated the area, casting long shadows and lighting up the sky in garish hues.

"What's in those giant storage tanks?" he asked, curious about the port's usage.

"Fuel," said Fromoth Trun, his eyes darting about nervously. His padded fingertips plucked at the folds of his robe. "Let's go, Commander. The wind is favorable." He signaled to the frog-faced crew to assist Deke.

He loaded his equipment onto the launch assigned them. He would have liked to explore the port but was eager to do his dive. It had been too long since he'd been underwater and he craved the freedom of the sea. Grabbing Mara's hand, he strode up the ramp onto the launch after the crew finished hauling the rest of their gear on board.

Fromoth Trun gave the order to cast off and they sped away, zipping across the waves at high speed. Deke reviewed the dive plan with the hired guide, a pudgy-faced fellow named Porvir Cash.

Mara stood on the deck and gripped the railing. She squinted at the wind and breathed in the salty air. Darkness encroached upon the night like an inky cloud.

"Will you be all right when I go below?" he said, hoping she'd be safe with the crew.

She turned toward him, her hair whipping about her face. "I'll be fine. I'm worried about you. You'll be down there alone. Who knows what may happen?"

"I won't be alone. Cash will be with me, and you'll be up here, making sure the boat is waiting. Anyway, I'm used to night dives."

Unable to keep his distance, he moved closer. "I appreciate your concern." He placed his hands on her hips. The rolling motion of the boat rocked him against her.

"Get away," she said, a warning gleam in her eye.

He saw the rapid pulse throbbing in her throat and grinned. "I know you want me. Say it, Mara."

"Conceited oaf. You're the one who can't keep his hands off me." Glancing over his shoulder, Mara stiffened. "Fromoth Trun is watching us."

Deke stepped away. Resetting his mind toward the business at hand, he strode toward the mini-levitator that held his equipment. He was letting Mara distract him again when his focus should be on the job. His movements brusque, he began preparing for the dive.

Mara observed him a moment before turning back to the railing. The deck lifted and dipped as they sped across the swells. Her stomach lurched as a high crest jarred the hull. This might be Deke's element, but it wasn't hers.

Her world had large, forested continents. She'd rarely seen the ocean when she was young. What was it like to grow up on a water planet where the populace lived in floating cities? Deke had mentioned his work at the research institute on Eranus. He'd paid a stiff price to sacrifice two annums of his life by enlisting in the SEARCH force. Would this stint help him achieve the exalted position of chancellor?

She should admire his dedication, and yet it bothered her that his single-minded devotion didn't include her. She was losing her heart to this man, and he wouldn't admit any feelings of reciprocation. How long would she have to wait? Could Master Keenan have been wrong about them?

No, you've seen the rose-colored light. Deke simply couldn't accept what she had to offer. She'd given him her body. What else would it take to make him realize they were linked on a higher spiritual plane?

Chapter Twelve

Deke braced his legs on the heaving deck of the launch and knelt to retrieve the neoprene wet suit he'd brought from the *Celeste*. Stripped down to his swim trunks, he felt the chill of the night air on his skin. A thrill of excitement raced through him as he went through the familiar motions of suiting up for a dive. He couldn't wait to explore the underwater environment on Yanura. Being away from home distressed his system, and he yearned for the watery depths that were part of his soul. Besides, the scientist inside hoped for new discoveries below the surface.

The snug-fitting wet suit and hood warmed his blood as he reached for his buoyancy compensator jacket, regulator, and cylinder system. The vest fastened with a series of front clips. After adjusting his equipment, he secured a waterproof dive computer on his wrist. It served multiple functions, including decompression guide, compass, and chronometer.

When he wore it on land, the device also served as a backup communicator for his datalink. The instrument had one additional purpose that had been designed on Eranus, but Deke hoped he wouldn't have to use it that way.

Cash signaled to him, and he strapped on his full face mask. The mask attached to the regulator that connected to his tanks. It left him air space to speak into a built-in comm device while also breathing freely from the air mixture in the tanks. A knife, underwater lights, and a dive slate for taking notes completed his ensemble. The last items to go on were his heavyweight belt and fins.

"Commander? Can you hear me?" Cash's raspy voice sounded in his ear. The amphibian had strapped on a mask that would enable them to communicate. Being able to extract oxygen from his blood-rich gills, he didn't need diving gear. His moist skin, webbed feet, and natural abilities would aid him.

"Won't the cold water bother you?" Deke asked, eyeing Cash's meager swim trunks. Even though they were amphibians, the Yanurans were cold-blooded creatures, meaning they were sensitive to exterior temperature changes.

Cash's tawny eyes gleamed with amusement. "Our species has adapted to the cold saltwater environment. Are you ready?"

Deke gave a thumbs-up sign before remembering he was among aliens. He hoped they didn't consider the gesture to be an insult.

Cash nodded brusquely and led him to an interior cabin where a moon pool was designed in the bottom, allowing for ease of entry into the sea. The Yanuran went first to demonstrate the technique. Following after him, Deke rolled through the rounded hole into the water and sank into the welcome liquidity. A wave of exhilaration charged through him as he turned and kicked in Cash's direction. He easily matched his guide's progress as they swam downward.

Seaweed fronds reached toward the surface like tree-high spikes. This variety was called merl, and according to what Fromoth Trun had told him, it didn't grow anywhere else. Similar to kelp beds on other worlds, the undulating masses of merl thrived in shallow waters of the temperate zone. The plants required strong light and a rocky bottom for anchorage. Colorful fish, crustaceans, and sea urchins made their homes in the crevices. As Deke descended the murky depths, he was careful not to get entangled in the hundred-foot-high greenish fronds.

"They can grow up to a foot a day," said Cash, pointing out the gas-filled bladders that kept the fronds afloat. "This water is cool and rich in nutrients, factors necessary to the growth of merl. Here you see one of our largest submarine forests. Yanura has many others, and we've discovered a wide variety of uses for the plants."

He pointed to a tall, supple stalk. "The stipes carry sugar alcohols—the product of photosynthesis—from the upper blades, which are exposed to sunlight, to the dimmer sections below. The merl are secured to the rocks at the bottom by branched holdfasts."

Deke gave a wide berth to a sea otter that glided past. He slowed his progress to savor the watery environment. This was where he belonged. He loved exploring the mysterious depths, no matter the world.

At the bottom, he spied colorful strawberry anemones, sponges, and hardy fungus corals. The holdfasts that attached the merl to the underlying rocks teemed with clams, snails, brittle stars, and crabs.

He drifted upward toward the middle range of the forest, observing a bright orange garibaldis patrolling its territory. Knowing the eight-inch-long fish would defend its turf, he veered away, marveling at the expanse of the forest. In the tallest canopy, the fronds hosted epiphytic algae and animals such as hydroids, cnidarians, and bryozoans. The marine life was as diverse as the species found in a rain forest on land and just as fascinating.

He propelled himself toward Cash. "You say these things can grow a foot a day?" he said.

The Yanuran grunted his affirmation, his bulging eyes luminous in the light from Deke's lamp. "They grow upward to a hundred feet each season."

"How are they harvested?"

"Trained workers cut the most mature stalks, leaving enough for next season, although we've successfully replanted forests in other parts of the world. As a ranger, my job is to protect the underwater environment."

Deke gazed at him thoughtfully. On Eranus, his mother's family owned Drylon, a global cosmetic company. They had no such scruples. A by-product of kelp was an important ingredient in their secret formulas. To harvest the plants, they snipped strands and streamers several hundred feet long by automated machinery that transported the cuttings to barges. Since the reproductive parts of the plants were not preserved, entire beds were destroyed in this manner. Drylon didn't care if the marine life that depended on this submarine forest was ravaged as well. They could always replant the crop.

As director general, Deke's father had granted the company special privileges, a concession made in return for his wife's wealth. Deke disdained his father's compromise. One of the reasons why he wouldn't accept funding from his mother's family was because of their disregard for ecological factors. He'd been involved in lobbying for stricter environmental controls before leaving Eranus and intended to resume his efforts when he returned.

Eranus's original inhabitants had poisoned their world with toxins and had to seek life elsewhere. Strict antipollution measures had been put into effect by subsequent colonists. But lately, Drylon's powerful influence had undermined the laws. If Deke became chancellor, he'd promote conservation to ensure that marine life was better protected. It made achieving the position all the more important to him.

Suffused with passion for his projects, he didn't realize immediately that Mara was sharing his head space. He sensed her presence and frowned with annoyance. *Not now!* Yet warm pride struck him as he felt her support for his goals.

Bewildered by the emotions she engendered in him, he lost sight of Porvir Cash. Glancing around, he realized with panic that he'd strayed from their last position and had no idea where he was. It was Mara's fault for distracting him again, dammit. Where in Zor was his guide?

"Commander," said a familiar voice in his ear.

Deke was so relieved to hear from Cash that he barely noticed Mara's hurt departure from his mind. As he waited for the Yanuran to join him, he spied something that reflected brightly in his halogen light. Curious, Deke aimed his lamp downward to get a closer look. A strange outcropping of white rocks met his gaze. Kicking vigorously, he followed a ridge several meters long and noticed more of the white rocks, jagged and gleaming in the unnatural light.

"What are these? They're strewn all over this area." he asked his guide.

Cash appeared in front of him, his large eyes glittering. "It's a mineral conglomerate. The nutrients in this water are rich and diverse. They're replenished seasonally by up-swellings of colder water laden with organic matter and by mineral runoff from the land. So much food is available that marine species grow here that thrive nowhere else. Same goes for those rocks. Careful, an eel is just behind you."

Deke stilled his movements while the creature swam past. A young harbor seal weaved its way through the cool merl stipes, its whiskers white in his underwater light.

"I see another rocky ridge over there. How far out does that one go?" Deke swam over, intrigued by the surreal beauty of the white rocks nestled at the base of the green merl stalks.

The Yanuran motioned that it was time to begin their ascent. "The forest stretches for several kilometers. We couldn't possibly tour the entire area."

Deke peered closer, examining a set of flaws in the rock face. It almost appeared as though someone had chipped away at it with a tool.

Cash tapped his arm. "Come, we're running short on time."

"What happens to the merl after it's harvested?" Deke asked as they swam back toward the undulating masses of merl.

"A company called Seabase Pharmaceuticals produces medicinal products from the merl along with other marine resources. Their ongoing research aims to discover new therapeutics. Vyclor got its start many annums ago when early tribes brewed a tea from the dried fronds and noticed it slowed signs of aging."

Deke swung around to face him. "What about Turtle Ravage? My friend was researching a vaccine here for this disease when he disappeared. Did your laboratories ever complete those studies?"

Cash shrugged. "You'll be going to Seabase Pharm's plant

from here. You can ask your questions to them in person. Follow me."

Deke had no option but to comply, ascending slowly and stopping at the intervals prescribed by his dive computer. A competent guide, Cash brought them up directly under the moon pool.

****

Mara could tell from Deke's flushed face that the underwater sights had impressed him. She stood by as he stripped off his heavy equipment. When he faced her dripping wet in his swim trunks, she handed him a towel supplied by one of the boat's crew.

As the engines coughed into life and the launch picked up speed, she gripped the back of a chair bolted to the deck. His chest glistened with water that ran in rivulets down his taut abdomen and into the banded waistline of his trunks. Aware that Cash and the others were involved in a consultation elsewhere, she wished they could prolong their moment of privacy. She wanted to feast her eyes on him as long as possible.

"How about drying my back?" he said airily, tossing her the towel and turning around.

She swallowed convulsively. Gods, his shoulders were so broad! She dried him off quickly, dismayed at how easily her heartbeat raced and her fingers trembled from the contact.

"What did you see down there?" she asked, trying to get her mind off his rippling muscles and bronzed skin. It took her full willpower not run her fingers through his damp hair, down his supple neck, and along his wide shoulders.

"We'll talk after I get dressed," he said curtly.

Bending over, Deke reached for his knit shirt and pants, having opted to wear more leisurely clothes than his uniform for the outing. His position gave her a sublime view of his tight derriere perfectly outlined by the clinging wet swim trunks.

Her eyes widened when he began to strip them off. Choking,

she whirled around so her back was to him. Her ears picked up every sound he made as he pulled on his clothes.

"You did it again," he said quietly.

Pivoting, she stared at him. He hadn't sounded pleased. Fully dressed, he glared at her, a hostile gleam in his eyes.

"What do you mean?" Fearful of his response, she moistened her lips.

"You invaded my mind. I lost my sense of direction."

"I-I'm sorry. All of a sudden, I was in your viewpoint. You were excited about something. I think strong emotion might be the trigger for these separations."

"So what does that mean? I shouldn't feel anything? Because of your intrusion, I got isolated from my guide. I could have drifted miles away from the boat."

"But you didn't. What did you see down there?"

He took her cue to change the subject and related his findings. "I'd like to know more about those rocks. One section looked as though a chunk had been removed. Maybe we'll learn more at the pharmaceutical plant." He strode onto the deck, precluding any further private discussion.

She gazed after him, dismayed by his disapproval. She'd hoped to share his excitement, and instead he'd made her feel like an item tossed in a disposer.

Slumping her shoulders, she despaired of ever gaining his affection.

****

When they reached land, Lixier Bryn met them with a skim craft, whisking them to their next destination. Seabase Pharmaceuticals owned a vast complex of buildings designed as interlocking diamond-shaped structures. Illuminated against the darkness of the night sky, the triangular walls shone with a brilliant golden glow.

"Tell me about the water-based industries on your planet, Commander," said Fromoth Trun as they approached the main entrance.

"Our main commerce is in undersea mining and mariculture," he responded. "We also have our prime research facility, the Institute for Marine Studies."

"Ah, yes. I heard you were competing for the chancellorship. You're in a unique position with your father, Jon Sage, being director general of Eranus. And your mother's family owns a majority share of Drylon. I understand they use an extract from kelp by-products in their secret formula."

Deke should have figured the Yanuran leader would check up on him. "Yes, this is true."

The Yanuran leader cast him a sly glance. "It might be expedient for us to arrange an exchange of scientific data."

"Sorry, but I'm not authorized by the Eranus government to negotiate on their behalf. I'm here as a representative of the Coalition."

He kept his tone mild as he pondered the meaning behind his host's words. Did Fromoth Trun hope to learn the ingredients for Drylon's popular line of cosmetics? The Yanurans weren't in that type of product, as far as he knew. Why else would Fromoth Trun have mentioned the topic?

"It's something to consider when you become chancellor," Fromoth Trun suggested.

"Thanks; I'll keep that in mind," Deke said in a dry tone.

Mara poked him. "I didn't realize your family was part of the Drylon dynasty."

"It's my mother's business. I don't care to talk about it."

In truth, she'd been so intent on researching Deke's credentials that she hadn't paid much attention to his personal background when she had looked up the database on his planet. Now her curiosity was piqued. Every woman she knew used at least one of Drylon's skin-care products.

They stopped at a set of massive steel doors where a bevy of officials greeted them. Cozen Jaak, president of Seabase Pharmaceuticals, gave a brief welcoming speech. He led the tour, explaining how their researchers gathered plants and animals that showed disease-fighting potential. Their scientists tested these specimens for therapeutic effects, potency, side effects, and other relevant data.

"We've had particular success lately with sea whips and their anti-inflammatory properties," Cozen Jaak said.

"We have a similar program on Eranus." Deke paced down a corridor beside the official. Fromoth Trun and Mara followed behind with a small entourage. "Our research ships are equipped with advanced laboratory facilities. If our biochemists find a plant with medicinal promise, a quantity will be harvested and sent to the institute. There the plants are purified and analyzed, followed by more testing including in vivo trials if indicated. In many cases, we've identified the chemical structures so the drugs can be produced synthetically."

"You should consider my offer," Fromoth Trun said. "Our worlds could benefit from a mutual exchange of scientific information."

"Medical research is only one of our interests at the institute. We have departments in geology, microbiology and other disciplines. Our researchers pursue a wide variety of studies."

The Yanuran leader pursed his lips as he gazed at Deke thoughtfully. "Who provides your funding?"

"We're supported by a foundation, but most of us obtain our own research grants."

"What is your particular area of study, if I may ask?"

"I've been investigating deep-sea vents. They're a rich source of life, and the possibilities are endless for new discoveries."

The Yanuran narrowed his eyes. "I suppose your family supports you in your efforts."

Deke gave a noncommittal grunt in reply. He was revealing too much about himself. His vulnerabilities would become evident, unless Fromoth Trun already possessed this information and was simply sounding him out. He liked that notion even less.

"Where is Vyclor manufactured?" he asked, switching subjects.

"Right here," Cozen Jaak answered, taking him by the elbow and propelling him ahead of the others. "Vyclor had its origins in herbal medicine," the president explained, guiding Deke and the rest of their party past a series of immaculate laboratory facilities. White-robed workers, visible through glass windows, were intent over tables laden with scientific instruments.

"Vyclor is given to everyone routinely beginning at age twenty," Cozen Jaak said after they'd toured several other sections and retired to a conference room. They took seats around a rectangular table. Deke and Mara accepted an offer of cool fruit drinks and sweet grain wafers. They could use the sugar boost to help fuel them through this long nocturnal cycle.

Dr. Parannus, head of the science section, elaborated. "Once several dosages have been ingested, the drug cannot be discontinued without painful withdrawal symptoms, including the possibility of death. This is due to the altered metabolic state of the recipient. In other words, once started, the drug must be continued for life."

Dr. Parannus was a large Yanuran with a broad, flat-topped skull and an enormous belly. Obviously he ate more than one meal a day, Mara thought to herself as she observed him. The Yanuran helped himself to some of the wafers intended for the guests and crunched them noisily in his mouth.

"You mean Vyclor is addictive?" Mara asked, her interest soaring at this revelation.

"Not in the usual sense of the word. It's more like a thyroid medication that some humans must take in order to maintain metabolic stability."

"But your people don't need Vyclor for health reasons," she pointed out.

"Most of us consider it worth the risks in order to extend our lives. It's changed our entire society."

"What about side effects?" Mara hadn't seen the data on Vyclor, but she assumed Deke had this information.

The scientist bowed his head. "Sterility is an unfortunate

result. Those of us who want children breed during the first few mating seasons before the critical dosage is reached."

Sitting across the table, Deke nodded. "A lot of people I know would feel the same way. They'd jump at the chance to extend their lives regardless of the risks involved."

He was right, Mara thought. The Yanurans would make a killing in profits if Vyclor were offered on the galactic marketplace. Those white crystal rocks Deke had noticed during his dive provided the basis for a compound used in Vyclor production. This compound was combined with an organic matrix obtained from merl to produce the drug.

Even if the Yanurans licensed production to offworld companies, they'd still possess the only sources of raw materials. They stood to gain a fortune if the Coalition granted them approval status.

"What about toxicity trials?" she asked. "Did you run them on other species?"

Dr. Parannus nodded. "We had no trouble obtaining volunteers. As Commander Sage saw from his preliminary review of our data, Vyclor appears to be safe for humans."

"Porvir Cash told me the merl is harvested by hand," Deke said, drumming his fingers on the table. "Where do you house the workers, and how is the merl transported to the surface? Maybe we could apply some of your methods on my home world."

Dr. Parannus's complexion darkened. "It's all handled offshore. Here, I've prepared this data card for you to take with you. You may review these additional studies on Vyclor in the comfort of your room. I assume you brought your own datalink?"

"Of course," Deke said, wondering why Mara was waggling her eyebrows at him. Was she alerting him to something the fellow had said?

As he accepted the data card outstretched in Dr. Parannus's hand, a server knocked against him, spilling fruit juice down the front of his shirt and pants. The data card slipped from his wet fingers onto the floor.

"I'm so sorry, sir." Crouching, the server swooped up the fallen object from the ground and handed it to Deke.

"You fool," Dr. Parannus said, "look at what you've done."

A spreading stain wet Deke's clothing. "It's all right. I brought some extra outfits in my bag."

The server wrung his hands. "May I bring you some fresh lava cakes? I am not usually so clumsy, and I wish to make amends."

"Dr. Delain Crug, is that you?" Cozen Jaak inquired, squinting at the fellow. "What are you doing away from the chemistry lab?"

"I requested the post. It is not often we have the honor of greeting such illustrious visitors."

"Get back to your department," Cozen Jaak ordered, his skin mottling. He turned to Dr. Parannus after the server left. "Did you know about this?"

The scientist lifted his chin. "Certainly not. I don't deal with people from his division."

"Check him out. There's no reason why he should have been allowed in here. We'd better schedule a review of security procedures."

Fromoth Trun turned to Deke and gave him a crocodile smile. "Shall we go, Commander? I have a few more places to show you before we retire for the morning."

"Yes, I'm ready to move on. Thanks so much for the tour," he told the others. "It's been educational."

Eager to review the Vyclor data, Deke was dismayed they weren't returning to the burrows right away. They took the skim craft and had to put up with another two hauras of visiting some bland industrial sights and public edifices.

Mara kept yawning, reminding him they'd slept little since their arrival. Finally, after a particularly long and boring dinner in their honor given by the City Science Council, they returned to the underground complex with dawn nearly breaking.

"Hedy and Wren haven't returned," Mara remarked upon their arrival at their assigned suite. "I hope they're okay. So tell me, after today's informative tour, are you prepared to recommend Yanura for Coalition membership?"

Deke, who'd been unbuttoning his shirt to get comfortable, stopped and gaped at her. "Why would I?"

"Because everything we've seen today confirms Fromoth Trun's claims about Vyclor."

"Does it? We need to speak to some ordinary citizens to get their opinions, and we've yet to meet with any of the Wort faction. We've seen what Fromoth Trun wanted us to see."

"I think he's been very accommodating. He's shown you the seaweed farms and the production facilities for the drug. What more is there?"

"Did you send me a signal during our session earlier?" Deke countered.

"Dr. Parannus's skin darkened during your discussion. I sensed he was being deceptive."

Deke finished removing his shirt and tossed it onto a chair. "That proves my point, which is that Fromoth Trun and his cohorts are concealing something from us."

"Nonetheless, they deserve a fair evaluation based on objective evidence."

Deke shook his head. Mara's convictions were strong, but her view was tainted by her own personal bias which she refused to acknowledge.

"When are you going to stop being so trusting?" he said, rubbing his neck. He longed for a shower and eight hauras of sleep. "These people have secrets. We know this from Larikk's disappearance."

"You still don't know for certain what happened to him." She pursed her lips. "Jallyn can't be on Yanura. The Croags don't have any reason to hold her. As for the Worts, Fromoth Trun said they have no objections to Coalition membership."

"We need to verify that for ourselves." Deke sank onto the wide sitter to yank off his boots. "I'm not satisfied with what we learned today."

"Why not?" Mara kicked off her low-heeled shoes and sat in

a chair opposite him. She sagged back against the cushions, her face weary. They both needed some rest.

"Fromoth Trun asked me too many personal questions. My family connections have nothing to do with our mission. No one really told us how the harvested merl reaches the production facility. The seaweed is cut by hand, so they don't have automated equipment. And then there is the matter of the security breach. That fellow, Delain Crug, wasn't supposed to be waiting on us. I gathered he's one of their chemists."

"Maybe we'll think better after we sleep. What's happened to Hedy and Wren?" A worried frown creased her brow.

He shrugged, rising. "They have their datalinks. Wren would contact me if there's a problem."

"Deke, wait." Standing, she held out her hand to stop him. "We need to talk… about us."

He snorted. "What's there to say?"

"I didn't mean to distract you during your dive. The separation just happened."

He noted the distress in her wide eyes and part of him softened.

"Fine," he said, "We'll let it go. Good night, or good morning, whichever it is."

She moved closer until she stood directly in front of him. He sniffed the sea scent in her hair. "Don't I get a goodnight kiss?"

His gaze lowered to her lips, full and inviting, and he felt his loins stir. "Mara, I can't just kiss you and leave it at that. Please don't do this to me. Hedy and Wren might return at any moment."

She radiated a smile of pure feminine power. "I'm willing to take that chance."

His body surged with desire. "All right," he agreed against his will. His body already anticipated her essence charging into him with her own sexual energy.

Despite his intent to resist her charms, he couldn't avoid the magnetic pull of her attraction. Cursing under his breath at his own weakness, he followed her into the sleeping chamber and stripped off the rest of his clothes.

Chapter Thirteen

Mara was in a deep slumber when someone banged against her lounger and cursed, waking her. Her lids flew open and she regarded Hedy through bleary eyes. Her roommate was struggling to get undressed. The clothes she wore were soiled and torn.

Mara's consciousness resurfaced. After her fast and furious lovemaking with Deke, they'd each retired to their own rooms. She had no idea of the time or whether it was night or day outside.

"What happened to you?" she asked Hedy, her tongue feeling like cotton.

After pulling on a knee-length nightshirt, Hedy gazed at her with horror-stricken eyes. "We were touring a museum when a bomb went off. It was horrible! Smoke billowed everywhere. Windows smashed and masonry tumbled from the ceiling. A group of female docents were killed." Hedy sniffled, a lone tear running down her cheek.

"Good God. Are you all right?" Mara sat bolt upright, coming fully alert.

"Yes, thank the stars. When we made our way to the exit, gunmen fired at us from the street. We were trapped. An army unit engaged the terrorists and helped us to leave."

"Why didn't you notify us?"

"We didn't want to worry you."

"For heaven's sake, you should have let us know. Did Wren tell Deke?" Glancing at her chronometer, she saw several hauras had passed since she'd gone to bed. It was nearly noon.

"He's informing him now." Hedy's eyes misted. "He was so

wonderful, Mara. He shielded me with his body when the debris rained down. Fortunately, the explosion happened in another section of the museum. The guide had decided to bypass that wing because there was a new exhibit she wanted to show us."

Mara rose to get dressed. "You were lucky, and Wren's actions prove he cares for you. At least he acknowledges it, even if he doesn't… if he won't… you know."

Hedy gave a dismissive wave. "Something weird is going on in this place. After today, I'm willing to agree with Deke's suspicions. There's a reason why so many armed guards are around. Fromoth Trun must have been expecting an attack."

"You're right. We'll have to be more watchful. Don't worry, we'll find out what secrets these people are hiding."

****

Deke's fists clenched as Wren related the sequence of events. "Son of a belleek, I knew something was off about the Yanurans. Terrorists! We need to get to the bottom of this, and I know just who to ask."

He entered the living area and activated the communicator, demanding an audience with Fromoth Trun. Without bothering to tidy himself, he hastened into the corridor, his hair askew and his shirt untucked. He'd awoken when Wren had barged inside their room and had thrown on his clothes while his colleague spoke.

Mara rushed after him into the tunnels. "Wait, I'm coming with you." At least she looked better put together with a pullover sweater and long skirt. She'd tied her hair into a low ponytail.

His jaw taut, he gave her a curt nod. Maybe she would sense some emotions from the Yanuran chief of state now that she knew they couldn't trust him.

The planetary leader greeted them in the anteroom of his private quarters. His fingers plucked at his voluminous robe after he gave the pair a welcoming bow.

"It was an unfortunate incident," he said in a mild tone upon Deke's inquiry.

"Our friends were nearly killed. A group of docents died. And you call this unfortunate? Do you have any suspects? Is that why we've been escorted everywhere by security personnel, because you've been expecting trouble?"

Fromoth Trun winced at the barrage of questions. "I haven't wanted to concern you with our internal affairs, but we're involved in a border dispute with the Worts. They've been extending their tree roots, destroying our burrows in outlying districts. With their terrorist tactics, they mean to coerce us into granting them rights to more land."

He gave Deke one of his characteristic sly smiles. "It's a domestic matter, Commander, one that can be easily resolved once we have access to Coalition resources. We need to perform a satellite survey in order for our boundaries to be objectively defined. I'm sure the Worts would honor the results as would my people. Considering the urgency of the situation, I implore you to send an immediate message to the Admissions Committee recommending approval of our application."

Deke wasn't satisfied with Fromoth Trun's response. Would people involved in a simple border dispute resort to terrorism? Of course, wars had been fought for less. But why would the Coalition team be targeted? He felt certain the bombers had singled out Hedy and Wren, being aware of their itinerary. If both sides wanted a ruling over their boundaries, wouldn't the Worts support Coalition membership? Attacking the visitors would ensure their rejection, not acceptance. It didn't make sense.

He leveled a firm glare at the Yanuran leader. "I insist on talking to the Worts myself to confirm your claims. Besides, I still need to discuss Larikk's disappearance with them. He vanished in the Alterland, which is their habitat."

And there was still the matter of locating Jallyn. Speaking of which, Mara hadn't done a separation lately to see if the child's status had changed. He'd have to ask her to do one once they were back in their suite.

"It is impossible to arrange such a meeting," Fromoth Trun said, his complexion darkening.

Mara stepped forward. "The Admissions Committee would look favorably upon our recommendation if we attended a conference with the Worts," she offered, smiling sweetly. "I'm sure you could arrange something amenable to all parties."

Fromoth Trun flicked out his tongue to catch a darting insect. "The Worts do not consort with outsiders. I told you they prefer to keep to themselves. Currently, we are unable to communicate with them."

"So we'll go to them in person," Deke stated.

Fromoth Trun shook his head. "It's a fearsome route through the jungle to reach the Alterland. You can't fly there. The vegetation is too thick and the landmarks are hidden beneath the canopy."

"That doesn't matter. You can get us a good guide."

The Yanuran's mouth twisted. "If you insist on this absurd plan, I'll see what I can do. It will take time to make the necessary arrangements."

"Make it soon," Deke warned him. "In the meantime, what's on our schedule for tonight?"

"You're to attend a concert at the Grand Amphitheater. Your presence will have a beneficial effect on the populace."

Deke suppressed a grimace. "Fine; we'll see you later. I'll expect you to have our travel arrangements made by then."

Outside in the corridor, Mara spoke in a low tone. "Our situation just got a lot more precarious. I sensed hostility in Fromoth Trun. It's almost as though a curtain lifted and I could detect his true feelings."

"I'm not surprised. Likely he'll arrange for us to have a convenient accident along the way. Maybe his people set the bomb and not the Worts. He might want us to believe they're responsible to set us against them. But we'll play the game by our rules, and not his, from now on."

****

Once they were back in their suite, Deke asked Mara to perform a separation. "Do it quietly, here in the living area so we don't awaken Hedy or Wren."

Mara slipped into her room to retrieve the infant's blanket. In the living area, she sat on the sitter while Deke perched on the edge of an opposite chair. Closing her eyes, she began her journey along the astral plane.

Her essence transcended the limits of time and space as she floated, lighter than air, above her body. Deke's aura was clearly visible from this vantage point. His cords of energy radiated toward her, attracting her like a magnet. How tempting it would be to go to him, to merge her psyche with his. But she had a job to do and it didn't involve personal desires.

Focusing her mind, she visualized Jallyn with her delicate features, smooth skin, and tiny hands and feet. Again, as before, an unpleasant force tugged at her expanded consciousness. It drew her like a cosmic vacuum that wanted to suck her into the great void. The force yanked at her spirit when she resisted its pull. She entered Jallyn's life space with a sense of relief.

High stone walls met her gaze above the sides of a crib. Jallyn must be lying on her back. This place was different from before. A casement high up on the wall showed trees outside. Suddenly, a frog face came into view as someone peered at her.

Mara's shock was so forceful that she nearly ejected from Jallyn's essence. With an effort of will, she remained. This person's features differed from the people she'd met so far on Yanura. His brown skin with ugly bumps was unfamiliar to her. As though aware of her presence, the frog face bared his teeth in a malevolent grin.

This must be the source of evil she'd been experiencing. Her breath caught in her ethereal throat as she waited to see what he would do next, but someone's voice distracted him. He turned away and disappeared from Jallyn's vision. Voices argued in the background, and then all went quiet. Left alone, Jallyn stirred with discomfort. Her fanny felt wet. She needed a diaper change.

Upset by the experience, Mara separated and returned to her own body. Her eyes closed, she tried to make sense of what she'd seen. She didn't hear Deke calling her name until he shook her by the shoulders to get her attention.

"Mara, snap out of it."

She stared at him and took a deep, shaky breath. "Jallyn's in danger. There's someone with her who has hostile intent. He's a Yanuran but different. His skin is brown and covered with bumps."

Deke's eyes narrowed. "It's a Wort. Their faction must have Jallyn. We'll visit them with or without Fromoth Trun's support."

Mara couldn't believe it. So the Yanurans did have Jallyn. Was Fromoth Trun aware of this? Yet how could Jallyn have been brought here if not on his ship? That would mean the statesman was acting in collusion with the Worts, not in opposition to them. And what about the terrorist attack that had nearly killed Hedy and Wren? If the planetary leader was involved, it would undermine his goal to join the Coalition.

Perhaps that incident had been staged to make them think the Worts and Croags were at odds. It would mean everything Fromoth Trun had told them was false. But what would he hope to gain by such a scheme?

She'd been a fool. Deke had been right all along to suspect these people.

"I need some fresh air," she told him. "Do you want to come along?" They should continue their conversation outside, where surveillance devices might not be listening in. Deke had done a sweep of their quarters when they'd arrived, but more bugs might have placed in their absence.

"I could use a change of scenery," Deke said in a bright tone, quickly catching on to her plan. "I believe we passed a beach on the way to the pharmaceutical plant. Let's see if we can get transport there. It'll be good to take a break."

Fromoth Trun, annoyed at having his rest disturbed again, gave Deke a terse reply. "If you wish to go for a swim, Commander, our lake is close by."

"I prefer the ocean, if you don't mind. I miss being away from the water."

Giving a resigned sigh, the Yanuran agreed. "You'll be dropped off. It's too hot and sunny for any of our people to remain with you. We'll monitor the area through long-range sensors. Oh, and a word of warning—don't turn your back on the sea."

"What's that supposed to mean?"

"We call it the fire coast. You'll find out why. If you're thirsty, try the seagrapes."

Deke could almost picture the Yanuran grinning as he signed off. Puzzled, he wondered what Fromoth Trun's veiled hints had meant, but he was too eager for a dip in the ocean to care. All worries evaporated from his mind at the idea of plowing through the waves.

He glanced at Mara's attire. "I don't suppose you've brought along a swimsuit?"

Her brows lifted. "I didn't think we'd have time to go swimming."

"It doesn't matter," he said, allowing his gaze to roam her length. "I'm sure we can improvise."

****

An haura later, they found themselves alone on a sandy stretch of beach. Mara gazed at the clear, sparkling water and was glad for the respite from their problems. Danger might lurk on the horizon, but for now they could enjoy the peace and serenity. The calm before the storm, she thought, wishing she could relax. Fromoth Trun's deception made her uneasy.

"Want some ray-block lotion?" Deke offered after rummaging in the knapsack he'd brought. He'd laid out a blanket provided by the Yanurans and erected a shady awning secured by four sturdy poles. Stripped to his swim trunks, he stood before her in his bronzed masculine glory.

"Don't you use sun film?" She kept her gaze purposefully averted.

172

"We use lotion on Eranus. It's one of Drylon's most popular products," he admitted in a grudging tone.

She leveled her direct gaze on him. "Why do you always speak of Drylon with such resentment?"

"I don't agree with their politics."

"Such as?"

Deke sat on the blanket and applied the lotion to his arms. She couldn't help following his movements as he smoothed the cream over his hair-sprinkled skin.

"Drylon doesn't care about preserving the environment," he said, squinting up at her.

Her shadow fell over him and she moved in order to see him better. That was a mistake. Now he was rubbing the lotion on his muscled thighs. She swallowed hard, dismayed when an answering heat rose within her.

"Do you want me to put some on your back?" she foolishly offered. Not that he needed it. His broad back was so tanned, he couldn't possibly burn. But there were harmful ultraviolet rays to screen out, and Yanura didn't maintain a protective shield.

"Sure," he said, flipping onto his stomach. He closed his eyes and rested his head on his folded arms.

She knelt beside him, squeezing a line of lotion onto her palm. Just his nearness made her breath quicken and her pulse thrum with excitement. "Tell me more about Drylon," she said in an attempt to remain impersonal.

Seemingly in a relaxed mood, Deke responded readily. "Drylon uses automated harvesters to reap the kelp on Eranus. It destroys the plants in the process. They replant the crop without caring about the organisms dependent upon the kelp forest for food and shelter. It's a tragic situation that could be avoided with more conservative efforts. I've been lobbying for stricter regulations but don't have the clout to fight them. If I win the chancellorship, I can gather the necessary support to address the issue on a higher level."

"Where does your mother fit into this scenario?"

"She's an administrator. All she cares about is increasing profits."

"I can see how you two would clash."

"I won't take credits from her to fund my research, not that she's offered. She's aware that I'll oppose her if I become chancellor."

"What about your father, the director general?" Mara asked.

"He'll do whatever my mother says. There's not much love in their marriage. She married him for the concessions he could give the company. He wanted her for the wealth she'd bring to his position. They're a perfect pair. Both are users."

"Is that why you've never married, because you're afraid of getting stuck in a similar situation?"

He sat and twisted to face her. "The women on Eranus only care about me because of my influential parents. I've never met anyone who liked me for myself… until you."

His words captured her heart, because they were exactly what she felt. No one appreciated her unique qualities. As she met Deke's gaze, she was startled by the tenderness in his expression.

"I know you return my regard," she told him in a soft voice.

"Maybe… but your ability still disturbs me. When are you going to invade my mind again? I can't deal with the uncertainty."

She noticed his anguished expression. "Yet you want me, don't you?"

He reached out and traced a line down her arm. "I can't help it. You drive me wild."

She ignored the pleasure coursing through her at his teasing touch. "So why won't you accept your feelings? You'll see you have nothing to fear."

Mara understood she tempted him and yet he was still terrified of her. Accustomed to being in control, he was put off by her ability to jump into his head without warning. Or perhaps he equated sharing his feelings with losing his identity. The only way he knew how to express himself was through sex.

Discouraged by their lack of progress, she began to rise, but his hand on her arm stilled her.

"I'm sorry," he blurted, his pleading eyes asking for her patience.

Despite his fear, he obviously yearned for the closeness they could share. And that realization brought her hope.

She expanded her consciousness and was pleased to see his channels opening. If only she wouldn't slam them shut with her unexpected visitations. Yet as she pressed her mouth to his, she determined to let him express himself in the only way he knew. Later, maybe he'd come to accept her gift.

The gentle lapping of the waves and the cries of birds faded into the background as she yielded to his embrace. The shade provided by the overhead awning made their position comfortable, and the soft carpet of sand beneath the blanket helped her to relax.

His tongue plunged inside her mouth, sending sensations of delight twirling through her. She entwined her arms around him, clutching tightly.

Then suddenly he released her and sprang back.

"Let's go for a swim," he suggested. "I need to cool my skin."

Her eyes lit on his sexy dimples. When he grinned at her like that, she'd do anything for him. "I don't have a swimsuit."

"No problem. Raise your arms." He tugged at her top.

"What are you doing?"

His eyes blazed. "Did I ever tell you about my private island on Eranus, the place I go when I need to be alone?" At her negative response, he went on. "There's a beautiful beach with the most powdery amber sand you've ever seen. I like to go swimming… in the nude."

He removed her top in one swift motion. Her heart thumped wildly. Now that she knew what he intended, she couldn't suppress her excitement. She swallowed in eager anticipation of his next move.

"You have such lovely skin," he murmured, kissing her bare shoulder. "You smell so good, just like that spicy fragrance in the air." He looked around, sniffing. "What is that scent?"

Rising, he stalked over to a short, squat bush laden with small purplish fruits. "Are these the seagrapes Fromoth Trun mentioned?"

She stood and joined him. "I suppose. Look, they're all over the beach. Do you think they're safe to eat?"

Deke pulled his datalink from his knapsack and ran a quick scan. "This says they're edible. I am hungry all of a sudden." After replacing his instrument, he plucked a cluster of grapes off a branch and plopped them into his mouth. "Delicious. You should try some."

She ate a few of the plump grapes, savoring their sweet flavor. Before the two of them realized it, they'd picked the bush clean. A warm flush crept from Mara's toes up along her legs to her torso and neck.

"I'm hot," she said, her skin burning. She could barely breathe from the intense heat.

Deke's face reddened. "Me too. Let's cool off." He turned toward the sea and dashed away after discarding his swim trunks on the sand.

"Wait for me!" Mara shed her pants and charged after him. It wasn't until she watched him swim his laps and return toward her that she realized her fervor wasn't satisfied. The burning hadn't abated. She needed him.

The feverish look in his eyes told her he felt the same affliction. "Mara—"

"I know." She fell into his arms, laughing as salt water sprayed her face.

The warm sea enveloped them, caressing them as they embraced. Beneath their feet, the furrowed sand tickled her toes. Occasional schools of tiny fish swam past, but neither one paid any attention. All Mara knew was the pressure of Deke's lips on hers and the feel of her breasts pressed against his bare chest.

But even as the idea that she should remove her underwear entered her mind, she was already discarding her remaining garments. And so it was they came together in a writhing wave of passion.

****

Her eyes closed, Mara reveled in the aftermath of love, her aura still partially associated with Deke's. It was a wondrous feeling as they rocked together in the gentle surf, their limbs entangled and their minds sharing a warm feeling of satiation.

A taste of sea salt lingered on her lips. She wanted to stay there with Deke, to enjoy the ocean even as the waves grew rougher and began lifting them off their toes.

She sensed Deke's fear before separating from him. Snapping her eyes open, she stared in the direction of his shocked gaze.

"What in Zor is that?" he cried.

A slate gray cloud was rolling in, its edges sharply delineated against the bright blue sky. Similar to a fog, it obliterated the sunlight, darkening the sky as it expanded. As they watched in horror, the clouds became more agitated, roiling and churning like plumes of volcanic ash.

"Let's get ashore." Deke grabbed her arm and propelled her toward the beach. An orange glow blossomed in the sky as the clouds ignited and fire spread toward the horizon. The water reacted with a violent boiling motion just as she and Deke reached the sand. He secured their awning and pulled down a flap to protect them from the storm outside.

The phenomenon lasted about half an haura, during which time they sat terrified and perplexed by the sudden change in climate.

After the warm air dried her skin, Mara pulled on her clothes. Finally, the whipping wind and roar of the water subsided. Peeking outside, she noted the sea had returned to its former calm.

Deke wiped his brow with the back of his hand as they emerged into the sunlight. "Now I know what Fromoth Trun meant by calling this the fire coast. I wonder how often that happens. Why did he let us come here if he knew it was dangerous?"

"He did warn us, remember?" She glanced at the shells and seaweed that had been tossed onto the beach.

"That fire was nothing compared to the heat that consumed me after I ate those grapes," Deke said. "Do you think Fromoth Trun knew the effect eating them would have on us?"

"Are you implying he meant for us to go into the water to cool off? If so, he must have known this would happen."

"That's another point against him." Deke donned his swim trunks, collapsed the awning and packed their supplies. Then he activated the signal that would summon transportation. "It's time to head back to the burrows. I hope Hedy and Wren have had enough of a rest. We've got work to do."

****

After a long and satisfying slumber, Hedy awoke to a strange sound coming from outside her closed bedroom door. Sitting up and groggily rubbing her eyes, she listened carefully. There it was again. *Whoosh—whoosh—whoosh.*

She charged out of bed, spared a moment to visit the sanitary, and then threw open the door. Still in her nightshirt, she gaped at Wren, who was pacing the living area, his magnificent wings extended at his back. Apparently, he was exercising them, and the noise she'd heard was his huge wingspread cutting through the air.

"What are you doing?" she said, her racing pulse slowing to normal.

Wren halted, his face coloring. "Sorry, did I wake you?"

"Yes, but this view is worth it."

She was disappointed when Wren pinched his face and folded his wings back inside his shirt slits. Suns! She'd have liked to caress those incredible feathers, to run her fingers through the stiff vanes and stroke the length of them. It was almost as good as stroking other parts of him, maybe even better. Now that was a titillating idea. A small smile played on her mouth as she imagined herself performing that other activity.

"How do you feel, Doctor?" Wren asked, deliberately walking away from her and taking a seat on the lounger.

She spotted an opportunity and bounded down beside him. "I'm still upset about the bombing," she moaned dramatically, putting a hand to her brow in remembered terror. "All those injured people, and I couldn't use my skills to help them."

She felt bad about her helplessness in the situation and shocked that it had happened at all. Wren didn't have to know that her reaction was exaggerated.

"It appears Commander Sage was wise to prepare us for unexpected contingencies," Wren remarked, his voice gruff.

He was trying terribly hard not to look at her, she thought bemusedly. She inched closer and spread her nightshirt along her leg. The lure worked. Wren gave a quick glance in her direction and then stiffened his spine.

"I'm frightened, Wren," she went on, playing her role for all it was worth. "What if we're attacked again? I don't feel safe on this planet." She touched his arm, an imploring expression on her face.

He cursed under his breath and snaked his hand over to pat her thigh. "I'll see you come to no harm. You're safe with me. I couldn't bear it if anything happened to you."

Her heart soared with joy. He'd admitted his need for her! Raising her face, she said, "Kiss me, Wren. It's the only way I'll be able to forget about everything."

His hazel eyes glittering, he lowered his head, his mouth ravaging hers with a desperate need. Wrapping her arms around him, she felt she'd never get close enough to this man.

A tumult of emotions shook her as their mouths engaged in a passionate dance. Dear heaven, she loved the big Polloxite. A tear of happiness trickled down her cheek. Wren noticed it and issued a low growl before deepening the kiss. She yearned to go further and fly with him toward the pinnacle of passion.

But would he go with her? Or would he still deny his attraction due to childhood traumas?

The door to their suite swung open with a crash. Wren sprang away with a guilty flush as Deke and Mara strode inside looking disheveled.

They took in the situation at a glance and shared a knowing look with each other. Their obvious amusement aggravated her.

"Why couldn't you have waited until later?" Hedy snapped. Now she'd never know how far Wren might have gone.

"We gave you sufficient time to rest," Deke drawled, his gaze keen, "although it appears you decided to use the time in a more interesting pursuit."

"You can be damned annoying, do you know that?" She stood and straightened her nightshirt, not feeling in the least embarrassed by her informal attire.

Deke's grin widened. "I have been told the same thing by someone else you know." His teasing glance turned toward Mara.

Hedy's friend rolled her eyes at him. "I thought we had work to do."

"That's right. You can tell them what happened at the beach. I want to check the data Dr. Parannus gave me. Wren, any new developments?" At his navigator's negative shake of the head, Deke said, "Check the room for bugs again and then pack our supplies. We need to be ready to move out."

"I'll get right on it." Wren rose and straightened his shoulders.

Deke disappeared into their room. Mara waited until Wren did a sensor sweep of the living area before she told them what had happened during the trip to the shore.

"That sounds horrible," Hedy said upon Mara's conclusion. "It certainly seems as though Fromoth Trun knew what would happen if you ate those fruits."

"Yes, it does. I need to take a shower and you should get dressed. We have plans to make."

****

Deke wasn't smiling an haura later when he strode from his room to where the others were gathered in the living area. "Everybody, listen up. I have news."

When they were seated and attentive, he mentioned the data card given to him by Dr. Parannus. "The information about Vyclor validates what we've been told. The drug works as an antioxidant, counteracting a harmful free-radical by-product called protein carbonyl that is thought to contribute to the aging process. Toxicity trials have accounted for variant responses in different species, which was one of my concerns. Depending upon the population, rates of drug metabolism can vary widely. Usually a response is influenced by genetic factors, structural variations in the binding receptor sites on the body, and environmental factors such as diet. But in Vyclor's case, all oxygen-dependent species should be able to metabolize the drug properly."

He paused for dramatic effect, eyeing each one of his crew members in turn. "It seems logical and conclusive, doesn't it? If it weren't for something unusual that I noticed, I'd probably have been satisfied. However, two items are included that obviously don't belong in this data stream. A close-up photograph shows a bunch of dead bodies and it's accompanied by a set of coordinates. The dead people look like Worts but I can't be certain."

Mara, seated on the couch, clasped her hands in her lap. "What does this mean?"

Deke shrugged. "There's some sort of industrial facility in the background. We need to visit this place without Fromoth Trun's knowledge."

"Did Dr. Parannus make this addition?" Hedy asked.

"It might have been inserted by him or by someone else. We have no way of knowing."

Mara's eyes widened. "Remember that Delain Crug fellow? He conveniently knocked the data card from your hand when he spilled that drink on you. When he leaned over to retrieve it, he could have switched cards. I'll bet he's the one responsible."

Deke gave her a nod of acknowledgement. "It's a distinct possibility."

"So what's next?" Wren asked from his perch on the edge of a chair.

"We could return to the pharmaceutical plant on some excuse and try to find Delain Crug, but if he's involved, it would put him at risk. I'd rather go directly to this location. Here's what I propose."

After relating his plan, Deke contacted Ebo on the ship and

relayed his instructions. A short time later, a call came through from Fromoth Trun's secretary.

"We've received notification from Defense League Command that they've received a distress call from the Regaluch system. The *Celeste* is the closest ship, Commander. You have orders to investigate the distress signal."

"I'm so sorry. Will you kindly notify Fromoth Trun that our mission here will be delayed?" Deke said with a forced note of disappointment in his voice.

"He'll be expecting you to return as soon as you complete your assignment."

"Naturally. Have you alerted spacedock to prepare for a launch?"

"I will notify them at once. Please make haste. I know our honored leader will be eager for your return so you can complete negotiations."

"We'll be as quick as we can." Deke cut off the commlink and gestured to his friends. "Pack your bags. We're going to see some action for a change."

Chapter Fourteen

"I can put her down over there," Deke suggested, piloting the shuttlecraft toward a small hammock, one of the few patches of higher ground dotting the swampy landscape. "We can't get any closer to the coordinates, or we'll risk being seen on visual."

Seated beside him in the copilot's chair, Wren nodded grimly. They shot past a field of tall brown sawgrass and veered toward a clearing just before the brush thickened. In the distance, a cluster of tall chimney stacks indicated the location of the industrial complex that was their target.

Deke used the ship's molecular alteration program to reconfigure their vessel as a boat. He brought them to a shuddering halt on a strip of land bordered by a large canal, a dirt road, and an evergreen forest. In the night, their spindly white trunks must look like ghostly wraiths rising from the swamp. Right now, the shadows cast by the trees looked cool and inviting.

The air was thick with humidity as they emerged into the bright sunlight. He glanced at the murky water in the canal. Green vegetation covered the surface where hardly a ripple showed.

No one was in sight, which was what they'd hoped when planning their excursion for the daytime hauras. To the south, tall brown grasses with serrated leaves stretched in an endless expanse broken only by an occasional bush or squat tree. Water glistened throughout the grassy plain. In the opposite direction, a swampland forest crisscrossed a network of waterways.

Whichever path they chose, they couldn't go on foot.

Deke eyed his crew members who'd dressed in dark cloaks

to disguise their alien forms. His gaze settled on Mara's slim figure, and a warm, appreciative glow lit him as he watched her. She moved with the grace of a dancer, and his loins hardened remembering their sensual duets in the physio lab. It hadn't been an easy decision to bring her along.

He'd wrestled with himself over her assignment. He needed Ebo and Wren as members of the landing party, and Hedy was essential as medic. Did he dare trust Mara not to get into trouble if left alone on the ship? In the end, he'd decided she should come along. He didn't wonder whether that was the real reason or whether he'd hesitated to include her because of her gift. It would cause trouble if she jumped into his head at a critical moment. But he finally decided to add her to the away team because she might be useful with her empathic powers.

Refocusing his thoughts, he decided which way to go. The forest would provide better cover, plus he'd spied a dirt trail. "Let's go that way," he said, moving on.

His team took positions behind him single-file while he set the pace. The brush lining the path was thick with silver-branched bushes, red-leafed trees, squat palms, and white-trunked evergreens. He glimpsed a sausage tree with its oblong-shaped fruits hanging down from vine-like branches. From his review of Yanura's plant life, he knew they were edible.

A pungent aroma hit him as they approached a curve in the trail. He halted and motioned for Ebo to take point. The Sirisian elongated his neck to peer around the corner.

"It's a fueling station," Ebo said, his turbaned head covered by his cowl.

"A fueling station for what?" Mara asked. "There's nothing here."

As they neared the structure, Deke pulled the hood further over his head and hunched his posture to mimic the Yanurans. A rustling noise from behind told him his crew were doing the same.

Several strange-looking conveyances were docked at a slough that ran around the back of the station. Yellow water lilies floated on the shallow water, its stillness broken only by an occasional fish that surfaced. A gentle breeze caressed the hairs on his arms.

"Who goes there?" called a gruff voice from within.

"We're travelers," he responded. "Are your vessels for hire?"

Fifteen minutes later, Deke emerged from the outpost and headed toward the dock. Putting Mara's linguistic expertise to use, he'd hired one of the airboats without—he hoped— arousing any suspicions. The scruffy Croag who ran the station hadn't even given him a second glance after being offered a generous payment. He'd even given directions to the industrial plant in a bored tone as though new workers came through there fairly often.

Deke climbed into the flat-bottomed boat with its bright blue meraninum hull rising out of the water. In the front, a protective windshield curved upward, shielding the rows of black plasticine benches behind it. From the flat deck behind the passenger seats rose the supports of another seat that towered over the rest. This was the pilot's chair. Behind it, at the rear of the boat, sat a powerful engine. It drove a gigantic propeller blade captured in a metal frame that supported the pilot's chair.

"I'll drive." Deke indicated the others should take the passenger seats facing forward.

With a grunt, he climbed to his post and donned the goggles and earphones provided by the station owner. He located the starter button and jabbed it with his forefinger.

With a cough and a sputter, the powerful engine roared into life, drowning out all other sound. *Great, we'll be heard for kilometers.* So much for a stealthy approach to their target.

Wren threw off the mooring lines, then jumped into the boat after the others. He took a seat next to Hedy, snaking his hand in her direction. Deke noticed Mara cast an envious glance their way and felt a surge of dismay that he couldn't comfort her in a similar manner. Damn the woman. She constantly distracted him.

Clenching his jaw, he gripped the throttle and carefully eased the stick forward. The twin air rudders shifted and the boat moved ahead. Now all he had to do was navigate the maze of waterways to reach their destination.

After a turn ahead, he increased speed, shooting down a narrow waterway bordered by tall grasses. Wind whipped at his face as the vibration from the motor shuddered through his body. He felt like whooping with exhilaration. What a ride!

He couldn't see his crew's reaction since their backs were to him. Their vessel bumped over a mound of black muck and his seat rose, then dipped, as the boat skimmed over the water at high speed. A flock of white long-necked birds took flight at the noise but his attention was diverted by a series of turns. Soon they were rapidly approaching the hammock where the Croag had told him to dock.

He cut the motor and sideslipped the airboat into a slough beside a short wooden pier. A couple of other boats moored there bobbed in the current. He felt a rush of silence as the engine noise stopped and the vibrations ceased. Removing his earphones and goggles, he scanned the area from his high vantage point.

An oasis of tall palms, flowering bushes, and fruit-laden trees met his gaze. But the idyllic scene was marred by a sulfuric odor in the air. Wrinkling his nose, he descended from his perch. An orange-beaked bird stood feeding in the shallow water, seemingly undisturbed by the intrusion.

At least no one was there to greet them, he thought gratefully as he mustered his team. They headed down a winding dirt trail that led toward the towering stacks from the industrial complex. Sweat dripped inside the skinsuit he wore under his cloak. The silver suits, impervious to sensor scans, were standard-issue uniform for sensitive missions. They were hot as Zor on a day like this but they were invisible to radar. All of his team members wore one, and glancing back, he saw they looked as flushed and uncomfortable as him.

A huge fence loomed in front with a guardhouse at a gated entrance. He drew his group to a halt before they could be spotted. A hasty conference ended with Mara splitting off from the group.

She sauntered toward the gatehouse, her cloak gone. With her wavy hair loosened from its braid, her seductive walk, and the skinsuit that clung to her curves, she appeared a vision of loveliness. But would the lone Yanuran guard be tempted by the human female? Deke squinted as he aimed his weapon from behind a tree.

Mara called out to get the guard's attention. Another Yanuran joined him. So there were two people on duty. Hopefully they were the only ones, Deke thought as he pressed his finger on the trigger.

Pop—pop!

The guards went down without a sound. At his nod, Wren went to work on the gate, first jamming the electronic alarm circuitry, then disengaging the locking mechanism. The gate swung open in silence.

They entered the grounds through an archway. On their left was the guardhouse, and on the right was a small, nondescript building. Before them stretched a series of gravel roads connecting numerous structures with varying shapes.

All of the buildings had an unfinished look to them, as though they were temporary. Most were constructed of cinder block or corrugated metal with a small sprinkling of brick. Each building was numbered. They were interconnected by a series of huge white pipes. The piping varied in diameter and had joints where it took sharp ninety-degree turns.

Some of the pipelines were supported by metal super-structures. All of the buildings had outdoor stairwells for fire escape.

Spherical constructs that were separate from the larger buildings dotted the landscape. They struck a chord in Deke, but he couldn't recall where he'd seen something similar.

He checked out the first building that was smaller than the rest. It held a bin with safety glasses, another one with rubbery overshoes, plus row after row of hanging coveralls. He appraised the room then gazed at his crew questioningly.

"What do you think?" he asked.

"This must be a dressing area for the workers," Mara replied. "We should put on these outfits. They'll easily fit over our cloaks. It will help if we're dressed like everyone else."

He nodded his agreement. "Wren, you'll stay with the women. Wait here and make sure no other guards come by to impede our exit. Ebo, come with me."

Properly suited up, Deke and Ebo moved out. Each new location they scouted brought with it a new smell, none of them pleasant. Deke felt like gagging half the time but suppressed the reflex.

The cylindrical storage tanks were painted white to reflect the heat, and each one had a metal staircase running up its side. The spherical ones stood apart like outcasts and again he wondered at their purpose. A water treatment plant, recycling center, and bimanthium crystal-powered generator told Deke the facility was self-sufficient. But what was produced here?

Something nagged at him, telling him he'd seen buildings like these before. Outside each larger cluster of buildings was a small upright structure painted in bright yellow. He entered one, curious as to its use. Inside were sinks and shower spigots.

Showers? Rubber shoes? Coveralls and safety glasses?

A proverbial lightbulb went off in his head. This was a chemical plant.

Halting in shocked surprise, Deke wondered what kind of chemicals were produced there. Fertilizers? Industrial solvents? Something to do with their pharmaceutical industry?

Now he remembered seeing similar buildings at Drylon's production facilities, but the extent of safety precautions here went well beyond the bounds for everyday household solutions.

These products must be more dangerous. Those showers were for emergency use along with the sinks for cleansing the eyes. Those spherical constructs that stood apart from the others must store the products.

Great suns! A sinking feeling took hold of him as he observed the laborers conduct their business. In his mind's eye, he saw those dead bodies pictured on the data card. Were they from here?

His gaze surveyed a flat expanse in the distance. Whoa, was that an airstrip? He gestured to Ebo to accompany him as he headed that way. A set of tracks paralleled their path. Several rolling platforms stood poised on the tracks. These trolleys contained torpedo-shaped cylinders with a red warning symbol painted on their sides.

"I'd like to take one of those with us for analysis," Deke said to Ebo from the shadow of a nearby building.

"They're too big, sir," the Sirisian replied, his face red from the heat.

"I know. We'd need to obtain a mini-levitator."

"How about checking out one of the larger buildings instead? We might locate one of the laboratories and find some answers there."

"Okay, we'll try that first."

They were approaching a casement on the side of a structure to check for an easy means of entry when a harsh voice stopped them cold.

"Halt! Who are you, and what are you doing snooping out here? Turn around slowly, and keep your hands where we can see them."

Deke turned to face a pair of frog-faced guards holding shooters aimed at their chests. He exchanged a glance with Ebo and gave an imperceptible nod.

****

Mara bit her nails with anxiety. Why were Deke and Ebo taking so long to return?

She'd taken to counting the ants crawling past on the dry ground in order not to worry, but she couldn't help feeling concerned when the minutes ticked by and there was no sign of them.

If only she could do a willful separation to check on Deke's well-being, but she didn't possess any of his belongings and hadn't yet reached the point of being able to direct their spiritual contact. She found herself wishing one of their spontaneous occurrences would happen, but it didn't. Agonized, she turned to Wren.

"Maybe you should go after them," she suggested, pushing a stray wisp of hair from her face. She'd rebraided it and twisted it on top of her head.

Wren stood squinting in the sunlight, peering in the direction they'd gone. "Be patient. The commander will return when he is ready," he said confidently.

She grimaced. She didn't like this mission. Being an open, honest person, she liked to deal with people without reservations, and the deceit they'd used on Fromoth Trun bothered her.

What if Deke were caught? How would he explain their presence here? Then again, what was this place, and why had someone tipped them off to it by inserting the coordinates on that data card?

She shook her head, too worried to think clearly. Leaning against the hot stucco exterior of the wardrobe building, she wallowed in the anxiety that clouded her mind.

I should meditate, she told herself. *I wouldn't feel the heat so badly and it would take my mind off Deke's absence.* But she couldn't concentrate. Her gaze fixed on the path Deke and Ebo had taken to where it rounded a curve and became lost to view. Off to the side, Hedy and Wren held a quiet conversation.

She glanced up when footsteps thudded in their direction. Her heart leapt with relief as Deke and Ebo tore around the bend. Their boots kicked up dust in their wake. Their faces were red and sweaty and their expressions edged with desperation.

"Move it," Deke shouted. "They're right behind us."

Encumbered by her weighty outfit, Mara trundled through the gate with the others and dashed down the path toward the dock. As soon as they reached the airboat, Wren threw off the mooring lines while Deke climbed onto the pilot's seat. He jabbed at the starter button and the engine roared into life just as a loud claxon clanged, announcing their presence.

"We can't let them catch us," Deke hollered.

Mara barely heard him as she flung herself onto a seat. She and Hedy helped divest each other of their coveralls as Deke pushed the throttle forward.

They eased along the slough. Soon they were skipping along at high speed and appeared to be in the clear until another airboat intersected them at a canal.

Laser fire zinged past her ear.

With a shriek, Mara crouched in the bottom with Hedy while Wren and Ebo returned fire. She hoped Deke knew where he was going. The waterways were shallow and could be hazardous at this speed to a pilot unfamiliar with the territory.

She spared a glance his way, disturbed to note his grim face. He'd managed to don goggles and earphones but she could tell by the set of his mouth and his taut posture how critical he considered their situation. If he got hit, or the propeller became impaired, they'd be in big trouble.

She didn't care to contemplate a trek through the muck with the Yanurans in pursuit, nor could she even bear to think about Deke being wounded.

Her eyes widened at another thought. Why were they being pursued by armed Croags in airboats? Deke and Ebo must have discovered something significant.

It could be nothing more than tightly guarded industrial secrets, but those dead bodies on that data card implied a more sinister scenario.

Her breath caught in her throat as a sizzling beam of red light shot past, melting the edge of the boat where it hit.

With a snarl, Wren fired back, and a rapid volley ensued. Deke swerved as they reached a narrow river bordered by tall grasses. Cobwebs brushed Mara's face as she tried to peer over the edge, but whenever she rose, the vibrations made her teeter. Other waterways veered off from this one.

Deke revved the engine and swerved left, away from another airboat that had joined the pursuit and was heading straight at them.

They hit a pile of muck, and she grabbed at Hedy as the boat rose under them and then fell with a jarring thud.

Without losing speed, the boat flew toward a forested section of the swamp where twisted white shapes rose out of the dark water. Her teeth rattled from the engine's vibration and she clenched them together, but it didn't help. It felt as though her bones were being shaken loose.

Hedy poked her arm, her eyes wide with fright. "Mara, is that where we're heading?"

The swamp's dismal depths loomed ahead. Moss dripped from overhanging tree branches. Fallen logs and other debris carpeted higher patches of ground.

Surely Deke won't drive us into that obstacle-ridden lagoon? Tall, cone-shaped stumps stuck up from the murky brown water.

They veered right, and Mara swallowed hard, wondering if Deke knew what he was doing. They had to lose those Yanurans. As she crouched on the deck, clutching at Hedy with both hands, her thoughts raced.

What was produced in that foul-smelling factory in the middle of a swamp? It couldn't be a waste treatment site so far from civilization. How about a normal industrial process that smelled so bad no one wanted it near their homes? But that didn't seem likely considering the tight security.

The ghostly swamp flashed by on their left. She risked another glance at Deke. His face was abnormally white, his lips pressed tightly together.

She felt an uncontrollable urge to merge with him and offer her strength but knew it would break his concentration, even if she could manage to initiate the separation.

Certainly, it would help if she could control her power. Then he wouldn't have to be afraid of her, and she could offer solace when needed. But she wouldn't take the chance of disrupting his thoughts. Those woody growths permeated the swamp, and he had to pay attention to their passage.

Her ears caught Wren's whoop of exultation, and she snapped

her head around. One of the boats pursuing them had hit something in the water and flipped over. The Yanurans floundered in the shallow water and then they were lost to view.

Deke raced the boat toward a dark green spot indicating higher ground. Behind them, a second boat followed but at a distance. As they approached the small island, he slowed their speed until they could make out the patches of thick tropical vegetation that provided a shady cover. Here he cut the engine and slipped the airboat into a small cove. The vibrations ceased abruptly along with the deafening roar.

"We'll wait here," Deke said, having taken off his earphones. "It's too far to circle around these hammocks. We'd waste too much fuel. Wait until that other boat comes into view, then fire at its propeller," he told Wren and Ebo.

As they settled in to wait, Mara and Hedy slumped into their seats. At the water's surface, reeds and cattails swayed in the breeze. A turtle sat motionless on a slime-covered rock. Gnarled tree roots, broad leaves of tropical plants, and tangles of vines formed a dense entrance to the interior. Mara inhaled a sweet floral scent, grateful to chase away the unpleasant odor from the industrial plant.

"What was that place?" she asked Deke. His gaze scanned the watery expanse, his goggles hanging from a strap around his neck. A light breeze whipped his hair into his face.

"We'll discuss it later," he replied, his voice terse.

Seated high above them, he appeared powerful with his muscled body, broad chest, and confident posture. He didn't look anything like the sensitive science scholar she knew him to be inside. *This is the warrior*, she realized grudgingly. *This is the soldier who'd snuffed out all the Hortha guards on that mission with Wren to the planet Souk. This is the SEARCH force leader in charge of our mission.*

She should have listened to his advice regarding the Yanurans. Now look at them. They hadn't accomplished any of their objectives other than learning more about Vyclor, and even that might be a scam.

"Get ready," Deke ordered as a droning hum sounded in the near distance.

When the noise grew into a roar, he put on his goggles and earphones. The other airboat thundered past. Deke pressed the starter button, kicking the engine into life.

He whipped the boat out of the cove and into the marsh. The other vessel skimmed over the sawgrass in front of them. Deke moved the throttle and they shot after the other boat.

Wren took aim and fired. His laser bolt hit home, knocking the other boat's propeller off balance. Their vessel settled onto the grassy marshland, its engine making sputtering sounds before quitting altogether.

Deke careened down another slough to avoid them. Several turns later, he slowed their speed, finally reaching a halt. After cutting the engine, he removed his earphones.

"Um, Wren, can you get a fix on our shuttle's location?"

She didn't like the sheepish look on his face. "Don't tell me we're lost?" she asked. Her skin itched, and she scratched at a reddish bump. Suns, what kind of insects did they have here? None of them had thought to wear repellant.

Wren stood on the flat deck. Hedy gasped as his wings sprouted from his back.

"Sorry," Wren said, his face reddening. "I had to stretch. Just a minute, sir, and I'll get you that information."

"How?" Hedy asked, her eyes wide. "There aren't any landmarks here that we would recognize. One canal looks like another. Wait, I get it. Your datalink must have a program that detects the shuttle's beacon."

"True, but I use another method." He grinned at her, a bright, engaging smile that lit his entire face. "My species has a highly developed sense of echo location."

"Oh," Hedy said in an awestruck tone.

After flapping his wings a few times, Wren refolded them into his back. He emitted a series of high-pitched squeaks and then fell silent, listening for echoes the others couldn't hear. "The shuttle lies in that direction," he told Deke, giving an approximation of the distance.

"Hang on," Deke said, replacing the earphones on his head.

Mara groaned. Her temples throbbed as the shuddering vibrations and deafening engine noise resumed. She couldn't wait until they reached the *Celeste.*

****

Deke had planned to return the airboat to the fueling station but feared a reception committee might be waiting for them. Instead he drove directly across the swamp to where the shuttle rested, still disguised as a watercraft.

In his mind's eye, he visualized the guards aiming their shooters at him and Ebo back at the complex. Ebo had elongated his arms, snatching the shooters from their opponent's hands before they realized what was happening. A few well-appointed kicks and punches had brought the Croags down. The siren had intensified the hunt for intruders and ensured their pursuit.

Shaking off the memory, Deke ordered his crew into the shuttle and heaved a grunt of relief. Within minutes, he'd lifted off and steered through the atmosphere toward their ship.

Each one of them gave an exclamation of pleasure as they disembarked the shuttle in the *Celeste*'s cargo bay.

He surveyed his scraggly team. They looked hot, bedraggled, and fatigued. Knowing they'd like to shower, grab a meal, and rest, he grimly gave his orders.

"Set course for Revitt Lake City," he told Ebo.

Mara stared at him. "We're returning so soon?"

Deke observed the disappointment on her face. "We've seen evidence of nasty chemicals being produced at that plant. We didn't see any dead bodies, but the implication is that the Croags might be testing those chemicals on the Worts. We have to talk to them. If Fromoth Trun hasn't made any arrangements, we'll seek the Worts on our own. We shouldn't tip his hand just yet when he might know where Jallyn is being held."

Jallyn. Mara squeezed her eyes shut, a flood of anxiety overwhelming her. She felt Deke's hand on her arm, sensed his flow of compassion, and gained strength from his presence. Opening her eyes, she noticed the other crew members had already left for the upper levels. She and Deke were alone.

"I'm sorry for being so stubborn. You were right all along about everything," she told him. Her defense of Fromoth Trun no longer seemed rational. Deke's arguments had been valid from the start. She'd been too biased by her own sense of righteousness to think clearly.

Deke drew her into his arms. "Mara," he said, burying his face in her hair, "I'll make sure this turns out all right. We'll get Jallyn back."

"I was so worried when you and Ebo didn't return right away." She tilted her head so she could gaze up at him.

Before she knew what was happening, she'd jumped into his viewpoint, staring at her own pink lips and yearning to take her right there on the cargo bay floor.

Abruptly, he released her and stepped away. "Don't do this to me. Don't make me so crazy for you that you steal my mind."

"But I thought you liked it when we're together."

His expression softened. "I like the physical aspects, but everything I've been working toward for my whole life dissolves into nothing when I'm with you. That's what scares me. Even our purpose here fades into insignificance when we're linked. I need you to keep your distance if I'm to focus on our mission."

"You're denying the inevitable. We're meant to be together."

His movements jerky, he jabbed the panel to summon the turbolift. "You keep saying that and I don't understand why. I'm not able to give you what you want."

"It's what you want, too. Can't you see that?"

"What I want is to be left alone." His eyes narrowed as he cast her a glance. "I'm going to work. Please do me a favor and stay off the bridge."

"You're shutting me out. That's unfair." She couldn't help her accusatory tone. He wouldn't even give them a chance.

The lift arrived with a *whoosh*. He stepped inside, and when she didn't follow, he departed without another word. Mara stood staring after him, wondering how they'd ever close the deep chasm between them.

197

Chapter Fifteen

Deke berated himself as he sat on the bridge of the *Celeste* peering out the viewscreen during their approach to Revitt Lake City. Why was Mara so damn persistent? Any other woman would have backed off by now. Why did she keep bothering him?

Stroking his jaw, he tried to understand what she hoped to gain. What if he did agree to let their relationship work itself out? Maybe he'd ask her to return to Eranus with him. If she stayed there as his mate, she'd have to give up her diplomatic career. Was she willing to sacrifice her life's work to be with him? Of course, they hadn't talked about it, nor was he even ready to consider the idea, but what would she say given the choice?

He pursed his lips, mulling over the notion of bringing her home. His parents expected him to settle down with a girl from one of the wealthier families on Eranus. How would they react to a woman like Mara? Her exotic beauty and unnatural ability would make her stand out in any population. Would they react with the same horror as Pietor's parents?

Despite his wish to be free of her, he couldn't bear to see her hurt. Hopefully his father would be more tolerant. As leader of the planet, Jon mingled with people from different worlds at diplomatic functions and was used to socializing with aliens. So was Deke's mother, but Palomar would be disappointed he hadn't chosen a mate who could bolster the family fortune.

Deke realized he knew little about Mara's background other than the struggles she'd had throughout her childhood. Her parents might still be living. What kind of work did they do? If she had other relatives, how did they regard her? And why should he care? He couldn't live with the woman, knowing she'd invade his privacy when least expected.

And yet the idea, once introduced, wouldn't disappear. It continued to nag at him, producing visions he didn't want to see—showing her his favorite cavern by the Whispering Dunes; proudly introducing her to his colleagues at the institute; teaching her how to dive and sharing the wonders of Treasure Cove. He'd sit down to dinner with her and she would tease him about his choice of seafood.

Maybe she'd serve him an iced jelly, her sarong clinging tightly to her hips, her long raven hair cascading down her back as she sauntered toward him, a seductive gleam in her eyes. By the corona, he was tempted—

"We've received clearance for landing," Ebo said, breaking his daydream.

"Proceed," he said, compressing his mouth. Satisfied that Ebo could handle the maneuvers, he glanced at Wren, hunched over his nav console. He wondered what was going through the Polluxite's head.

Wren acted as though he enjoyed Hedy's attentions even though his manner of showing it was gruff. Suddenly curious, Deke swiveled in his chair to face his friend.

"What are you going to do when this is over?" he asked.

Wren glanced up, startled. "Sir?"

"What are you going to do about Hedy?"

Wren's face colored. "I haven't thought that far in advance."

"I don't know what I'll do about Mara. I suppose I can call on her when I visit Bimordus Two."

Wren raised a layered eyebrow. "And how often will that be?"

"Not too often if I win the chancellorship."

"What's that?" Wren's tone sharpened.

Deke cursed inwardly as he realized he'd let slip his secret. Oh, well. His crew would find out sooner or later. "I enlisted in the

Defense League for only two annums. It's not a career track for me. Are you familiar with the Institute for Marine Studies on Eranus?"

"No, sir, I am not."

"Ebo?" Deke asked, thinking the Sirisian might have heard of it. At the fellow's negative shake of his head, he continued. "The chancellorship will be vacant several months from now. I've applied for the position. I'm trained as a marine biologist."

Wren's expression of surprise was almost comical. "But your military exploits are well known. I've heard stories—"

"Those incidents occurred within the past annum and a half. Before that, I worked at the institute. I joined the SEARCH force so I could improve my diving skills while earning points with the selection committee. There's so much I could do as chancellor in terms of conservation."

Wren's hazel eyes regarded him solemnly. "Mara knows about this, I assume?"

Plowing a hand through his unruly hair, he nodded.

"Have you asked her to return home with you?" Wren performed a few calculations on the nav computer as he listened.

A glance out the viewscreen showed them to be on course for the spaceport. "Why would I do that? I said I could call on her when I visit Bimordus Two."

"Which won't be very often. I don't think Mara is the type of female to abide that kind of relationship for long."

"What about you and Hedy?" Deke countered.

"She knows how I feel. Our relationship cannot work." Wren lifted his chin in the air, his gaze defiant.

"But you wish you could have her, don't you?"

"Aye, more than anything. All I can think about is when will I see her next. Her sweet face dances before my eyes during every waking moment. Her lilting voice plays music in my ears. She drives me crazy, but I cannot touch her." He glared at Deke, his expression wild. "Would you have ever guessed a woman could cause such distraction?"

Deke nodded, amused. "I have the opposite problem. Mara drives me crazy when I do touch her." And here he was thinking of her again when he should be deciding what to say to Fromoth Trun. Blast, that woman tormented him.

"There's no easy solution, is there, my friend?" he said. "We were better off before we met the ladies."

Wren studied him, his demeanor serious. "Do you really believe so, Commander?"

Disconcerted, Deke shuffled his feet. "Maybe… I don't know. I'm confused by it all."

"You know what that means, don't you? Being so obsessed by a woman that you cannot think of anything else?"

"What are you getting at? Spit it out, man."

"You're in love."

Deke gave a disbelieving grunt. "I am not."

"I know that's how I feel toward Hedy. It is a curse upon me that I cannot tell her, for that would be my undoing. But you can tell your woman and reveal your heart to her."

"You're unhinged, Wren. I am not in love with Mara."

Before Wren could contradict him, he whirled away, distraught and unsure of himself. Wren's vision is biased by his own amorous inclinations, Deke thought. He's vastly mistaken about me. I want to bed Mara, not wed her.

Furiously pushing away such disturbing notions, he focused his thoughts on Fromoth Trun. It was much more comforting to think about his work than to analyze his feelings regarding one insistent and beautiful woman.

****

The Yanuran leader greeted Deke and his team in the spacedock landing bay.

"Responding to the distress call did not take you very long, Commander." Fromoth Trun's moist green skin darkened to a murky brownish color.

"It turned out to be a false alarm," Deke answered smoothly. "Have you made the arrangements I requested?" Tucking his hands into his uniform pockets, he sauntered forward until he stood within centimeters of Fromoth Trun's frog face. The fishy odor that assailed him made him suck in a sharp breath, but he didn't let his reaction show on his face.

"I was waiting for your return. We didn't expect you back so soon." The Yanuran fingered his voluminous robe, his glittering amber gaze darting to the casements. Outside, the sun descended in a brilliant crimson display.

Deke's mouth tightened. "We've packed our gear. We're ready to go. Just get us a guide."

"I'll have to contact the chief councilor for the Worts. He'll want to arrange a proper reception."

"Forget the reception. We'd rather arrive unannounced. Now about the guide…"

Fromoth Trun glanced at Wren and the women who waited patiently behind Deke. They all wore insulated khaki treksuits. Deke had put on his uniform, replete with gold braid and service medals, hoping it would make him appear more intimidating.

"You must be hungry after your journey. Join us at our repast before work hours begin," Fromoth Trun suggested, his manner obsequious. "We'll discuss this further. Have you read the material I sent you regarding Vyclor?" At Deke's nod, he went on. "The drug will benefit everyone. Why don't you make this easy and recommend our approval to the Admissions Committee?"

"I understand how the sale of Vyclor would benefit your people, Your Excellency. I'm not so sure how it would serve anyone else. I'd like to hear the Worts' opinion on the subject. They do take Vyclor, don't they? Didn't you say the entire population uses it?"

Mara cleared her throat behind him, and he wondered what emotions she was sensing in Fromoth Trun. The Croag leader was probably involved in that secret project in the swamp. Deke didn't need her psychic ability to realize it would be dangerous to reveal their knowledge. They still didn't know what that project signified, but the Worts might be able to tell them.

"Yes, that is so," the Yanuran said, making a sweeping gesture toward the exit. "Let us retire to the burrows. You can avail yourselves of our hospitality for the night. By morning, you might see things in a different light."

Deke squared his shoulders. "We aren't interested in your delay tactics. If you don't provide us with a guide, we'll proceed to the Alterland ourselves. Even though we can't fly our shuttle in, we'll find a way. It would help if we had your cooperation."

His steely tone made it clear that he'd recommend an immediate denial of Fromoth Trun's application if their team was refused aid.

The Yanuran got the message. "Very well," he said with a shrug. "I have someone in mind who can serve your needs."

****

Several hauras later, a winged pod transported them to the Alterland, a tropical rainforest deep at the base of the highest mountain range on Yanura. Their driver deposited them at Camp Selva, a research site run by a pharmaceutical company. The property, basically a clearing in the jungle close to a stream, consisted of twenty bamboo cottages with thatched roofs and a separate cooking hut.

Mara surveyed their surroundings. glad her team had the foresight to bring along a supply of flame torches. Since the Yanurans could see in the dark, public lighting was conspicuously absent. Light from the planet's twin moons barely illuminated the scene. Fortunately, dawn was about to break and soon the sun would kiss the horizon.

The four members of their landing party stood viewing the silent encampment. Ebo had stayed behind under Deke's orders to take the *Celeste* into orbit and monitor communications. As she peered at a grotesque black insect scurrying by, Mara had a distinct wish to join him. Nonetheless, her excitement grew at the prospect of learning more about a new culture.

The downside was being near Deke for several days. Even though she'd seen the invisible cords binding them, Deke's continued denial of his feelings battered her. Was it worth the effort on her part to try to make him see the light? She'd touched the loneliness hidden inside him and knew he needed her as much as she needed him. If only she could convince him to give their relationship a chance.

Make the best of it and get your act together. You have a job to do.

The dank air smelled of rotting vegetation. As the sunrise brought a pink blush to the sky, vapor swirled through the thick tree canopy. Cicadas hummed in unison and strange birdcalls filled the air.

Deke strode over to the only Croag who wasn't in a hurry to retreat to his bungalow. The fellow stood by the stream, holding a makeshift fishing pole that dangled in the water. He wore a wide-brimmed hat, a pair of baggy pants, and a loose-fitting frock coat that had seen better days.

Deke called out a greeting in Jawani, the standard Coalition language, but the fellow ignored him.

Mara joined them. *"Rogi Kwantro,"* she said, gratified to get a curt nod in response. Trying the Croag dialect, she said, "We're supposed to meet a guide to take us into the interior. Can you direct us to the person in charge?"

With a laborious sigh, the fisherman laid his pole down and rose to face them. "I've been hired to take you inland. Folks in these parts call me Slime." He aimed his glistening amber eyes in their direction. "How much you payin'?"

"I thought Fromoth Trun had set the terms," she stated.

"The only agreement he made was for me to be here. Now how much?"

"What's he want?" Deke demanded. Sweat trickled down the sides of his face. He didn't look very comfortable in his khaki treksuit. He'd changed out of his uniform but in this heat it wasn't much of an improvement.

"He's asking how much we'll pay him."

Deke cursed. "Fromoth Trun is trying to make this difficult, isn't he?"

"I wouldn't think so. He wants us to approve his application."

"Then he's sure going about it in an odd manner. Tell this frog face we'll pay him a hundred credits to take us to the nearest Wort village."

She translated, glad that her skills were proving useful. She glanced at Hedy who was holding a hushed conference with Wren beside one of the cottages. This trip wouldn't be easy for her friend, either. Wren was being just as stubborn as Deke about their relationship.

Their potential guide lifted his fishing pole and cast the line into the water. "Not worth the effort for that paltry amount. It's an arduous trip."

Deke's face reddened. "Offer him five hundred."

"Five thousand," Slime countered after Mara relayed his message.

"Two and a half thousand," Deke said.

"Three thousand and a crate of live torgus larvae when we're finished."

Deke acquiesced, contacting Lixier Bryn via datalink to confirm the transfer of credits. "Your food will be flown in when we're picked up," he told the fellow. "How soon can we leave?"

Slime packed up his fishing supplies. "By first lunar light," he replied in standard Jawani.

"So you do speak our language," Deke said, lifting his brows.

"Never said I couldn't."

"We have to travel during the day. We can't see at night like you can."

Slime's complexion darkened. "That'll cost you extra."

"Fine, we'll pay you five hundred credits more upon our safe return."

The Yanuran drove a hard bargain, Mara thought as the team sorted their gear and prepared for the trek. Slime stored his fishing equipment and gathered his rucksack. Taking point, he led the team down a dirt trail that wound into the jungle.

It rained not long after their start, a sudden torrential downpour that made their path slippery. Mara slogged her way through the mud, wishing she had webbed feet like their guide. Exposed tree roots and rocks made the hike treacherous.

Slime didn't have to worry about the sunlight drying out his moist greenish skin. A pale, diffuse light filtered through the dense jungle canopy that towered a hundred feet or higher. A multitude of insects presented him with ample meals, and his long tongue flicked out to catch treats along the way.

This wasn't Mara's idea of fun. The trip would be worth it if they found Jallyn or learned more about the conflict between the Croags and the Worts. The only thing that bothered her was Fromoth Trun's reaction if they did learn the answers, but it was a waste of time to worry about that now. Being careful of her footing was more important.

She admired the ease with which Deke made his way through the dense foliage, as though he'd grown up in this type of environment instead of on a watery world. He hacked away with a machete, marking their route should they need to make a hasty retreat. Sweat poured down his face but he wasn't short of breath. His muscles must be accustomed to the exertion.

Thank the stars he'd ordered her and Hedy to work out in the physio lab. They'd never have been able to keep the pace if it weren't for those fitness sessions. The memory of her initial rebellion arose to bring an embarrassed flush to her face. Deke had been right again, she admitted. She was beginning to realize his counsel was wise on many subjects.

They spent part of the night in the shelter of their tents, but none of them slept much. The raucous cries of birds of prey and howls of wild animals kept them awake. Rising before dawn, Deke ordered them to move out by the light of their flame torches.

When not mired in muck, they watched their path for fallen tree branches and other debris. Slime warned them not to go near the huge brown blobs attached to nearby trunks. Swarms of biting insects lived inside and they wouldn't want to disturb the nests.

"We're getting near Wort territory," he announced on the third day.

Mara breathed a sigh of relief. Exhausted and hungry, she longed for the comforts of her air-filtered office on Bimordus Two. At least Hedy seemed to be holding up well. Her friend actually appeared to be enjoying the trip, but maybe that was because Wren was so solicitous to her comfort. In contrast, Deke was trying his best to ignore Mara, assisting her only when they had to cross a particularly hazardous stretch of land.

"That's odd," Slime said, abruptly coming to a halt.

She bumped into Deke ahead of her, then leapt back. "What is it?" she asked, hearing nothing except the hum of insects.

Slime pointed to the ground. "See those markings? It means dangerous bogs are up ahead. This isn't how I remember the trail. Somebody has changed it."

She frowned. "I don't understand."

Slime peered at her. "I'd planned to take you as far as the river but now that won't be possible. We'd have to cross into Wort territory by land, and it isn't safe. The brown skins use poison darts on strangers if you arrive unannounced. I'm done here."

"Now wait a minute," Deke said, holding up his hand. "We hired you to take us all the way."

"You follow this other path, and you'll get there. *Rogi Kwantro,* humans. You're on your own." He turned and loped away, disappearing back the way they'd come.

A whooshing noise from behind made Mara utter a cry of alarm. She spun around and realized it was Wren flapping his wings.

"Whew!" Wren said. "I thought I'd never get the chance to stretch."

"Stars, Wren," Hedy squealed. "You have to stop tempting

me that way." She observed him with an enthralled look on her face.

Deke rolled his eyes in Mara's direction and she grinned back.

"Should we make camp here for the night?" she suggested. "I'm tired. We could all use a rest."

He rubbed his unshaven jaw. "I'd like to reach the Wort village before it gets too late. Let's take a brief break, then continue on."

After a snack, they lifted their packs and trudged off down the alternate trail Slime had pointed out. A short distance later, Mara began to feel uneasy.

"You don't suppose there's another reason why Slime didn't want to go along with us, do you?" she asked Deke, who'd taken the lead.

The wild cries surrounding them seemed to have gotten louder and rustling noises brought shivers to her spine. Was it her imagination or were they being watched?

Deke stopped in his tracks. "Slime was telling us stories," he reassured them, picking a worm off his pants leg as easily as if it had been a speck of dust. "I don't believe the Worts would cause harm to random visitors. Do you?"

Before she could voice her opinion, the ground opened up beneath their feet and swallowed them whole.

****

A musty odor invaded Mara's awareness as consciousness returned along with her full senses. She blinked open her eyes, warily surveying her surroundings.

Deke was out cold beside her. They lay on a bed of reeds on a wooden floor in some sort of hut. Daylight streamed in through an open doorway, beyond which she could make out the shapes of tall leafy trees. Hedy and Wren were sprawled in another corner.

Daylight? They'd been unconscious all night?

She tested her limbs, grateful to note a lack of injuries from their fall. The pit hadn't been very deep, but as soon as they'd landed, a pungent-smelling vapor had overwhelmed them.

Concerned about Deke, she checked the pulse at his throat. It felt strong and regular. Her gaze swept across his face to where a lock of hair had fallen across his forehead and she brushed it aside, letting her fingers linger on his skin. His lashes were thick and silken. Sparing a glance at his slack jawline shadowed by dark stubble, she rested her gaze on his mouth. His lips were curved with a permanent upward tilt that appealed to her.

He stirred, and she moved away, afraid he'd discover her staring at him. Hoping to learn some answers, she crept toward the opening to peer outside.

By the Light! Their hut was set among the treetops far above the ground. Entwined in the rainforest canopy were dozens of structures like theirs with precarious ladder bridges swaying between the dwellings. Steamy humidity permeated the air.

She swatted at a hungry mosquito, dismayed to find several welts already on her neck and bare arms. The repellent she'd applied earlier must have worn off. She hoped Deke had brought an extra supply, but that was the least of their concerns. How were they to get down? Their hut didn't possess any ladders that she could see.

Trickles of perspiration ran down the sides of her face as she leaned over the platform's edge. She sucked in a breath as she spotted a brown-skinned Wort shimmy up a nearby tree, clinging to the bark with thick disks on his fingers and toes. How had she and the others been brought up here? And what did the Worts plan to do with them?

A squeaking sound drew her attention. Conveyances drawn by ropes and pulleys hauled goods to and from the structures and the ground. A few cottages stood at ground level, likely the cooking huts. Smoke rose from holes in their thatched roofs. A spicy aroma drifted her way, and she realized her stomach felt empty.

She could use a drink to quench her thirst and had to use the sanitary, but there weren't any facilities that she could see. Besides, how would they get down from there?

A loud groan pierced her ears and she swung around to see Deke sitting up and rubbing his forehead.

"I feel like I've been run over by a roadbuilder," he griped. "What is this place?"

His narrowed eyes scanned their surroundings as he rose unsteadily to his feet. The top of his head touched the ceiling and he grunted his displeasure. Wren and Hedy were just beginning to stir in their corner and he spared a glance in their direction.

"Careful," Mara cautioned them as they stood, teetering confusedly. "We don't know how sturdy these wood planks are."

Although the flooring seemed able to bear their weight, the Worts obviously were smaller than their burrow-dwelling cousins, the Croags. They certainly hadn't provided their human visitors with any familiar amenities.

"That gas must have really knocked us out. Did you just wake up?" Deke asked her. At her nod, he scratched his head. "We should have taken more precautions. If I'd—"

"Deke," she interrupted before he could continue, "we're here. Accept it."

"We're in a Wort village, I presume?" He stalked to the open platform outside and peered around. "How in Zor do we get down from here?"

She gestured in frustration. "We could shimmy down the tree like the natives," she joked.

To her surprise, Deke appeared to weigh the option seriously, but then his steady gaze caught hers. "We need to speak to the Worts."

Hedy moved to join them. "You may not have noticed, but our equipment is gone."

Deke patted his pockets. "So are my datalink and my weapons."

It appeared the Worts had been thorough in their search. None of their knapsacks were evident in the hut.

"I need to stretch my wings," Wren said, pacing back and forth, the top of his head brushing against the ceiling. "There's not enough room in here."

"And I need to use the sanitary," Mara confessed. "What are we going to do? We can't wait hauras until they decide to talk to us."

"I don't think we'll have to," Deke said, pointing.

A lanky Wort swung through the open doorway on a vine and plunked himself down on the reed-strewn floor.

Chapter Sixteen

"Rogi Kwantro," the brown-skinned male said, pounding his fist on his chest and bowing. A woven tunic and shorts covered his athletic body. "I am Onus Hahn, a member of the village council."

Mara was surprised he spoke in standard Jawani. Following Deke's example, she extended a similar greeting.

"Why have we been brought here in such a disagreeable manner?" she asked, her tone imperious to cover her unease.

She'd noted the pistol strapped to the Wort's belt. At least the fellow exuded less of a fishy odor than his city-dwelling cousins. She supposed living so far from the sea might prove the discriminating factor in that regard, or else their diet made the difference. They might eat more fruits and nuts while the Croags consumed more seafood.

Onus Hahn's keen tawny eyes regarded her. "You are the spokesperson for your group?"

She deferred to Deke. "Commander Sage is in charge of our expedition," she said. "I'm Mara Hendricks, a cultural specialist in interstellar relations. Dr. Te'larr is our medic and Lieutenant Wren is… an administrative aide."

She didn't want to name him as the ship's navigator. It might not be wise to imply they had a starship hovering in orbit. If the Worts thought they were siding with the Croags, then revealing an armed presence could work against them. It was bad enough that Deke and Wren had been caught bearing arms, although trekking through the jungle presented its own hazards.

The tawny eyes glanced in Deke's direction, giving him a

cursory appraisal. Mara tried to get a sensory reading but couldn't pick up any vibes, and the Wort's impassive expression told her nothing.

"For what reason do you intrude upon our land?" he asked, eyeing her attire.

Since she was dressed identically to her teammates, she wondered at his close perusal. Someone must have searched them while they were helpless. He must know she wasn't armed.

"We're here as official representatives of the Coalition government," Deke said. "It is imperative we discuss several issues important to us both. Our visit is friendly. There was no need for you to mishandle us."

"My apologies." The Wort bowed politely but his voice lacked any hint of regret. "We are not accustomed to having offworlders seek us out, and we must protect ourselves against… certain foes."

Mara wanted to question his statement, but her personal needs took precedence. "May we, um, have the use of your private facilities?" Flushing embarrassedly, she hoped he'd get the hint without further explanation.

"It's damned hot up here. Isn't there a place on the ground where we can talk?" Deke said.

She shot him a look of reproach. His attitude wouldn't help their cause. Smiling sweetly at Onus Hahn, she tried to ameliorate the effect of Deke's demanding tone.

"Commander Sage wishes to meet with your leaders."

The Wort narrowed his eyes. "We'll proceed to the Council Hall. I will summon our elders."

At the open doorway, he signaled for a conveyance slung on a rope. While helping them to step onto the platform, he darted his sticky pink tongue out to snare a gnat.

Once on the ground, Mara and the others followed Onus Hahn toward a rectangular wood building set on stilts in the center of the village. As they passed by various structures, the residents turned their heads in surprise. She was stunned that many of them bore arms, males and females alike. Were they engaged in warfare, and if so, with whom? Or was it mere precaution from the wild beasts that roamed the jungle?

Hedy poked her on the arm. "Mara, their features are similar to the terrorists who fired upon me and Wren in town."

Her eyes widened. She'd almost forgotten the incident in her eagerness to speak to the Worts about Yanuran politics. They could be among the very band of ruffians who'd tried to kill Hedy and Wren. It certainly would account for their weapons if the Worts were waging their own brand of terrorism against the Croags. And if that were the case, how would they regard a group of Coalition representatives?

Onus Hahn led them inside the building. A circular conference table took up the center space. "Sanitary facilities are in the rear behind that partition. Make yourselves comfortable while I round up the others and arrange for refreshments."

While he was gone, they held a hushed conference.

"I don't trust them," Deke said, his expression grim. "This is the same region where Larikk disappeared. You can see they don't take kindly to strangers. Be on the alert and watch for a means to escape."

"The Worts were the ones who attacked us in town," Hedy told him. "What will they do with us now?"

Mara gave her a sympathetic glance. Her friend appeared wilted, drained of her usual energy. She must be feeling the result of the heat and anxiety.

"We should ask these people about that attack ourselves. Maybe it's a different faction that's involved."

"Another thing," Wren cut in. They whipped their heads in his direction. Usually he preferred to listen silently, speaking only when he had something important to say. "Did you notice how there were no youngsters in this village?"

Mara gasped. "You're right! How very odd." An image of Jallyn came to mind, bringing with it the harsh reality of their situation. "By the Light, do you think they know where Jallyn is being held?"

"You can ask them," Deke suggested in a sardonic tone. "You're so willing to believe in the goodness of people's souls. See how much they're willing to admit."

Challenged, she glared back. "And you're too eager to mistrust them. Try having an open mind, Commander. You might be able to deal with them more effectively if every word out of your mouth isn't laden with hostility."

"Let's try to get our bags returned," Hedy urged. "I'd like my medical equipment back." She took Mara's arm. "Come, you said you needed to use the sanitary. I'll go with you."

Inside the facility, Mara finished her business, then turned to Hedy after they both washed their hands. "He's as pigheaded as ever," she announced, twisting her long hair into a braid.

"Who is?" Hedy's green eyes regarded her innocently although a small smile played across her mouth. Tugging her outfit into place, she smoothed it over her hips.

"Deke suspects these people of all sorts of dire doings."

Hedy snorted. "And you don't? Sweetheart, do you need an awakening? I hate to admit it, but I agree with your lover boy."

Her cheeks heated at the term. "We haven't even spoken to their council yet. These Worts may know nothing about Jallyn or Larikk or who attacked you and Wren the other day."

"Are you calling Fromoth Trun a liar? Because if you believe the Worts are innocent, then you're saying the Yanuran leader has been telling fibs."

She planted her hands on her hips. "I'm not saying they're innocent. Gods, you're just as blind as Deke. All I want is for both sides to get a fair evaluation."

Hedy gave a long sigh. "I swear, Mara, someday you'll wear me thin. You're obsessed with fairness because you were never treated that way. Deke is willing to listen to them. He's going into this with his eyes open, that's all."

"No, he's not. He views the Worts as hostiles."

"I can understand why. Didn't you see the weapons they're carrying? And their manner of greeting visitors isn't exactly courteous." Hedy began walking out.

"Wait," she called, stricken that she might have offended her friend. "All right, I admit Deke is right to be wary. Is that what you want me to say?"

"No," Hedy said, turning to regard her. "I just want you to be prepared."

Be prepared. Those were Deke's words. And hadn't he been right before?

Maybe she should listen to his advice. Being too trusting was one of her faults, as he'd so readily pointed out to her. It wasn't always appropriate to give the other person the benefit of the doubt, especially when they were at a disadvantage.

Her senses alert, she strode into the meeting hall to take her seat next to Deke at the round table. Hedy joined Wren next to them. A trio of Wort females entered and placed a selection of fruits and nuts and a pitcher of drinking water with crude cups in front of them.

Mara drank greedily. She felt better after using the sanitary and splashing cold water on her face, but her treksuit stuck to her body in the humidity. The hall was open to the air, and a slight breeze blew through but it didn't cool her skin.

This is why I never cared for the tropics. She wasn't fond of heat, humidity, and bugs. She much preferred the temperate zone of her home on Tyberia, where the nights were cool and even in summer the temperatures never soared to sweat levels.

She was surprised when Deke reached over to squeeze one of her hands. A flash of tenderness on his face was quickly hidden as Onus Hahn strode inside accompanied by four other male brown-skins.

The females who'd served them took places around the table, causing her to raise her eyebrows. Gender equality seemed to be the norm everywhere on Yanura, a practice she wished other worlds would emulate.

Deke withdrew his hand from hers but then rested it on her thigh under the table where no one could see. She wondered if he sought reassurance by touching her, or if he was attempting to provide her with courage. Either way, the contact warmed her heart and made her soul yearn to break free and merge with his. It was all she could do to sit still and act composed with the Worts staring at them.

Onus Hahn began cleaning his teeth with a splinter of wood. "Explain your purpose in coming here," he ordered, directing his statement at her.

Deke responded before she could get in a word. "Fromoth Trun seeks membership in the Coalition of Sentient Planets. As planetary potentate, he represents the central authority. How much of a voice do your people have in the government?"

One of the elder females replied. "I am Onus Laang and I sit on the Wort Elective Caucus, which is our main governing body. We agree with the Croags in our form of government."

From the corner of her eye, Mara saw one of the younger females nervously drum her fingers on the table. She was fairly attractive, with large brown eyes and an upcurved mouth. Her dress was a pretty shade of rose enhanced by a white apron. For a moment it looked as though she would say something, but then her expression clouded and the moment was lost.

"How do your people feel about membership in the Coalition?" Mara asked, staring at the female. The Wort averted her eyes, focusing her gaze on the table.

"As a group, we have no objections to joining the Coalition as long as our privacy is respected," said one of the elder male members. "Our territorial integrity must be honored. The Croags seek to push us from our land by cutting down our trees."

"Fromoth Trun says the opposite," Deke countered, leaning forward. "He claims you're destroying their burrows by extending tree roots into the underground network."

Onus Hahn's face mottled as he cut into the conversation. "Not so! We can show you proof of the damage his people are causing our habitats."

"Fromoth Trun says a satellite survey would settle the boundary dispute."

The Worts cast surreptitious glances amongst themselves. "That is so," agreed Onus Laang. "If Coalition membership is granted, our dispute would be solved. We can arrange for a comm-link, Commander, should you wish to contact Bimordus Two."

"I'd like my own datalink returned, thank you, and our other equipment."

"Of course." Nodding to the younger Wort, Onus Laang gave Deke a sly smile. "My apologies for the inconvenience. Since you came from Croag territory, we couldn't be sure of your loyalties. Your items will be returned at once."

Deke tightened his mouth, and from the pressure of his hand on her thigh, Mara could tell he wasn't satisfied with the flimsy excuse for their reception. Thankfully he let it go, changing the subject with his next statement.

"Fromoth Trun offered the drug Vyclor as an economic incentive so Yanura can be granted special trade status," Deke said, his mild tone disguising the tension radiating from his body.

"That's a generous offer," Onus Laang crooned, "Otherwise, we'd have to wait the standard probationary period before being granted trading privileges. We cannot afford the time. As Fromoth Trun says, the satellite survey is the definitive means to achieving peace."

Onus Hahn leaned forward, folding his webbed hands on the table. "Shall I show you where his people have destroyed our forest? The plant and animal life dependent upon the tall trees have perished in that area. It will be the fate of our entire habitat unless the Croags are stopped. They will only listen when the Coalition shares its advanced survey techniques."

"The Coalition will not grant approval when I tell them how our team was attacked by terrorists in Revitt Lake City," Deke countered. "Fromoth Trun claims your people were responsible. He says you wage a terrorist war in order to be granted extra land."

Onus Laang's eyes narrowed. "We are a nonviolent people. I know nothing of this attack. Fromoth Trun lies! He must have staged the act himself to prejudice you against us."

"Maybe there are those among you who take it upon themselves to—"

"My people would never resort to terrorist tactics." Her skin mottled. "It is not of us that he speaks. It is the—"

"*Golongus!*" called Onus Hahn in his native tongue.

Onus Laang's lips compressed. "Forgive me, Commander. I get upset over the situation."

The young female Wort returned with their supplies, interrupting the conversation. After piling the knapsacks in a corner, she resumed her seat and sat quietly, her eyes averted from Mara's probing stare.

Wren coughed, adjusting his position. He looked fidgety and uncomfortable, and Mara wondered if he'd had a chance to spread his wings while she and Hedy were in the sanitary.

"What about your friend?" Wren asked Deke, giving him a pointed stare.

Deke nodded. "Larikk, a colleague of mine, vanished in the Alterland three annums ago. Have you any information about him that you can share?"

"An inquiry has already been completed," Onus Hahn snapped. "His death was ruled an accidental drowning."

"Did it occur near here?"

The Wort shrugged. "I am not familiar with the details."

Mara sensed prevarication, but then Hedy cut in, disrupting her train of thought.

"Where are the children?" the medic asked, her tone meek.

Mara suppressed a smile. Medicine was Hedy's forte, not matters of state. She had to be feeling disoriented by this entire situation, but at least Wren offered her some consolation.

"Pardon?" Onus Hahn said, his expression bewildered.

"The youngsters. How come we see only adults? Where do you house the children?" Mara clarified.

The young female Wort gave a choking sputter, abruptly cut off by a stern glance from Onus Laang.

The elder council member beamed widely, her smile expansive. "They live in separate dwellings."

"May we visit them?" she asked, wishing to confirm that statement.

"I'm afraid not. We don't want them exposed to outsiders. The contamination would dilute our culture."

She got a distinct sense that Onus Laang was lying and wondered how much of the truth about anything had been spoken in this room. The young female exchanged a quick glance with her, then lowered her eyes. Mara got the impression she'd speak in private if given the chance, but how to arrange it?

"What is your name?" she asked in a kindly tone.

"I am called Onus Laola, mistress." She darted a nervous glance at Onus Laang. "I am honored to be the newest council member, but I have much to learn."

"Thank you for fetching our belongings."

"I regret the necessity of taking them from you. It was our intention—"

"That's enough," Onus Hahn interrupted. "Would you care to see where our trees have been cut down by the Croags?" He addressed his offer to Deke. "Once you see the destruction, you'll agree it is imperative to relay approval of our admission status to your superiors."

Mara felt suspicious of his insistence. He sounded like a parrot of Fromoth Trun. Both of them blamed each other for the border dispute but felt admittance into the Coalition would solve their problems. Or would it? What if they wanted to be granted special trade status for some other reason? What could they possibly hope to gain?

They'd reap huge profits from putting Vyclor on the market, she reminded herself. But how would they use the credits gained? Would they purchase something that wasn't accessible through other means?

Accompanied by the village leader and a squad of armed males, she and the others were taken via winged pod to a sector where whole tracts of trees had been ravaged, leaving nothing but loose soil easily dislodged by a strong wind. The devastation sickened her.

"How could anyone do this?" she cried. "Even if these trees weren't your home, it's a massive rape of the land, not to mention the wildlife that would have lived in those trees."

"Talk to Fromoth Trun," Onus Hahn urged. "The Croags use wood from our trees to make their furniture, which is widely prized throughout the land, but they destroy our environment in the process. Ask him why he's engaged in a purposeful annihilation of our homes. Now will you contact your government and recommend approval of our application? Use of the Coalition's resources is the only way we'll stop this destruction."

Deke's face darkened, and she feared he was going to blurt out something offensive.

"Is there a direct route to Revitt Lake City from here?" she asked hastily.

"Let's return to the village and we'll discuss it."

She felt discomfited by the watchful stance of the armed guards who'd accompanied them. The escort reminded her of the security detachment Fromoth Trun had provided, and that in turn brought to mind a subject that troubled her.

"If your people were not responsible for the terrorist attack on Hedy and Wren, then who was?" she asked, breathing in the dank air. She felt wilted from the heat and humidity and longed for air-conditioned comfort. Truly, she preferred her role in the city to field work, although she'd never pass up the chance to learn personally about a new culture.

Onus Hahn's skin darkened, emphasizing the ugly raised bumps that dotted his arms. "I wouldn't know, mistress. But let us not waste any more time here." His gaze darted about nervously as though expecting those same terrorists to pop out of the ground. "We'll be more comfortable continuing our discussion in the council hall."

Deke gave her a questioning glance. She gave a brief nod, indicating they should comply. Perhaps she'd find the opportunity to talk to Onus Laola.

"Can we stay in your village for a few more days?" she asked. "We'd love to learn more about your people."

"We'd be honored," Onus Hahn replied, although his reluctant tone said otherwise.

Their guest quarters were much more luxurious than the hut in which they first awoke. Two bungalows high in the treetops were accessible by a rope-and-pulley conveyance. The two lodgings were linked by a short log bridge. Twin beds that could be pushed together to form a wide lounger or separated to serve as couches made up the interior along with a wood bureau, a small table, and chairs. Oil lanterns were provided for later when it got dark.

Onus Hahn showed them how to use the conveyance and pointed out the closest sanitary on the ground below. Running water was available from a spigot in a corner connected to a pipe leading outside to a central storage tank.

"Our lifestyle is simple but it suits our preferences," he explained. "We work during the late afternoon and evening hauras when the sunlight wans and the moons rise. Our rest time is between midnight and noon. While you're here, I'll make sure flame torches are lit after dark. I hope you'll join us tonight for our main meal. In the meantime, if you need anything, blow this horn." He indicated a tubular object by the open-air entrance. "I'll also have netting brought over to screen your openings." His tongue darted out to catch a fly as he made his departure.

"Yuck," Hedy said as soon as he'd left. "I can just imagine what creepy crawlies they'll give us to eat."

"If there's a pond nearby, maybe they'll have freshwater snipes on the menu," Deke said with a teasing grin.

Mara's stomach contracted. "Hopefully, they'll have fruits and nuts like they gave us earlier."

Wren searched through their bags. "Our weapons are missing, Commander."

Deke frowned. "I'm not surprised. Something strikes me as very odd about this place."

"Me too," Mara agreed. "They're awfully insistent on Coalition approval, same as Fromoth Trun." She loosened her braid, finger combing her hair. Deke's gaze followed her movements, and she itched to feel his fingers on her scalp.

Hedy's gaze rested upon them. "Wren, let's go to our place," she said, indicating he should grab his equipment and follow her to the other hut.

"Huh?" Mara and the men responded in unison.

Hedy squeezed the Polluxite's arm. "We have things to discuss," she said, signaling him with her eyes. "Mara, you don't mind if we aren't roommates this time, do you?"

"Um, I guess not."

Wren glanced from Hedy to Deke and Mara and his visage reddened. "Yes, doctor, you are right. We have things to discuss." As an afterthought, he raised a layered eyebrow at Deke. "With your permission, sir?"

Deke's mouth twisted wryly. "Go ahead, enjoy yourselves."

Mara's jaw dropped. She hadn't expected him to approve. She watched with dismay as Hedy and Wren tramped across the short bridge and disappeared into the open doorway beyond.

"Why did you agree?" she asked, seeking clarification.

"Why shouldn't I?" Deke busied himself unpacking his supplies. His broad back stretched taut the material of his treksuit.

Moistening her lips, which had suddenly gone dry, she said: "I thought you preferred to avoid my company."

He straightened, giving a resigned sigh. "I can no more avoid you than I can avoid thinking. I'm just confused, Mara. You invade my mind even when you're not there, if you get the gist of my meaning."

His eyes burned into her and she looked away, discomfited by his close scrutiny. "I've been trying not to push you."

"But I still feel the pressure. What if we let things go along? What then?"

Now she was confused. "I don't understand."

"Would you go back to Eranus with me?"

Hope flared within her. "Is that an invitation?"

"It's a matter of curiosity. If we decided to stay together, what were your plans?"

Deflated by his impersonal attitude, she mumbled her reply. "I hadn't thought that far ahead."

"Are you telling me that for all your claims that we're meant to be together, you've never considered what it means?"

She shrugged helplessly. "I never really thought that you would—"

"What?"

"Accept me," she finished lamely, her head lowered.

For a long moment he didn't answer; then he strode over and rested his hands on her shoulders. "Mara, look at me."

She lifted her face to gaze into his soul-searing brown eyes.

"If we were a normal couple, I'd take you home in an instant. But it's more than that. You have a power that goes beyond my comprehension. When I'm with you, I lose my sense of self."

"But I don't intend for you to lose anything. The two of us can be stronger together. You don't have to be alone anymore."

"I'm used to being alone and to having my thoughts to myself. I don't like someone else being in my head."

"I can't read your mind," she reminded him gently.

"No, but you're aware of what I'm feeling." His hand reached up to smooth her hair. "It's hard to resist when I'm with you. I don't mind the enhancement during sex, but—"

She pulled away. "That's not fair! You can't use me to heighten your pleasure and then cast me off."

He stepped closer, his eyes luminous with desire. "You can't deny that you like it, too."

"Maybe so, but I want more than that."

"I can't give you more."

"Can't, or won't?"

Drawing her into his arms, he buried his face in her hair. "I really don't know what I want."

The moment was broken by the arrival of their mosquito netting, which made an effective privacy screen on the casements and entrance. When left alone again, Mara turned to Deke, who was testing the mattress on one of the beds.

"I didn't bring anything to change into other than a clean treksuit," she said.

Deke grinned. "That's all right. You don't have to wear anything to bed." His expression sobered. "I won't take advantage of you. It's your choice, Mara. You know my limits."

He'd certainly made them clear. He was still willing to have sex with her but nothing more. Depressed, she picked up her knapsack and fumbled through the contents.

"Look, I'm sorry," he said, his voice earnest. "You're right, I'm not playing fair. I really don't understand what you want from me. What's in this for you?"

She gave a wan smile. "It's not a matter of gain. I can't help the way I feel."

How could she explain the yearning to be as close to him as possible on all levels of their existence? Her need went beyond the physical realm.

Deke dashed a hand through his ruffled hair. "Gods, you drive me crazy. What am I going to do with you?" As soon as the words left his mouth, the idea of what he'd like to do showed in the fevered gleam in his eyes. "Hedy and Wren had the right idea," he said, rising and sauntering towards her.

"Now just a minute. You said you wouldn't take advantage of me." But even as she protested, her blood heated and her senses whirled dizzily.

"Did I tell you how much I love your hair?" He halted in front of her and grasped a few strands in his hand. "It feels like silk." He took some in his other hand and brought it forward, letting her hair flow over the rise of her breasts.

Her pulse quickened as he stared at her chest. His nearness weakened her knees and sent a flood of desire coursing through her.

As though he sensed her reaction, a slow smile curved his mouth. "You want this as much as I do, don't you?"

When his heavy-lidded gaze met hers, her resistance melted. "Yes," she said, barely recognizing the husky tone as her own. The temptation to join with him was too strong. If he would accept her this way, so be it.

She lifted her face. "Kiss me," she demanded.

He took her mouth eagerly, plundering her sweetness without any trace of gentleness. She felt his hunger for her even as she parted her lips to receive his tongue. Their kiss mingled until they became one, writhing against each other.

Deke edged her toward one of the beds. They fell upon it with their limbs entangled, mouth to mouth, unable to separate either physically or spiritually. Mara reveled in the feel of his hard body against hers but it wasn't enough. She craved contact with his naked flesh.

It took them a moment to shed their clothes and then they were back, entwined on the firm mattress, their mouths clamped together. Deke's hands roamed her body and she moaned from the sheer pleasure of it. Everywhere he touched, her senses flared and ripples of ecstasy radiated through her.

She gripped his back, clutching at it, relishing the hard strength of his muscles as he moved against her. Her breasts pressed flat against his hairy chest and the feel of him aroused her even more. Grinding against him, she felt his engorged organ prod her thighs. She parted her legs, wanting him at once and yet wishing this would never end.

Her eyes closed, she concentrated on the sensations of his mouth on hers, his tongue exploring her depths. Merged with his psyche, she felt his pleasure from the contact between them, and his wish to prolong their delight as long as possible.

With an iron will, he restrained his powerful urge to thrust into her. Knowing that he wanted her to be satisfied hurtled her further into the inferno of desire.

His hands found her breasts and she gasped with delight as he teased her nipples into taut, aching peaks. That he knew what to do to please her because he could feel her reactions increased her desire. She arched her back, thrusting her breasts more completely into his practiced hands. A sound of pleasure escaped her lips as he gently massaged her, his thumbs stroking her nipples. Tingling sensations shot through her.

He shifted his position, moving his mouth to her nipple, suckling it with his swirling tongue. Her head lolled back and she spread her legs, so intense was the ache between them.

Deke's hand found her secret folds of flesh and obliged her need, his circular strokes sending her into a spiral of lust.

She reached for his shaft, gratified to hear his sharp intake of breath. It was amazing how incredible it felt from his viewpoint, the pressure of her hand on his swollen tip. She caressed the petal-soft skin and didn't stop when his head raised and he gazed at her with passion-filled eyes.

"I don't ever want this to end," he rasped.

"Me, neither."

She raised herself over him, the temptation to take him too strong. She lowered herself onto his stiff member, smiling when his head fell back and he moaned with pleasure. She slid down the full length of him, reveling in the fullness of their union.

"By the stars, I've never felt such wonder," he said, his voice barely above a whisper.

She felt his intense need for gratification and began moving her hips, tantalizingly slow at first, then spiraling to a speed she couldn't control. Her own lust took hold of her and propelled her into a pool of hot, molten desire. It rushed her down a river of passion until her body jerked in a climactic splash of ecstasy. Deke joined her climax, his spasms mixed with hers in her mind.

When done, she rolled off him and sprawled on the narrow bed at his side. Her mind took longer to separate. Contentment snared both of them, the web of their desire loosened but not abated.

His hand grasped hers. "Gods, Mara, I don't want to let go of you," he murmured.

"It feels right, doesn't it?" Her voice trembled with emotion.

His eyes closed, he admitted his affirmation silently, and she picked up on it in his mind.

"Then why do you resist our being together?" she whispered.

"Because I'd be tempted to stay in this village. You and me… in our own hut. Why should we leave?" His lids flew open and he thrust her from his psyche. "I resist because this is the result. You make me lose focus. Have you forgotten about Jallyn and why else we're here?"

She sat and reached for her clothing. "Of course not. But there's no harm in us taking momentary pleasure in each other. You said yourself we could enjoy sex if nothing more."

He slid off the bed and stood. "I'm not sure I still feel that way. You've taken over my thoughts. I want you even when we're not in the same room together. I can't function when I'm so distracted."

"Our merging would strengthen us if you'd accept it."

Even as she spoke, her heart sank. In the throes of passion, Deke wanted her. He shared in the pleasure of their joined souls when they made love. But when reality intervened, he cast her aside like a pariah.

"I've got work to do," he said, his cold tone cutting her as sharp as any knife. "But let me set things straight. I do care for you, but I need more time. I'm not sure—"

"No, you're not sure of anything, including how you feel about yourself. As for me, I know when I'm not wanted."

She yanked her clothes on and had just finished fastening her treksuit when someone lifted a corner of their netting and tossed an object inside the hut.

Chapter Seventeen

Deke's purposeful stride took him to the fallen object by the door. "It's a rock with a note tied around it," he said, untying the piece of paper.

"What does it say?" Mara asked.

He frowned as his eyes scanned the message. "Take a look for yourself."

She grabbed the note from his outstretched palm. The words, scrawled by hand, jumped out at her: *Go home! You bring danger here.*

"What does this mean?" She gazed at Deke, alarmed by the warning. "Are we in danger, or does it mean trouble will follow us to the village?"

"I don't know, but we'll find out." He dressed hastily and took the note from her, tucking it into his treksuit pocket.

She stopped him with a hand on his arm. "Wait; it might be better if we pretend we never got this message. I'd like to explore the village, and if we proceed normally, we might find someone willing to talk to us." The councilwoman came to mind who seemed to have something to say. "Aren't you curious as to why everyone we've seen carries a weapon?"

For a long moment, Deke stared at her. "You're right. It reminds me of Fromoth Trun's security detail. You'd think these people were expecting an attack."

"Onus Hahn said the Worts were not responsible for the terrorist incident that nearly killed Hedy and Wren," she reminded him. "If these people were not involved, who else is behind these assaults?"

"We're not going to find any answers by hanging around here. Let's get Hedy and Wren and move out."

****

Hedy and Wren seemed glad for the excuse to leave their hut. From the flustered look on the Polluxite's face, Mara surmised Hedy must have been giving Wren a hard time. She and her friend fell behind the men as they descended via the rickety rope-and-pulley contraption to the ground.

While most of the Worts maintained living quarters in the trees, their workplaces were located at ground level. Mara spied an older female painting flowers on an intricately designed porcelain basket. She hastened over to inspect the wares. The people had come out to work during the late afternoon hauras when meager sunlight filtered through the leaves.

"These are lovely." She ran her fingertips along the curved rim of a vase displayed on a shelf. The statuettes, vases, pitchers, and other items consisted of a creamy translucent material. "I do sculpture work myself and I've never seen a base like this before. How do you get the iridescent tint and smooth texture?"

The Wort's face crinkled with pleasure. "The white clay comes from the Lorn province to the north. I use a special process to create this result."

"I'm impressed." With a series of well-placed questions, Mara encouraged the crafter to describe the skills of her friends. Rope making, basket weaving, and making kalucha nut jewelry were popular pastimes. As for industries, collecting gold lace and researching natural resources for the large pharmaceutical concerns were their main occupations.

"Gold lace?" Mara queried, scratching an itch on her neck. "What's that?"

"It's a filament secreted by the walloie larvae. Harvesting it is a delicate business. We have to be careful not to harm the organism. Our trained guild members work the filament into lace."

"So your businesses are organized into guilds?"

"Aye, mistress. The master guilder serves as chief. Below him are journeymen such as myself. We train through an apprentice system."

Mara was familiar with other cultures that used similar practices. Still intrigued by the beautiful porcelain objects, she asked the woman about the glazing process.

Across the square, Deke observed her conversing with the Wort female, He admired how easily she got along with people. Charming the artisan seemed as commonplace to her as steering Fromoth Trun's flattery into meaningful dialogue.

Whether she spoke with a planetary leader or an ordinary citizen, Mara's skills served her well in conducting interviews. Not only did she assist him by acting as his interpreter, but she complemented him by taking the edge off his bluntness with her diplomatic aplomb. Sometimes he lost patience with people like Fromoth Trun, and Mara was handy to have around in those instances. She reminded him to exercise tolerance, as she would fondly say.

Like a ship on a stormy sea, her calm serenity offered a refuge. The temptation to seek harbor with her lingered in his consciousness, drawing him toward her like a diver in a whirlpool. The only thing that kept him from being sucked under was his fear that he wouldn't be able to surface. Yet beneath the depths awaited a sea of contentment such as he'd never known and wouldn't ever discover with another woman.

Her arms moved in graceful arcs as she spoke to the craftswoman. Seeing her so animated brought to mind her talent as a dancer and skill as a sculptress. Her varied interests and quick wit guaranteed she'd keep any man on his toes.

"Commander!" Onus Laola's voice startled him out of his thoughts.

Deke whipped around and spied the young female council member hurrying toward him. Garbed in a bright yellow dress, her head was devoid of the fancy bonnet preferred by her city-dwelling cousins.

"Rogi Kwantro," she greeted him with a slight bow. "If you and your friends will follow me, you can join us for our evening meal."

****

"The pottery lady was telling me how she creates her beautiful pieces," Mara said to Onus Laola as they strolled ahead of the others. "She received her training from the master sculptor beginning at age fifteen. Is that the norm for learning a craft?"

"Yes, there's a set apprenticeship followed by a certification exam."

Rounding a bend, Mara was delighted to come upon a communal dining hall in a hut apart from the council chamber where they'd met earlier. The large open-air structure set on stilts was situated next to the cooking hut.

At Onus Laola's direction, she and her friends climbed a short flight of steps to enter and sat themselves around one of several long rectangular tables provided with carved wooden chairs. Other Worts began filing in as a loud gong clanged to announce the dinner haura.

Onus Hahn, smiling broadly, introduced them as "Coalition visitors eager to learn about our culture."

Their attempts to ask pointed questions were skillfully parried, but she managed to coax Onus Hahn into discussing economics.

"We sell our gold lace, prized porcelain, and certain plant and animal products with medicinal properties to the Croags. In exchange, we buy sluer oil that fuels our generators. We don't use too many electrical devices, but we like our water purifiers, waste disposal system, and cleansing units."

"Why not use fabricators?" Deke asked. "Then you could make foods not available in this region."

Mara gave him a sideways glance. His hulking presence gave her a measure of security. An undercurrent of restraint came from the Worts and she sensed they were purposefully steering the conversation in a direction more to their liking.

"Fresh, natural foods are healthier than artificially synthesized molecules," Onus Hahn replied. "We believe if a society relies too heavily on technology, it loses sight of its origins."

"I disagree." Deke hunched forward. "On Eranus, we use the most advanced technological tools available, but our laws protect the environment. We value our resources and seek to preserve them."

"But your laws are not all-encompassing, are they, Commander?" Onus Laang said from across the table. Slurping from a bowl of conkfish soup, she eyed him warily. "Isn't it a point of contention that your automated kelp harvesters destroy the crop in the process of cutting the stipes? Weren't you involved in an effort to modify this practice?"

Deke stiffened. "How do you know about that?" He shook his head when offered a second helping of pureed nog fungus.

"We try to stay informed. An exchange of scientific data between our worlds would benefit us both."

From the way Deke's eyebrows arched, he knew they were baiting him. But for what purpose? Mara wondered.

Onus Laola commented from farther down the table. "We have other medicines besides Vyclor that your people would find helpful, plus by-products of our plants that are used in commercial applications. Pharmaceutical research is our main industry, and we've made many discoveries."

Wren cleared his throat loudly. Having been engaged in conversation with a hefty male Wort at his side, he'd broken off his dialogue to listen to their debate. Hedy was being unusually quiet and Mara had the feeling she was deliberating how to get Wren into her bed when they were alone again.

Deke hadn't missed Wren's signal. "Speaking of pharmaceutical research," he said, "what happened to my friend Larikk?"

"An unfortunate accident," Onus Hahn replied, dropping a live slug into his mouth. "He was last seen heading in the direction of Dead Wort's Marsh."

"Where is that?"

Onus Hahn waved a dismissive webbed hand in the air. "It's a dangerous place with deadly bogs and hungry predators. We warned him not to go, but he ignored our words of caution. When a search party was sent to track his movements after he failed to report in, they found his notebook by one of the ponds. We assumed he leaned over too far to collect a specimen and toppled in. The stinger eels would have taken care of him."

"Stinger eels?" Deke said harshly. The look on his face was one of skepticism, and Mara didn't blame him. Why were they being given this information now?

"The eels live in the ponds. Their sting paralyzes a victim. We figured your friend drowned."

"His body was never recovered," Deke pointed out.

Onus Hahn bent his head, a sorrowful look on his frog face. "Are you aware of what eels do, Commander? They'll enter your body through an orifice and consume you from the inside out. There wouldn't be any remains."

"What happened to his notebook?" Deke asked in a choked tone.

Horrified by the images the Yanuran's words provoked, Mara patted Deke's leg under the table to offer solace. She sensed how distraught he felt over the painful memories of his friend that were compounded by feelings of guilt. He considered himself responsible for Larikk's being there.

"His research notes were sent to Seabase Pharmaceutical's central office. He'd completed his work on the vaccine."

"Why wasn't I notified? And why are you telling me this now?"

Onus Hahn's tongue flicked out and caught a flying insect for his dessert. "The inquiry into Larikk's death was distressful to us. But I wish to demonstrate our good intentions, because we would benefit from Coalition technology as much as our Croag cousins. It would be unfortunate if a misunderstanding between our peoples colored your judgment. I'd be happy to set up a commlink so you can send an affirmative message to your superiors."

"I'll think about it," Deke replied.

Mara sensed his surge of anger and felt they'd learned as much as they could during this session. There were still too many unanswered questions before their final decision, such as how the Worts had access to information supposedly known only to the Croags.

According to Fromoth Trun, the two races rarely communicated with each other, yet some of Onus Hahn's phrases seemed a duplicate of the Yanuran leader's convincing arguments. She still felt they weren't being told everything.

"Let us head to the Ceremonial Circle," Onus Laang suggested, rising abruptly. Her movement signaled an end to the meal. "We have a special entertainment planned for you tonight."

Onus Hahn gave a loud croak, his version of a belch. He fell into step behind Deke and Mara as they descended the stairs outside the hut. As the oppressive humidity hit her full force, she felt as though she could have sliced the moist air with a knife.

The sun had descended but the temperature was still warm, bringing sweat to her brow. Sounds of the jungle intruded upon her consciousness. Whistles, howls, and whoops came from every direction, startling her so that she grabbed onto Deke's arm. Torches had been lit for their benefit, illuminating the paths around the village. Streaks of green light blinked in the darkness of the jungle beyond where the black shapes of trees loomed like eerie shadows.

They followed Onus Laang to a large clearing where a series of cut logs had been arranged in a broad circle. Hedy and Wren were close behind. They were holding hands, and Hedy had a satisfied expression on her face. Mara wondered what had occurred between them to erase her friend's glumness but she didn't ask.

Their friends took a perch on the opposite side of the circle from where she and Deke were seated. Onus Hahn flanked Deke while Onus Laang took her place at Mara's side.

"We celebrate the seasons in a series of ritual dances," Onus Laang said. "Our most talented performers have prepared a demonstration for you."

Mara clapped. "I love native dances. Maybe I can learn a few steps." The idea of dancing in the sticky humidity brought to mind her need for a shower.

"Excuse me," she said embarrassedly, leaning toward Onus Laang so no one else could hear, "but where do your people go to wash? I used the sanitary but didn't see any shower facilities."

Onus Laang gave a warbling shout of laughter. "Forgive me, mistress, but your ignorance of our ways is most entertaining. When we wish to bathe, we swim in one of our natural pools. The rainforest is abundant with ponds and streams fed from higher mountain areas."

"I didn't bring a swimsuit."

This statement brought forth another burst of uproarious laughter. Eyes turned in their direction and Mara felt Deke's questioning gaze boring into her.

"What's so funny?" she snapped.

Onus Laang smiled at her. "We have no need for such modesty. Our mating urge comes only once an annum, unlike you humans who are constantly influenced by your hormones." Her speculative glance flickered toward Deke. "If you like, I can have someone show you one of our bathing pools in the morning."

"Thanks, I would appreciate it."

A commotion from one of the nearby huts drew her attention and with relief she noticed a group of dancers emerge. They wore short-skirted tunic outfits with feathery trim.

Deke tapped her arm. "What was that all about?"

"I need to take a shower. A swim in the local pond seems to be the norm."

"Sounds good to me," he said with a wicked grin.

A staccato drumbeat reached her ears as a trio of Wort musicians struck up a tune. Shifting her attention to center stage, she was thrilled to count eight Worts in the dance troupe. They paired off into male-female combinations and gyrated to the blood-rushing beat of the music.

An elder Wort whom Mara hadn't met before sauntered up to her and Deke while they watched the performance. He offered them each a ceramic goblet.

"This heat must be making you thirsty," he said in a gravelly voice. "We have a special drink made from anquilla blossom nectar. Do you smell the flowers? Their petals open only at nightfall."

Mara had noticed the heavily perfumed air. During the day, a profusion of flowers was evident in the forest. Vibrant purple, white, bright red, and tangerine predominated. Many of the flowers grew as epiphytes, plants that depended upon other plants for their foundation. They could be found at all levels among the treetops.

She'd been too preoccupied before to enjoy the beauty around her but after a few sips of the sweet fruity drink, her senses heightened. Sounds of rushing water came from a distance and strands of bamboo creaked in the intervals between musical numbers. She expanded her awareness to the surrounding jungle until she felt at one with nature. It was a harmonious feeling that made her regret not having meditated more on this trip.

"Mara, are you all right?" Deke's sharp tone broke her reverie.

She smiled at him, feeling somewhat tipsy. "I'm fine."

The rhythmic drumbeat vibrated through her bones and stirred her senses. A peculiar lightness filled her limbs. In the center of the circle, the dancers whirled in a fast tempo, their feet prancing with lightning swiftness and their arms outstretched. Her pulse accelerated to match the drumbeat.

"Come on," she yelled to Deke, pulling him upright. "Let's join them."

The Worts croaked their approval as she dragged Deke into the center. Flickering shadows created by the torches cast a glow that excited her further. She looped her arm through Deke's in a manner that wouldn't allow him to escape and laughed when his awkward shuffle made him stumble over his own feet.

"You can do better than that," she admonished. "Remember our duets on the *Celeste*?"

His eyes smoldered at the memory as he caught her around the waist. "No one else was watching us then."

"So pretend we're alone." In a daring move, she shimmied against his body, pleased when his gaze dropped to the cleavage exposed through the unbuttoned top of her treksuit.

His lips tightened and his eyes glittered as he matched her movements with the grace of a panther.

"You're doing great," she told him, fluttering her eyelids as she'd observed Hedy do.

Thinking of Hedy, she wondered what she and Wren were up to. They sat on a log, leaning into each other with glazed looks on their faces. They both appeared in a daze, as though a light push would topple them over.

Deke grabbed her hand and twirled her around, spinning her senses so that she lost her ability to reason. His wild laugh made her giddy with delight. Around and around they spun, whirling to the insistent beat of the drum.

The rush of water in the background grew louder until it became a pulsating roar. It took a moment for her to realize it was the blood throbbing in her ears and not the noise of a distant waterfall. She didn't resist when Deke pulled her into his arms to plant a firm kiss on her mouth in front of everyone.

"I believe you have enjoyed enough of the dance." Onus Hahn tapped Deke on the shoulder. "Follow me, Commander. I know you wish to express your appreciation for our hospitality, and I have made arrangements for you to do so. Mistress, you may join your friends. They are retiring for the evening. You must be fatigued after such a long day."

Disengaging herself from Deke's side, she nodded numbly. She felt uncommonly tired and her head reeled dizzily.

"Go along," Deke said, the warmth of his voice penetrating her hazy mind.

As directed, she stumbled after Hedy and Wren, who were tottering arm-in-arm down the path toward their treehouse.

Deke turned to Onus Hahn, patiently waiting for his attention. "Where to?" he asked jauntily, vaguely aware of an odd ringing in his ears.

"This way." Onus Hahn led him through the flickering shadows of the village as the dancers and audience dispersed.

Leaves from the encroaching jungle brushed his face as they wound down a narrow path at the edge of the enclave. Strange birdcalls pierced the air, and the hoot of an owl provided a distinct background to the droning chorus of cicadas. He should be wondering where the Wort was taking him but didn't care.

Onus Hahn halted in front of a lone hut on stilts. "In here, Commander," he ordered, his tone bereft of its former friendliness.

Deke took a deep breath of the heavily scented air before climbing the short flight of steps into the interior. His eyes widened in surprise at the sophisticated communications array in front of him. A young Wort who was on duty leapt up at their entrance.

"We've set up a link to Bimordus Two," Onus Hahn said. "I thought you'd like to tell your superiors how cooperative we've been and how we support Fromoth Trun's application to join the Coalition." He handed Deke a microphone.

"Why, sure." Deke grabbed the device. His expansive mood made him want to share his joy, but he couldn't remember who to ask for at the other end. "Um, what do I say?"

"Ask for Deleth Goor on the Admissions Committee," Onus Hahn replied.

Deke's finger hesitated on the button that would transmit his voice message. "I don't know." He wavered, wanting to please his host, but a fraction of his mind told him to resist.

"*Nahmrabi!*" Onus Hahn muttered angrily in his native tongue. Stepping closer, he thumbed the control for Deke. "Speak, human."

Something snapped inside his head. "No, I won't." Deke cut the link and dropped the microphone on the counter.

Onus Hahn's eyes blazed. "I expected you to cooperate."

"Expected or planned?" A cloud seemed to lift from his mind, but he hadn't the strength to pursue his renewed clarity of thought. "I'm finished here. I'll rejoin my friends."

Turning on his heel, he strode toward the door and fumbled his way down the steps. Surprisingly, Onus Hahn didn't try to stop him. Wondering why he felt so strange, Deke wandered in the direction from which he'd thought they'd come.

It wasn't until he came to a guard post at an unfamiliar section that he realized he was lost. One of the guards obligingly led him to the guest hut and saw that he was safely ensconced inside.

Mara was fast asleep, sprawled across her cot. Deke didn't bother to check on Hedy or Wren. He collapsed onto his bed, falling into oblivion even before his head touched the pillow.

****

The softness of the pillow cradled Mara's head as she tossed restlessly in her sleep. Her dreams were nightmarish visions of Jallyn being guarded over by hostile Worts. They were dancing around her crib, their faces streaked with war paint, loud battle croaks warbling from their throats. And then she was dancing with Deke. They whirled round and round, laughing in each other's arms, oblivious to the Worts and to Jallyn's frenzied cries.

Jallyn! Mara bolted upright, her forehead beaded in sweat. Rays of sunlight pierced the interior of the hut. Bird songs filled the air from outside.

Deke was sprawled on his lounger lying on his back. She'd meant to wait up for him but drowsiness had overwhelmed her and she'd collapsed on her bed. She wondered what had transpired between him and Onus Hahn.

Not wishing to disturb him, she went to her knapsack and retrieved Jallyn's blanket. It was imperative to learn how the babe was faring when bad vibes from her dream lingered in her head.

Clutching the blanket in her hands, she sat on the edge of the lounger and closed her eyes. An image of Sarina popped unbidden into her mind. Before she could focus her thoughts, she was zooming through astral space and jumping into her friend's viewpoint.

The low lighting in Sarina's sleeping chamber meant it was night on Bimordus Two, but Sarina was awake, her eyes open. She rolled onto her side and bumped into Teir.

Mara withdrew her essence, not wishing to intrude on their privacy. Thank goodness Teir was home so Sarina didn't have to bear her burden alone anymore. She needed the closeness of family during this terrible crisis.

Heaving a sigh of relief, Mara concentrated on receiving vibrations from the baby's blanket. The infant's frequency attuned to her higher consciousness, drawing her in until they merged.

"How much longer do you intend to let this farce continue?" said a gruff male voice in the Wort dialect.

The baby was lying on her back, her gaze focused upward toward the ceiling. She couldn't see the speaker but could sense his dark presence. A shiver racked Mara's spirit body. It was the same evil essence she'd encountered before.

Another male replied. "He hasn't given us an answer yet. I'll wait as long as necessary."

"I say kill the child now and be done with it."

"Not while the Coalition team is on Yanura. They might find out about us."

"So what? If they do, we'll accomplish the same goal."

"I disagree. We'll lose our leverage. You'll follow my orders on this, Kromas."

Mara gasped. The males were arguing over Jallyn's life. One of them wanted to kill her. The other meant to keep her alive, but for what purpose?

She tore herself from Jallyn's consciousness, hurtled through the astral plane and landed back in her physical body.

"Deke, wake up!" She prodded him on the shoulder. He

didn't budge, so she shoved him again. Mumbling something she couldn't decipher, he rolled sideways.

She had rarely seen him sleep so soundly. The only other time she remembered him out cold like this was after they'd been gassed in the jungle pit on their way to the Wort village.

By the Light! Was that why she'd conked out so easily last night? A vague recollection of dancing wildly with Deke remained in her mind, but she'd attributed it to her dream. Now she recalled the dancers and musicians along with the syrupy drink she'd gulped down in her thirst.

Could the beverage have been laced with a drug that made them all woozy? It would account for her lack of inhibitions in front of the Worts. And now that she considered the idea, it would also provide a reason for Hedy and Wren's peculiar dazed state.

Why had Deke been singled out to go with Onus Hahn? Curious to learn what had transpired between them, she debated how to rouse him. He was snoring lightly but she resisted the impulse to push him off the bed.

She could enter his essence, although then she ran the danger of succumbing to his state of slumber. If he did awaken, he'd be angry at the invasion. The only other option made her smile as she smoothed her fingers through his hair and breathed in his musky masculine scent.

Speaking of scents, neither one of them smelled very good. Hadn't Onus Laang offered to send someone to show her the bathing pools this morning? Wrinkling her nose, she decided it was a necessary excursion.

Meanwhile, she stretched out beside Deke and stroked his bare arm while willing him to wake up. His eyelids fluttered open, and he focused his bleary gaze on her.

"Morning," he said, his tone husky.

"Get up. I have something to tell you."

"In a minute. Come closer."

Her gaze dropped to his stubbled jaw and then to his lips. Unable to resist, she leaned in to kiss him. And then she was in his arms, being kissed wildly and passionately. She wanted to preserve the moment, to enjoy the sensations he evoked in her. As she relaxed in his embrace, she willed herself to stay out of his head so she could savor the intensity of her own response.

Was that how he felt? Whenever she joined with him, he was forced to share his feelings. It didn't matter that their union enhanced their physical pleasure. She was stealing his privacy. Wasn't he entitled to keep his emotions to himself?

Deke murmured her name, adjusting his position so he could reach her throat. He flicked his tongue out, tickling her neck so that she lost control. Her psyche merged with his, her passion swirling in a haze of need. They shed their clothing and came together in a frenzy of lust until ecstasy claimed them.

****

Their passion satisfied, Mara slid to her side so Deke wouldn't see her confusion. Was that what it was like for him? Having his mind invaded, never knowing when his feelings would be vulnerable to her? No wonder he wanted to shut her out. She'd thought he would welcome her presence. No one truly wanted to be alone, and in their joined state, he'd never have to suffer loneliness.

But perhaps she'd been wrong. She had no right to intrude upon him against his will. Yet what could she do? Lacking control over her ability, she couldn't just cut herself off from him, nor did she want to. They were still bound on a spiritual level no matter how hard either one of them tried to deny it. It was their destiny to be together.

Forcing herself back to the present, she opened her mouth to tell Deke about her mental visit to Jallyn and her theory about a drugged drink, but before she uttered a word, a loud thud sounded from the platform outside their hut.

"Mistress, are you in there? It's Onus Laola. I've come to take you to the bathing pools this morning."

Mara leapt off the bed and grabbed her clothes. "I'll be right out," she cried, pulling on her underwear and a shift dress. Conscious of Deke's eyes on her back, she spared a glance at his naked body stretched out on the bed. "Do you want to come? We could both use a dunk in the pool."

He swung his legs over the edge of the bed and reached for his treksuit. "I need to contact Ebo and bring him up to date on what's been going on." He kept his voice low so Onus Laola wouldn't overhear. Rummaging in his sack, he pulled out his datalink. "You go on ahead. I'll catch up to you later."

She hesitated as a sudden premonition of danger invaded her. "Please come now. I… I'll feel safer with you along."

"Ask Hedy and Wren to go with you. They could probably use a good cleansing."

When he turned his back to her, Mara gave up her attempt to persuade him. She was probably being nervous over nothing.

Holding a small bag with a set of fresh clothes, she pushed aside the mosquito netting and emerged onto the outdoor platform. A light mist caressed her face. It must have rained during the night. The sound of dripping water almost drowned out the ever-present drone of cicadas. A damp smell hung in the air and moisture tipped the leaves of nearby trees.

"Rogi Kwantro," the Wort said with a bow. Onus Laola wore a mauve gown with a white apron. Her frog face beamed a friendly smile.

"I appreciate your coming to get me so early," Mara said after repeating the greeting. "Isn't this normally your sleeping period?"

"I don't require many hauras of rest. It is better we go now, before the pools get crowded."

Mara nodded at Hedy's hut. "Would you mind if I asked our friends to join us?"

"I would be honored by their company as I am by yours."

Mara experienced a moment's doubt. She'd lose the advantage of being alone with Onus Laola if her friends accepted the invitation. But there was also safety in numbers, and she didn't know how far they had to go to reach the pools.

As she crossed the log bridge, she heard sounds of arguing coming from within the other hut. Uh-oh. It sounded as though there was trouble in paradise.

"Hello," she called out. "I'm going to the pools. Anyone care to join me?"

"I will," Hedy yelled back, a petulant note in her tone.

"Me, too," Wren's voice boomed.

The two charged out, colliding at the entrance as though they were so eager to depart from each other's company that they couldn't maneuver properly.

Wren held the netting aside for Hedy to pass. She stalked past him, her nose in the air.

What a contrasting pair, Mara thought with an inner smile. Hedy never failed to express her emotions, while Wren continued to deny his. She couldn't wait to get a report from her roommate on what they'd been fighting about.

Speaking of reports, she'd forgotten to ask Deke about his meeting with Onus Hahn last night. Hopefully, she would remember the subject later when he rejoined her.

Right now, her objective was to get clean, she reminded herself, stepping onto the conveyor with her companions. The jungle was swathed in mist, and as they descended to the ground, a dank aroma scented the atmosphere.

The village was devoid of movement on the upper residential levels but the wildlife made up for the stillness of the settlement.

As they passed a strand of creaky bamboo, Mara spied a long-legged spider suspended on a glistening web. Monkey-like catarrhines cheeped overhead as they leapt from branch to branch. Their movement caused rain droplets to splatter from the trees. On one limb, a lizard with a curly tail sipped water from a cup created by a pink bromeliad.

"This area is so pristine," Mara remarked, following a dirt trail behind Onus Laola.

"It may look peaceful but the jungle has hidden dangers," Onus Laola said. "We maintain guard posts at various checkpoints."

"Is that why my friends and I fell into a pit on our way here? You've set traps, too?"

"Yes, that was an unfortunate incident."

As they proceeded, Mara brushed away a vine that dangled from a figaras tree, a variety familiar to her from her studies. The vine was elastic and strong and could be woven into rope. Boulders became more prominent as they followed an incline toward the sound of rushing water.

Suddenly, they came upon a narrow river. A scarlet-beaked bird rummaged for food among reeds along the bank.

They followed the stream until they came to a grotto with rocky cliffs on either side and a spectacular waterfall. The water tumbled over a series of boulders and then into a quiescent pool. Sunlight dappling through the foliage glistened off the water, making it sparkle like thousands of gemstones.

"Here we are," Onus Laola said. "Do you like it?"

"This is where we are to bathe?" Wren inquired gruffly.

Mara grinned at the look of dismay on his face. "I'll bet you expected a sanitary facility complete with sonic showers, didn't you?"

"No," Wren sputtered, "but I, um, expected some segregation for privacy."

"Is the water cold?" Hedy asked.

"It's cool in the morning until the sun heats the water. Spend as much time as you need. I'll take a quick dip before you go in." She proceeded to strip in front of them.

Wren's face reddened and he turned away.

"Come on, Wren," Hedy cooed. "Get into the spirit of things. Look, I'm taking off my tunic. What are you waiting for?"

Wren coughed. "I need to heed a call from nature." He dashed off down the trail in the opposite direction.

"Don't be long," Hedy cried after him.

Onus Laola plunged into the pool and dove under the surface. Mara took a longer time getting unclothed than Hedy, who stood before her stark naked.

"What's going on between you and Wren?" She cast a surreptitious glance at their surroundings, hoping none of the Wort guards were nearby to observe them.

Hedy sighed. "The man refuses to budge on his attitude. I don't know what to do. I've tried everything and he still resists me."

"Wren may be the first guy who hasn't fallen at your feet. Maybe that's why you're so infatuated with him."

"It's more than an infatuation. I can't get him out of my head. I'm looking at him all the time, wondering what he's thinking and trying to figure out how I can get his attention. I know he wants me, but he won't admit it."

"It could be you're trying too hard. You have to let things play out naturally."

"You may be right. Come on, let's test the water. I don't like standing around here so exposed."

Mara descended to the pool's edge where Onus Laola was just emerging from her swim. She dipped her foot in. "It's lukewarm. Let's go." Careful of her footing on the pebbled bottom, she ventured farther.

The sound of rushing water was music to her ears. As a child, she'd liked to sit beside a waterfall and imagine herself as one with the droplets of water cascading over the rocks. How free she would feel if she could tumble over the edge and soar into space like her spirit body. Was that what it would be like for Wren if he could fly?

Remembering Hedy's story about the ascension rites on his planet, she felt sad for Wren that he'd never achieved that milestone. She wondered what Hedy could do to encourage him, but her own situation with Deke precluded giving her friend any advice.

She certainly wasn't having much success on her own. With that glum thought, she stepped into deeper water and shrieked as the liquid surrounded her up to her neck.

"Come on, Hedy! It feels good once you're in," she yelled, flopping onto her stomach and beginning a series of strong strokes.

The waterfall produced a steady spray of mist. Still able to touch bottom, she stopped a safe distance from the cascade and scrubbed her hair as squeaky clean as she could get it. Splashing sounds from nearby told her Hedy had joined her.

"Look, Onus Laola is leaving," Hedy said.

Sure enough, their guide trudged down the path with their dirty clothes in hand. Her brownish body gleamed with moisture.

"Onus Laola, where are you going?" Mara called.

"I am taking your soiled clothing to the laundry. You'll be all right. Wren should be along at any moment. I'll return in a short while."

"No matter," Hedy told Mara as they watched the Wort retreat into the forest. "We brought clean clothes in our sacks, and she left us some towels. Listen, I have an idea that might work on Wren."

A few moments later, Mara climbed the bank of the stream and dried herself off with one of the towels their guide had provided. When she was done, she donned a clean set of underwear and a fresh treksuit. She set off in the direction Wren had gone and found him examining a strange plant with raised white dots on its glossy leaves.

"Hedy's in trouble and she needs you," Mara said, her tone urgent.

Wren's startled glance met hers. Then he gave a howl and charged down the path.

****

His heart thudding in his chest, Wren wondered what had happened. Was Hedy in trouble in the river? Could she have slipped on one of those slick rocks and injured herself? His breath caught in his throat as he imagined her floating unconscious in the water.

She meant more to him than he could admit and it would crush him if any harm befell her. It would be his fault for leaving her unattended. Never mind that their relationship wasn't going smoothly. It was still his responsibility to look after her.

"Wren!" Hedy hollered when he neared the riverbank.

He reached the water, took one look at her floundering in the current, and plunged in, clothes and all.

"Hang on, I'm coming," he shouted, pushing through volumes of water with his powerful strokes. Swimming had been one of his favorite pastimes on Pollux. He'd hoped the exercise would influence his ability to fly but his theory had failed.

"My foot's caught in a tangle of weeds," Hedy called.

He swam up to her, and she swooned into his arms. "By the moons of Agus Six," he swore as his hands felt the soft flesh beneath his fingers. She was naked! He tried to suppress his surge of desire but to no avail. Her movements caused him to shudder but he dared not let go.

Evidently she wasn't a strong swimmer and needed his help to reach the shore. But he was touching her in places he considered sacred. Were her moans expressions of fear or of pleasure? And were her tremors from the trauma or his nearness? He couldn't tell and didn't want to know.

Unable to keep his need for her in check, he let his hands roam to her belly. His physical response to touching her was immediate. He was mad for the woman. If only he was whole, he'd lay her on that bed of moss by the riverbank and—

His fantasy became reality when their feet touched bottom and Hedy twisted in his arms. Her mouth clamped on his as she pressed her nude body firmly against him.

"You've saved my life. I'm yours, Wren," she said against his lips, her hot breath teasing him into submission.

His eager fingers followed a path of their own to her breasts. As though he'd just been offered a gift from heaven, he stroked her twin peaks even as he plundered her mouth.

By the gods, how sweet she tasted. And yet, he hadn't earned the right to have her.

She writhed against him, draining his battered willpower.

He'd been able to refuse her in their hut when she kept finding excuses to touch him, but now he couldn't hold out any longer. If he succumbed, would any of his honor remain, or would he live the rest of his days in shame?

Suns, he already lived in the wake of his disgrace. Hedy still wanted him, no matter what he'd done. She'd promised to stay by his side regardless of the future. But wouldn't he taint her with his dishonor if they lay together?

A solution came to mind as a yellow-feathered bird swooped over the water and plucked a fish from under the surface. He'd satisfy Hedy's need but would withhold his own satisfaction. Content with this decision, he slid his palm downward. Just the idea of where he was about to touch her made his pulse rate soar.

"Oh yes," Hedy said, swaying against him.

The rush of the waterfall and the pounding of his heart thrummed in his ears like an orchestral piece at its crescendo. But before he could progress any further, Mara emerged from the path at a hard run, her face red from exertion.

"Wren, come quick," she cried.

Instantly alert, he sprang apart from Hedy. "What's wrong?"

"It's Deke. I've just been pulled into his viewpoint. He's in terrible danger."

Chapter Eighteen

Deke contacted Ebo via datalink just after Mara and the others left for the pools. Alone in the hut, he exchanged status reports with his communications officer.

"We're in no immediate danger that I can discern, although I wouldn't trust these Worts beyond my own nose. Have you been able to make sense out of their messages?"

"I'm reading a high frequency of coded missives between various locations, but the ship's computer hasn't been able to provide a translation."

"Keep trying. You've got a fix on our location, right?"

"Aye, sir. I have a locator alert set for all four of you."

"Good. Contact me if anything significant occurs. Sage out." He replaced the datalink in his knapsack, thinking he'd join Mara for a swim, when a loud crashing thud made him whirl toward the open doorway.

Someone had hurled another rock inside the hut.

He dashed to the outdoor platform, hoping to catch the sender, but the village remained quiet and he didn't see so much as a moving shadow. Glancing up, he peered at the mist-enshrouded tree canopy and smiled grimly when a swinging vine caught his attention. Blasted frog faces. They could maneuver through the trees like catarrhines.

Returning inside, he scooped up the rock and untied the attached note. His eyes hastily scanned the scrawled message:

Come alone. I have vital information you'll want to hear.

Directions were enclosed.

Tossing the rock aside, he debated whether to bring his knapsack. His weapons were gone, but he could always summon his teammates with the datalink.

No, he couldn't. They'd left everything here except for their clothing.

Just to be sure, he went over to Wren's hut and rummaged through his navigator's belongings. Sure enough, Wren had left his datalink behind. No one could activate them without their personal codes, but Deke deemed it wise to advise his crew not to leave without their equipment next time.

Figuring he could use the emergency backup link on his dive computer to call Ebo if necessary, Deke descended the hut via the conveyance to ground level.

No one stirred in the sleepy village. He was grateful for the mist as he took off in the direction indicated. Later he'd insist their weaponry be returned. It was something he should have done before and hoped he wouldn't pay for his negligence.

The idea that this was a trap entered his head, and he grew increasingly uneasy as he followed the jungle trail. The instructions were clear, using landmarks such as a huge banyan tree by the south edge of the communal dining hall, and dead logs crisscrossed at a ninety-degree angle by the stream farther on.

He left the village proper and found himself on a muddy path cut through the thick foliage. The mist freshened his face as he sniffed in moist, dank air that smelled of rotting vegetation.

His boots squelched the soggy earth as he trudged on. Insects buzzed his ears. Orchids, anthuriums, and other flowering plants he couldn't identify splashed bright colors against the greenery. A brilliant blue terin flashed by, stopping to hover over a large white blossom. The bird used its long bill to drink the nectar, reminding him of the drink he'd ingested last night.

He'd certainly behaved strangely, dancing with Mara in front of a bunch of natives and nearly acceding to Onus Hahn's demands. Had there been something in that sickly sweet beverage that had affected him?

"Aaarooo!" sounded a fierce noise from above.

Deke nearly jumped out of his boots. Grabbing a big stick from the ground, he glanced upward. Branches rattled and leaves and twigs rained down in an avalanche of debris. A giant somu nut crashed where he'd been standing a moment before. If it had hit him on the head, the impact of the weighted nut could have killed him.

A male barrulu glared down at him from the somu nut tree. Shaking its shaggy mane, the creature thrust out its lower jaw and bellowed at him.

He moved on. Soon he reached a section where the muddy ground sucked at his boots. It looked like a wetland dotted with stands of palms. When he came to a kapok tree with cathedral-like buttresses, he halted at its base. This was the location given to him in the message.

"Commander," someone called out in standard Jawani.

He spun in the direction of the voice. An elder Wort female emerged from behind a cluster of tall reeds. The wild-growing grass had feathery flower heads and strap-like leaves. Sedges and rushes clogged the banks of a nearby pond, and he could see how easy it was for the Wort to blend in with her surroundings. Her brown skin color and forest green tunic matched the colors of nature.

"Who are you?" he demanded.

The Wort's expressive amber eyes assessed him. "You came alone? No one followed you here?"

"As far as I know, nobody saw me leave the village."

"Good. Sit down." She lowered herself onto a fallen log.

He inspected a flat tree stump for bugs. Seeing none of immediate concern, he plopped down onto the makeshift seat. "You said you had valuable information for me."

"I am Raisa, Onus Laola's grandmother. It is for her sake and the sake of her child that I speak to you."

"Her child?" He frowned in puzzlement.

"She had a male child six annums ago. As is our way, he was

taken to be raised by the jakoon." Raisa's eyes narrowed. "It is time for this sacrilege to end. Our children must be returned to our care."

"I don't understand. Who are the jakoon? Where are the children taken?"

"The jakoon are Croags who supervise the upbringing of our young. The children are kept until maturation, when they are sent home. If we were to resist, the Croags would cut off our supply of Vyclor. You must end this practice. Make it a condition of Yanura's acceptance into the Coalition."

Deke stiffened. "It always comes back to Fromoth Trun's application, doesn't it? Did someone put you up to this?"

Raisa stood abruptly, her eyes flashing. "I risked my life in coming here and you dare to insult me? I should have told the NARCs myself where to find you."

"NARCs? Who are they?" He rose, squaring his shoulders. Maybe now he'd get some useful answers.

The Wort stared at a line of ants crawling on the ground. "The National Revolutionary Congress are activists who seek to end Croag dominance in our political affairs. They refuse to take Vyclor on a routine basis as do other Yanurans."

Deke tilted his head. Could this be the faction that held Jallyn? "What do they want?" he asked, his tone neutral.

"Everyone should have freedom of choice regarding Vyclor. The central government must include representatives from all of our peoples. And forced conscription of our children must end."

"Conscription? What do you mean?"

The female jabbed a finger at him. "The NARCs have Jallyn, and they're using her as a pawn to force Fromoth Trun to agree to their terms. If the Croag leader refuses, Jallyn will be killed and her death blamed on his people. The Coalition, informed of his treachery, would reject his application for admission."

Deke opened his mouth to ask another question, but just then a beam of red laser fire cut through the air. With a choked cry, Raisa toppled over.

Frog faces jumped out of the surrounding grasses, flanking

him on all sides. Deke's hand automatically went to his hip but he hadn't any weapons. Being outnumbered and outgunned, it was a moot point anyway. The Worts bristled with shooters, laser rifles, and gas grenades, making him wonder who'd supplied them with armaments. Woven tan tunics covered their bodies and all six of them were males.

"Your death will further our cause," the largest of the group snarled, stepping closer, his weapon aimed at Deke's chest. "The Coalition will be informed of your demise. They will reject Fromoth Trun's application."

One of the smaller men glanced at his leader. "I thought our orders were to capture the human, not kill him."

"I give the orders here," the red-eyed Wort said.

"Forgive me, Kromas, but our goals are to force the Croags to accede to our demands. If you murder this man and the girl child, you'll defeat our purpose."

Kromas's skin darkened, and he turned to fire before the speaker had a chance to react. The Wort crumpled to the ground without a sound.

"You're next," the rebel leader said, swinging his shooter toward Deke. "Like your friend Larikk, you'll meet your end in Dead Wort's Marsh."

As his finger moved on the trigger, Deke used the only means available to save himself. He grabbed at an overhanging vine and leapt upward, kicking the shooter out of Kromas's hand. Landing behind the big Wort, he whirled around and punched him in the small of his back.

The Wort grunted and doubled over, and Deke used the opportunity to chop at his thick neck. His subordinates attacked, pummeling Deke in the stomach and ribs.

He tossed one of the assailants over his shoulder. The fellow landed with a loud splash in the pond. With a shriek, he disappeared beneath the surface.

A hit on the jaw made Deke reel backward, right into the crushing embrace of Kromas. Kromas's arms tightened around his chest while three of his troopers approached with evil grins on their frog faces.

Ignoring the painful vise squeezing his rib cage, Deke tensed his muscles, preparing to bend his knees and toss Kromas into the pond with his crony.

Before he could make his move, an essence invaded his mind. Mara's fear reached him and he froze, immobilized by her emotion. His paralysis gave Kromas and his friends the advantage.

Before he could recover, Kromas forced him toward the pond's edge.

"The eels will get you as they did Larikk. Join your friend in the deep." The rebel lifted him and tossed him through the air.

As he tumbled, he activated a switch on the dive computer strapped to his wrist. He crashed through the surface of the water, covered with green algae and round lily pads. Just before he went under, he sucked in a gulp of air.

While the cool liquid swallowed him from view, Deke wheeled around, diving deep and swimming in a direction away from the bank with the rebel soldiers. He remembered seeing a thick cluster of reeds and made out their stems in the murky environment. Something slithered past his leg, about two feet long and solidly built.

The dangerous inhabitants of Dead Wort's Marsh didn't threaten him. In fact, being tossed into the pond was his lucky move of the day. His dive computer contained a protective device that emitted a personal energy screen. The electromagnetic force shielded him from any electrical charges. The eel's sting, if it attacked, would be neutralized and have no effect on him.

Ignoring the slithering creatures that bypassed him as he swam, he reached a cluster of reeds and grabbed one at its base, ripping it from its roots. Putting one end in his mouth, he gave a quick prayer to the Great Almighty and blew his remaining air through the hollow reed. At the other end, a flower head must have popped off, because when he tried to take in a breath of air, his lungs filled with ease.

Using the reed as a snorkel device, he swam farther from the enemy. The series of interconnected ponds stretched for some distance. Hopefully, they would think he'd gone down like their comrade-in-arms, never to surface again.

He could breathe through the hollow tube as long as necessary. The light was low down here, but he could make out large roots lying on the bottom, stems extending upward to the flat-leafed lily pads on top. Fish with whiskers swam past and a crab crawled along the sandy bottom.

He couldn't keep his eyes open for long or they started burning, so he closed them and rested his boots on the sand. The water temperature was cool but it wasn't cold, so hypothermia shouldn't be a danger if he didn't stay down overly long.

After a short while, he would surface and see if any NARC soldiers had stayed to stand guard. Settling into position, Deke wondered how long he'd have to wait.

****

Mara charged down the path toward the village, her heart pounding as she wondered what had happened to Deke. When she'd jumped into his viewpoint, she caught a glimpse of brown Wort faces, a giant kapok tree, and the body of a village woman sprawled on the ground. What had alarmed her the most was sensing the same dark presence she'd felt around Jallyn.

Fear spurred her onward, and she didn't stop to answer Wren's bombardment of questions as he and Hedy caught up to her.

"Later," she shouted.

When they reached the village, she ran into a kitchen hut where smoke billowed from a cooking fire. She asked the female in there for directions to Onus Laola's hut.

"Mara, what's going on?" Hedy demanded in a huff. Still wet but attired in the treksuit she'd brought along to the pond, she patted her dripping hair with her towel. Wren had gone off to check the dwelling Mara shared with Deke to see if he'd left them a note.

Briefly Mara related what she'd seen, then she grabbed a nearby rope ladder and began climbing.

Onus Laola's hut was empty of occupants. Built into a tree, several rooms rose on different levels. Mara felt guilty peeking into the private areas but she had to find their guide for advice on where to search for Deke.

One room at an upper rise caught her attention. It held a small bed and a wood bureau that displayed a holographic photo of a young Wort male. The picture was propped next to a jagged white rock. A ripple of surprise tore through her as she studied the picture.

Did Onus Laola have a child, and if so, why hadn't she mentioned the boy? Where was he living? Mara couldn't help drawing a parallel to the situation with the Croags. Where were all the children? Could Sarina's baby be at the same place as the Yanuran young?

She had too many questions and few answers. She wasn't satisfied with the rationale given for Larikk's death. Deke believed data was being withheld about Vyclor. And what of that chemical plant? Could it truly be a facility for manufacturing sluer oil, which the Croags traded to the Worts for gold lace? If so, how did one account for the dead bodies on the data card Deke had been given?

Rubbing her hand over the jagged white rock, she puzzled over the mystery of it all. Even this rock seemed to ring a familiar mental bell but she couldn't remember its significance.

"Uh-oh." A piece broke off in her hand. Now what should she do?

She had to cover the evidence of her visit. After stuffing the broken edge in her pocket, she turned the rock so the rough surface faced away from the open portal. Wiping her sweaty palms on her treksuit, she turned to go.

Halfway down the ladder, she spotted Onus Laola heading her way, her arms laden with their clothes.

Mara jumped down the last few meters. "Onus Laola, I was looking for you."

"And I have been searching for you. I did not expect you to return to the village on your own."

"Deke is in trouble and we need to find him."

Onus Laola thrust the bundle of neatly folded clothing at her. "How do you know this?"

"I had a vision." Mara explained what she'd seen.

The Wort female's expression turned thoughtful. "He's at Dead Wort's Marsh. We must hurry. Come, I'll show you the way. Leave your clean laundry on my conveyor."

Wren hustled toward them, his brow furrowed. "The commander left us no messages," he said. "Here, Doctor, I've brought your medpack."

By the time they reached the wetland, Mara was perspiring and her treksuit stuck to her back. What had happened to Deke? Was he all right?

She berated herself for not keeping an item of his so she could do controlled separations. His intense emotion had drawn her into his lifespace before, but now when she wanted to reassure herself of his well-being, she wasn't able to do so. It was frustrating, and she fumed at her helplessness.

They burst into a clearing and stopped in their tracks. Facing them was a series of ponds with tall reeds on the banks swaying in a light breeze. And there was that huge spreading tree she'd seen in her mind's eye.

Mara spotted the body first and her heart leapt into her throat. With a stifled cry, she dashed forward. A wave of tremulous relief passed through her as she noted the female Wort's features. But where was Deke?

Twisting her head, she searched the vegetation but saw no sign of him.

"By the grace of Mother Water," Onus Laola cried, her face assuming an unhealthy pallor. "It is Raisa, my maternal grandmother." Sinking down beside the old Wort, she covered her face with her hands.

Wren loped over to retrieve a fallen rifle. "I thought your people avoided Dead Wort's Marsh."

Onus Laola glanced at him with sorrowful eyes. "Our villagers avoid this area. We keep busy making crafts, herb gathering, and fishing. We are not warriors, although we carry arms for protection. Likely that weapon was dropped by a soldier in the National Revolutionary Congress, or NARC as we call it. They probably lured Commander Sage here and attacked him."

"What is this group?" Mara asked, staring at the pond. A ripple creased its surface, originating from a cluster of tall grasses at the opposite end of the pond from where they stood.

"NARC is an extremist splinter group made up of citizens who refuse to bow to Croag rules."

"Why the secrecy?" Hedy asked. She'd been running a diagnostic on Raisa, and now she straightened with a resigned look on her face. She switched off her mediscan unit and put it away.

"NARC uses terrorist tactics to force Fromoth Trun to agree to their demands," Onus Laola replied, a melancholy note in her voice.

Mara nodded grimly. "They must have been responsible for the bombing attack at Revitt Lake City. It follows that Fromoth Trun didn't want us to find out about them because Deke would recommend a denial of his application due to political instability."

"Exactly." Onus Laola's sad eyes roamed to Raisa's still form. "My grandmother hoped to help our people. She was always saying our children belonged at home."

"Where are they?" Mara's tone was unduly harsh, but it was tiring to keep repeating the same questions. "And why didn't you mention you have a son?"

"I cannot give you any further information. It might endanger my child." Onus Laola sprang to her feet and wrung her webbed hands.

"Did these rebels capture Commander Sage? Do you know where the NARC command base is located?" Wren demanded.

Onus Laola pointed north toward the higher mountain ranges. "They live in the Cloud Forest. It is a treacherous route by foot." Her expression turned pleading. "Please do not inform Onus Hahn or Onus Laang about my role in this. It is bad enough that Raisa was involved. I can tell you no more. I'll make up an excuse for my grandmother's death and return to retrieve her body for burial."

A gloomy silence fell over the threesome as they were left alone with the corpse. Mara stared at the pond, wondering how they would ever track Deke to rescue him. Nothing about this mission was going the way they'd expected.

As she considered their options, a mountain of water erupted from the pond. She shrieked as a blackened creature reared its head from the depths.

"Mara, is that you?" asked a familiar voice.

"Deke?" She couldn't believe her eyes. The apparition washed the mud from its body and a dirty, sodden Deke emerged from the water.

"Commander! We thought you'd been captured," Wren said, his face breaking into a relieved grin.

They exchanged information, bringing each other up to date on their findings.

"You should have come with us to the pools," Mara chided. "Now look at you. You're a mess."

Deke squatted on a log and peeled off his boots. With a grimace, he shook them upside down to remove the muck inside.

His cold gaze met her concerned one. "If you hadn't jumped into my head again, I'd have won this fight. It was a mistake to add you to the away team when you lack control over your ability. It's continually jeopardizing our mission. As soon as we can, I'm sending you back to the ship."

Mortified, Mara stared at him. She'd thought he'd be happy to see her. After all, it was her vision that led them to him. Now he was blaming her for his predicament?

He squished his feet into his wet boots and stood, glowering at them. Even Hedy and Wren were struck speechless by his outburst. They stood mutely by, stunned expressions on their faces.

"As you can see, I didn't need any help. If Mara hadn't invaded my mind, I could have fought them off and hopefully kept one alive to question him. Now the only information we have to go on is what Raisa told me."

"What do you mean, Mara invaded your mind?" Wren asked slowly. He seemed to be the only one unaware of Deke's meaning.

Deke shot her a venomous glance. "You know of her ability to separate? She does it to me, intruding on my privacy with her mental powers. It can happen at any time without warning. In this instance, her interference put me into a life-threatening situation."

His scorn cut her like a thousand knives, and it was worse because he disparaged her in front of their friends. Moisture pricked her eyelashes, and she bit her lower lip to hide her hurt. Not that she could seem any more despicable in their eyes. Hedy averted her gaze but not before Mara saw her friend's pitying glance. Wren continued to study Deke with an obscure expression.

"How about using your ability for our benefit?" Deke said with a sneer. "Can you tell us where Jallyn is yet? Do a reading and tell us what you see."

A reading… as though she were some sort of smarmy ghost-chasing medium.

"I need her blanket for that, and it's in our hut. But I have this piece of rock from Onus Laola's dwelling." Casting aside her impulse to respond to his snide remarks, she focused on the importance of their mission and withdrew the rock from her pocket.

"By the Light," she whispered when she'd landed at the other end of her astral journey. She was in a child's viewpoint, presumably Laola's son. He was swimming underwater, gathering specimens of similar white rocks. They appeared crystalline with a glittery surface.

All around him swam other Yanuran children of mixed races. The younger ones used a tool to snip the stems of stalk-like plants with balloon-shaped protuberances.

"Those are air-filled sacs that keep the merl afloat," Deke explained after she'd come out of her trance and given a report. "The youngsters must be harvesting the merl farms. But why the secrecy about the process?"

"If what Raisa said is true," Wren offered, "the children are being taken to work the farms against their parents' will. The Worts don't protest because they're afraid the Croags will cut off their supply of Vyclor."

"Do you think Jallyn is being held with the Yanuran children?" Mara asked.

Deke gestured for them to proceed back to the village. "No, the NARCs have her. Our first priority is to rescue Sarina's child. A moderate faction among them hopes to press Fromoth Trun into agreeing to their demands. But this Kromas character wants to kill the baby and end any chance for conciliatory talks. We have to get to Jallyn before Kromas makes a move against her."

Mara fell into step beside him. "Did you learn anything new about Larikk's death?"

Deke's face was stony as he replied. "The NARCs were responsible for his disappearance. They didn't say why they'd wanted him dead."

Had he kept one of his attackers alive to question him, Deke might have found out. But thanks to her influence, he'd lost the chance. Deke did not speak the words but Mara heard them as clear as that bird squawking from the branches.

She compressed her lips. By the stars, it was his strong emotions that drew her to him. The occasions were just as disruptive for her. If only she could make him understand the ties that bound them, he might not view her with such loathing.

****

Deke glimpsed the forlorn look on Mara's face and tightened his jaw. Knowing she was hurting made him feel lousy, but it was the only way for him to maintain control over this mission.

He hated himself for becoming distracted and allowing his attackers to get the upper hand. This wasn't the first time she'd interfered in his affairs, nor would it be the last unless he got rid of her. But they were stuck on this planet together. What was he to do when he couldn't live with her and felt bereft without her? Was there some compromise they could reach?

Feeling guilty over the despicable way he'd treated her, he cast her a sideways glance. She looked beautiful even in her distress. Her eyes glistened and her glorious hair hung down her back. She walked beside him with her chin in the air, her confident stride disguising the emotions that must be churning inside her. As a diplomat, she'd learned to hide her feelings well.

With sudden insight, he realized his feelings toward her were as ambivalent as his own dual roles. Scientist or warrior, which was he?

He'd tried to deny the fighting instinct that made him so formidable on commando raids. Being a soldier reminded him of his father and the constant nagging he'd experienced as a child to engage in competitive sports. And yet now that Deke had a taste of combat, he could almost say he enjoyed the challenge, and it horrified him. As a scientist, he valued life and sought to preserve it. Was he becoming so like his father that in time he'd make the same unethical choices?

Great suns, he hoped not. But it made him wonder if he'd be fit to assume the role of chancellor should he get the position. Was it beyond his ability to reach a middle ground in disputes? The job required a diplomat as well as a scientist and leader, and maybe he wasn't cut out for it… at least, not alone.

He needed someone like Mara who could steer him down the proper path, curb his aggressive tendencies, and help him maintain his moral compass. With her experience, she was perfectly qualified to advise him in negotiations. But would the sacrifice to his privacy be worth it to keep her at his side?

He marched silently down the trail, glad she couldn't read his mind. No conclusions came to him except that he had to apologize for his callousness.

"We'll gather our gear and leave for NARC territory," he told his team. "Don't mention our plans to anyone in the village. Sympathizers might be among them. I'll ask Onus Hahn for our weapons back and give him an excuse for our absence."

"That old Wort by the cluster of berries has a pile of ropes he's made from woody vines," Wren mentioned. "I'll see if I can buy some from him. They might come in handy."

"Speaking of berries, I'm starving," Deke said. "We'll need to eat before we go. Mara, you can arrange to have meals prepared for us. Doctor, collect your equipment and get anything else you might need from the villagers. I saw you eyeing the herb lady's assortment earlier."

Once they reached the settlement, Deke split off from the others to find Onus Hahn. The Wort leader believed his story that they were heading back to Revitt Lake City. Deke said they would proceed by land in order to gather valuable plant specimens along the way. Likely the fellow would contact Fromoth Trun and Deke didn't want the Yanuran leader expecting them any time soon.

After a quick meal, he conferred with his crew and decided which trail they'd follow. His regret over his actions toward Mara made him morose, and so it was with a brusque gesture an haura later that he led his team onward.

Chapter Nineteen

The thick jungle closed around the landing party with an eerie stillness. Deke took the lead as they proceeded single-file along a trail roughened with rocks and tree roots. His backpack bulged, full of food and supplies he'd purloined from the Worts. He'd obtained enough to hold them for several days, but hopefully their journey wouldn't last so long.

As he trudged along the narrow path, brushing leafy branches and vines off his face, he mentally reviewed their stock that included mosquito netting, portable flame torches, dry socks and underwear, an extra treksuit each, plus a couple of machetes. Wren had his preferred nutritional supplements plus the ropes he'd bought from the villager, while Hedy had her medkit. Mara's pack held her personal items plus a few extra supplies for the group.

Somehow it no longer mattered if he won the chancellorship. Saving Jallyn from harm was more important. He'd reassessed his goals, and being with his friends and pursuing research that mattered were more meaningful. He wondered what place Mara held in his future. He wasn't sure where she would fit in but knew that he couldn't go forward without her.

****

Challenged by Deke's silence as he led the team through the jungle, Mara compared him to the trees. Like those signposts of the rainforest, he was tall, firm, and unyielding. Inside each tree trunk was a living core, giving oxygen as it received sunlight and moisture through its leaves. Vines twisted like gnarled ropes hanging from tree limbs. Mosses and epiphytic plants grew upon other plants, while flowers provided brilliant splashes of color among the greenery.

How could she reach Deke's heart when he begrudged her even the slightest consideration? She'd given him everything and he gave back nothing in return.

No, that wasn't true. He'd shared his hopes and dreams. It was possible she knew more about him than he understood himself. But that didn't aid her cause. She lacked the experience to break his barriers.

Practice your meditation. Master Keenan's words drifted into her mind like dust motes on dappled rays of sunshine. She needed to expand her consciousness in order to tighten the bonds between their chakras. But she couldn't concentrate on that now.

She watched her footing during their uphill hike along the mountainous trail. It was hot and breezy, making her grateful when Deke called a halt at a lookout point where ridge after ridge of unbroken jungle met their gaze. Wiping the sweat from her brow, she turned to Hedy.

"I'm glad we had those fitness sessions on board the *Celeste* or I'd never make it."

Hedy's chest heaved from exertion. "Your dancing keeps you in shape. I'd never have made it if Wren hadn't pushed me halfway up the hill." Her glance fell upon the Polluxite who paced back and forth, flapping his magnificent wings. He didn't even appear winded.

Neither did Deke. He stood off to the side, giving Ebo a report via datalink. Mara recognized the stiff set of his shoulders. As leader, he bore the responsibility for them all. She yearned to merge with him and offer support.

"Let's move out," Deke said curtly, terminating communications. "We'll make camp at nightfall. That should give us another two hauras."

She groaned. "I'm hungry. When do we eat?" Their meal of

fruit and fish in the Wort village hadn't provided her with enough energy.

"Here, take these." He passed around a snack of bananas and nuts.

They refilled their canteens with fresh water from a gushing mountain stream. The cold liquid felt good sliding down Mara's throat, as did the fine spray of mist that cooled her skin. She was loath to budge but when Deke gave the signal, she gamely packed away the remnants of her repast and slung her backpack over her shoulders. Already her muscles ached and she knew it would only get worse. The soggy humidity added to the discomfort.

The path took them from a rocky incline to a tract along a river and then it diverged into a quagmire of greasy clay and mud. Water glistened on leaves, and dripping noises accompanied the chirping of birds and the cheep of catarrhines overhead.

Once or twice she glanced back, thinking she sensed someone watching, but the stillness of the jungle met her gaze. Plodding along, she caught a glimpse of a furry gray animal peeking at them from a thick cluster of reedy platwhacks. Then the trail took a downward curve.

Up and down the hills they went at a steady pace. One stretch hugged a slope and below they saw a rushing river boiling over a bed of boulders.

Deke stopped when they came upon a dilapidated house constructed of roughly hewn boards. The wood sagged with rot, but the abandoned dwelling would provide shelter for the night. Deke ordered them to make camp.

Hedy passed around a handful of igoob leaves. "Rub these on your skin. It'll keep the insects away," she said.

Deke and Wren produced a meal of boiled elephant-ear roots. The starchy plant food tasted like potatoes with a nutty flavor. It filled their stomachs and left them satisfied, albeit tired from the day.

They prepared the hut and claimed spaces inside. Rain drummed on the tin roof and insects buzzed outside the netting they'd strung across the open doorway. Wren stayed awake, taking the first watch, while Mara and the others drifted to sleep.

****

Mara awakened at the first hint of dawn. Rising, she saw Deke had fallen asleep by his post at the door. His expression appeared peaceful.

Not wishing to disturb him, she brushed past, lifting the netting out of her way. Beside a large tree, she relieved herself and cleansed her hands and face in a running stream. A flat rock beckoned to her and she sat, facing the forest. It had been a long time since she'd meditated like this, surrounded by the beauty of nature. She began a series of exercises, mental and physical, designed to open and charge the chakras.

Her consciousness expanded as she experienced the connectedness of everything around her. The universal energy field flowed through her until she could see the shimmering vortices of her auric layers. They pulsated with each breath she took.

A ripple in the force attracted her attention. Glancing over her shoulder, she noticed Deke stumbling from the direction of the hut, a groggy look on his face.

"Mara?" he called.

"I'm over here." She waved and stood to watch him approach.

With her heightened perception, the rose-colored arcs that sparked between their chakras were electrifyingly real. With pleasure she noticed they were thickening at the lower levels, meaning Deke might be beginning to accept her. A leap of joy filled her heart.

His auric bodies glowed with energy. As he neared, a finger of light reached out from his emotional layer, stretching toward her.

Her astral being separated from her essence and flew toward

him, ready to envelop him with her love. Immediately his light extinguished, and she was thrust back into her physical body.

I caused him to withdraw, she realized. He was still walking in her direction, unaware that anything other than a verbal exchange had passed between them. He must have perceived her as a threat. He'd sensed her aura was about to invade his mind. It must be disturbing to someone of his limited perception.

If only I could let him call the shots. What if she reined in her response and tightened control over herself? Could she prevent the separations?

"What are you doing out here?" he asked, his tone gruff. "I got worried when I woke up and you weren't inside."

She thrilled at the concern implied by his words. His hair was unkempt, his jaw shadowed by stubble, and his treksuit rumpled. But for all his dishevelment, he looked spectacular.

"I needed some time alone," she replied.

His clear brown eyes held hers. "I've been meaning to talk to you. I'm sorry about the way I acted yesterday. I was rude and thoughtless, and I've no excuse other than I get scared when I lose control over this situation. I don't know how to deal with it… or you."

She traced her finger along his jawline. "It's my fault, too. I haven't been trying hard enough to control my separations. If I respond less intensely to events that affect you, perhaps that will help."

Deke caught her hand and kissed her palm. "I don't know if I like that idea. Even when I want to resist you, I can't. You're like a wood nymph come to tempt me. When I'm near you, my mind goes numb and my body reacts the only way a man can respond to a beautiful woman."

She shuddered at his sensual tone of voice. His mere presence had the power to weaken her knees and vaporize her reason. Steeling herself against his allure, she closed her eyes when he bent his head to kiss her.

The pressure of his mouth on hers strengthened her desire, but she continued to resist the onslaught to her senses. If she limited her response, she might prevent another separation.

Deke's mouth hungered for hers. As he pressed his lips against her mouth, he pulled her close and reveled in the softness of her body. She was the Light personified—beauty, grace, compassion, and intelligence encased in a loveliness that had no parallel. His desire exploded and he moaned her name, scraping his fingers through her thick hair.

But what was this? Instead of her usual enthusiastic, almost wanton response, she was barely moving her mouth under his. Nor did her chest heave with excitement. Did she no longer find him desirable? Had he hurt her so badly that he'd killed her passion?

A wave of panic swept over him. So intense was it that he became frightened. Lifting his head, he gazed at her with a puzzled frown. "Mara, what's wrong?"

Her long lashes flicked open. Her eyes, wide and dark as an eclipsed sun, stared at him in confusion. "What do you mean?"

"You're not... I mean, you don't seem interested." He dropped his hands and moved back.

For a moment she didn't answer. Then a sympathetic smile curved her lips. "I was trying to be less responsive. I thought it might prevent me from separating if I exercised better self-control."

"But you said it was my strong emotions that drew you to me."

"That is so, but I can do my part to rein in my feelings. Perhaps you should try to restrain your reactions, too."

He stared at her. "Restrain my reactions? Are you crazy? Don't you know what being near you does to me?"

Mara merely shrugged. "It's your choice, Deke. I'm offering you an option. You hate it when I jump into your head. If we both act more dispassionately, it may help avoid another occurrence."

"But..." He trailed off lamely.

Speechless, he didn't know how to respond. What if she never entered his persona again? Wasn't that what he wanted? He thought long and hard while she kicked at a fallen branch on the ground, and decided he wasn't happy either way.

He couldn't abide her invading his mind but didn't want to lose the incredible sensation of being united with her. Yet he couldn't have it both ways. Either he accepted her fully, sacrificing his right to mental privacy, or he'd have to reject her completely.

"I don't care for your option," he blurted. "I like the way you are when we make love. I don't want you to inhibit your response to me." He paused, struggling with his own confused feelings. "I'll try it your way. I'll let you into my mind… whenever you want to come." If he was willing to receive her, maybe the experience would seem less intrusive.

Her keen eyes probed his. "You're not ready yet. I still sense reluctance and fear. You have to be the one to take control, not me."

He didn't understand what she meant but didn't care. Her feminine scent overwhelmed his resolve. The sun had risen and a heavy mist drifted into the valley. The meager sunlight caught the droplets of moisture and illuminated them in a luminescent glow from behind that made Mara look like a goddess with her hair streaming down.

A surge of blood rushed to his groin. By the corona, if he was to be the one to take control, he wanted her, here and now.

"Mara, be mine," he mumbled, grasping her by the shoulders.

Crushing her into his embrace, he lowered his mouth to hers. She must have sensed his wild need because her lips parted and her arms coiled around him.

She gave herself willingly to his embrace. Spiritually they were already connected, and now he'd begun to reach out to her on an elemental level. It was happening the way she'd hoped, and she didn't want to do anything to disrupt this new status.

Accordingly, she let him make all the first moves and tightened her resolution not to separate until he wished for it. Even if she found herself hovering in her astral body, she'd exert all her force of will not to enter his essence until he summoned her.

And he did summon her while his hands desperately roamed her back and his mouth plundered hers with a mad intensity that thrilled her.

"Mara…"

She could almost hear the unspoken words. They were like the wind, a whisper in her ear. The spiritual call broke her restraint and she merged with Deke's energy signature. She felt his arousal and knew he wanted to give her all that she'd given him and more.

Her breath caught in her throat as he lowered her onto a carpet of moss. As the mist drifted over them, erasing their surroundings, he peeled off her treksuit and undergarments and discarded his own.

"Gods, you're exquisite." He kissed first one breast and then the other.

Clutching at his hair, she tangled her fingers in the soft waves as though they were a lifeline and she were drowning. He took his time, teasing each nipple into a taut peak and massaging her other breast with his hand. His tender touch drove her wild, more so when they shared their reactions. The dual delight made them mad with passion.

He shifted his position and their mouths clamped together. Tasting his hot breath inflamed her senses, and her desire skyrocketed. Splaying her hands across his broad back, she rocked her hips, pushing against his engorged organ.

Take me now, she pleaded in silence.

As though he'd heard, Deke thrust into her in one hard motion. For a moment, he suspended movement, as though he wanted to relish her tightness and experience the fullness he brought to her. She could barely breathe, so taut was the knot of tension inside her. When he slid out and in again at an agonizingly slow pace, she dug her fingernails into his skin.

The inferno that had been building inside her rushed toward the surface. As he drove deeper into her body with a grunt of male glory, she reached her climax. Her shuddering spasms brought him over the edge, and his seed spurted into her.

Yes, Mara thought. *I am yours.*

I know, Deke's mind responded. *You are mine… and only mine.*

She sensed his possessiveness, and a surge of joy filled her. He recognized how right it felt for them to be together.

But now wasn't the time to count her blessings. They still had a job to do, and she didn't dare distract him any longer.

As soon as she'd broken their spiritual link, she rolled off him. "The daylight is dispersing the fog. We'd better move on."

Deke lingered to kiss her lightly on her tender lips. "We'll talk later… about us. I'm still not sure where I want this to go, but I know I can't risk losing you. We'll work something out."

Great suns, what did he mean? Did he not intend to ask her to come home with him? And if she did get an invite, what about her job on Bimordus Two?

Troubled, she pulled on her clothes, casting a surreptitious glance at the forest surrounding them. Strange animal warbles and hoots accompanied the sound of dripping water. The air was fresh with the scent of rain. When the mist rose, it promised to be a lovely sunlit day.

So why did she have a sudden premonition? Was it because of what Deke had said?

A chill racked her body but she shrugged off her irrational fear, excusing it as anxiety over his remark. It wasn't a sense of real danger that bothered her, more like a question of where their relationship was going.

Deke still hadn't made a commitment to her. What role did he see her playing in his life?

The time for debate was over. Striding toward the ramshackle hut, she wondered if Hedy and Wren were awake. Deke walked quietly beside her, deep in thought.

His mind was already focused on the mission, she figured. If only she could cast him from her thoughts so easily. But given her serious disposition, that was impossible. Her problems preoccupied her to the exclusion of all else, and even Jallyn's precarious situation paled beside her yearning for Deke's acceptance.

He was right. Their relationship was proving to be a distraction neither of them needed.

****

After breaking camp, Deke led the others along the trail up a rigorous incline. He should have been thinking about the upcoming confrontation with the NARC rebels but instead was replaying his lovemaking with Mara in his imagination.

His loins stirred as he relived the feel of her pliant body against his. It was difficult to concentrate on their mission when all he could think about was when they'd lie together next.

Trudging along the mountainous path, he used the pretense of wanting to discuss a plan of action with Wren to move ahead of the women. His backpack felt heavier today, and even though the sunlight reaching the ground was dim, his body was bathed in sweat. The mist had lifted, leaving a heavy humidity that made breathing laborious on the rough path they followed.

"You're sure we're heading in the right direction?" Deke queried his navigator.

Wren appeared winded by the climb through rock-laden trails, or maybe it was the occasional glimpse of a precipice and a huge drop-off to the side that made his face pale and his breath come short.

"I got a rebound echo from up there," he said, pointing.

Deke nodded grimly. "The mountaintop could be crawling with rebels. We'll have to be careful. I wish we didn't have to protect the women. We should have sent them back to the ship."

Wren glowered at him. "Don't let Mara hear you say that. She'd be sure to present an argument."

Deke gave him a sideways glance. "I still don't know what to do about her when this is over. How about you and Hedy?"

Wren's lips tightened. "It is not my choice. I cannot pursue her."

"Mara told me how she found the two of you at the bathing pool. She was sorry for the interruption."

Mara had related the story yesterday during one of their rest breaks when she and Deke had a moment alone.

"I thought Dr. Te'larr was in distress," Wren explained, his face coloring. "When I came upon her under the waterfall, she was floundering in the lake and hollering for assistance."

"So you jumped in, clothes and all, while she was stark naked." Deke chuckled. "It was a come-on, you big oaf. And you fell for it."

"She was so alluring, I couldn't help myself."

"Maybe you need to lie with her to cure your problem. Have you considered that possibility?"

Wren shook his head vehemently. "I have not passed the ritual test. I cannot take a mate until I do."

"Well, in my opinion, you're wasting the chance of a lifetime."

They passed under a rocky overhang and Deke glimpsed a small, furred animal drinking from a pool of rainwater. The trail cut through a steep section of soggy forest and his boots squished through the muck. The fresh smell of wet leaves mixed with the scent of rain-washed soil.

Mushrooms and molds sprouted on fallen logs and even the insects were coated with fungus, so damp was the forest in this area. Wren tramped beside him, lost in thought. The women talked quietly behind them, keeping the pace.

The top of the mountain appeared unexpectedly. One minute they were enclosed by the lush jungle and the next they'd broken into a nearly barren area dotted with stunted trees. To the west, the shiny reflective surface of an ocean was visible, and to the east were the dark green lowlands. A strong wind blew up, flapping their clothes and ruffling their hair.

"We'll stop here," Deke ordered, bringing his party to a halt. "Wren, do an inventory on our supplies. I'll notify Ebo of our progress."

Pulling out his datalink, he conferred with his officer, informing Ebo they were about to enter hostile territory.

Wren checked the charges on their weapons and wiped off the moisture while Hedy stood by him on a nearby rise. Mara waited for Deke to finish his conversation with Ebo.

"Do you wish to do a separation to check on Jallyn?" Deke asked when he'd cut the comm line.

"Not now. I'll wait until we're closer. Do you really think we have a chance of rescuing her?"

He squinted in the bright sunlight. "I've worked with heavier odds before. We'll save her."

The reassuring words were barely out of his mouth when Hedy's shrill scream pierced the air.

Chapter Twenty

"Kill them!" Kromas ordered in standard Jawani. He pointed to Mara and her friends who stood in the central hall of a huge stone fortress built into the mountainside, the ancient lair of a tribe from Yanura's distant past.

Hedy's scream had signaled an attack by hidden sentries who'd risen from what turned out to be artificially constructed boulders at the lookout point where they'd stopped to rest.

Having been divested of their weapons and marched to the rebel stronghold, they were now the center of a heated argument. Armed insurgents surrounded them, and an uneasy grumbling pervaded the National Revolutionary Congress's command center as their leaders wrestled for power.

"We'll keep them alive for now," countered Ragger Minn, a thinly built Wort with a yellowish tinge to his brown skin. "We can use them as a bargaining tool against Fromoth Trun."

Dressed in a short belted brown tunic with an animal fur thrown over his shoulders, he radiated an aura of command. Mara realized he could be a formidable opponent even though he favored sparing their lives.

With her wrists bound behind her back, she couldn't reach out to Deke for reassurance. He stood beside her, rigid with tension, doubtless figuring the odds and trying to determine a means of escape. She'd prefer using diplomacy rather than violence. Certainly, it was worth a try.

"Excuse me." Her voice rang loud and clear in the cavernous hall. Dozens of bulging eyes shifted in her direction. "What exactly are your demands to Fromoth Trun? Perhaps we could help you obtain them."

Kromas's mouth split in a sneer. "Fromoth Trun doesn't listen to us. Why should he hear what you have to say?" He paced closer, eyeing her as though she'd make a tasty meal.

"He wants to be admitted into the Coalition," Deke ventured, glancing at her with a nod of approval. "Our welfare is important to him. If you tell us what it is you want, we can mediate between you."

"Yanura must not be accepted into the Coalition," Kromas shouted, spittle forming at the corner of his mouth. "Killing you and the infant will ensure that never happens."

Mara's breath hitched. "Jallyn is here? Can I see her?"

Kromas stuck his face in front of hers and she sniffed his foul breath. "You'll be joining her soon enough." He swiveled his head to regard Deke with unbridled hostility. "How did you escape the stinger eels in Dead Wort's Marsh? I thought we'd left you for dead."

Deke gave a cocky grin. "I scared them off."

Kromas stepped over and backhanded him. Deke stumbled backward.

"Stop," Ragger Minn said. "You are out of line. Do you wish to be forcibly removed from this council?"

Kromas's eyes narrowed as he slowly spun around. "Try it, *vermuchak.*"

Ragger Minn met his gaze with a burning stare and seemed to grow in stature. "Do not upset my patience. Our demands to Fromoth Trun are valid. It is the reason most of us are here. Are you saying you oppose our goals?"

Tension cut through the air. Finally, Kromas answered. "I don't agree with your slow methods of achieving them, especially considering the current crisis."

"Will somebody please explain what's going on?" Mara cut in. Their lives were at stake and she didn't understand why. "And can't you unbind us? My fingers are going numb."

Ragger Minn nodded to an associate who cut their corded bonds. Mara rubbed her chafed skin, wishing Hedy could apply a balm, but their knapsacks had been confiscated.

"Our demands to Fromoth Trun are threefold," Ragger Minn said, glaring at the prisoners. "Every Yanuran is routinely administered the drug Vyclor beginning at age twenty. After several initiating dosages, the drug must be continued for life. If stopped, the withdrawal symptoms can cause a painful death. Since the Croags operate the merl beds and processing centers, they control the supply of Vyclor. No one dares oppose them for fear of getting their dose of the drug cut off."

Mara nodded. "We understand. Go on."

"Taking Vyclor should be a choice. Not everyone wants to extend their natural lifespan through artificial means, and forcing Vyclor on the entire populace gives the Croags too much power. They abuse their authority and exploit our young. That's our strongest point of contention."

"Can you elaborate?" Mara tilted her head, glad they'd opened a dialogue.

The rebel leader hunched his shoulders, his eyes boring into hers. "Our children are taken from us shortly after birth. They're forced to live in underwater communities and to harvest the merl. This agreement goes back for generations, but who can protest it? The Croags allow no one else to participate in governmental decisions. We only want a voice in government and the right to make decisions that affect us."

Deke jabbed a finger in the air. "Then why did you abduct the Great Healer's child? You're guilty of a heinous crime. How do you rationalize this action?"

Kromas straightened. "Tell them about the missiles, Ragger Minn. They'll see that sometimes violence must be met with violence to make a stand." An approving mumble sounded from the watching crowd.

Behind Mara, Wren grunted, and she wondered if he was uncomfortable. It had been several hauras since he'd opened his wings and he might be feeling the tension of confinement in ways other than the rest of them. He'd be mortified if his wings erupted in front of their captors.

Ragger Minn strutted toward Deke and her attention diverted to him. "We received intelligence reports that the Croags had found a new use for their pharmaceutical research division. Their labs produced a weapon of incalculable danger, and they were preparing missiles to launch an offensive against us. This is why our tactics turned desperate."

Deke's eyes widened. "What kind of weapon? And how far away are they from being able to launch it? Where did they get the technology to build missiles?"

Ragger Minn scratched his ear disk. "The Croags have created a chemical weapon using genetic manipulation of the drug Vyclor. The destructive agent, when inhaled in droplet form, causes the reverse effect of the anti-aging mechanism. The victim's metabolism accelerates, and he dies of heart failure within minutes. They've used our captured comrades as test subjects. We've holophotos of their dead bodies as evidence."

So that was what those bodies signified on the stolen data card. Glancing at Mara, Deke saw comprehension dawn on her face.

"Do you know where the Croags are stockpiling this stuff?" He had the feeling he knew the place even if the rebels hadn't a clue.

"Yes," Kromas growled, "but the place is too remotely situated for us to attack, and anyway, it's the missile site that concerns us more. The warheads are already locked in. All the Croags await is a detonation device that would be available once they had access to Coalition technology."

No wonder Fromoth Trun is in such a hurry to get special trade status. "The Coalition doesn't sell detonators or other war-making devices," Deke said.

Ragger Minn made a dismissive gesture. "Once he earns enough credits from the sale of Vyclor, Fromoth Trun can buy them on the black market. Where do you think he got those missiles? I believe he bought them from the Rakkians."

Deke's pulse accelerated. "It was two Rakkians who stole Jallyn from her nursery."

"Joro and Pruet." Ragger Minn smirked. "You should know the Rakkians are a stinking race who hire their services to anyone willing to pay the price. Their technology is also available but it's much more expensive."

"I hired the assassins to steal the child for us," Kromas said. "They hid her in a special sensor-reflective insulated cabin inside their ship at the spaceport on Bimordus Two. The Defense League was fooled into chasing after the three vessels that launched following the abduction. Two days later, the Rakkian ship lifted off without arousing suspicions, and they delivered her to us."

Deke nodded. "So Fromoth Trun was being truthful. He didn't know anything about the abduction at the time of his launch."

"Correct," Kromas replied, "but he found out about it soon enough when we told him we'd kill the child and place the blame on him if he didn't accede to our demands."

Hedy cleared her throat. "When he wouldn't listen, you attacked me and Wren in the city, didn't you?"

Ragger Minn glowered at her. "Your deaths would have impeded his relations with the Coalition. It was Kromas's idea, not mine. Having the baby is enough leverage to bear."

"And it's not working," Kromas responded. Voices of approval rose to join his. "Fromoth Trun refuses to yield power. I say kill them all and notify the Coalition that Fromoth Trun is responsible. That'll put a halt to his grandiose plans."

Loud murmurs erupted, putting forth arguments for both sides.

"If you kill us," Deke cautioned, "you'll face Coalition retribution. They won't just target Fromoth Trun. The Defense League will wreak havoc on your entire planet. This jungle will be made uninhabitable for eons."

"We are listening, human, but I fear you are not hearing us," Ragger Minn said, a resigned look on his thin frog face. "Take them below while we decide their fate," he ordered. Troops immediately surrounded them.

"Please, may we see Jallyn?" Mara asked.

"You may assume responsibility for her care," Kromas growled. "The brat has been giving her Rakkian caretaker a headache ever since she arrived, and her squalling makes us all edgy. She's yours for as long as you are here. And if I have my way, that won't be for long."

****

Kromas's evil snorting laughter echoed in Mara's ears as the guards led them through twisting corridors into the depths of the fortress. The air grew cold and damp, and she shivered in her treksuit. Where were they being taken?

Something hit her with the force of a tidal wave. She stopped, stunned. It wasn't anything material. She'd sensed it in her mind. And now she was being tugged mentally in a forward direction.

With faltering steps, she proceeded along. Deke steadied her by the elbow, giving her a sharp glance. Their armed escort prevented any conversation.

The chamber they were led into had a vaulted ceiling, cold stone walls, and a casement high on one side. She recognized it instantly. The baby's crib stood by a wall, and a basket heaped with supplies rested on the floor beside it.

At their entrance, a woman with brown hair knotted into a low bun rose from her chair. Her violet eyes regarded them with surprise.

A baby wailed, making Mara wince at the assault to her ears. She rushed forward to where Jallyn howled in her crib.

As soon as Mara peeked over the rim, the baby stopped crying and gave a happy gurgle. Mara's mental tension eased, and she sensed the child's acute relief at glimpsing a familiar, friendly face.

"We've found you. Poor baby." She scooped Jallyn into her arms and buried her face against the baby's soft cheek. Tears stung her eyes. She couldn't believe they'd found the child. At last, Jallyn was safe.

Or was she?

Holding the infant, she glanced at the guards. The troop commandant was addressing the caretaker.

"Your duties are terminated. Transport back to Rakkia has been arranged. Gather your belongings and go see Ragger Minn for final payment."

With a grateful bow, the woman left for the adjoining chamber. A few moments later, she returned carrying a large satchel. "I am ready," she announced, and the troop escorted her from the room.

A loud click signaled the latching of an electronic lock from outside. Mara and her friends glanced at each other.

Deke broke the morose silence. "How is Jallyn? Is she well?"

Mara tickled the baby. "She looks healthy."

Her senses picked up the infant's contentment in her arms. Jallyn's communion with the universal energy field must be strong. No wonder the caretaker complained of headaches in her presence. Jallyn must have been bombarding her with hostile mental vibes.

Kissing the baby's forehead, she thought she'd never experienced such joy.

"What do we do with her?" Deke asked.

From the corner of her eye, she noticed Hedy and Wren disappearing into the adjacent chamber. "We have diapers and formula." She tilted her head to indicate the basket on the floor. "And I see a vapor unit and a synthesizer by that wall, so we can cleanse her cloth diapers and refill the bottles. All she needs is right here."

Hedy emerged in time to hear her last sentence. "I wish I had my medkit to examine her. The other room holds a wide lounger, plus a cooling unit with food and water."

A flapping noise told Mara that Wren was exercising his wings. "Wren needs his nutrient drinks."

"I can survive without it for several days," the Polluxite said, appearing in the doorway.

"What happens now?" Hedy asked with a frown.

"We wait." Mara nuzzled the baby's neck and sat in the lone chair. "Jallyn, my sweet," she murmured, tweaking her tiny fingers. At least Jallyn's footed sleeper kept her warm.

"We may have found her," Deke said curtly, "but that doesn't mean we're going to get out of here alive."

Mara wished she could gauge his emotion. At first, she'd sensed strong affection emanating from him, but now he seemed irritated. Was he jealous of the attention she showed the child? She wanted to laugh at the absurdity of that notion, but the sober look in his eye told her she might be on track. Either that, or he figured their chances of survival weren't too high.

****

They slept fitfully through the night, snacking on food in the cooler and discussing different options for escape. In the morning, Mara packed the infant's supplies in a carryall they'd found in a closet. Now footsteps approached from outside.

Deke straightened his shoulders while Mara enveloped Jallyn in her arms. Hedy and Wren stood side by side, their faces wary.

The lock clicked, and the door swung wide. Facing them was the same troop commander and his escort.

"We have arranged for your transfer to Revitt Lake City. You may bring the child," he added, nodding at Jallyn.

So Ragger Minn had won out, Deke thought. He presumed they were being sent to Fromoth Trun to plead the case for the rebels. A denial of the Yanuran's application was inevitable due to political instability.

His relief was short-lived. As soon as they emerged from the fortress into the mist-enshrouded forest, Mara put her hand on his arm.

"Something is wrong," she whispered.

He adjusted the sack on his shoulder that held Jallyn's supplies. "What do you mean?"

She glanced at the encroaching jungle with frightened eyes. "They haven't given us back our equipment, nor has Ragger Minn spoken to us. I don't like it."

They resumed their climb up the rocky incline. The raucous cries of birds and the occasional howl of a wild animal emitted from the heavy vegetation. The rising sunlight barely penetrated the thick foliage to lift the mist. Mara clutched Jallyn tightly in her arms, afraid of stumbling.

Suddenly, their trail ended in a rocky precipice. The troops stepped back, laser rifles drawn and pointed at them.

"What is this?" Deke said, while Mara's breath hitched.

"Kromas has decreed that you are to die. It is for the good of the people." He raised his arm to give the order to fire.

At that moment, a squad of war-painted Worts jumped out from behind the surrounding trees, screeching battle cries. Fighting broke out and laser fire zinged back and forth as the attackers engaged the troops. An alarm sounded as another wave assaulted the fortress.

Deke pushed Mara to the ground, covering her body with his. Mara cradled the baby to protect her.

"Hedy," Wren yelled, charging after her as she ran from the melee.

Rocks and fallen logs obstructed his path but he agilely avoided them, his fear for Hedy spurring him on. Running along the rocky promontory, he was heedless of the soldiers chasing after them.

"Stop!" he shouted at her. "This track is dangerous. The ledge could crumple any minute."

One moment she was in view, and the next, she was gone.

Laser bolts singed his ears, but Wren paid them no heed. He teetered at the edge of the precipice and glanced down. His blood went cold as horror rippled through him.

Hedy's body tumbled through the air. Far, far below were jagged rocks. She would be impaled.

Without a moment's doubt, he spread his wings and leapt off the cliff. If he couldn't fly to save her, then he'd join her in death.

As he began his freefall, a wondrous thing happened. His wings started flapping. Up and down in a series of powerful strokes, they beat rhythmically just as they did when he was exercising them.

Instinctively, he furled them back, streamlining his body so he was able to dive downward with startling speed. And then he was below Hedy, swooping her limp form into his strong arms.

He soared upward, realizing she had fainted but glad she was safe. He broke out of the mist into the blinding sunlight just as her lids fluttered open. She regarded him with amazement.

"Wren, you're flying."

"Aye, so I am," he answered, his voice tremulous. "Because of you, Hedy Te'larr, I am a whole man. I would like nothing more than to demonstrate my deep gratitude. However, I cannot abandon my friends. I shall put you down and go to help them."

"Don't you dare leave me behind. Mara's in trouble, and I'm coming along." She clung to him, careful not to obstruct his powerful wings.

He landed a short distance away so no one could see their approach. He and Hedy closed in on foot, assessing the situation from behind a clump of bushes.

A contingent of Croags had arrived and taken command. The rebels were subdued. Deke, Mara, and Jallyn appeared unharmed.

Deke appeared to be in a heated argument with the Croag officer in charge, but no one was pointing shooters at him, so Wren assumed everything was under control.

"What's going on?" he asked after revealing his presence.

Mara rushed to her friend's side. "Hedy, where have you been? I got worried when you disappeared."

Still clutching Jallyn in her arms, Mara appeared disheveled, her treksuit splattered with mud and her damp hair plastered to her face. It had rained in the short interval they'd been away.

Hedy gave a secretive smile. "I'll tell you later. What happened here?"

"Apparently, the Wort warriors from the village followed us," Deke explained. "They notified the Croags of the location and both launched a joint attack. Will you look at this shuttle?" He gestured to a sleek metal vehicle parked in a clearing. "It may be an older model, but it's still functional."

"Sir, if you don't mind," the Croag officer said with a stern expression.

"He wants us to board the shuttle but won't explain where we're going," Deke told Wren.

"Fromoth Trun wishes a dialogue with you," the soldier commented.

"I'll bet he does." Deke drew his crew aside for a quick conference. "We know too much, and Fromoth Trun is a desperate character. I say let's head back to the *Celeste*. I should notify the Admissions Committee about this situation and ask for instructtions."

A Wort ran up to them, delivering their knapsacks, which Deke had insisted be returned. A hasty inspection showed everything present except for their weapons and datalinks.

"Where's my comm unit?" Deke demanded. "I need to contact my ship." He glanced up, straight into the barrel of a shooter pointed at his chest. The Croag officer had drawn his weapon.

Instinctively Mara moved closer and he draped a protective arm around her shoulder. Hedy gasped as other Croags surrounded them, and Wren's string of expletives rang in the steamy morning air.

"Board the shuttle as you're told," the Croag said, his stance militant.

"Fromoth Trun will regret this," Deke promised, shouldering his knapsack on one side and the baby's carryall on the other.

The infant started squalling and Mara squeezed her close, murmuring reassuring words in her ear. But the child with the sign of the circle on her palm must have sensed danger, because she wouldn't let up.

Deke cast Mara a sympathetic glance but was unable to help. Worried about how he'd get his team safely off planet, he marched in front of the others toward the waiting shuttle.

At least he still had his dive computer strapped to his wrist. He could use the backup datalink to call Ebo, but first it might be smart to see where they were headed.

Maybe Mara could use her diplomatic skills to talk Fromoth Trun into freeing them, although Deke had a bad feeling that wherever they were going, it was a one-way trip.

"Move." The Croag officer prodded him along by shoving the shooter into his back.

He grunted his displeasure, resisting the urge to turn around and punch the fellow. Getting beaten into submission wouldn't aid their cause. Gritting his teeth, he strode up the ramp into the vessel, glancing back at Mara to make sure she didn't need his assistance.

Once inside, he took the seat assigned him and strapped on his safety restraint as the crew began flight procedures. Mara sat beside him, stretching the harness to secure herself and the child. Hedy and Wren were situated behind them.

A jolting lurch initiated the journey and the sky tilted outside the viewport. They soared toward the heavens but the journey was short. Soon they'd vectored away from the mountains and taken a sharp dive downward, toward the sparkling aqua sea.

As the hiss of pressurized air reached her ears, Mara's throat constricted. The sharp angle of descent made her queasy. This vessel must lack the inertial dampeners that the shuttle from the *Celeste* had to make the ride tolerable.

"I feel sick," she said to Deke, as the baby wailed. The loud noise in the small space increased her discomfort.

"Hold your nose and blow," he suggested. "It'll help equalize the pressure."

The sea's surface loomed toward them and they plunged through the waves, the shuttle's vibrations altering as it adjusted to the fluid environment. Silvery fish and marine mammals swam past their viewport in a blur. As they neared the seabed, a structure in the distance became visible through the murky water. It appeared to be a series of interlocking spheres and cylinders.

"By the Light, it's an undersea city," Mara said, gaping at the sight.

Deke pressed something on his dive computer. She guessed he was recording the depth and coordinates. The shuttle slowed, rocking side-to-side as the pilot lined up with a connecting port.

A loud clanging noise signaled they had docked. Grating sounds reverberated in the cabin as the locking mechanism activated.

"Return to Seabase One after we depart," the troop commander told the pilot. "We'll call you if you're needed again." He rose, along with the three soldiers who had accompanied him. "Follow me," he said to Deke and his team.

Mara unfastened her restraint and stood, glad to ease a cramp in her leg. Jallyn had stopped crying, having worn herself out and fallen asleep in Mara's arms.

"Do you feel all right?" Deke asked, a solicitous frown on his face.

"I'm better, thanks." Her stomach had settled now that they'd landed. She didn't speak as they were herded through the hatchway into a service chamber with an array of equipment.

Hedy touched her elbow from behind. "I don't like this place."

"Neither do I." Mara clutched Jallyn tighter to her chest as they were prodded onto a pneumatic platform. The troop leader pulled a lever and the platform descended.

Three levels down, they came to a stop. A familiar frog face stood waiting to greet them in a maintenance area.

"Rogi Kwantro," Fromoth Trun said, beating his chest with his fist and bowing elegantly as though they were on a diplomatic tour. "Welcome to Habitat Oceania."

"What is the meaning of this?" Deke demanded, stepping forward.

"Ludack, you may report to the duty station with your troops," Fromoth Trun addressed the officer. The Croag saluted and led his soldiers through a hatchway into another section.

"Commander Sage, you should be grateful we rescued you from the rebels. They planned to kill you and the child."

"You knew about Jallyn all along, didn't you?" Mara asked, her voice tense.

Her arms were getting tired from holding the baby. Jallyn, still asleep, breathed softly through her tiny nose, her sweet scent making Mara's heart melt.

"The National Revolutionary Congress contacted me shortly after Jallyn's arrival on Yanura," Fromoth Trun answered. "I'd hoped to resolve the situation without troubling you."

"How absurd. Why do you think we were sent here? Investigating your claims about Vyclor was only one reason. We were also searching for Jallyn." She shifted her position. "By any chance, did your plans for resolving the situation include—"

"We need to return to our ship," Deke cut in, casting her a warning glance. "Lieutenant Ebo has a fix on our position. He'll take certain prescribed actions if I don't report in."

"You can contact him in a short while," Fromoth Trun said in a smooth tone. His brown skin darkened, which Mara had learned meant he was being untruthful. "First, allow me to show you around our undersea community. You're from a water world. I'm sure you'll appreciate our unique habitat."

The Croag gave Mara and the others a cursory glance, as though dismissing their importance. "Perhaps your friends would care to refresh themselves while we talk. We can improvise a cradle for the child so she can sleep in peace."

Miffed at Fromoth Trun's attitude, Mara lifted her chin. "We'd be interested in the tour also, thank you. Which way shall we go?"

The Croag glared at her. "Very well. Follow me." With a swish of his robes, he proceeded through a series of compartments separated by hatchways. He left a fishy odor in his wake.

Deke took the lead beside the Yanuran potentate. She followed behind, sensing hostility directed at the Coalition team, including Jallyn. It didn't bode well for their future, and she figured they'd be smart to consider a means of escape.

Gods, to think she'd believed everything Fromoth Trun had told her on Bimordus Two. What a naive fool!

No wonder Deke had scorned her initial assessment of the Yanurans while on board the *Celeste.* She may have been right about Fromoth Trun's innocence regarding Jallyn's abduction, but he'd been informed as soon as the NARCs received the baby from the Rakkians hired to capture her. He'd hidden the truth from them and even now was planning to launch missiles armed with chemical warheads at the rebels.

The Croag led them through the habitat, pointing out the sights as though they were welcomed guests. They passed through a series of laboratories, data centers, machine shops, and living quarters that covered all three levels. Finally, they came to an observation lounge with floor-to-ceiling windows.

Mara nudged Deke. "Look at those Yanurans swimming through that maze of plants. They're children."

Deke turned a questioning glance on Fromoth Trun.

"Indeed, you are correct. Our young are born with gills. Because they must breathe underwater, we bring them here. It is convenient to use them as a labor force to harvest the merl. At puberty, the young Yanurans develop lungs and are reunited with their mothers to live on land."

Mara glowered at him. "The Wort villagers are not pleased with this way of life, nor are the NARCs. They claim you conscript the young of many races."

Fromoth Trun's skin mottled, and he made a sweeping gesture. "The children must live somewhere, and we provide them with an entire underwater city. We even bring teachers down from the surface to instruct them. Adults come in shifts, adjusting their lifestyles in order to enter the watery environment."

"How do you communicate?" Deke asked. Beside him, Mara

handed Jallyn over to Hedy. The baby stirred, making whimpering noises.

"The children have an inherent ability to communicate with each other underwater. As adults, we use a hydrophone device built into a face mask."

Deke nodded, that form of communication being familiar to him. A hydrophone sent out high-frequency sound waves. On Eranus, they used a headset that picked up mastoid bone sound transfers using a similar principle.

Gazing out the window, he studied the youngsters swimming around outside. The habitat he and the others stood in was filled with pressurized air. Adult Croags who came here to work with the young would need time to adapt to the change in environment. Although they were amphibians, they'd gotten used to living on land.

That meant there would be air locks, an important factor he stored away for later use.

Fromoth Trun explained how the young labor force cut the merl stipes and loaded the harvest onto platforms that rose to the surface. From there the cut stalks were transferred to a ship that went to a processing center. Communities like this one were stationed all around the globe at offshore regions rich with merl farms.

"The crystalline rocks are used to make Vyclor, aren't they?" Deke said.

Fromoth Trun nodded. "Our youngsters load the bits of rock into bins, which are then transferred to the surface." He gazed at Deke thoughtfully. "Your friend Larikk first introduced us to the idea of putting Vyclor on the galactic marketplace. He offered to help us get it approved in exchange for a cut of the profits. The NARCs killed him, hoping to discourage other offworlders from taking advantage of us."

"If Vyclor was put on the market, how would you use the profits?" Mara asked.

"We'd buy harvester machines so our children wouldn't be

forced to do this work. That's why we're so anxious for early trade status. We wish to make reforms that will ease the burden on our young. Commander, I'll set up a commlink so you can send a message to the Coalition approving our admissions status, and then you can all leave." He beamed at them, clearly expecting Deke's acquiescence.

Deke's eyes narrowed. "I don't know that I'm ready to give my approval. In fact, because of the political situation with the rebels, I might recommend a rejection of your application."

Fromoth Trun bristled. "I said we're willing to make reforms. Once we have the harvesters, we can sit down with the NARCs to discuss their complaints."

"The conscription of the young is not their only issue," Mara explained. "They demand representation in the central government and an end to routine distribution of Vyclor. They say everyone should have freedom of choice regarding administration of the drug."

The Yanuran leader scowled at her. "If they wish to die young, that is their business. It was decided long ago that the population as a whole would benefit from the treatment. But these are issues that can be discussed later, after we obtain the harvesters."

When Deke got occupied in observing a group of youngsters working within clear view of the observation window, Fromoth Trun addressed Mara in a low tone. "Breathing this pressurized atmosphere for any length of time could harm the human child. I suggest you use your private time to convince Commander Sage of the sincerity of my request."

He turned to the others and spoke loudly. "Feel free to wander on your own and explore the wonders of our community. Of course, you have nowhere to go should you decide to leave." His croaking laugh rang harshly in her ears. "I'll show you to your guest quarters. You can order meals and they will be delivered to your suite. Do you have enough supplies for the infant?"

"We have what we need for now," Mara responded as they

fell into step beside the Croag leader. She realized Fromoth Trun wouldn't let them go unless Deke complied with his demands. Even then, they might experience an unfortunate accident on their way to the surface. She didn't believe they were in any immediate danger, but they should use their free time to formulate an escape plan.

Deke agreed wholeheartedly when she voiced her concerns in the privacy of their sleeping quarters. The suite held a large room with dormitory-style beds and a sitting area with a table and chairs, softly cushioned loungers, and a music center.

Mara ensconced herself on one lounger to feed Jallyn. Having helped Sarina enough times, she was familiar with infant care. Jallyn suckled happily on her bottle that was pre-filled with formula, and Mara thought how fortunate Sarina was to have a child with such a sweet disposition.

Deke and the others sat at the table. "Fromoth Trun wants those harvesters, but I'm not sure freeing the youngsters of their burden is the real reason for his request," Deke said.

"He didn't mention the satellite survey or the border dispute with the Worts," Wren pointed out. "That was his prior excuse for getting accepted into the Coalition."

Deke drummed his fingers on the table. "According to the rebels, he needs detonators in order to launch missiles against them. Once the Croags achieve Coalition membership status, he'll sell Vyclor and use the profits to buy these devices on the black market."

"Wait a minute," Mara said, wiping the baby's mouth with a burp cloth. "There used to be a farm near my home on Tyberia. If I recall, the harvesting machines had activator mechanisms."

"By the stars, so do our kelp harvesters," Deke said. "I'll bet Fromoth Trun plans to convert the starter mechanisms into detonators. The electronic components are similar." He shook his head in admiration of their adversary's plan. "He has everything in place—the chemical agent, the missile silos, and the targets. Now all he needs are the detonators to make it work. Great suns, he wants to join the Coalition so he can wipe out the opposition."

No wonder the NARCs kidnapped Jallyn, Mara thought. It was their last desperate hope to stop him.

"Fromoth Trun won't let us leave," Deke concluded. "He'll use the rest of you as leverage to force me into contacting the Admissions Committee and recommending approval status. Then he'll stage an accident to get rid of us… all except Jallyn, that is. He'll say her abduction was part of a Rakkian plot and he rescued her, but we were killed in the skirmish. He'll be regarded as a hero."

Wren's jaw tightened, and his brows drew together. "We should find a way out of here. Hedy and I can explore the place."

"I'll go out on my own, if you'll be okay," Deke said to Mara. She was obviously stuck there with the infant.

"Sure; I might take a nap if I can get Jallyn to sleep. Don't worry about me."

"Then I'll contact Ebo and give him a status report. Let's divide up and agree to meet back here in two hauras."

****

Deke prowled around with amazing freedom. The habitat personnel, advised they were a visiting inspection team sent by the Coalition, treated him to every courtesy.

"What happens if there's an emergency and you need to evacuate?" Deke asked a worker monitoring the atmospheric systems in the data control center.

Banks of video screens provided a three-hundred-and-sixty-degree view of the habitat's surroundings. On the opposite side from where he'd seen the Yanuran young, floodlights bathed the underwater environment in a yellowish-green iodide glow. A swirl of minute particles and marine organisms restricted visibility so that beyond the range of lights, the scene tapered into murky darkness.

The fellow glanced up. "We keep a transfer capsule docked in Bay Two. It's available for emergencies." He tapped a schematic diagram where it showed a red dot. "This capsule holds thirty people, but normally only twenty-five of us reside here."

Deke pointed to a similar blip in an adjacent bay. "What's this one?"

The frog face grimaced. "That capsule needs repairs. It's out of action for now."

"What's the problem?" Deke's tone was casual, but his heart thumped with excitement. Should the need arise, this might be their ticket out of there.

"The ballast system was damaged due to a hull tear, and the propulsion board short-circuited. We've put in a request for an electrical engineer, but one isn't due to arrive for another fortnight. The capsule hit a ridge of rock during its last transit."

"So normally you have only one of these capsules, but because of the damage, a second one was sent as backup?"

"That's right. You'd think the bigwigs at the surface would want to save money by fixing the older one, wouldn't you?" the frog face said with a frown. "They do what's easiest and not what's more cost efficient. It's typical for politicians with money in their pockets."

"Good luck," Deke told him with a pat on the shoulder.

As he exited the compartment, he decided he'd like to get a closer look at the damaged carrier. He went about it via a circuitous route in case his movements were being monitored. That way, it would seem as though he'd arrived at the docking bay purely by chance.

****

Deke had no sooner returned to their guest suite than Fromoth Trun summoned him.

"Commander, would you care for a beverage?" the Croag offered in his private quarters. He wore his usual gaudy robes of office.

"No, thanks." Deke stood with his hands clasped behind his

297

back, wondering what the Yanuran leader wanted. Would he offer a bargain to let them all go? Or would he threaten harm to Deke's friends if he didn't cooperate?

"I have a comm panel in here with a link set up to Bimordus Two," Fromoth Trun said. "You may notify your superiors of our gracious hospitality and extend your team's approval of our application."

Deke set his jaw. "I can't do that."

"Why not?" The Croag's skin mottled, his reaction when displeased.

Deke pressed his lips together. He didn't care to reveal the extent of his knowledge regarding the chemical warfare offensive, because that would erase any pretense between them. If he hoped to be treated with civility and not clapped in irons, he'd better come up with a good reason for his delay.

"I, um, was thinking about your previous offer," he said, meeting the Croag's amber gaze. "You'd said our worlds—Eranus and Yanura—might benefit from a scientific exchange. You make a valid point. Not only does Eranus possess the harvesters you require, but we have other advancements that would benefit your people."

Noting an interested gleam in Fromoth Trun's eyes, Deke warmed to the subject and rattled off a list of what his people could provide. This included speed thruster packs for underwater divers, a liquid breathing medium that prevented nitrogen narcosis, a prototype winged submersible for deep-sea exploration, ROVs—remotely operated vehicles—that performed difficult mechanical operations underwater.

"Besides our technology, we have our mining industry. Manganese nodules are only one of the rich mineral resources we can offer. On the other hand, you're way ahead of us in pharmacological research and aquaculture."

Fromoth Trun stared at him. "I thought you said you have no authority on Eranus."

"Not now I don't, unless I win the chancellorship. But there's always my father. I'm sure I could convince him to listen. We still need Larikk's vaccine for Turtle Ravage disease, among other things you could trade."

"So you wish to make a private deal?"

Deke gave him a wily smile. "Yes, I do. It would benefit us both."

Sometimes it took a bit of crookedness to snare a crook. He prayed Fromoth Trun would swallow his bait.

The Yanuran leader studied him. "I'll confer with my ministers. You are certain obtaining the harvesters from Eranus wouldn't be a problem? This would have to take place in the immediate future."

"No worries. I'll make it a priority."

"We'll still want to join the Coalition to reap the benefits of all the member worlds, but you and I can reach an agreement in the interim." His eyes narrowed to slits and his mouth twisted. "Of course, if you're bluffing, our medical researchers always have need for human subjects for their experiments. Your friends are expendable if you betray me."

Deke suppressed his surge of anger and forced a conciliatory note into his voice. "My deal is a better one. We'll both profit from it, and no one else needs to know."

"I'll get back to you on my decision. You are dismissed, Commander."

Deke was escorted back to his room, surprised when the guards didn't take up a post outside their door. Fromoth Trun probably figured Deke's team had nowhere to go.

"That's what he thinks," he muttered under his breath.

Mara sprang from her seat on the lounger where she was holding Jallyn. "You're back! I was getting concerned. Hedy and Wren were here already. They went to the rec room to watch a Katuba tournament."

She'd changed into a short tunic dress and Deke's gaze drifted to her bare legs. "I'll save my story until they get back."

"In that case," she said, rising and thrusting Jallyn into his arms, "you can hold her for a while. I need a break."

"Hey, I don't know what to do."

"You'll figure it out." And with those taunting words, she vanished inside the sanitary.

"Blast, now what?" He stared at the child's face. Her tiny mouth puckered and her eyes pinched and she began to cry. "Be quiet," he said, rocking her.

When his motion had no effect, he fumbled for a bottle in the supply bag, then jabbed the nipple at her mouth. Her howls grew louder.

"Drink," he tried again in an authoritative voice. Her face reddened and her squalls increased to ear-piercing shrillness.

"Having a problem?"

Hedy's voice made him whirl around. She had returned with Wren and stood in the open doorway, grinning at the sight of him holding the infant.

Relieved, he rushed forward. "Here, she's all yours." He plopped the wriggling babe into Hedy's outstretched arms.

Hedy took the bottle and stroked the nipple against the baby's cheek. Jallyn's mouth grasped onto it, and she suckled in contented silence.

"Thank goodness," Deke said, embarrassed to be defeated by a child.

"What did Fromoth Trun want? Mara told us he'd summoned you." Wren's long stride carried him into the room. At the cooler unit, he took one of his Cal drinks and gulped down the contents.

Deke shut the door and swiped a hand over his face. "We've got trouble."

Wren grunted. "Like, we don't know that already?"

Deke gestured for him to do a sweep for hidden surveillance devices. "Fromoth Trun has upped the stakes," he said upon the all-clear signal.

Mara emerged, looking refreshed and lovely with her wavy hair spread over her shoulders. He ignored his surge of desire and repeated his conversation with the Yanuran leader.

"If I don't get him those harvesters, he's threatened to offer you to his medical researchers as test subjects. We may only have a few hauras before he sends for me again. Here's what I have in mind."

In a terse tone, Deke related his escape plan.

Chapter Twenty-One

"Do you have everything you'll need?" Mara asked Deke.

His earlier inspection of the damage to the disabled transfer capsule had shown what was required to fix it, so he'd assigned everyone a list of items to acquire before they'd split up. He had instructed his team to meet him at a vacant storage bay he'd discovered earlier.

The timing of their escape would be tricky. The entire plan depended upon how quickly Deke could repair the emergency capsule.

He studied the heap of tools in front of him. Hopefully none of the Croags would have reason to visit this remote corner, but in case they did, he set Wren to work fashioning a miniature heater so they could show something for their efforts. Their excuse was the low temperature in their guest quarters being too uncomfortable for them. Hedy stayed in their room to care for Jallyn and to warn them if Fromoth Trun called for Deke.

Squatting by the stash of supplies, he checked the cable cutters, pneumatic drill, couplings, fishnet, pressure lines, foam sheeting, gum matrix, and other assorted odds and ends. The group had pilfered the goods from various places such as the machine shop, science labs and maintenance modules. He hoped they wouldn't be missed for a while. By that time, his team should be long gone.

He laid out the long-sleeved clothing Wren had obtained by complaining of the chilly temperature. Using Hedy's thermal tissue regenerator as a welding tool, he melded the edges together into a one-piece suit and hood. Spraying the suit with the rubbery matrix made it waterproof.

If his body temperature dropped, he'd lose dexterity, and with the delicate maneuvers he needed to perform during his splashdown, he couldn't afford to take extra risks. Body heat dissipated much more rapidly in a watery environment than in air.

After instructing Mara to weld some hooks and snaps onto his belt, which he took off for her to work on, he examined the gas cylinders he'd confiscated from an emergency station along the way. He hoped they'd be adequate for their purpose.

Using the pneumatic drill, he punched holes in their outer walls, threaded the hose lines through, and sealed the connection with a waterproof sealant. This would provide him with access to the air tanks once outside.

That part assembled, he glanced at his chronometer. They should start back to their room soon.

"I'm finished," Wren stated, holding up his miniature heating device. "Can I return to our quarters?"

"Go ahead. Mara and I will be along shortly."

Once they were alone, Mara expressed her doubts. "Are you sure this will work?"

He spread his hands. "No, but we have to take the chance. If we delay, Fromoth Trun will force me to approve his application and then he'll kill us all. We don't have any options. If we don't make a break for it, we're dead."

"Can't Ebo do something from the ship?"

"He'll stage a diversion when we're ready to make our move, but he can't retrieve us until we surface."

"Your part is too risky. I'm afraid for you."

He glowered at her. "You acted like this before you went to the pools with Onus Laola, and I ended up getting attacked because you jumped into my mind."

She propped her hands on her hips. "That wasn't my fault."

He liked the way her eyes flashed when she was angry, but he couldn't afford to be distracted. "None of the rest of you can do my job. I have to plug the ballast hole in the transfer capsule and fasten on a buoyancy device to get it to the surface. If I don't have total concentration, I'll fail. My mind must be clear. Do you understand?"

She nodded, her lips compressed.

"Good. Now help me pack these things so we can go."

****

In their suite, Hedy was just putting Jallyn into her makeshift crib for a nap. She glanced up to catch Wren gazing at her with an unfathomable expression.

"What is it?" she asked.

The stubborn fellow hadn't said anything personal since they'd arrived here, and she hoped he still wanted her after their escapade together. Now that he regarded himself as a whole man, he might decide to pursue other females, most likely from his own species.

"I was picturing how you will look holding *our* child," he responded, his tone gruff as he stepped forward. "Hedy Te'larr, would you do me the honor of becoming my mate?"

"What?" Her heart leapt into her throat.

"You've healed me, and you already had my deep affection. I cannot live without you."

She pressed a hand to her chest. "Oh, my. This is so sudden. I'm not sure… Yes, I am. Of course, I'll be your wife if you'll have me."

Later, when he eased his desperate kisses to allow her a breath of air, she said into his ear, "How about us getting a headstart on creating that child of ours?"

He shook his head. "We must wait for the proper time."

Her glance swept the bedding. "Why not now?"

"This isn't how Polluxites initiate their coupling." And he told her how his kind did it.

"That *is* worth the wait, isn't it?" she said, her breath coming short at the idea.

The door burst open and they sprang apart with guilty flushes. Mara and Deke strode into the living area.

Mara noticed the look Hedy and Wren exchanged, and her conviction grew that something significant had occurred between them. Could Hedy have broken Wren's cultural barriers?

"How's Jallyn?" she asked, strolling forward.

Hedy's color deepened. "She's asleep. Did you and Deke finish what you had to do?"

"Yes, we're done. Do you have the baby's bag packed in case we have to move fast?"

"It's ready. I'd like to give Jallyn another feeding before we have to move out."

"We may not have the time. Someone is coming," Deke said with a warning glance toward the open doorway. Footsteps sounded from farther down the corridor.

A pair of armed Croags arrived at their door. "Fromoth Trun wishes to see you and Mistress Mara," said one of them.

Deke's brows lifted. Why would the Yanuran leader request Mara's presence? Did he plan to use her as a hostage to convince Deke to approve their admissions status?

They had no choice except to obey. He'd assess the situation and decide on a response soon enough.

The Yanuran leader dispensed with civilities and got right to the point. "I conferred with my ministers. We decided there isn't time for you to contact Eranus to make the arrangements we'd discussed. Getting Coalition approval is a speedier route. We must obtain those harvesters." He thrust a microphone at Deke. "I've established a link so you can confirm your approval of our application."

"I'm sorry," he said, standing firm, "Based on the political problems facing your government and the violations of Coalition law, I have to recommend a rejection."

From the way Fromoth Trun's skin changed colors, Deke feared a nasty reprisal was in store for them. This might be their only chance to initiate an escape. He pressed a knob on his dive computer, sending Ebo the signal to activate their plan.

High-frequency sound waves bombarded the habitat, affecting only the frog people with their sensitive hearing. Fromoth Trun croaked and doubled over.

"Come on," Deke yelled to Mara. Grabbing her hand, he tugged her toward the door.

Ebo was about to aim a concentrated beam of goburon particles at the ocean floor. It would disrupt the current and possibly shift the habitat's foundation. They had to collect the others and reach the storage hangar before any of the watertight doors shut. Ebo would also jam the comm lines so the Croags couldn't send out a widespread alert about their escape.

"Fromoth Trun says to go to your emergency stations," he told the armed troops standing guard outside the room.

As he spoke, an explosion rocked the habitant and alarms started clanging. He and Mara rushed down the twisting corridors in the direction of their quarters.

Hedy and Wren were waiting. They held Jallyn and their sacks of supplies.

They sped toward the storage hangar. Once inside, Deke gathered his gear. "They'll expect us to head for the functioning capsule. We have to keep them busy while I repair the other one."

Accordingly, he used the pneumatic drill to create havoc along the way. The Croags, hands held to their ear disks to block out the piercing sonic barrage, scurried about as emergency teams responded. No one tried to stop them, but Deke figured that would change once Fromoth Trun regained control.

On their way to the air lock, they ran into their first snag. They had to descend to a lower level and the compartment below was flooded.

"I'll check it out," Deke said, reaching for his dive gear.

****

Mara held her breath as Deke submerged into the swirling water. He'd managed to find a portable light source which he had strapped to his forehead as a lamp, and slabs of flexible plastic clipped onto his boots made them into fins. He'd strung his tools onto his belt, providing easy access.

Covered in his manufactured wet suit with grease smeared on his face for added insulation, he appeared well-outfitted, but she knew unknown hazards faced him. She reined in her fear, not wishing to lose control.

When his head popped up, she breathed a sigh of relief. He paused on the top rung of the ladder from the lower level and removed his improvised face mask.

"It's clear at the other end, but I'll have to get you through this portion. You need to hold your breath for a short distance and then we'll share my air."

"What about Jallyn?" Mara glanced over her shoulder at Hedy, who cradled the infant in her arms.

"I'll encase her in a cocoon made from the spray-on matrix and can fill it with air. Tying on these wrenches will give it weight. You go first; then I'll bring her to you."

Mara gazed at him in panic. She'd have to swim through a flooded compartment? What if she lost sight of him and drifted away?

"Don't worry. I'll be with you," he said in a confident tone.

Gamely stepping forward, she cringed when the water covered her boots. She gasped from the cold temperature as she lowered herself further and the water soaked her clothes.

Darkness enveloped her as she submerged. Her heart pounded so hard, she thought it might burst. Deke guided her along, while she held her breath until her lungs burned. Then he gave her the mouthpiece.

Unfamiliar with the equipment, she choked in several short bursts of air. When her lungs eased, she gave him back the breathing apparatus.

They made it to a platform on the other side that stood clear of water.

"This lift runs by hydraulics but they're not functioning,"

Deke said. "We'll have to raise it manually. Wait here. I'll get Jallyn next."

Before she could praise him for his efforts, he vanished beneath the water's surface.

****

A short time later, they all stood on the platform. Deke released Jallyn from her makeshift cocoon. Wren helped him operate the manual cable system until they reached the upper level where they faced a double hatchway.

No one obstructed their path as they cracked the hatch and entered the bay that held the emergency escape vessel. The interior of the capsule presented an array of dials, screens, and sensors. Deke ran a quick check of all systems.

"There's enough battery power to sustain life support, but the propulsion system is fried. We'll have to use another means to get the capsule to the surface. Once I plug the hole in the hull, I'll fashion a lift bag from outside so the capsule can rise."

He didn't explain the rest, that he'd be in the water while his friends were inside the capsule. It would reach the surface without him.

After rattling off a quick set of instructions, he watched his friends board the vessel and seal shut the door.

The haunted look in Mara's eyes as they left him behind touched Deke's soul. He'd never known anyone to care about him as much as she did, and he felt guilty about the callous way he'd been treating her. But every time he saw her holding Jallyn, it made him imagine a life that he couldn't afford to think about until they were all safe.

Forcing aside his personal concerns, he focused his attention on the job at hand. He'd bolted together a piece of board with a lug-nut setup. Hoping it would work, he took the device to the hole in the hull. Once there, he pushed the rod threaded through the center into the hole to plug it. Then he tightened the wooden plate against the hull by turning the wings on the nut assembly. The final step was to apply sealant around the edges. Hopefully this jury-rigged device would keep water from gushing into the capsule during its brief ascent.

Next he had to deal with the buoyancy issue. Suited up, he flooded the compartment and opened the bay doors. It was time for Wren to do his part. He thumped on the hull, signaling his navigator. Deke stood aside while Wren released air through the rear vents. The thrust caused the capsule to skid forward to the edge of the bay.

With gloved fingers, Deke took the fishnet he'd stuffed with an expansive material, swam to the hose line, fitted on a connector, and filled the lift bag with air from an extra tank. Attaching it to a cable, he let it go.

Like a tethered balloon, the lift bag rose to the surface along with the ascent line. Hooking a loop onto the transfer capsule, Deke attached the loop to the cable. Now the vehicle should rise along the taut line.

All he had to do was wait for his friends to send the capsule back down.

As he watched it ascend, he didn't pay attention to drift. A surge of current caught him and swept him away. Like a rag doll, his body was thrust against a section of exterior piping on the habitat. A twisted cable pinned him in place.

Scores of poisonous sea urchins living on the habitat's outer rim pierced his improvised wet suit with their needle-like spines. Burning pain lanced his back as he fought to free himself from the tangled line. Panic made his breath come short.

He'd lost sight of the ascent line, and even if he managed to free himself, he might not find it before his air ran out. He'd prepared backup cylinders, but even so his total bottom time ran to fifty minutes assuming he could locate them. He'd used up more than a quarter of his time doing the repairs. Gods, what was he to do?

His struggles caused the cable to pin him in place more

securely. His hands, restricted by the gloves, couldn't grasp the cable cutters hooked to his belt. He tried to calm his breathing to conserve air.

Mara, where are you? I need you!

His plea made him understand what his soul had known all along. They were stronger when united. Then it was possible to accomplish anything.

By the stars, I can't exist without her. And if I don't get to the surface, I'll never get the chance to tell her.

Mara, help me! Come to me, my love.

****

Wren cracked open the hatch at the surface. He inflated an emergency raft then helped the women into it before turning back to flood the ballast as Deke had instructed.

He jumped into the raft just as the vehicle began to sink along its cable. When Deke joined them, Ebo would pick them up in the shuttle.

Wren's wings sprouted and he glanced at Hedy. "We're free," he shouted, enjoying the warm blaze of sunlight on his face.

Hedy's eyes danced with glee. "We have a few minutes until Deke arrives. Do you want to, um, you know?" She glanced toward the sky.

"Why not?" Turning to Mara, he said, "Would you mind taking Jallyn for a few minutes while we leave?"

Mara's jaw slackened. "Leave? Where are you going?"

"To heaven and beyond," Hedy called as Wren scooped her into his arms.

He took off, flapping his powerful wings to gain height. As they soared higher in the sky, his wings folded over, enclosing them both in a feathery embrace.

Stunned speechless, Mara stared after them until something tugged at her consciousness.

Mara, help me. Come to me.

With a cry of dismay, she fastened her gaze on the azure water. Deke was in trouble, she realized. *What can I do?*

She tried a separation, but it didn't work. Her essence remained physically grounded.

Come to me, my love.

Those last words broke her boundary. Her astral body separated and flew toward the source. Merging with his essence, she understood his predicament and felt his comfort at her presence.

****

Deke felt a warm glow as Mara's spirit melded with his and suddenly, he found the strength he needed. Gripping the cable cutters in his gloved hand, he snapped the line that had entrapped him and swam away. But where was the transfer capsule? He couldn't see it in the murky water, and according to his dive computer, he'd almost used up his bottom time. Did he have the power to make a controlled ascent?

You can do it.

Mara's faith cleared his mind. Grabbing a line reel from his utility belt, he tied off an end to a section of nearby piping and fed out the rest of the line so that it rose to the surface. He could follow this up without worrying about drift, and thus he began a slow ascent.

Stopping periodically to neutralize the nitrogen in his system, he saved his last reserve for the longest decompression stop at twenty feet below the surface.

By the time his head crested the waves, he was weak, dizzy, and shaking from pain, but his heart leapt in exultation. He'd made it. He jettisoned his gear and treaded water as the *Celeste's* shuttle veered in his direction.

A feeling of emptiness assailed him when Mara left his spirit to return to her body. He yearned to confess his newfound feelings, but when the shuttle hovered over his location, he had just enough energy to grasp the dangling ladder. Wren helped to haul him aboard.

The last thing he felt was a solid floor beneath his aching back before darkness overwhelmed him.

Chapter Twenty-Two

"I've discharged Deke from sickbay," Hedy said, standing in the doorway at Mara's cabin aboard the *Celeste*. "He said he was going to make a full report to Bimordus Two and then he needed to wash and change. He wants you to wait here for him."

Mara had visited Deke while he was healing, touching him mentally with her love. Using her expanded consciousness, she'd seen the strong bonds connecting them on every auric layer. The cords between their chakras were thick and flashed with the rose color of love. When had this occurred? Did it mean he'd finally recognized his need for her?

For the first time he had exerted control over one of her separations by summoning her. She had to believe that indicated his acceptance.

Once he had regained consciousness, he'd ordered Ebo to destroy the missile silos on Yanura before they set course for Bimordus Two. It was an action he'd have to rationalize to his Defense League superiors, but Mara would support him wholeheartedly.

She thought about how her outlook had changed on this trip. She'd been hardened to reality, but perhaps now she'd be more effective in her diplomatic role by being less gullible.

"Jallyn is asleep," she told Hedy, who was studying her curiously. They'd devised a makeshift crib in Mara's sleeping chamber. "Sarina can't wait until we arrive."

"I know." Hedy had been with her when Mara had contacted Jallyn's mother.

"The baby's aura is strong. I can feel her power and suspect she'll be able to do much more than heal people. She'll wield an awesome force when she matures."

"Sarina will guide her, and I'm sure you'll be there to offer your advice." Hedy gave a broad smile, reminding Mara that she still didn't understand what had occurred between Hedy and Wren on Yanura.

"Why don't you come in?" she invited her friend, smoothing her orchid sarong. Tired of tailored clothes, she'd chosen her native garb to relax in.

Hedy shook her head, a secretive gleam in her eyes. "Wren is coming off duty in another half-haura. I want to get out of this tunic and into something more comfortable."

"How was it that he could fly, Hedy? And did you two, you know, do it? When he wrapped his wings around you—?"

Hedy held up a hand. "The man is afraid of heights and that's what kept him from flying on his home planet. When I fell off a cliff during the skirmish at Cloud Forest, his wings sprouted and he saved me. He was spectacular, Mara. As for your other question, well, they do it differently on Pollux, at least for the first time." With a wink, she turned away.

"Wait!" Mara called, anxious for details, but Hedy had already vanished into her cabin across the corridor.

Heavy booted footsteps announced Deke's arrival into the crew quarters. He planted himself in her open doorway, looking as rakishly handsome as the first time they'd met.

"You look lovely," he said, his appreciative glance warming her blood.

"Thank you. How are you feeling?"

"I'm fine, thanks to you. I wouldn't have survived without your... intervention."

"I know." She studied him for any signs of illness, but he appeared fully recovered. Her gaze drifted to his alert brown eyes, freshly shaven jaw, and chiseled mouth then dropped to survey his muscular form encased in a crisp, clean uniform.

Aware of her scrutiny, he smiled at her, showing his even, white teeth and those ravishing dimples. Her heart thudded against her ribs as she gestured for him to enter. He shut the door and turned toward her. His overpowering presence filled the sitting room. She inhaled the spicy scent of his cologne, and her knees weakened with desire.

"I want to fill you in on what's transpired." A somber expression washed over his face. "Yanura was denied admission to the Coalition. Because of their involvement in Jallyn's abduction, they won't be eligible to reapply for five annums. During that time, they'll have to accomplish several reforms. Hostilities between the warring factions must cease. The Croags have to allow for representation of all races in the central government. Young people will be given freedom of choice regarding Vyclor, and child labor laws have to be initiated. A Defense League inspection team will supervise the dismantling of their chemical warfare apparatus."

"That sounds right. They have a lot of work ahead of them."

He nodded. "Restrictions on trade will compensate the Coalition for Larikk's death. However, I did contact the artisans we met and asked for samples of their wares. The economic commission might make an exception for their unique art works."

"That was generous of you. I'm glad the Yanurans will be moving forward. Will they be getting the harvesters so their young no longer have to work the underwater farms?"

"Yes, we've agreed to send an aid package. But enough about them. Here, I brought something for you." He rummaged in a pocket and withdrew a rectangular box.

Taking it, she turned it in her hands. "What is it?"

"On Eranus, when we wish to ask a woman to become our life mate, we offer her a gift that is symbolic of our future together. If she accepts the gift, it means she accepts the proposal. This one is only a hologram. The real item is being made on commission."

Her eyes widening, she pushed a button on the side of the box and a holographic image sprang into view. The delicate porcelain sculpture could only have been created by the Wort artisan she'd met in the village. It was a statue depicting a mother and child gazing lovingly into each other's faces, their arms entwined.

Tears blinded her as she regarded Deke. "It's beautiful. I accept your gift."

With a crooked grin, he stepped forward and clasped her by the shoulders. "There's a land basin in Eranus with pure white clay. I'd bet you could learn the technique for sculpting these things yourself, if you have any free time as a Chancellor's wife."

She stared at him. "You got the position at the Institute for Marine Studies? When did you find out?"

He gestured. "I received the call just before I left my cabin. You don't mind, do you? Because if you did, I'd reject the offer. I know how much your job means to you on Bimordus Two."

"We'll work something out. Being with you is more important."

Taking the box from her hands, he set it on a table. Then he drew her into his arms. "You're all I want and all I'll ever need. I realized that when I was trapped underwater. Survival only mattered so I could see you again. I want to be a part of you as you're already a part of me. Your gift is a special quality I'll always cherish."

"On Tyberia," she said, heat sizzling through her at his touch, "when a woman agrees to bond with a man, it's a done deed."

"Is that right?" Lowering his head, he brushed her lips with his. "I adore you. Let me show you how much I want you." And he proceeded to kiss her senseless.

Their psyches merged and she thought she'd die from the intensity of their emotions.

I love you. Deke's unspoken words reached her essence.

I love you, too, she sent back, and then all rational thought dissolved in the rapture of their embrace.

****

When the Elevation Ceremony for the Auranians began on Bimordus Two a few days after their arrival, Deke and Mara watched from the crowd. Sarina and Teir stood on an elevated platform, holding their baby between them. Suddenly a blinding light encircled them and radiated outward.

Mara felt an answering twinge within herself. Her consciousness expanded and she could see Jallyn's grown image shimmering before her eyes. It was more powerful than anything she'd ever seen. But the glowing form wasn't alone. Surrounding it were other beings, emitting the Light that permeated all of creation with warmth and love.

Joy filled her. Turning to Deke, she expanded her psychic energy and he melded with her. He shared her vision when another shape drifted into view.

She put a hand to her belly, knowing this was their own child, a son.

Jallyn's aura turned toward him and her spiritual fingers reached out. The boy child responded. Destiny awaited them.

THE END

Glossary

Activators - Circuitry used on spaceships during landing sequence.

Actuator Valves - Valves in propulsion system of sublight engines.

Aguar Plant - A weed-like plant favored by K'darr. Crimson leaves, fuzzy texture. Secretes a digestive enzyme in the dark that eats through fur and skin.

Alexipharmics - Pharmaceuticals.

Alpha Gomaran Two - A volcanic planet.

Amplexus - The Yanuran mating embrace that lasts for several days.

Annums - Years.

Aramus - A creature that looks like a rug and loves to be trampled.

Arbiter - A mediator.

Athos - Planet where siren song originated.

Auranians - An advanced civilization on Shimera whose people developed the power to manipulate their auras. Persecution forced them to leave the planet that was eventually destroyed. Glowstones identify their descendants.

Arcturian Brandy - An expensive brand. Teir's favorite drink.

Auricle - Sacred stone in the Great Hall on Bimordus Two. It's a glowstone from an ancient civilization on the destroyed planet of Shimera. Legend says one of their descendants will arise again in a time of great need. This descendant will bring harmony to the universe.

Bangus Tree - Shady tree with hanging roots like a banyan.

Baynor - Mayor on Tendraa.

Belleek - An ugly sea creature.

Bimanthium Crystals - A fuel source.

Bimordus Two - The seat of the Coalition central government. Five biosphere environments inhabit this barren planet. The capital city is in the Lifestyle biome called Bimordus Central. There's a Nutrition Pod, Rain Forest, Marine Habitat, and Biogenesis Research Center.

Biome - Sealed ecosystem.

Blood Crystal - A mysterious rock that conveys visions of the future.

Boks - A board game with colored tiles.

Borks - Animals who'll rip each other's throats out over a piece of meat.

Brambid - A flying insect.

Bremen - An affluent section of town on Vilaran.

Bungrats - A derogatory term used on Tendraa, refers to a rodent.

Bzoran cat - Type of aggressive cat with sharp claws.

Calgonite Ore - A valuable mineral.

Carellian Clay - A sculpting clay used to make pottery.

Carzen - A large, muscled animal that Souks ride like a horse.

Casement - Window.

Catarrhines - A monkey-type creature that lives in the rainforest.

Chirurgeon - Archaic term for a surgeon.

Circutia - Ilyssa's home world, a cultural and artistic nexus known for its friendly people. The Circutians are pacifists, abhorring all forms of violence.

Coalition - Coalition of Sentient Planets.

Coppenium - A mineral.

Cosh - A carafe of ale. A term of measurement, like a pint.

Crigellan - A species that is half-human and half-lizard.

Cr'ssian Soota Mud - A finishing polish for pottery sculptures.

Data Link - A portable data management device.

Deflector Shield - Ship's defense that protects against energy weapons and space debris.

Destiny - The vessel Rolf and Ilyssa take to Nadira. It's a Stinger-class ship equipped with warp-drive engines and two stabilizer fins attached to the main cylindrical-shaped body. The fins rotate horizontally for landings and lock vertically for combat and flight. Weapons include laser cannons, proton torpedoes, and concussion missiles.

Diamella - A clear crystal gemstone.

Dougger Gnat - A small, annoying insect.

Dromo - District leader on Souk appointed by Pasha.

Electrifier - Rod that emits an electrical charge used as a punishment device.

Eranus - Deitan Sage's home planet. People live on floating cities on vast oceans.

Fabricator - Matter synthesizer for food, clothing, and other essentials.

Farg - A deadly plague.

Field Relays - Circuitry controlling rate of descent in spacecraft.

Firestone - A brilliant, clear colored stone in gold, orange, or red.

Flamebrush - A bush with bright red thistles.

Flame lights - Torches powered by orellium gel.

Flavium - A mineral used in weapons production.

Flegymns - Fish that can devour a person in fifteen seconds.

Flyboard - Flying skateboard with handles.

Fodus Vine - A thorny swinging plant on Souk.

Fuel Capacitators - Storage for energy from charged bimanthium crystals.

Gecko - A creature with an exterior shell and antennae. They drink nectar for energy. They hire themselves out as mercenaries and often work for the Souks. Their gunships have a crab-like shape and carry laser cannons.

Gima - Mistress in Souk.

Glowstones - Stones that glow, like the ancient Auricle. These stones identify descendants of the Shimeran race who possess the ability to manipulate auras.

Halberd - A shafted weapon with a spike or axe-like cutting blade.

Haura - Hour.

Hazars - A pasha's private bodyguards.

High Council - Ruling body of the Coalition along with the Assembly.

Hiimma Birds - A high-soaring bird.

Holovid - A holographic video.

Hornet - A cruiser that takes Sarina to the science station on Timos.

Hortha - Bull-like creatures who use stun-whips as a punishment device. Speech sounds like buzzing noise. They act as guards for the Souks.

House of Raimorrda - Ruling class that crosses planetary boundaries.

Hovertram - Tram propelled by anti-gravity engine.

Humma bird - A songbird.

Igoob Leaves - Chew on them to repel insects.

Imperator - King on Nadira.

Imperatrice - Queen on Nadira.

Jaegger Beasts - Wild animals in the Uta Wastes, a desert plain on Vilaran.

Jakoon - Caretaker of the young on Yanura.

Jawani - Official Coalition language.

Jell Berries - Spicy berry on Souk.

Kather Sticks - A game with colored sticks and dice.

Katuba - A sport game involving a kick ball.

Kayoka - A white-faced monkey-like creature living in the Souk jungles.

Keela Blossoms - A white, fragrant flower.

Kookabur - A noisy type of bird on Souk that flies in flocks.

Koritah - A doctrine of proper social behavior for females on Souk.

Korions - An old enemy of the Coalition from its early formative years.

Kougra - A feline animal that likes to be cuddled.

Krach - Affirmative in Souk language.

Krecker - Souk slave laborer.

Krog - Battlecruiser and flagship of the Morgot fleet.

Lahar - A landslide of wet volcanic debris.

Lalith Leaves - An herbal remedy. When brewed like tea, it relieves congestion.

Landspeeder - A ground vehicle using anti-grav technology and turbo engines.

Laria - A term of endearment on Vilaran.

Laverbread - a mixture of seaweed, oatmeal, brown algae powder, raw placar fish and chopped fresh eels.

Lennox - A fat scavenger animal.

Levitator - Anti-gravity trolley.

Liana Vine - Tangled undergrowth vine.

Linear Actuator - A machinery part on a spaceship.

Lyphound - A beast on Souk. Used as a derogatory term.

Lypis Ice - A frozen fruit treat.

Marbelite - A white marble-like stone used in construction.

Mariculture - Agriculture in the ocean.

Marouche - A flying creature on Yanura that transports passengers.

Maug - A curse word used as an adjective.

Mediscan - Portable biomedical scanning device.

Meraninum - A lightweight, durable metal.

Merl - A type of seaweed that only grows on Yanura.

Mingka birds - Red jungle bird.

Mira - A respectful title for a female in Tendraan, like "ma'am" or "miss."

Mithridate - A fever-lowering medicine.

Moranian Flasher - A mixed alcoholic beverage.

Morgots - A warrior race from a distant solar system.

Mushgum - A quick-acting poison.

Mzips - Snake-like creatures.

Nadira - Lord Cam'brii's home planet in the Regulus star system. A lush, tropical world.

Nargot - A weasel-type animal.

Nutrium - An element that can combine with other elements in liquid form.

Omnus - Cerrus Bdan's ship.

Orellium - An organic substance used as a fuel because it burns for a long time and emits a cold light.

Oroxian Zinger - A mixed drink with fizz that tastes like cherries.

Pasha - Ruler of commercial cartel on Souk.

Parsec - A unit measuring distance.

Pastagillo Noodles - A pasta, like spaghetti.

Patima - Shawl.

Pest-House - A place where sick people are sent on Tendraa.

Petula - A term of endearment on Pollux.

Physio lab - Fitness center.

Piragen Ore - Metal used in spacecraft construction. Mined on Vilaran and Souk.

Pirium - A plastel used in spacecraft production.

Plastel- A strong but lightweight metal used in construction.

Platwhacks - Reedy plants that grow near marshes.

Pnimx Tusks - Contraband like ivory tusks.

Polluxite - Humanoid species with foldable wings. Home world is Pollux.

Pommus - A purple fruit, round and shiny like an apple.

Poultice - A soft, moist cloth filled with healing herbs applied to the body.

Posset-Drink - An herbal remedy on Tendraa.

Power Transfer Conduits - Part of a ship's propulsion system.

Preim - King of Vilaran. A descendant of the House of Raimorrda and sovereign leader of the Retti dynasty, the last Preim was overthrown in a bloody coup.

Provost - A governor on Vilaran; leader of a province.

Pyroclastic - Made up of fragments of volcanic origin.

Rabba - A wild animal on Souk.

Raker - Street cleaner on Tendraa.

Reeka Pears - A juicy pear with an expensive price tag.

Reflector - Mirror.

Reverse Levitators - Reverse anti-gravity field to slow aircraft on landing.

Rigelan Slug - A food delicacy eaten live.

ROF- Return to Origins Faction calling for secession of Coalition worlds.

Rorsh - A Tyberian monk.

Rubellis Gemstones - A ruby-like gem.

Sailbarge - Ground vehicle that flies with single propeller and sails.

Satrap - Military officer in Souk army.

Scramjet - A jet that travels at supersonic speeds.

Secondary Reactor Conduits - Backup system in sublight propulsion engines.

Sedit Beverage - Drink that induces calm.

Shimera - An ancient world with an advanced civilization whose people developed the power to manipulate their auras. These people called themselves Auranians. Persecution forced them to leave the planet that was eventually destroyed. Glowstones identify their descendants.

Shooter - A laser pistol with stun and kill settings.

Silverscreen - A filter that is impervious to sensor scans.

Sirisian - Race that has pink skin and an elastic body.

Siren Song - The power to mesmerize men through a woman's singing voice.

Skimmer - Surface vehicle with turbo boost engines and antigrav technology.

Slythian - A derogatory adjective for a low-life type of person.

Snipes - A freshwater fish eaten as seafood.

Snivel - Slithering creature like a small snake and just as lethal; lives in rock crevices.

Sol - Sun in Souk.

Solar Sailer - It's like a hot air balloon but with sails and a motor. A passenger basket is attached by cables to a rig of billowing sails.

Souk - A planet whose inhabitants have blue skin and dog-like facial features. They practice the slave trade and speak in guttural tones. Souk has two moons. Cerrus Bdan inhabits the Nurash Desert on one side of the Koodrash Mounts. The Thicket of Bayne is a jungle at the foot of these mountains. His brother Ruel's territory is on the other side of the range.

Souk Alliance - A syndicate of commercial cartels in the mineral-rich Capellan system.

Speedcraft - Planetside transports smaller than skimmer.

Speeder - A form of land transport that holds up to four people and resembles a bullet-shaped car with a glass bubble. Can fly at low altitudes with its anti-grav engine.

Spiral Town - Residence of High Council members on Bimordus Two.

Sulu Berries - A mulberry-type fruit.

Sumi - Souk word for slave.

Tangent Beams - Energy weapons array on starship.

Taurus - A volcanic planet where the Blood Crystal is hidden.

Techno War - A war on Tendraa stimulated by too fast progress into the technological age.

Tendraa - Mantra's home world. Ruled by a Liege Lord. Capital city is Lazore on the coast of the Bazmayan Sea. The planet is rich in flavium.

Theodolite - A precision instrument with a telescopic sight.

Thrum - A man-eating plant from Antiguas Two.

Torgus Larvae - A live food delicacy on Yanura.

Torrock - A desert beast of burden the Souks ride like camels or horses.

Tractor Beam Wheel - Towing beam on a spacecraft.

Tupella Blossoms - Flowers on Nadira with orange and red petals.

Turbolift - An elevator that goes horizontal as well as vertical.

Twyggs - Tree people.

Tyberia - Mara's home world.

Vacchus - Living crystal on the planet, Athos.

Vilaran - Teir's home world. Vilaran is a republic and one of the six founding members of the Coalition. Theal is the capital city. Vilaran is divided into provinces, each one ruled by a provost appointed by the central Parliament which is itself elected every eight years by the populace. Each province is divided into districts headed by a justice. The Centorian houses the provincial government. An elected president is head of state.

Valiant - Teir's ship, a remodeled freighter with gunports. It has three decks with a warp drive, sublight engines, and deflector shield generators.

Venice Treacle - A home remedy from Tendraa.

Vermuchak - A derogatory term on Yanura.

Vibril - A lead-like substance impervious to sensor scans.

Viewphone - A telephone with a video camera attached.

Viewscreen - Monitor window at the front of a starship.

Vorax - A scavenger bird.

Wagmint Tea - Mint tea.

Warp Drive - Faster than lightspeed propulsion.

Weri - Linen.

Wingboxers - Flying reptiles with yellow eyes, claws, and large wingspans.

Zandozor - A musical reed instrument.

Zor - A term for Hell.

Author's Note

I hope you liked Mara and Deke's story and will look for the other two books in The Light-Years Series – *Circle of Light* and *Moonlight Rhapsody*. It was huge fun to create the world of Yanura and its inhabitants. I especially enjoyed designing the exotic food scenes and various planetary settings.

****

For updates on my new releases, giveaways, special offers and events, join my reader list at https://nancyjcohen.com/newsletter. Free Book Sampler for new subscribers.

Thank you for taking the time to read my book. If you enjoyed the story, please consider writing a review at your favorite online bookstore. Reader recommendations are critically important in helping new readers find my work.

Warrior Prince Excerpt

Copyright ©2012 by Nancy J. Cohen

Here's a peek at *Warrior Prince*, Book #1
in The Drift Lords Series

"Hi, I'm Nira Larsen, here for an interview," she told the receptionist, whose solemn stare and black attire would have suited the funeral home she'd visited earlier.

"Please take a seat. We'll be with you in a few minutes." The woman's blunt-cut dark hair swung as she pressed a button on her console to announce Nira's arrival.

Nira glanced at the small waiting area with its threadbare carpet, row of vinyl seats, and musty odor. Why was no one else here? And why did this place appear so seedy, with peeling paint and grime-coated windows? Maybe she didn't want to work for people who treated their applicants with such disrespect.

Nonetheless, she'd like to land a position at Drift World. On her budget, she couldn't afford a ticket to the role-playing adult theme park, but getting a job there would solve that problem. Plus, she needed the money for other reasons.

She took a seat, an odd buzzing in her ears. It had started when she walked into the place. But even weirder had been the way the theme park's temporary employment office appeared to materialize out of thin air.

The address specified on the classified ad had taken her next to a popular café on Orlando's International Drive. Maybe she was just tired after her last two disastrous interviews, but she could have sworn this log cabin hadn't been in the parking lot when she'd arrived.

Her thoughts scattered when the inner door burst open, and an attractive blonde smiled at her. "Come in, Miss Larsen. My name is Algie Morar. I understand you're applying for a position as a makeup artist?"

"Yes, that's correct."

Nira followed her into a corridor marked by closed doors on either side. At the far end, the hallway opened into a large room from which low male voices rumbled in a strange guttural tongue. A curtain made of fabric strips obstructed the view.

The woman halted and opened a door, gesturing silently for Nira to enter. But instead of facing a desk and chairs as she'd expected for an interview, she spied a treatment table, sink, and counters like in a doctor's office. A supply of cosmetics lay spread out on the counter—brushes, eye pencils, powders, and other familiar tools.

"Wait here." Algie turned on her heel and left Nira alone. A moment later, she returned with a burly man in tow.

Nira's mouth fell open. The stocky fellow had oversized ears, a long bulbous nose, and abnormally large hands and feet. His small beady eyes glared at her from beneath bushy brows. He wore a workman's clothes, stained trousers and a plaid shirt.

"Jek is a test subject to see if you suit us for employment. See if you can make him look more normal," Algie said.

Nira stifled a nervous cough. Weren't those huge cauliflower ears prosthetics? "Um, I'm not sure I—"

"Use those supplies." Algie pointed to the counter. "Shadowing, for example, can de-emphasize certain features. You should know what to do."

The blonde sauntered closer. Her porcelain features were so refined, she could have been a model. She leaned inward, her ocean blue eyes shining brightly, her rosy lips parting as though about to confide a secret. Nira couldn't drag her gaze away. Her nostrils picked up a floral scent that held her spellbound.

It seemed so natural when Algie placed a palm on her arm like an old friend.

Nira sprang back as the buzzing sound in her head increased to painful decibels.

Algie's eyes blazed. "How are you resisting me?"

"What?"

"Never mind, just do as I said. Fix Jek to look more human."

More human? Nira shook her head. That annoying buzzing sound must be affecting her brain.

However, it didn't affect her instincts. An inner voice hammered at her to leave. She backed away, but at a simple nod from Algie, the door slammed shut from an invisible force.

"You're not going anywhere until I find out how you're blocking me. Jek, seize her."

The big man's beefy hand clamped onto her arm.

"Let me go." Nira fought to elbow him in the gut, but his strength overwhelmed her. He hauled her toward the treatment table. "Stop, or I'll scream."

The woman's sinister chuckle chilled her blood. "Go ahead. No one will hear you."

Jek thrust Nira against the hard metal table and pressed her in place with his thighs.

Algie sauntered closer. "You're different. You can block my spell. We haven't met anyone like you before. It could be a danger to us." The woman's smooth tone belied the enmity in her eyes.

Nira swallowed against rising alarm. These people must belong to some cult.

Get out while you can.

She stomped on Jek's instep, hoping to dislodge his grip. He merely chuckled and dumped her supine on the table.

"Help! Someone help me!" she cried when he reached for restraints.

Jek had secured one wrist in a leather strap when a crash sounded from outside in the corridor, followed by shouts and loud blasts. The door burst open, and black-clad masked figures poured inside. They aimed weapons at Algie, who repelled their fire by dodging aside in a blur of speed and then vanishing. Air rushed by Nira's ear. Then Jek was gone as well, leaving her at the mercy of these formidable men.

They stood in a huddle, murmuring in low voices. One of the gang slid his gaze her way and pointed at her.

"I'll take care of the woman," he said in a commanding tone. "Algie and her troops have probably vectored out by now, but search the place anyway and see what you can find." As the others scrambled to obey, he strode over to where Nira lay helpless on the table.

Wriggling against the strap holding her down, she cursed when it wouldn't give way. Now what? Was she a prize to be claimed by their leader? She cringed when he stroked her cheek.

"Who are you, little one? And how did you resist the Confounding?" His gentle tone surprised her.

"Untie me." She attempted to twist away, but he gripped her shoulder, holding her down. Flat on her back, she gazed into his intense turquoise eyes. She couldn't see the rest of his face, hidden by a hooded mask that covered his head. He smelled like pine trees and peat smoke. Calm trickled through her, quieting the buzz in her mind.

Strange that she didn't abhor this man's touch as she had Jek's. Far from it. She squirmed under his scrutiny, aware that her situation wasn't much better and yet she felt no fear. The stranger in black continued to study her, his eyes narrowed as though he contemplated a decision.

Banging noises sounded from outside as his men searched the building as per his orders. A single lightbulb glared overhead, casting the room into a surreal light. Dust motes floated in the air.

"I will release you, but you must come with us," the man said in a commanding tone.

Ice water sluiced through her veins. She didn't want to go anywhere with these fierce-looking men. "Look, I won't tell anyone what's happened here if you let me go home."

"I understand you are frightened. Be assured no further harm will come to you." He spoke soothingly, as though to a child. "I promise to keep you safe."

"Please, just set me free." She hated the way her voice quavered.

"How about if we make a deal? My men and I will take you home, but then you must listen to my proposal. We could use your help."

She nodded, having every intention of bolting for the door when on her feet. As he untied the strap around her wrist, tingling warmth raced along her nerves. Before she could jerk away, his strong hands grasped her by the waist and lifted her off the table.

Standing, she rubbed her arms, grateful for her mobility. Her glance skittered toward the exit. Unfortunately, the stranger obstructed her route. His tall physique overpowered the room.

"What's your name?" Maybe she could gain his sympathy.

"I am Zohar Thorald. Let us leave this place before the displacement field reactivates." While the man spoke in a soft tone, his authority brooked no arguments.

Nira assumed he must be a foreigner, judging from his stiff manner of speech.

He stalked into the hallway, calling for his comrades to follow. Nira trailed after him, frustrated when she still couldn't reach the main entrance. As if reinforcing her plight, Zohar snagged her elbow while he addressed his men.

"Find anything?"

"It's too late," one guy answered. "They must have taken anything of value before we arrived. It's almost as though they were expecting us."

The wall shimmered, and Nira blinked.

"Everyone outside." Zohar yanked on her arm, dragging her into the anteroom and out the front door. Daylight pierced her vision.

"My sunglasses. I left my purse in there. Let me go."

She twisted sideways but couldn't break his grip. No way

would she leave her Coach bag behind. It had been the first designer item she could afford, even if she'd bought it at the outlet store.

Zohar nodded to one of his men, who detached from the group and raced inside. He reappeared in the doorway and leapt onto the pavement just as the entire structure faded before her eyes.

"Okay, that wasn't real. I must be hallucinating." Nira accepted her bag from the man who'd retrieved it.

"No hallucination. You were nearly ensnared." Zohar prodded her toward a parked white van. "This is why you need our protection. Secure her." He handed her off to another masked man before heading toward the driver's seat.

"I have my own car. I can meet you wherever we're going." Nira thought it worth a try.

Zohar whipped around. "Give your keys to Kaj. He will follow us."

"I don't think so. Hey, what are you doing?"

One of the men flashed a pair of stormy gray eyes as he snatched her purse. He fished inside until he found her key ring. Tossing the bag back, he strode toward her vehicle as though it emitted a beacon. Along the way, he ripped off his mask. She got a glimpse of unruly wheat hair, even features, and a taut jaw before he turned his back on them.

"All right, how did he know that's my car?" She held her ground, refusing to budge.

"Your signals are strong, little one. You left your essence on your automobile. Even we are not immune."

Zohar tore off his hood, making her inhale sharply. If kidnappers competed for looks, he could win a spot in *GQ Magazine*.

Deep-set turquoise eyes sat under emphatic brows and above a straight, aquiline nose. A firm mouth spoke of a man who set himself high standards, his upper lip a bit narrower than its fuller bottom. He wore his dark brown hair swept back over a regal forehead like Captain Kirk on the original *Star Trek* show, although his hair was tussled from the mask.

He grinned, transforming his stern expression into one of devilish amusement. An answering coil of warmth rolled through her.

Okay, get a grip. You're trapped with four hunky guys who could easily overpower you, and you have no notion of their true intentions. She had to give them credit for rescuing her, though. Maybe they were undercover agents working with some federal agency on a drug bust case.

"Can we take off our masks, *rageesh?*" another man asked in a respectful tone.

Zohar shrugged. "Why not? The lady is one of us now. Tell me where you wish to go." His deep voice flowed over her like warm honey.

The police station, big guy. Unfortunately, she didn't know where one was located on International Drive.

She gave him her address while the rest of his men tore off their disguises. Crammed inside the second row of the van between two hunks, Nira clutched her precious handbag.

When her friend and mentor, Grace Miller, saw Nira trooping home with a gang of men, she'd probably call the cops herself.

Nira hoped so. Now that she was free to pursue her research, she didn't want anything to interfere.

Her glance dropped to her wristwatch. She'd received the timepiece from her mother as a gift when she lay on her deathbed, along with a confession that Nira had been adopted. This keepsake, left by her biological parents, remained the only clue to her true identity. It ran with no visible mechanism and no battery. She suspected it relied on solar energy.

Once Nira discovered the inscription on its face was runic lettering, she became fascinated with Norse legends. She studied comparative mythology in grad school, hoping to teach after she'd earned her doctorate degree. In the meantime, she meant to trace her origins but lacked the funding to carry out her plans. So far, she wasn't having much luck in finding a summer job.

She couldn't worry about that now. First she had to get away from these guys.

Twenty minutes later, they pulled up to the curb in front of Grace's house. As the driver of Nira's car joined them outside, the elderly lady meandered into the yard. She wore a loose patterned top with cream-colored pants and not a hair out of place on her teased gray head.

Nira's heart swelled with affection. Grace was a kindly neighbor who'd offered support when her mother died six years ago. After raising her two younger sisters, Nira had moved into Grace's house to save money. While the arrangement suited them both, Nira yearned for freedom, not to mention a measure of privacy. This was another reason why she wanted a job, to afford her own apartment. It would mean leaving Grace alone, though, and the eighty-two-year-old woman enjoyed her company.

"Nira, what happened? I didn't expect you back so early." Grace peered at Nira's companions. "Who are your friends?"

The one with rangy black hair and a beard spoke up. "We are…cousins."

"Really?" Grace propped her hands on her slim hips. "I didn't know you had any relatives besides your sisters, dear."

"No, I, uh—"

Zohar strode to Nira's side and spoke to her in an undertone. "If you need credits, I am prepared to offer you a job."

"Say again?" Leaning forward, Grace cupped her ear.

Nira shot Zohar an inquiring glance. She'd ask him what his remark meant later. In the meantime, she raised her voice so Grace could hear.

"These are cousins on my father's side. Since he walked out on us when I was eight years old, I never knew much about his family. I was quite surprised when they showed up." Glaring at Zohar, she waited for him to contradict her. He grinned back, a gleam of approval in his eyes.

"My word, you must be thrilled. Come inside and have some lemonade and cake." Grace surveyed their attire. "No doubt you'll want to lose those costumes. Your awesome guns add a nice touch, but they might frighten someone. Great choice of props, boys. I hadn't realized a science fiction convention was in town."

"This is Zohar," Nira supplied when he appeared at a loss for words. "Guys, meet Grace. She's a dear family friend."

"Where will you be staying? I know some budget hotels if you need a place." Grace's face lit up as it always did when she offered advice.

A hunk with golden blond hair and a youthful face had been speaking softly into his cell phone, or at least a device that looked like one. Switching it off, he regarded his leader. "Rayne has secured accommodations for us at a local hostelry."

"Oh, that's good. I suppose you'll want to visit the theme parks while you're here," Grace said as the sun broiled Nira's scalp.

Zohar cocked his head. "What is a theme park? Our objective is Drift World."

Grace wagged a finger. "Personally, sonny, I don't see the attraction in adults role-playing their fantasy jobs. Get a real one, that's my opinion."

"Grace, it's too warm out here. I'm going inside," Nira said. She snatched her keys from the carjacker and used the remote to lock her vehicle. Then she wheeled toward the front door, advancing only a few steps before she hesitated. These men seemed friendly, but was it wise to invite them in?

She turned toward Zohar. "Thanks for the escort home. Please don't feel you have to hang around on my account. You must have things to do."

"We still need to talk." A determined look on his face, Zohar gestured toward the house.

Her stomach sank. She wasn't going to get rid of him so easily. Maybe she could figure out a way to ditch these guys after cooling off inside.

Their leader accompanied her, his boots pounding on the hot pavement. The others crowded behind as she resignedly led the way.

Inside the foyer, Nira tossed her purse on a side table. As soon as Grace was out of earshot in the kitchen, she lowered her voice. "Okay, who are you and what do you want? And where are you from? You talk like foreigners."

"Our home is called Karrell." Zohar's eyes smoldered as he regarded her, his height and powerful shoulders making her feel small and feminine.

"Never heard of it. Must be a tiny country." She swept her gaze over their belted tunics, side arms, and tailored trousers. "You could pass for invaders from outer space. Are you sure you're not here for a convention? Or are you actors looking for jobs? Your outfits appear authentic. Or perhaps you're part of a SWAT team?"

"We are here to save your world, not invade it. What is this phrase, swat team?"

"I will research it, *rageesh.*" The man with a stubbled jaw, unkempt hair, and killer dimples could have been a double for Josh Holloway on *Lost*. Nira stared at him, wondering if this were some sort of reality show with hidden cameras.

"I told you not to call me that, Paz."

"My apologies." Paz bowed his head, making Nira wonder about his relationship to Zohar.

"What did you want to tell me?" she asked.

Zohar's gaze darkened. "We have much to discuss, but not a lot of time."

"Please, feel free to go and take your friends along with you. Your problems aren't mine, although I do want to thank you for rescuing me from those nutcases in that employment office. Just how did that place vanish, anyway? It was some sort of optical illusion, yes?"

"In a way. Look, you fail to understand the danger. We cannot leave you alone."

"I'm home now, so I am safe. I appreciate your concern, but I'll be fine."

He shook his head. "The Trolleks will come after you. They will follow your scent."

"What scent?" She sniffed the air. "Are you telling me I stink? I may have been running around in the heat, but—"

A grin transformed his face. "You misinterpret, little one. Your skin is fragrant, like purpura blossoms. It is a most pleasant scent and highly alluring."

Her cheeks flushed until she latched onto his other remark. "Trolleks? Who are they? And what did you mean when you mentioned credits outside?"

He raised an imperious eyebrow. "I wish to offer you a position as our local guide."

She gazed at him askance. Whoever these guys were, there wasn't any doubt in her mind that they needed help navigating the locale. Should she accept?

With her track record, it was likely to be the only decent job offer in her future. Her temples throbbed while she debated her response.

Right now, when she could finally search for her birth parents, she didn't need any roadblocks getting in the way. Was it worth tagging along with Zohar and his gang to earn the cash she needed for her research?

Maybe they were tourists from a backwater country, but that didn't explain their raid on the log hut or their assault gear. Something else was going on. Hooking up with them, even as their hired guide, could only spell trouble.

She stood tall, giving Zohar a level glance. "Sorry. Tempting as your offer is, I have to decline."

"Wrong answer." Zohar's jaw tightened as he reached for her.

Order Now at https://nancyjcohen.com/warrior-prince/

About the Author

Nancy J. Cohen writes the Bad Hair Day Mysteries featuring South Florida hairstylist Marla Vail. Titles in this series have been named Best Cozy Mystery by *Suspense Magazine*, won the Readers' Favorite Book Awards and the RONE Award, placed first in the Chanticleer International Book Awards and third in the Arizona Literary Awards.

Her nonfiction titles, *Writing the Cozy Mystery* and *A Bad Hair Day Cookbook*, have earned gold medals in the FAPA President's Book Awards and the Royal Palm Literary Awards, First Place in the IAN Book of the Year Awards and the *Topshelf Magazine* Book Awards. *Writing the Cozy Mystery* was also an Agatha Award Finalist.

Nancy's imaginative romances have proven popular with fans as well. These books have won the HOLT Medallion and Best Book in Romantic SciFi/Fantasy at *The Romance Reviews*.

A featured speaker at libraries, conferences, and community events, Nancy is listed in *Contemporary Authors, Poets & Writers*, and *Who's Who in U.S. Writers, Editors, & Poets*. She is a past president of Florida Romance Writers and the Florida Chapter of Mystery Writers of America. When not busy writing, Nancy enjoys reading, fine dining, cruising, and visiting Disney World.

Follow Nancy Online

Email – nancy@nancyjcohen.com
Website – https://nancyjcohen.com
Blog – https://nancyjcohen.com/blog
Twitter – https://www.twitter.com/nancyjcohen
Facebook – https://www.facebook.com/NancyJCohenAuthor
LinkedIn – https://www.linkedin.com/in/nancyjcohen
Goodreads – https://www.goodreads.com/nancyjcohen
Pinterest – https://pinterest.com/njcohen/
Instagram – https://instagram.com/nancyjcohen
BookBub – https://www.bookbub.com/authors/nancy-j-cohen

Books by Nancy J. Cohen

Bad Hair Day Mysteries
Permed to Death
Hair Raiser
Murder by Manicure
Body Wave
Highlights to Heaven
Died Blonde
Dead Roots
Perish by Pedicure
Killer Knots
Shear Murder
Hanging by a Hair
Peril by Ponytail
Haunted Hair Nights (Novella)
Facials Can Be Fatal
Hair Brained
Hairball Hijinks (Short Story)
Trimmed to Death
Easter Hair Hunt
Styled for Murder
Star Tangled Murder

The Drift Lords Series
Warrior Prince
Warrior Rogue
Warrior Lord

Science Fiction Romances
Keeper of the Rings
Silver Serenade

The Light-Years Series
Circle of Light
Moonlight Rhapsody
Starlight Child

Nonfiction
Writing the Cozy Mystery
A Bad Hair Day Cookbook

Order Now at https://nancyjcohen.com/books/

www.ingramcontent.com/pod-product-compliance
Lightning Source LLC
Chambersburg PA
CBHW052025220726
48293CB00015B/272